CREATED BY

**BRANDON
THOMAS**

AND

**KHARY
RANDOLPH**

SKYBOUND ENTERTAINMENT

ROBERT KIRKMAN
CHAIRMAN

DAVID ALPERT
CEO

SEAN MACKIEWICZ
SVP, EDITOR-IN-CHIEF

SHAWN KIRKHAM
SVP, BUSINESS DEVELOPMENT

BRIAN HUNTINGTON
VP, ONLINE CONTENT

ANDRES JUAREZ
ART DIRECTOR

ARUNE SINGH
DIRECTOR OF BRAND, EDITORIAL

SHANNON MEEHAN
PUBLIC RELATIONS MANAGER

ALEX ANTONE
SENIOR EDITOR

JON MOISAN
EDITOR

AMANDA LaFRANCO
EDITOR

DAN PETERSEN
SR. DIRECTOR, OPERATIONS & EVENTS

FOREIGN RIGHTS & LICENSING INQUIRIES:
CONTACT@SKYBOUND.COM

SKYBOUND.COM

IMAGE COMICS, INC.

TODD McFARLANE
PRESIDENT

JIM VALENTINO
VICE PRESIDENT

MARC SILVESTRI
CHIEF EXECUTIVE OFFICER

ERIK LARSEN
CHIEF FINANCIAL OFFICER

ROBERT KIRKMAN
CHIEF OPERATING OFFICER

ERIC STEPHENSON
PUBLISHER / CHIEF CREATIVE OFFICER

NICOLE LAPALME
CONTROLLER

LEANNA CAUNTER
ACCOUNTING ANALYST

SUE KORPELA
ACCOUNTING & HR MANAGER

MARLA EIZIK
TALENT LIAISON

JEFF BOISON
*DIRECTOR OF SALES &
PUBLISHING PLANNING*

DIRK WOOD
*DIRECTOR OF
INTERNATIONAL SALES & LICENSING*

ALEX COX
DIRECTOR OF DIRECT MARKET SALES

CHLOE RAMOS
*BOOK MARKET &
LIBRARY SALES MANAGER*

EMILIO BAUTISTA
DIGITAL SALES COORDINATOR

KAT SALAZAR
DIRECTOR OF PR & MARKETING

DREW FITZGERALD
MARKETING CONTENT ASSOCIATE

HEATHER DOORNINK
PRODUCTION DIRECTOR

DREW GILL
ART DIRECTOR

HILARY DILORETO
PRINT MANAGER

TRICIA RAMOS
TRAFFIC MANAGER

MELISSA GIFFORD
CONTENT MANAGER

ERIKA SCHNATZ
SENIOR PRODUCTION ARTIST

RYAN BREWER
PRODUCTION ARTIST

DEANNA PHELPS
PRODUCTION ARTIST

IMAGECOMICS.COM

EXCELLENCE VOLUME TWO. FIRST PRINTING.
ISBN: 978-1-5343-1862-5

PUBLISHED BY IMAGE COMICS, INC. OFFICE OF
PUBLICATION: PO BOX 14457, PORTLAND, OR 97293.
COPYRIGHT © 2022 SKYBOUND, LLC. ALL RIGHTS
RESERVED. ORIGINALLY PUBLISHED IN SINGLE MAGAZINE
FORMAT AS EXCELLENCE™ #7-12. EXCELLENCE™
(INCLUDING ALL PROMINENT CHARACTERS FEATURED
HEREIN), ITS LOGO AND ALL CHARACTER LIKENESSES ARE
TRADEMARKS OF SKYBOUND, LLC., UNLESS OTHERWISE
NOTED. IMAGE COMICS® AND ITS LOGOS ARE REGISTERED
TRADEMARKS AND COPYRIGHTS OF IMAGE COMICS, INC.
ALL RIGHTS RESERVED. NO PART OF THIS PUBLICATION
MAY BE REPRODUCED OR TRANSMITTED IN ANY FORM
OR BY ANY MEANS (EXCEPT FOR SHORT EXCERPTS FOR
REVIEW PURPOSES) WITHOUT THE EXPRESS WRITTEN
PERMISSION OF IMAGE COMICS, INC. ALL NAMES,
CHARACTERS, EVENTS AND LOCALES IN THIS PUBLICATION
ARE ENTIRELY FICTIONAL. ANY RESEMBLANCE TO ACTUAL
PERSONS (LIVING OR DEAD), EVENTS OR PLACES, WITHOUT
SATIRIC INTENT, IS COINCIDENTAL. PRINTED IN CANADA.

BRANDON THOMAS
CREATOR, WRITER

KHARY RANDOLPH
CREATOR, ARTIST, COVER

EMILIO LOPEZ
COLORIST

DERON BENNETT
LETTERER

SEAN MACKIEWICZ
EDITOR

ANDRES JUAREZ
LOGO, COLLECTION DESIGN

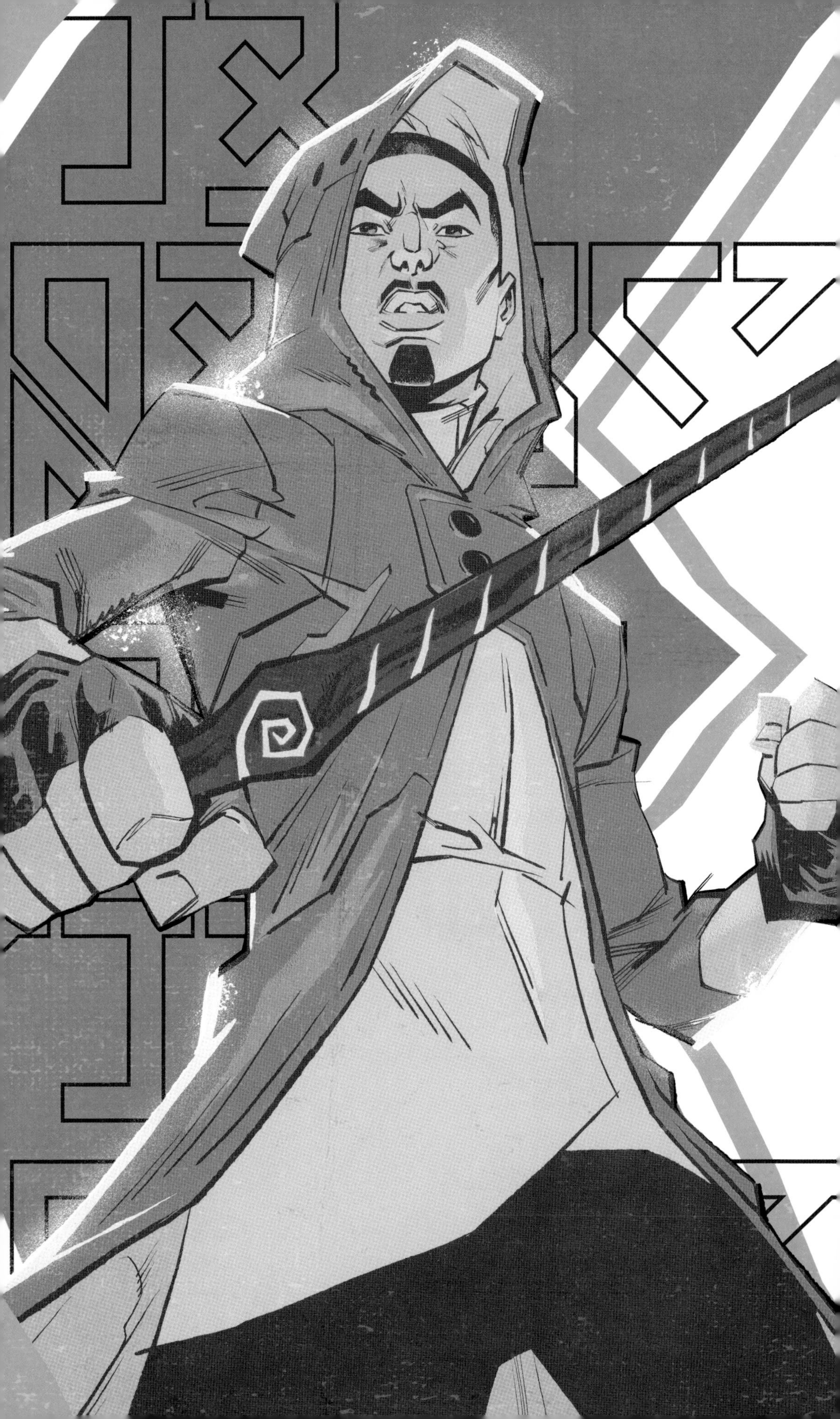

CHAPTER TWO
THE PRESENT TENSE

THE FOUR WALLS

I

THE PROTECTION AND DEFENSE OF THE
UNDESERVING IS NOT ALLOWED.

II

THE CREATION OF A MAGICIAN'S WAND
WITHOUT PERMISSION IS NOT ALLOWED.

III

THE CASTING OF SPELLS WITHOUT AN
APPROVED WAND IS NOT ALLOWED.

IV

THE USE OF MAGIC BY FEMALES
IS NOT ALLOWED.

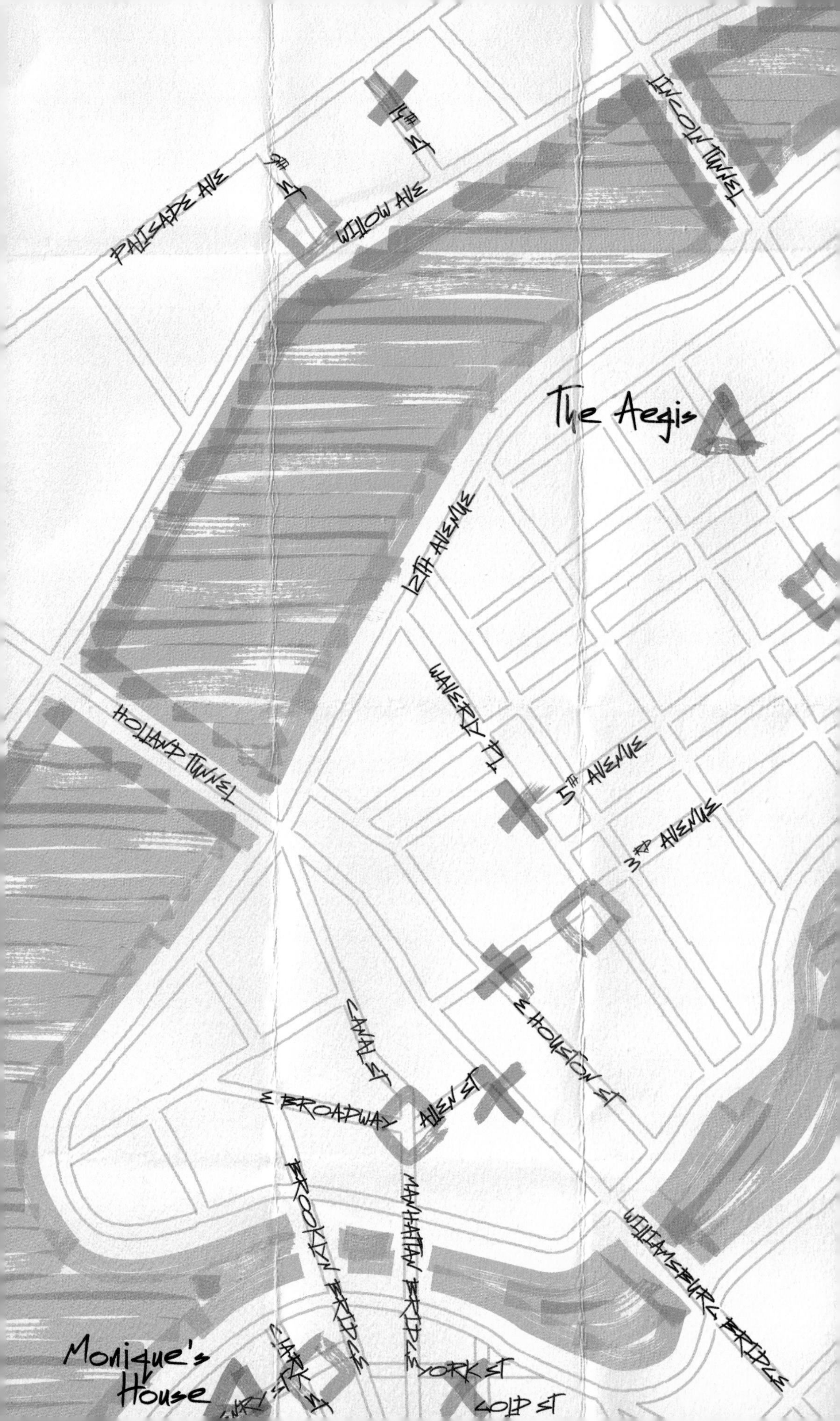
PALISADE AVE
9TH ST
14TH ST
WILLOW AVE
LINCOLN TUNNEL
The Aegis
12TH AVENUE
HOLLAND TUNNEL
WAVERLY PL
5TH AVENUE
3RD AVENUE
E HOUSTON ST
CANAL ST
E BROADWAY
ALLEN ST
BROOKLYN BRIDGE
MANHATTAN BRIDGE
WILLIAMSBURG BRIDGE
Monique's House
CLARK ST
YORK ST
GOLD ST

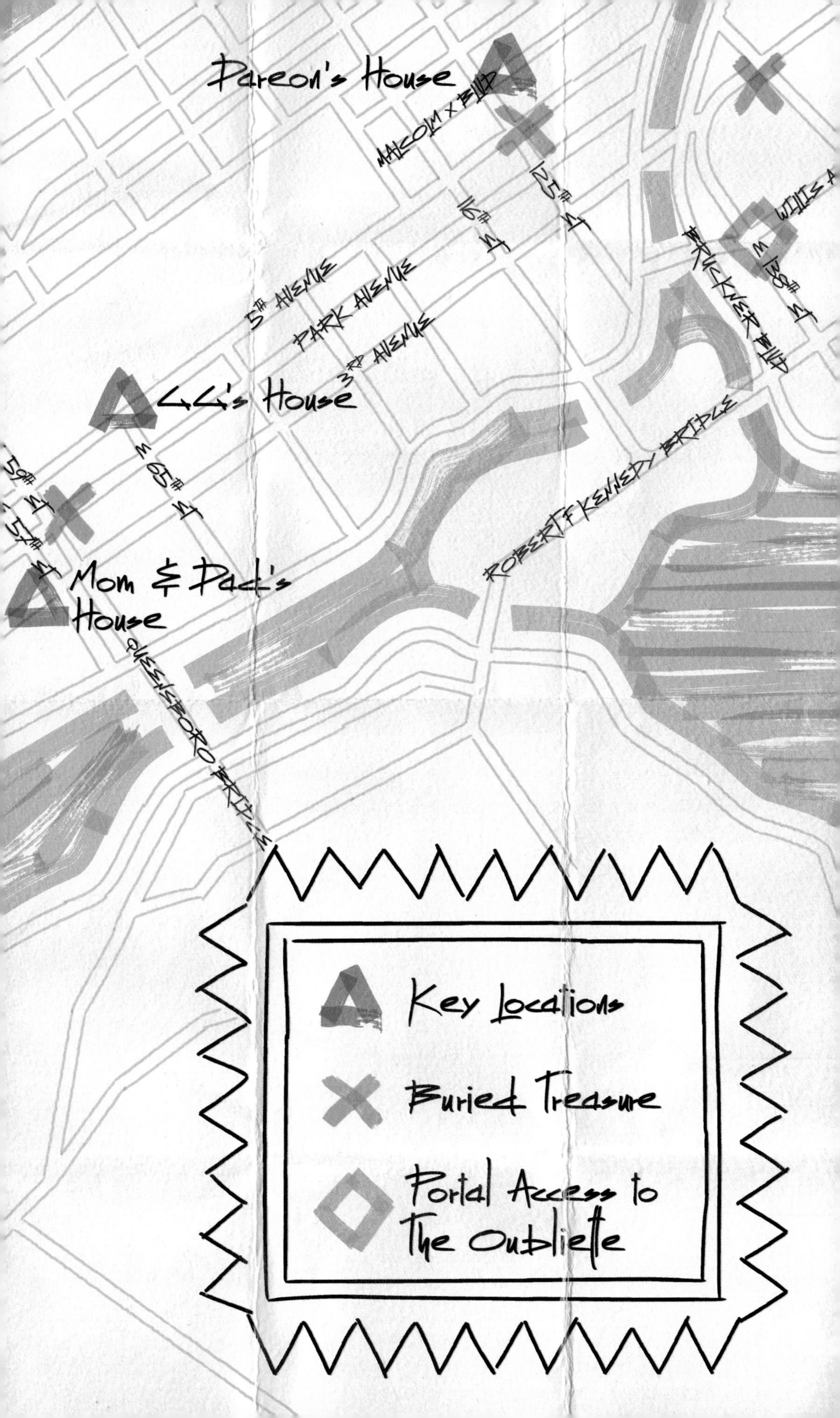
Dareon's House
MALCOLM X BLVD
125th ST
116th ST
E 138th ST
BRUCKNER BLVD
5th AVENUE
PARK AVENUE
3rd AVENUE
GG's House
E 65th ST
59th ST
Mom & Dad's House
QUEENSBORO BRIDGE
ROBERT F KENNEDY BRIDGE
Key Locations
Buried Treasure
Portal Access to The Oubliette

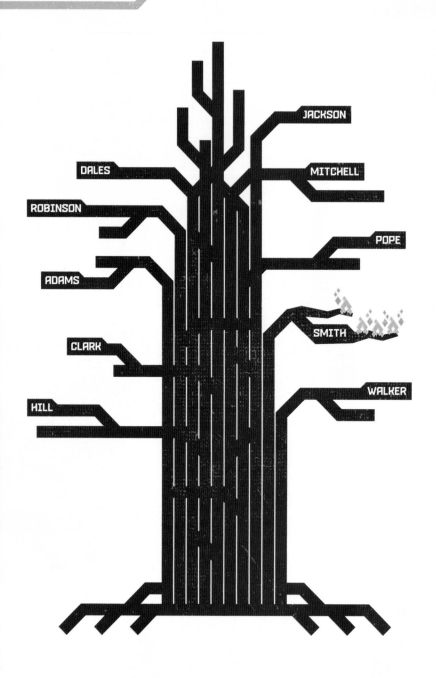

JACKSON

DALES

MITCHELL

ROBINSON

POPE

ADAMS

SMITH

CLARK

WALKER

HILL

THE TENTH

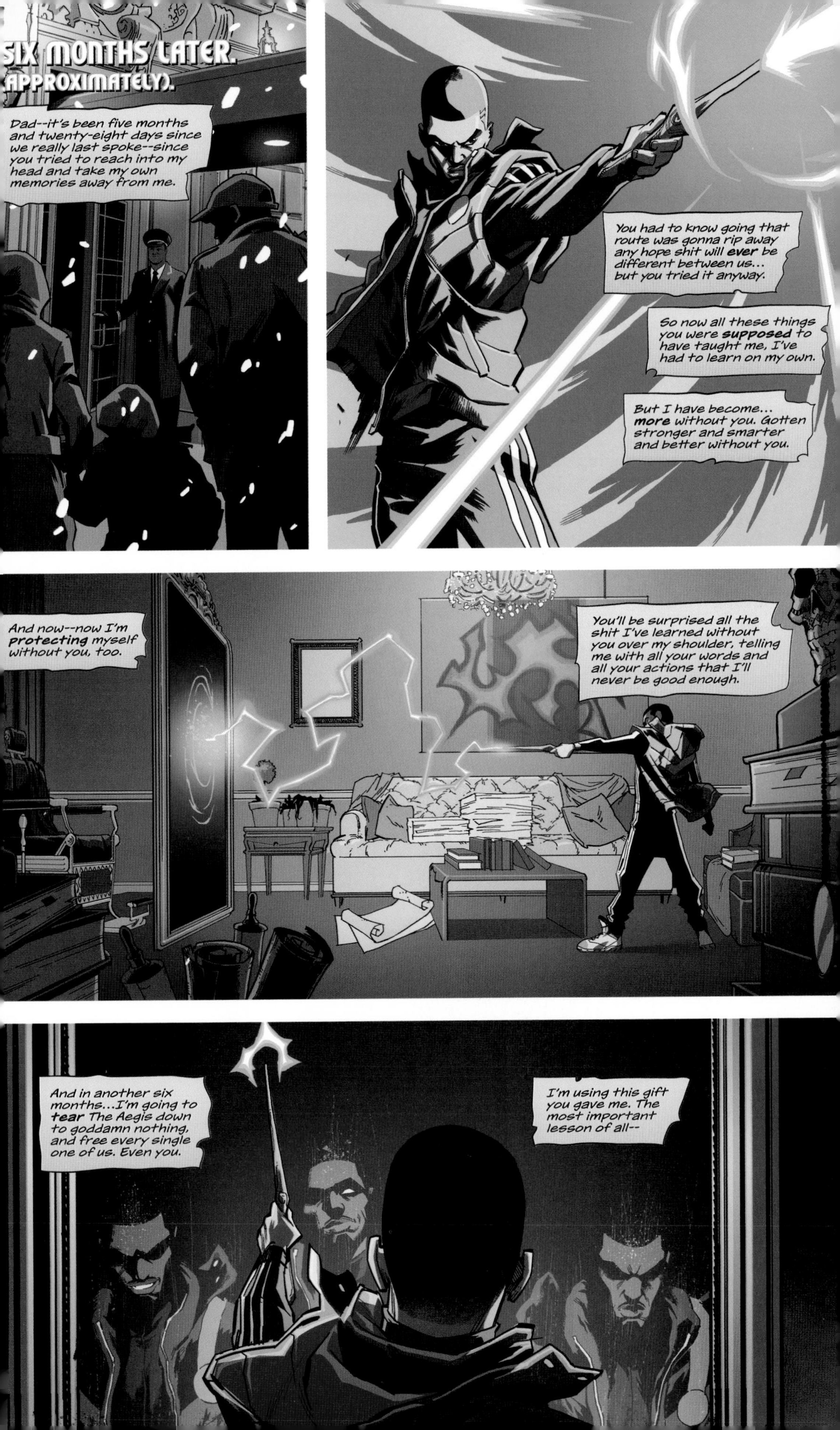
SIX MONTHS LATER. (APPROXIMATELY).
Dad--it's been five months and twenty-eight days since we really last spoke--since you tried to reach into my head and take my own memories away from me.
You had to know going that route was gonna rip away any hope shit will **ever** be different between us... but you tried it anyway.
So now all these things you were **supposed** to have taught me, I've had to learn on my own.
But I have become... **more** without you. Gotten stronger and smarter and better without you.
And now--now I'm **protecting** myself without you, too.
You'll be surprised all the shit I've learned without you over my shoulder, telling me with all your words and all your actions that I'll never be good enough.
And in another six months...I'm going to **tear** The Aegis down to goddamn nothing, and free every single one of us. Even you.
I'm using this gift you gave me. The most important lesson of all--

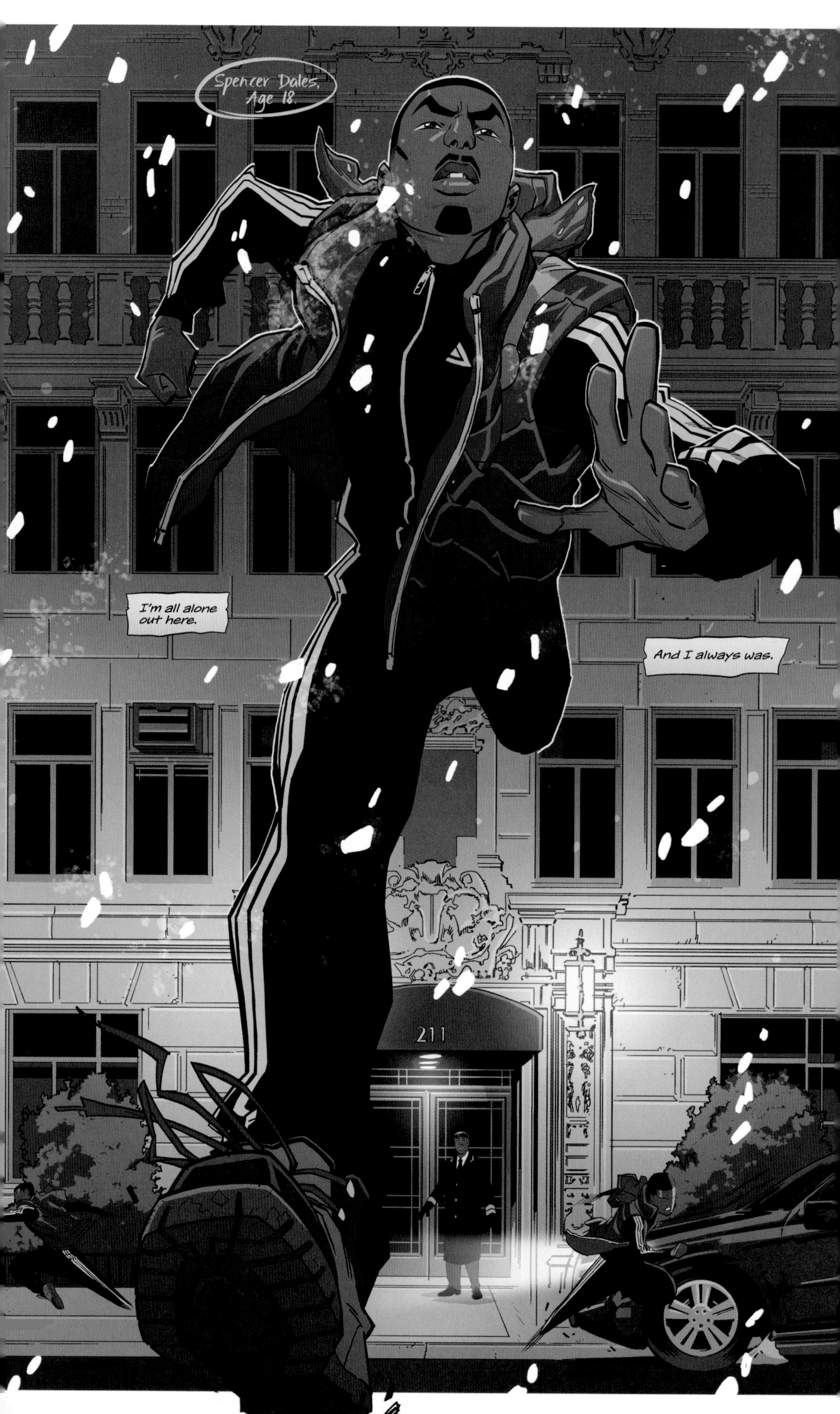
1929
Spencer Dales, Age 18.
I'm all alone out here.
And I always was.
211

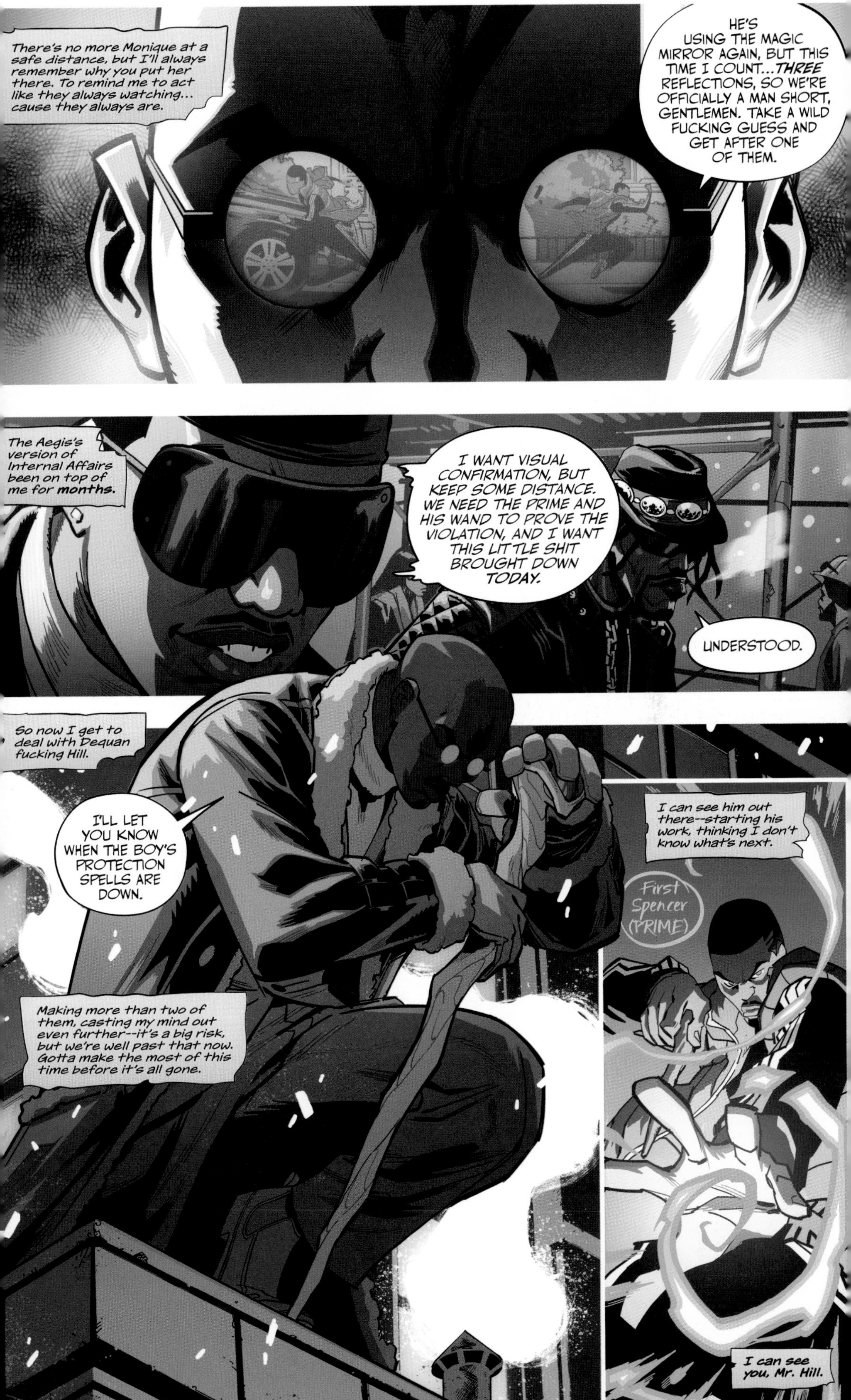
There's no more Monique at a safe distance, but I'll always remember why you put her there. To remind me to act like they always watching... cause they always are.
HE'S USING THE MAGIC MIRROR AGAIN, BUT THIS TIME I COUNT...THREE REFLECTIONS, SO WE'RE OFFICIALLY A MAN SHORT, GENTLEMEN. TAKE A WILD FUCKING GUESS AND GET AFTER ONE OF THEM.
The Aegis's version of Internal Affairs been on top of me for months.
I WANT VISUAL CONFIRMATION, BUT KEEP SOME DISTANCE. WE NEED THE PRIME AND HIS WAND TO PROVE THE VIOLATION, AND I WANT THIS LITTLE SHIT BROUGHT DOWN TODAY.
UNDERSTOOD.
So now I get to deal with Dequan fucking Hill.
I'LL LET YOU KNOW WHEN THE BOY'S PROTECTION SPELLS ARE DOWN.
Making more than two of them, casting my mind out even further--it's a big risk, but we're well past that now. Gotta make the most of this time before it's all gone.
I can see him out there--starting his work, thinking I don't know what's next.
First Spencer (PRIME)
I can see you, Mr. Hill.

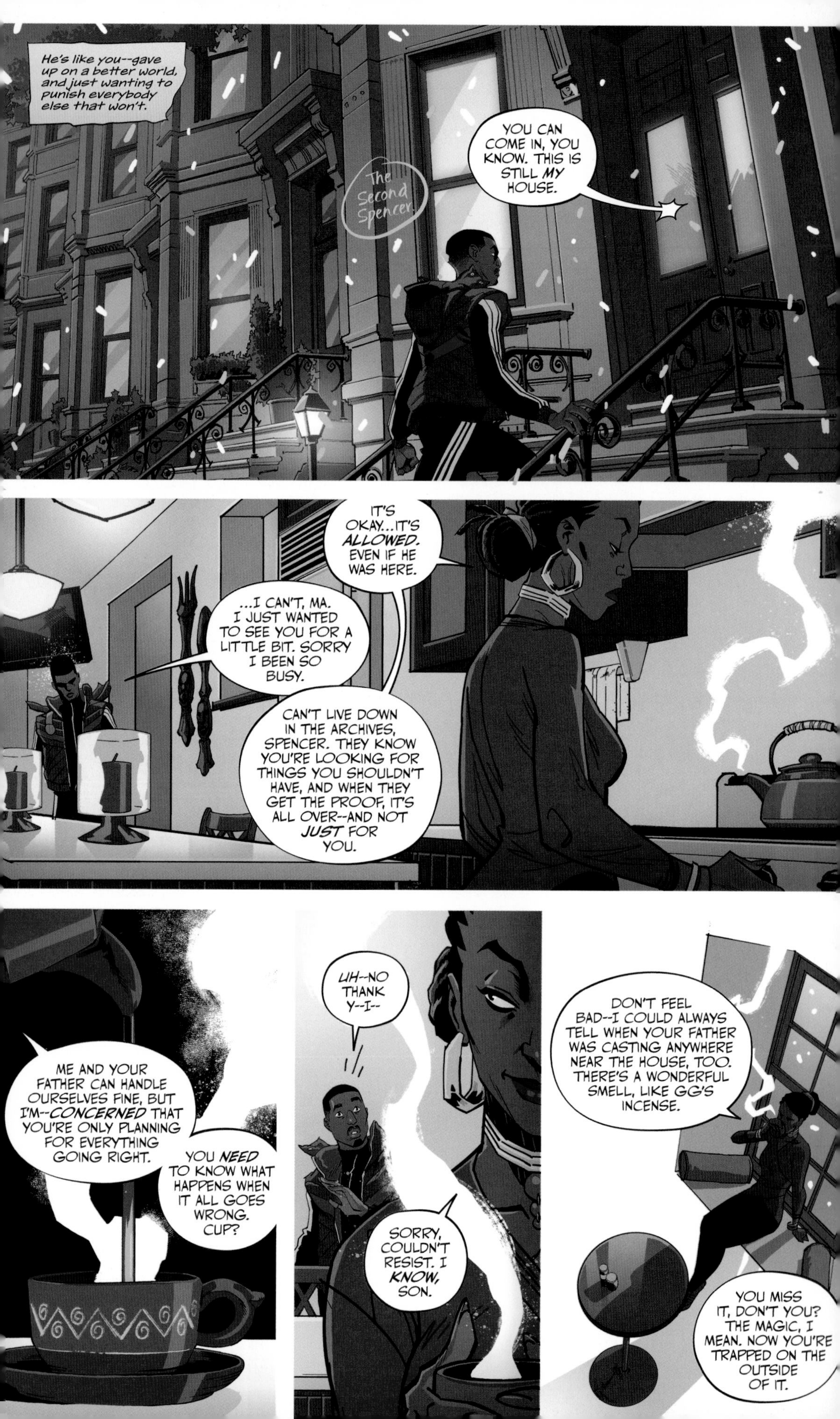
He's like you--gave up on a better world, and just wanting to punish everybody else that won't.
The Second Spencer
YOU CAN COME IN, YOU KNOW. THIS IS STILL MY HOUSE.
IT'S OKAY...IT'S ALLOWED. EVEN IF HE WAS HERE.
...I CAN'T, MA. I JUST WANTED TO SEE YOU FOR A LITTLE BIT. SORRY I BEEN SO BUSY.
CAN'T LIVE DOWN IN THE ARCHIVES, SPENCER. THEY KNOW YOU'RE LOOKING FOR THINGS YOU SHOULDN'T HAVE, AND WHEN THEY GET THE PROOF, IT'S ALL OVER--AND NOT JUST FOR YOU.
ME AND YOUR FATHER CAN HANDLE OURSELVES FINE, BUT I'M--CONCERNED THAT YOU'RE ONLY PLANNING FOR EVERYTHING GOING RIGHT.
YOU NEED TO KNOW WHAT HAPPENS WHEN IT ALL GOES WRONG. CUP?
UH--NO THANK Y--I--
SORRY, COULDN'T RESIST. I KNOW, SON.
DON'T FEEL BAD--I COULD ALWAYS TELL WHEN YOUR FATHER WAS CASTING ANYWHERE NEAR THE HOUSE, TOO. THERE'S A WONDERFUL SMELL, LIKE GG'S INCENSE.
YOU MISS IT, DON'T YOU? THE MAGIC, I MEAN. NOW YOU'RE TRAPPED ON THE OUTSIDE OF IT.

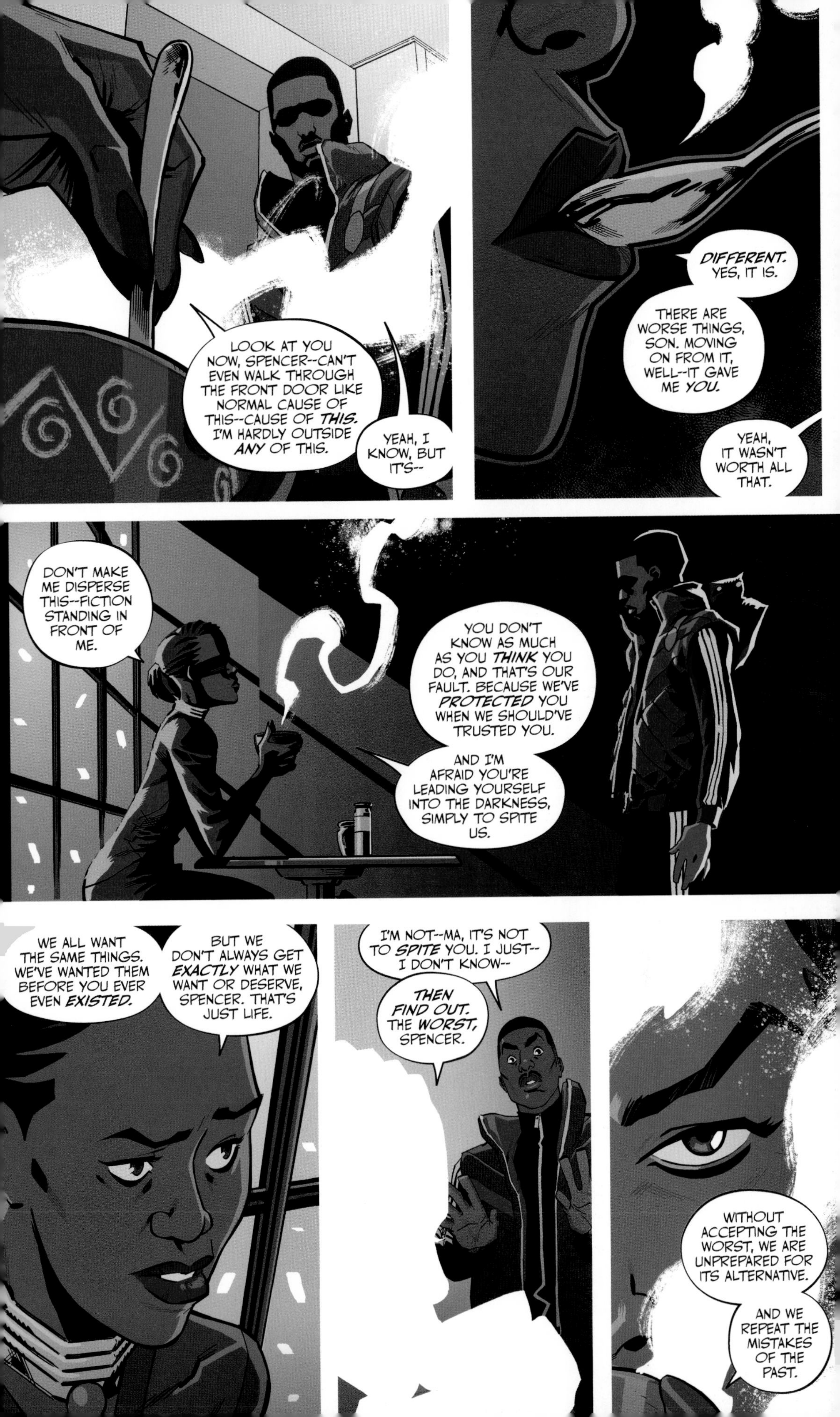
LOOK AT YOU NOW, SPENCER--CAN'T EVEN WALK THROUGH THE FRONT DOOR LIKE NORMAL CAUSE OF THIS--CAUSE OF *THIS.* I'M HARDLY OUTSIDE *ANY* OF THIS.
YEAH, I KNOW, BUT IT'S--
DIFFERENT. YES, IT IS.
THERE ARE WORSE THINGS, SON. MOVING ON FROM IT, WELL--IT GAVE ME *YOU.*
YEAH, IT WASN'T WORTH ALL THAT.
DON'T MAKE ME DISPERSE THIS--FICTION STANDING IN FRONT OF ME.
YOU DON'T KNOW AS MUCH AS YOU *THINK* YOU DO, AND THAT'S OUR FAULT. BECAUSE WE'VE *PROTECTED* YOU WHEN WE SHOULD'VE TRUSTED YOU.
AND I'M AFRAID YOU'RE LEADING YOURSELF INTO THE DARKNESS, SIMPLY TO SPITE US.
WE ALL WANT THE SAME THINGS. WE'VE WANTED THEM BEFORE YOU EVER EVEN *EXISTED.*
BUT WE DON'T ALWAYS GET *EXACTLY* WHAT WE WANT OR DESERVE, SPENCER. THAT'S JUST LIFE.
I'M NOT--MA, IT'S NOT TO *SPITE* YOU. I JUST--I DON'T KNOW--
THEN FIND OUT. THE *WORST,* SPENCER.
WITHOUT ACCEPTING THE WORST, WE ARE UNPREPARED FOR ITS ALTERNATIVE.
AND WE REPEAT THE MISTAKES OF THE PAST.

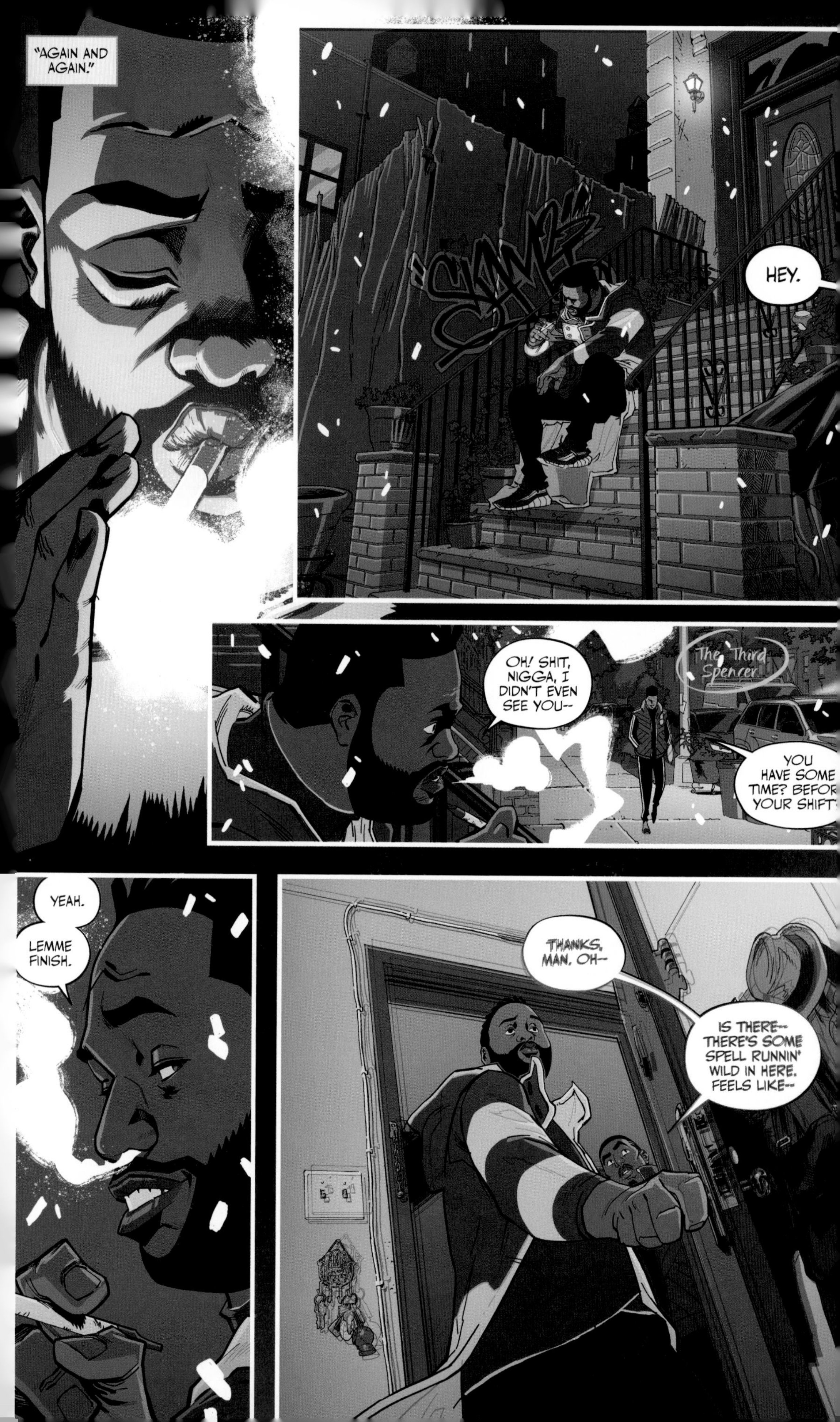
"AGAIN AND AGAIN."
HEY.
OH! SHIT, NIGGA, I DIDN'T EVEN SEE YOU--
The Third Spencer
YOU HAVE SOME TIME? BEFOR YOUR SHIFT
YEAH.
LEMME FINISH.
THANKS, MAN. OH--
IS THERE-- THERE'S SOME SPELL RUNNIN' WILD IN HERE. FEELS LIKE--

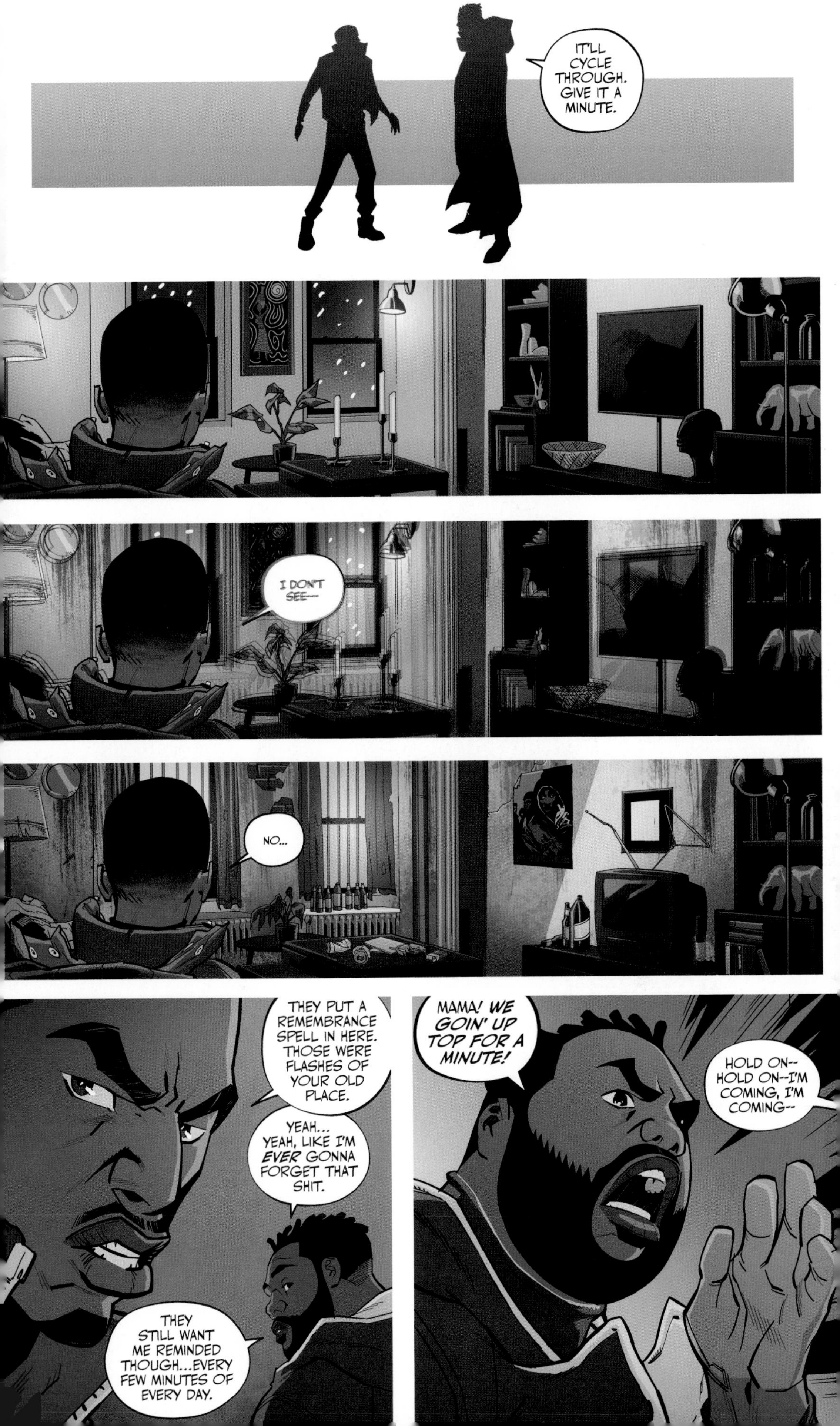
IT'LL CYCLE THROUGH. GIVE IT A MINUTE.
I DON'T SEE--
NO...
THEY PUT A REMEMBRANCE SPELL IN HERE. THOSE WERE FLASHES OF YOUR OLD PLACE.
YEAH... YEAH, LIKE I'M *EVER* GONNA FORGET THAT SHIT.
THEY STILL WANT ME REMINDED THOUGH...EVERY FEW MINUTES OF EVERY DAY.
MAMA! *WE GOIN' UP TOP FOR A MINUTE!*
HOLD ON--HOLD ON--I'M COMING, I'M COMING--

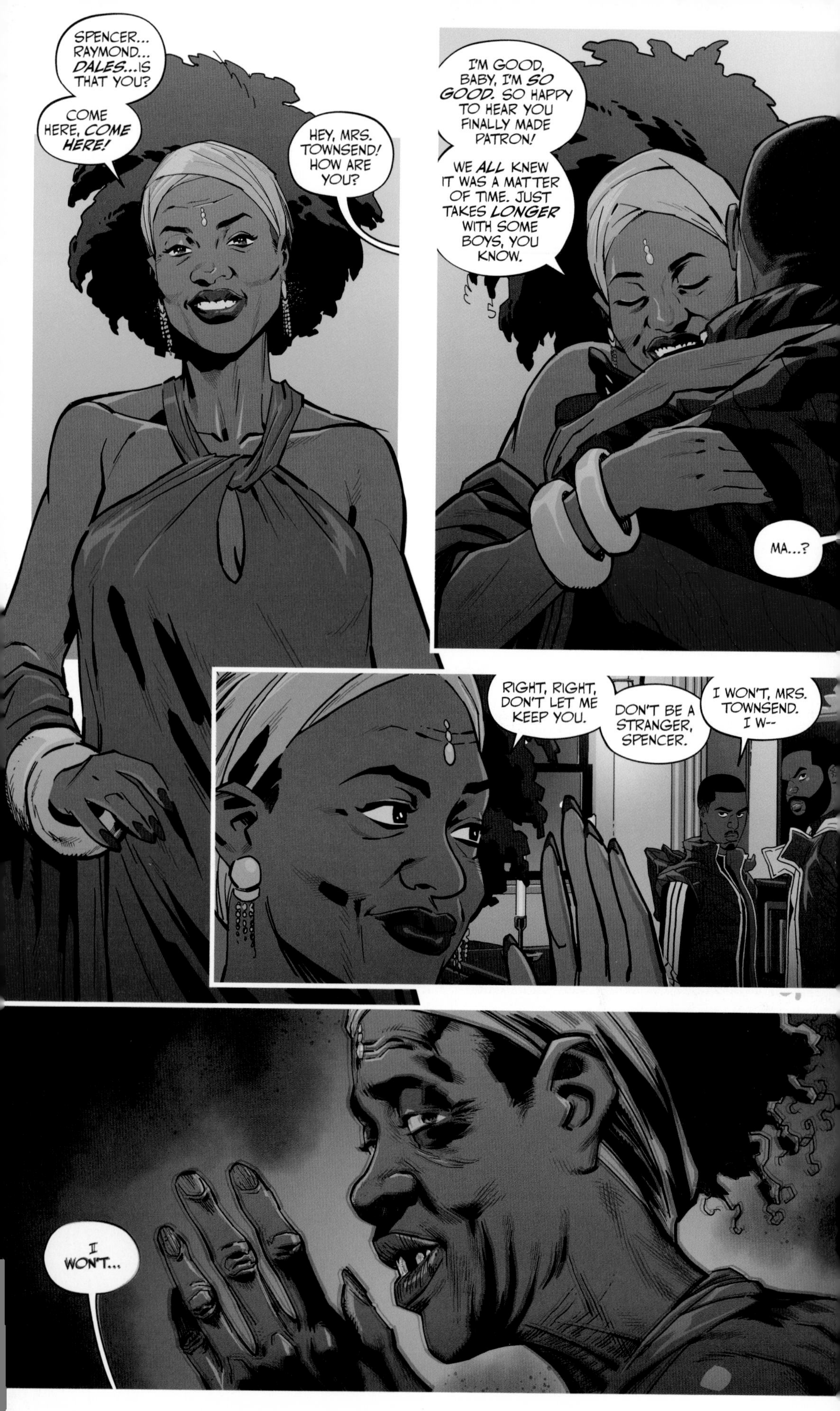
SPENCER... RAYMOND... DALES...IS THAT YOU?
COME HERE, COME HERE!
HEY, MRS. TOWNSEND! HOW ARE YOU?
I'M GOOD, BABY, I'M SO GOOD. SO HAPPY TO HEAR YOU FINALLY MADE PATRON!
WE ALL KNEW IT WAS A MATTER OF TIME. JUST TAKES LONGER WITH SOME BOYS, YOU KNOW.
MA...?
RIGHT, RIGHT, DON'T LET ME KEEP YOU.
DON'T BE A STRANGER, SPENCER.
I WON'T, MRS. TOWNSEND. I W--
I WON'T...

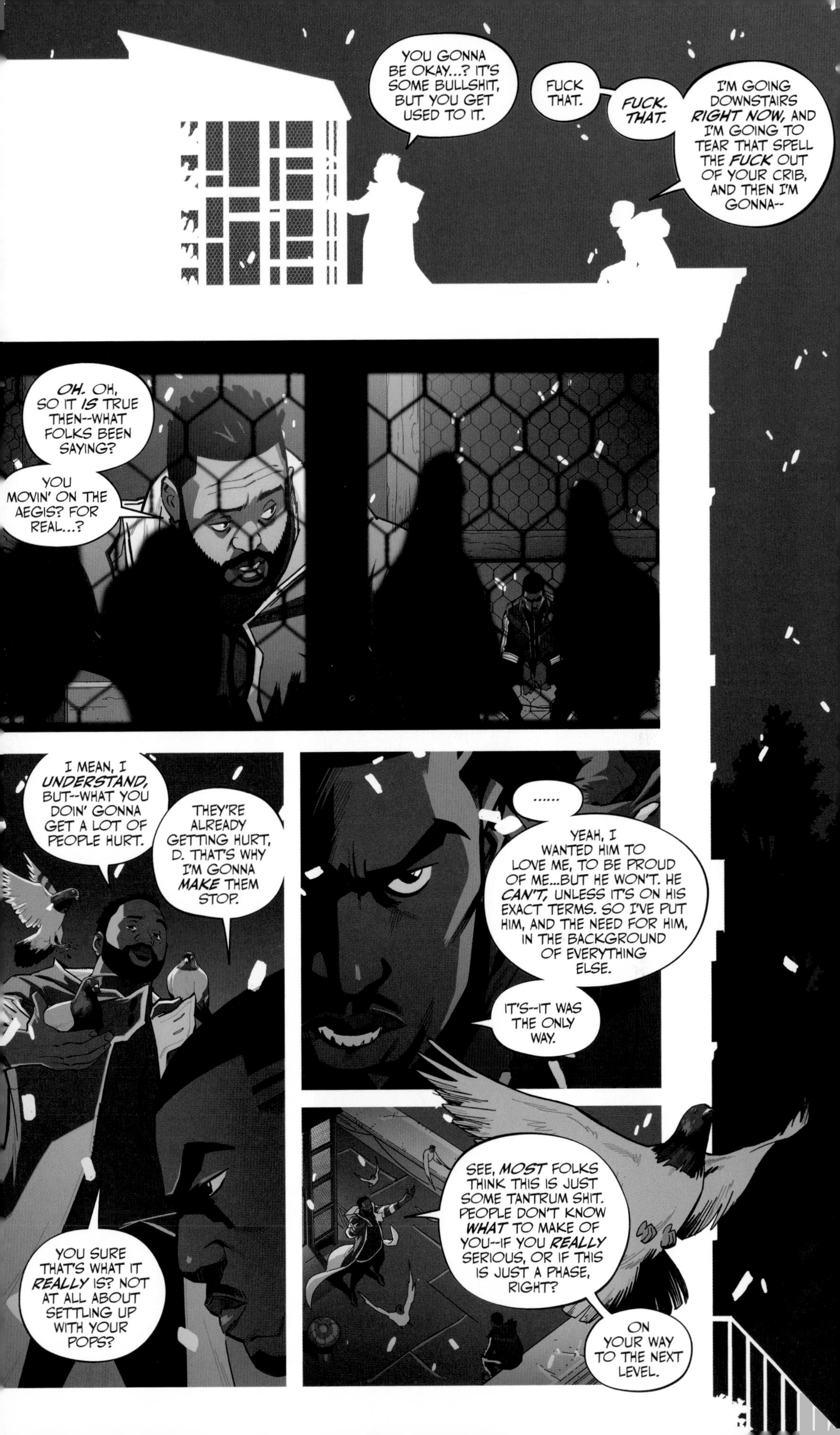
YOU GONNA BE OKAY...? IT'S SOME BULLSHIT, BUT YOU GET USED TO IT.
FUCK THAT.
FUCK. THAT.
I'M GOING DOWNSTAIRS RIGHT NOW, AND I'M GOING TO TEAR THAT SPELL THE FUCK OUT OF YOUR CRIB, AND THEN I'M GONNA--
OH. OH, SO IT IS TRUE THEN--WHAT FOLKS BEEN SAYING?
YOU MOVIN' ON THE AEGIS? FOR REAL...?
I MEAN, I UNDERSTAND, BUT--WHAT YOU DOIN' GONNA GET A LOT OF PEOPLE HURT.
THEY'RE ALREADY GETTING HURT, D. THAT'S WHY I'M GONNA MAKE THEM STOP.
YOU SURE THAT'S WHAT IT REALLY IS? NOT AT ALL ABOUT SETTLING UP WITH YOUR POPS?
......
YEAH, I WANTED HIM TO LOVE ME, TO BE PROUD OF ME...BUT HE WON'T. HE CAN'T, UNLESS IT'S ON HIS EXACT TERMS. SO I'VE PUT HIM, AND THE NEED FOR HIM, IN THE BACKGROUND OF EVERYTHING ELSE.
IT'S--IT WAS THE ONLY WAY.
SEE, MOST FOLKS THINK THIS IS JUST SOME TANTRUM SHIT. PEOPLE DON'T KNOW WHAT TO MAKE OF YOU--IF YOU REALLY SERIOUS, OR IF THIS IS JUST A PHASE, RIGHT?
ON YOUR WAY TO THE NEXT LEVEL.

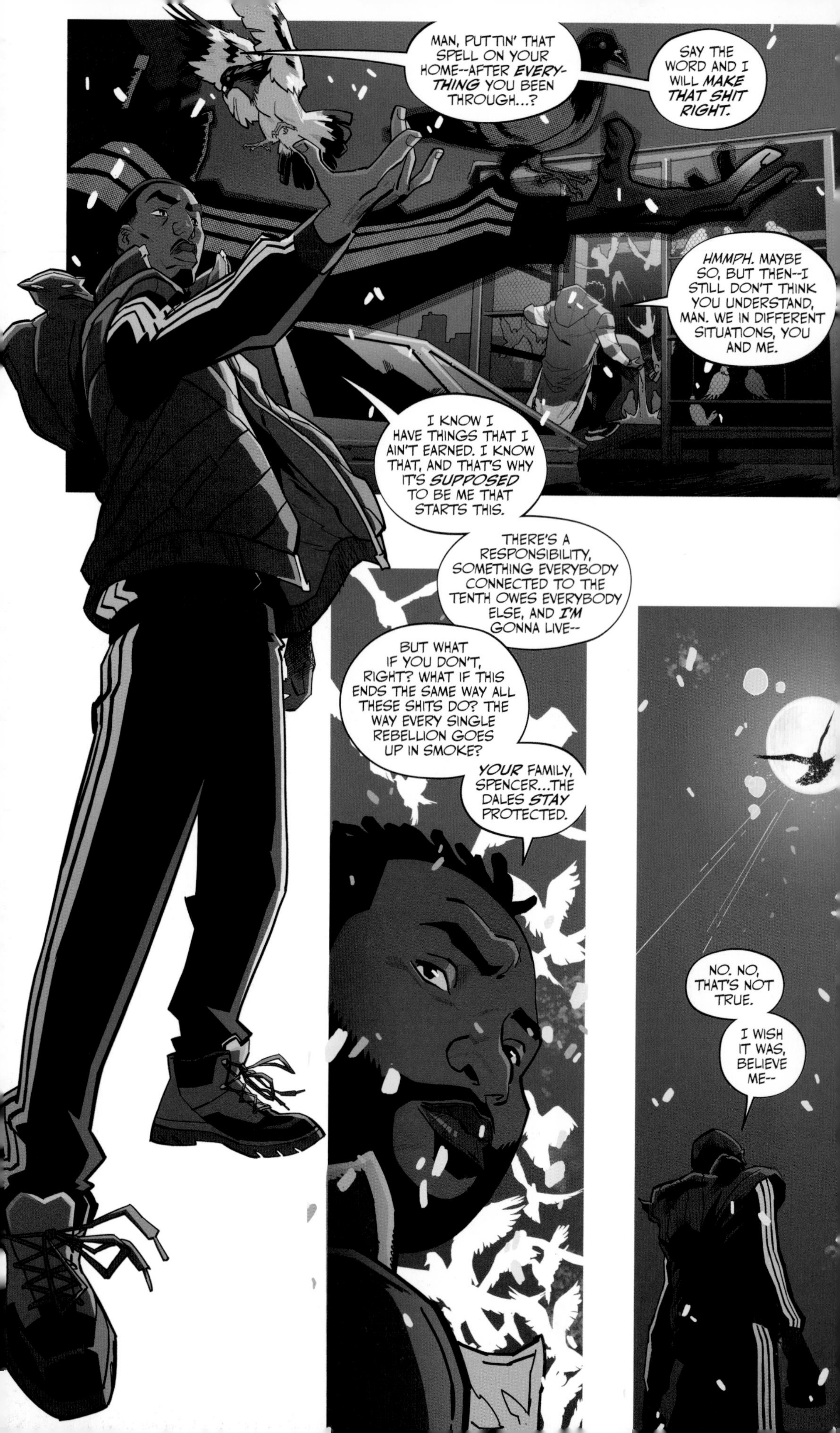
MAN, PUTTIN' THAT SPELL ON YOUR HOME--AFTER EVERYTHING YOU BEEN THROUGH...?
SAY THE WORD AND I WILL MAKE THAT SHIT RIGHT.
HMMPH. MAYBE SO, BUT THEN--I STILL DON'T THINK YOU UNDERSTAND, MAN. WE IN DIFFERENT SITUATIONS, YOU AND ME.
I KNOW I HAVE THINGS THAT I AIN'T EARNED. I KNOW THAT, AND THAT'S WHY IT'S SUPPOSED TO BE ME THAT STARTS THIS.
THERE'S A RESPONSIBILITY, SOMETHING EVERYBODY CONNECTED TO THE TENTH OWES EVERYBODY ELSE, AND I'M GONNA LIVE--
BUT WHAT IF YOU DON'T, RIGHT? WHAT IF THIS ENDS THE SAME WAY ALL THESE SHITS DO? THE WAY EVERY SINGLE REBELLION GOES UP IN SMOKE?
YOUR FAMILY, SPENCER...THE DALES STAY PROTECTED.
NO. NO, THAT'S NOT TRUE.
I WISH IT WAS, BELIEVE ME--

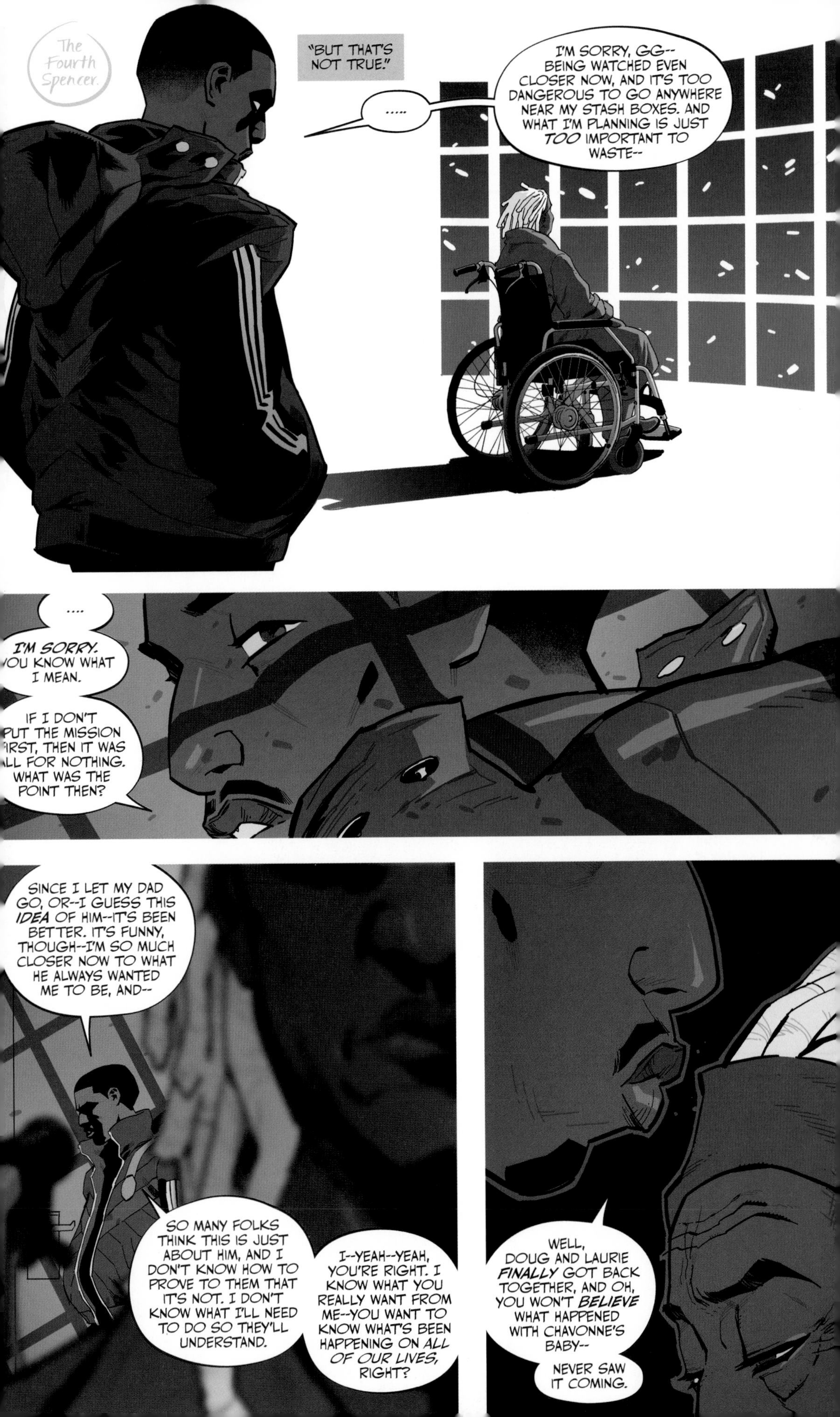
The Fourth Spencer.
"BUT THAT'S NOT TRUE."
.....
I'M SORRY, GG-- BEING WATCHED EVEN CLOSER NOW, AND IT'S TOO DANGEROUS TO GO ANYWHERE NEAR MY STASH BOXES. AND WHAT I'M PLANNING IS JUST TOO IMPORTANT TO WASTE--
....
I'M SORRY. YOU KNOW WHAT I MEAN.
IF I DON'T PUT THE MISSION FIRST, THEN IT WAS ALL FOR NOTHING. WHAT WAS THE POINT THEN?
SINCE I LET MY DAD GO, OR--I GUESS THIS IDEA OF HIM--IT'S BEEN BETTER. IT'S FUNNY, THOUGH--I'M SO MUCH CLOSER NOW TO WHAT HE ALWAYS WANTED ME TO BE, AND--
SO MANY FOLKS THINK THIS IS JUST ABOUT HIM, AND I DON'T KNOW HOW TO PROVE TO THEM THAT IT'S NOT. I DON'T KNOW WHAT I'LL NEED TO DO SO THEY'LL UNDERSTAND.
I--YEAH--YEAH, YOU'RE RIGHT. I KNOW WHAT YOU REALLY WANT FROM ME--YOU WANT TO KNOW WHAT'S BEEN HAPPENING ON ALL OF OUR LIVES, RIGHT?
WELL, DOUG AND LAURIE FINALLY GOT BACK TOGETHER, AND OH, YOU WON'T BELIEVE WHAT HAPPENED WITH CHAVONNE'S BABY--
NEVER SAW IT COMING.

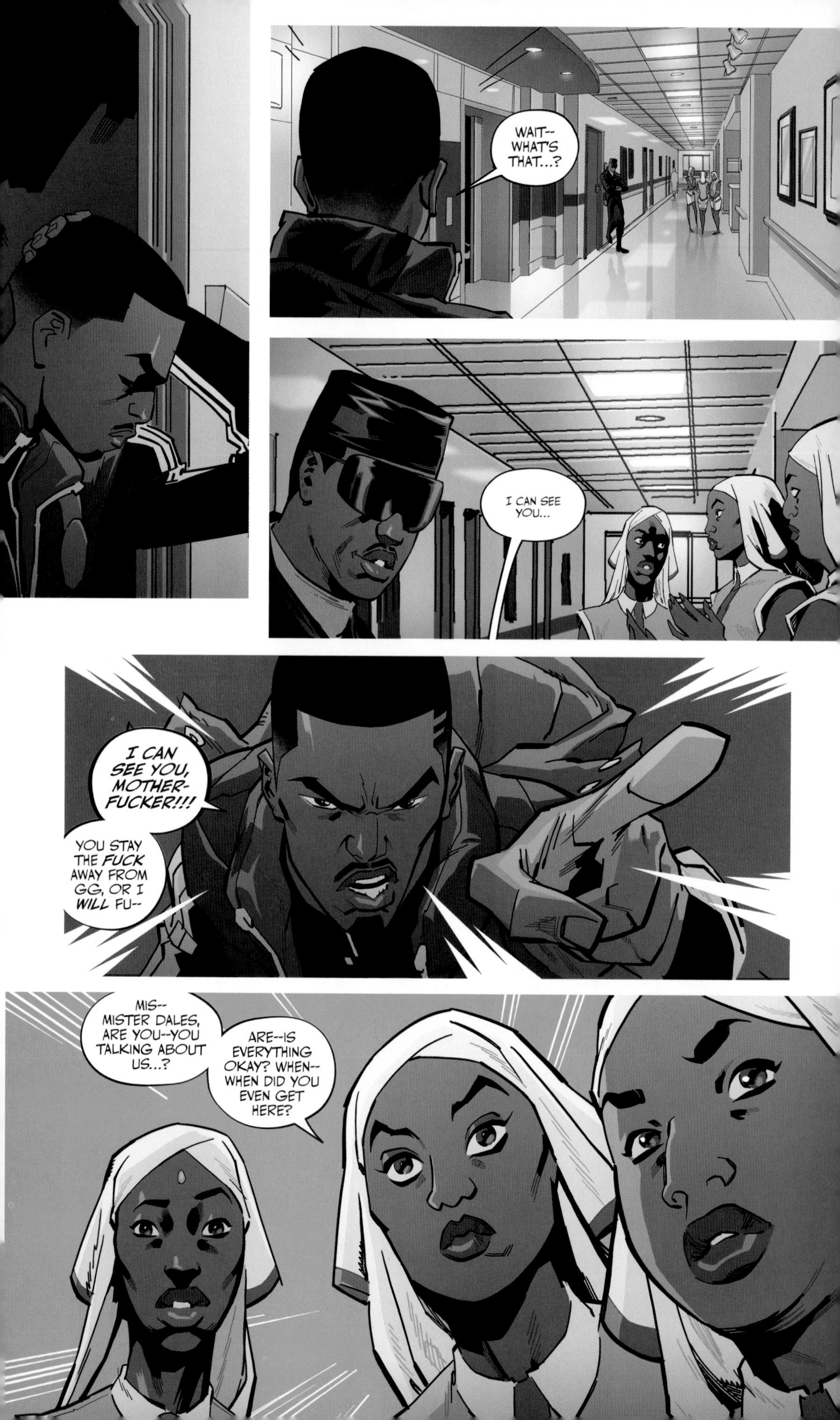
WAIT-- WHAT'S THAT...?
I CAN SEE YOU...
I CAN SEE YOU, MOTHER-FUCKER!!!
YOU STAY THE *FUCK* AWAY FROM GG, OR I *WILL* FU--
MIS-- MISTER DALES, ARE YOU--YOU TALKING ABOUT US...?
ARE--IS EVERYTHING OKAY? WHEN-- WHEN DID YOU EVEN GET HERE?

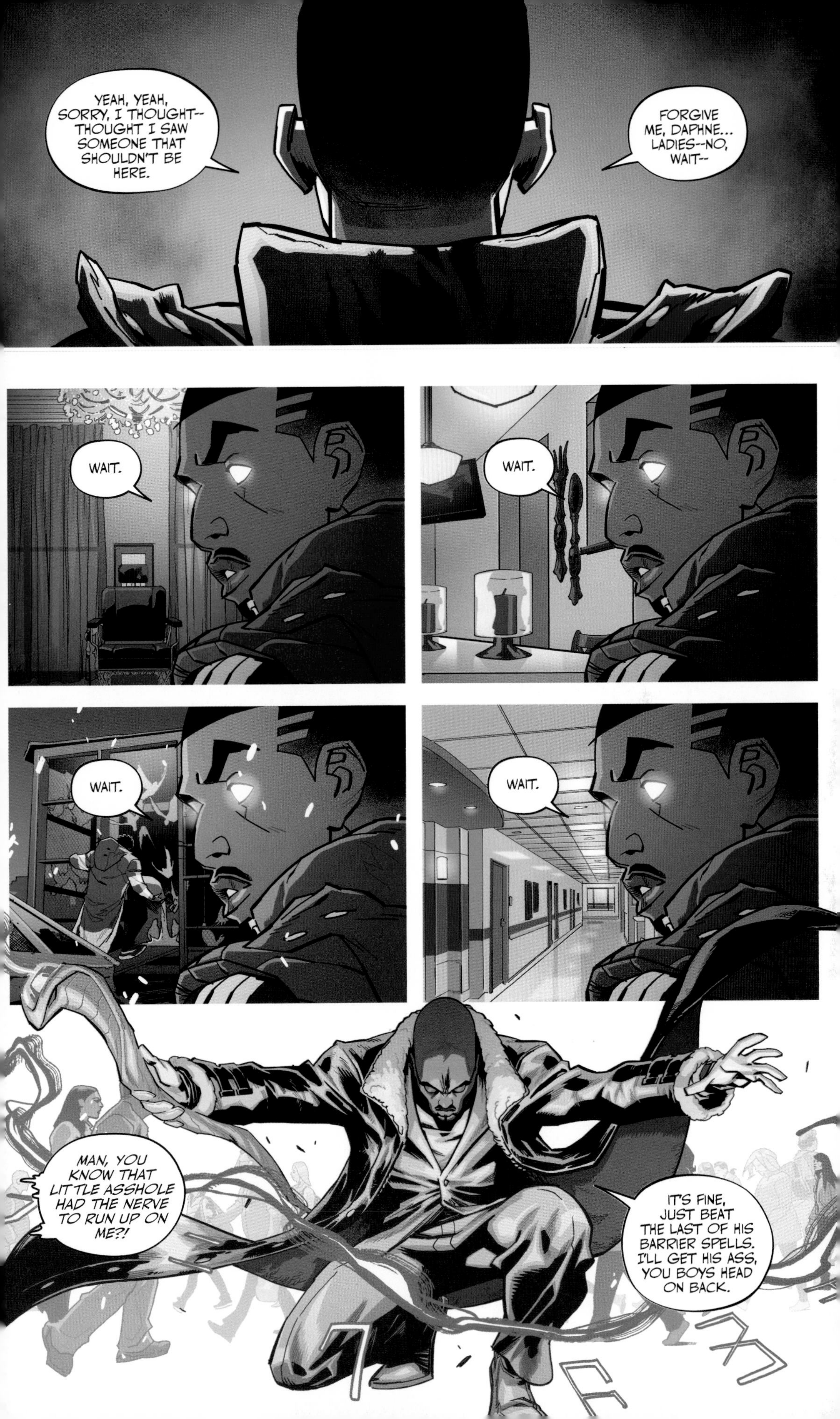
YEAH, YEAH, SORRY, I THOUGHT-- THOUGHT I SAW SOMEONE THAT SHOULDN'T BE HERE.
FORGIVE ME, DAPHNE... LADIES--NO, WAIT--
WAIT.
WAIT.
WAIT.
WAIT.
MAN, YOU KNOW THAT LITTLE ASSHOLE HAD THE NERVE TO RUN UP ON ME?!
IT'S FINE, JUST BEAT THE LAST OF HIS BARRIER SPELLS. I'LL GET HIS ASS, YOU BOYS HEAD ON BACK.

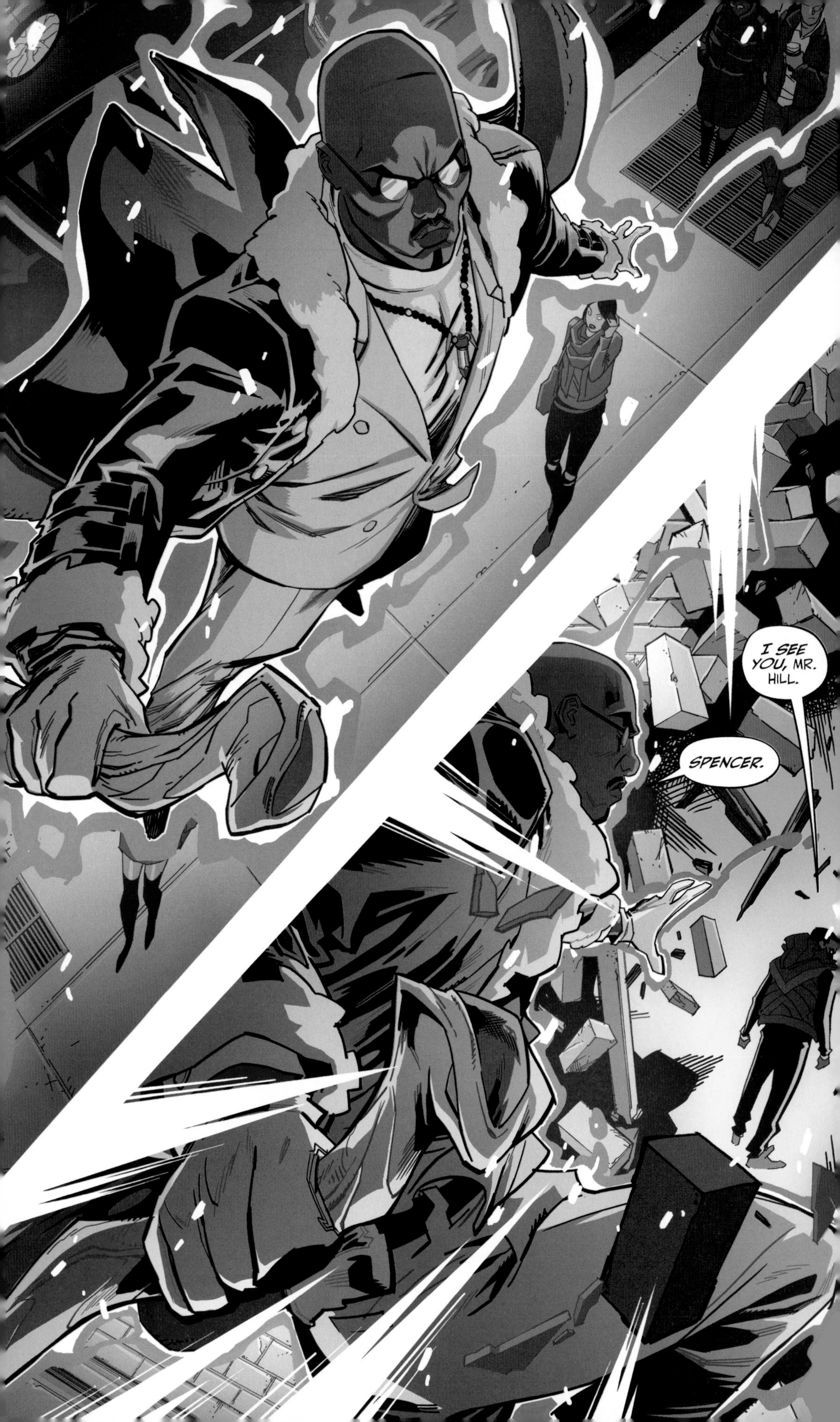
I SEE YOU, MR. HILL.
SPENCER.

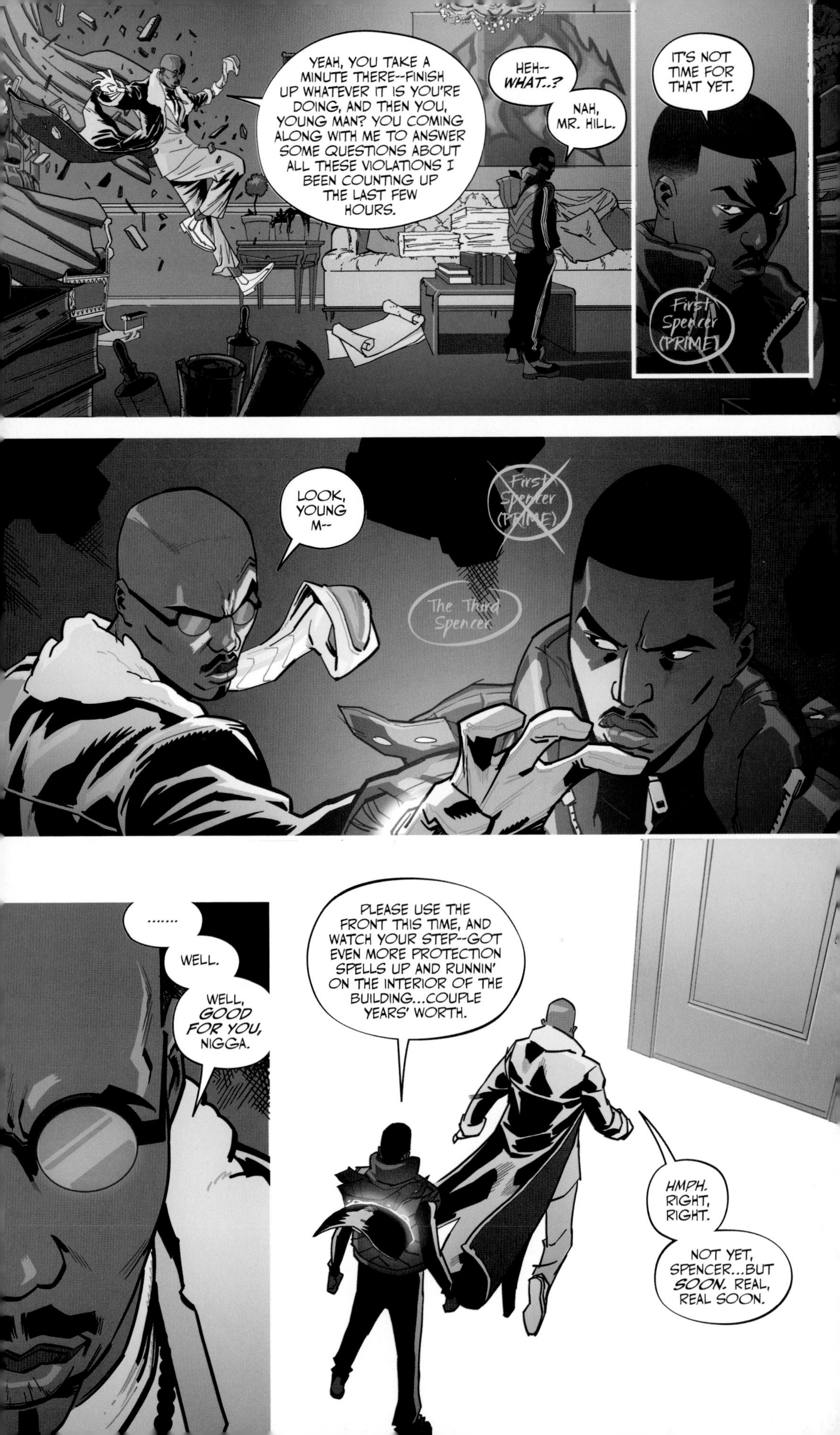
YEAH, YOU TAKE A MINUTE THERE--FINISH UP WHATEVER IT IS YOU'RE DOING, AND THEN YOU, YOUNG MAN? YOU COMING ALONG WITH ME TO ANSWER SOME QUESTIONS ABOUT ALL THESE VIOLATIONS I BEEN COUNTING UP THE LAST FEW HOURS.
HEH-- WHAT..?
NAH, MR. HILL.
IT'S NOT TIME FOR THAT YET.
First Spencer (PRIME)
LOOK, YOUNG M--
First Spencer (PRIME)
The Third Spencer
....
WELL.
WELL, GOOD FOR YOU, NIGGA.
PLEASE USE THE FRONT THIS TIME, AND WATCH YOUR STEP--GOT EVEN MORE PROTECTION SPELLS UP AND RUNNIN' ON THE INTERIOR OF THE BUILDING...COUPLE YEARS' WORTH.
HMPH. RIGHT, RIGHT.
NOT YET, SPENCER...BUT SOON. REAL, REAL SOON.

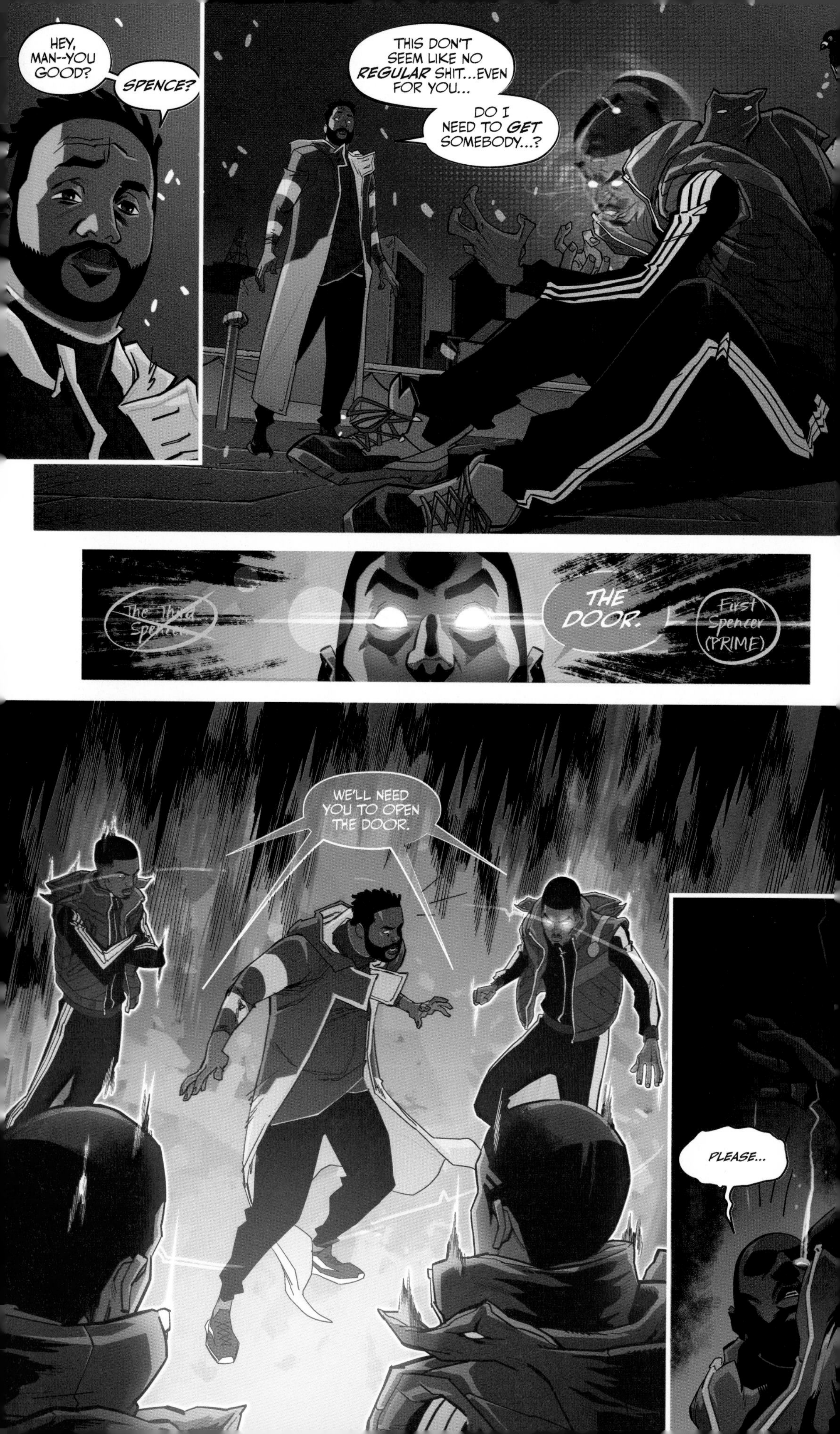
HEY, MAN--YOU GOOD?
SPENCE?
THIS DON'T SEEM LIKE NO REGULAR SHIT...EVEN FOR YOU...
DO I NEED TO GET SOMEBODY...?
The Third Spencer
THE DOOR.
First Spencer (PRIME)
WE'LL NEED YOU TO OPEN THE DOOR.
PLEASE...

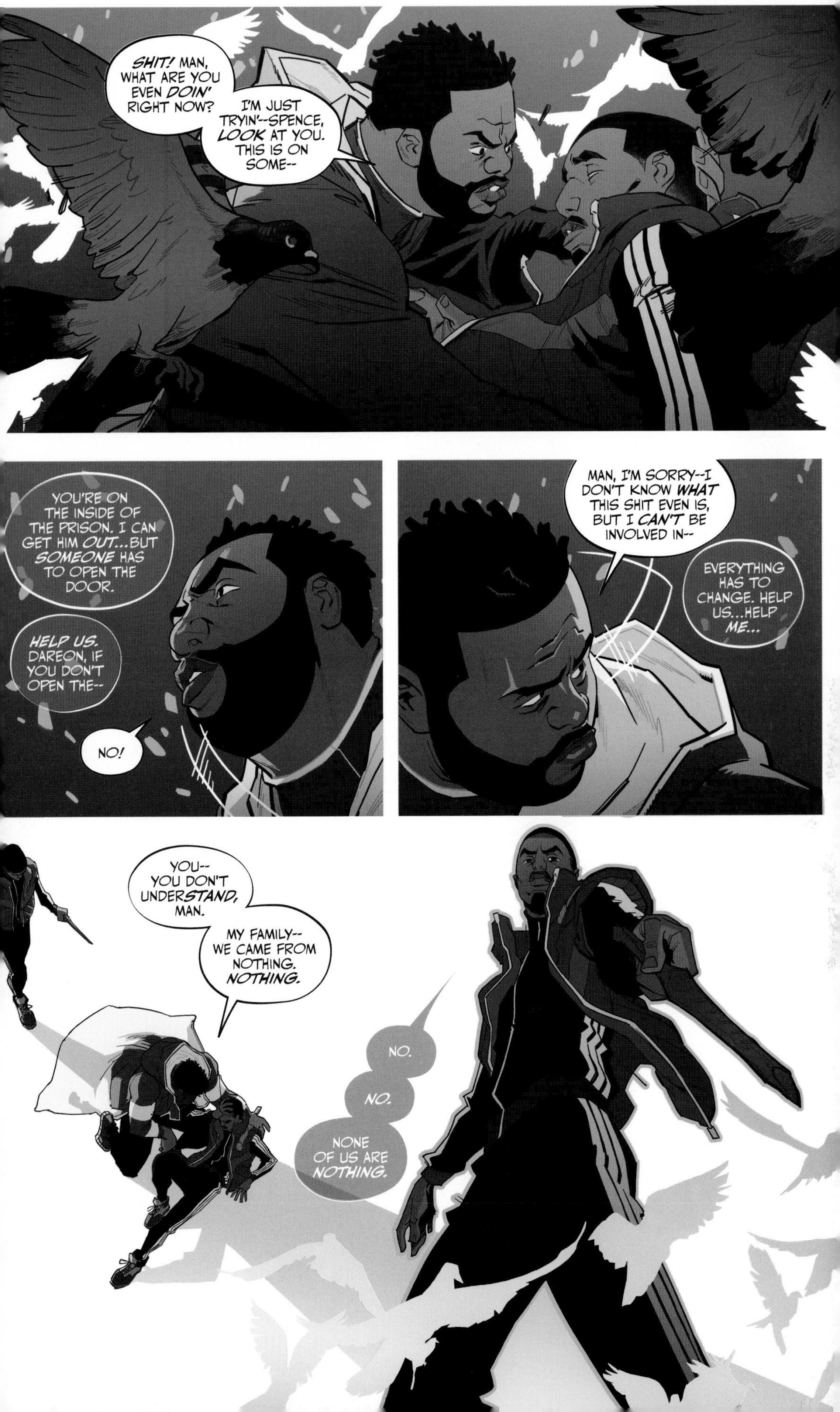

SHIT! MAN, WHAT ARE YOU EVEN DOIN' RIGHT NOW?
I'M JUST TRYIN'--SPENCE, LOOK AT YOU. THIS IS ON SOME--
YOU'RE ON THE INSIDE OF THE PRISON. I CAN GET HIM OUT...BUT SOMEONE HAS TO OPEN THE DOOR.
HELP US. DAREON, IF YOU DON'T OPEN THE--
NO!
MAN, I'M SORRY--I DON'T KNOW WHAT THIS SHIT EVEN IS, BUT I CAN'T BE INVOLVED IN--
EVERYTHING HAS TO CHANGE. HELP US...HELP ME...
YOU-- YOU DON'T UNDERSTAND, MAN.
MY FAMILY-- WE CAME FROM NOTHING. NOTHING.
NO.
NO.
NONE OF US ARE NOTHING.

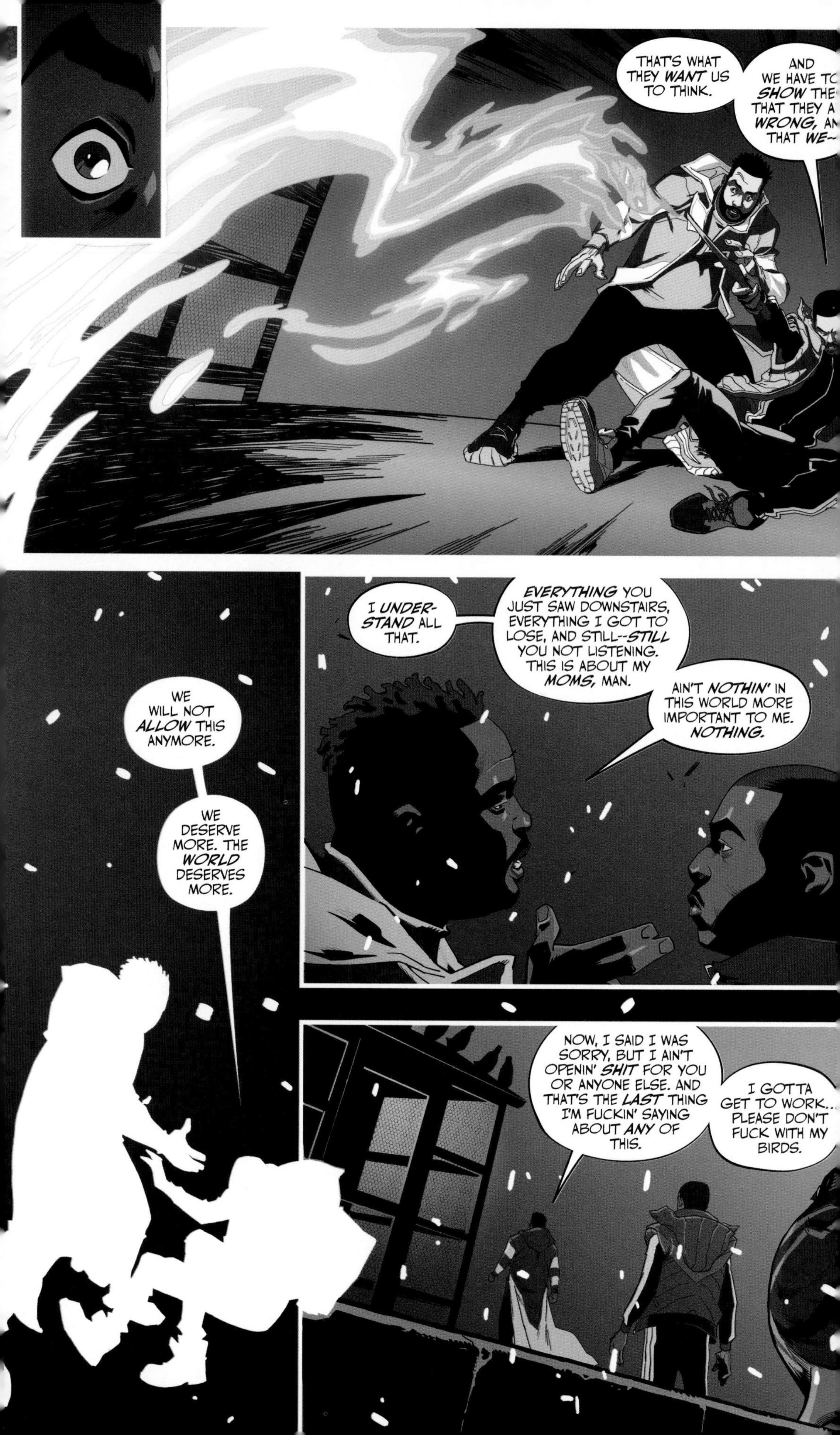

THAT'S WHAT THEY WANT US TO THINK.
AND WE HAVE TO SHOW THE THAT THEY A WRONG, AN THAT WE--
WE WILL NOT ALLOW THIS ANYMORE.
WE DESERVE MORE. THE WORLD DESERVES MORE.
I UNDER-STAND ALL THAT.
EVERYTHING YOU JUST SAW DOWNSTAIRS, EVERYTHING I GOT TO LOSE, AND STILL--STILL YOU NOT LISTENING. THIS IS ABOUT MY MOMS, MAN.
AIN'T NOTHIN' IN THIS WORLD MORE IMPORTANT TO ME. NOTHING.
NOW, I SAID I WAS SORRY, BUT I AIN'T OPENIN' SHIT FOR YOU OR ANYONE ELSE. AND THAT'S THE LAST THING I'M FUCKIN' SAYING ABOUT ANY OF THIS.
I GOTTA GET TO WORK... PLEASE DON'T FUCK WITH MY BIRDS.

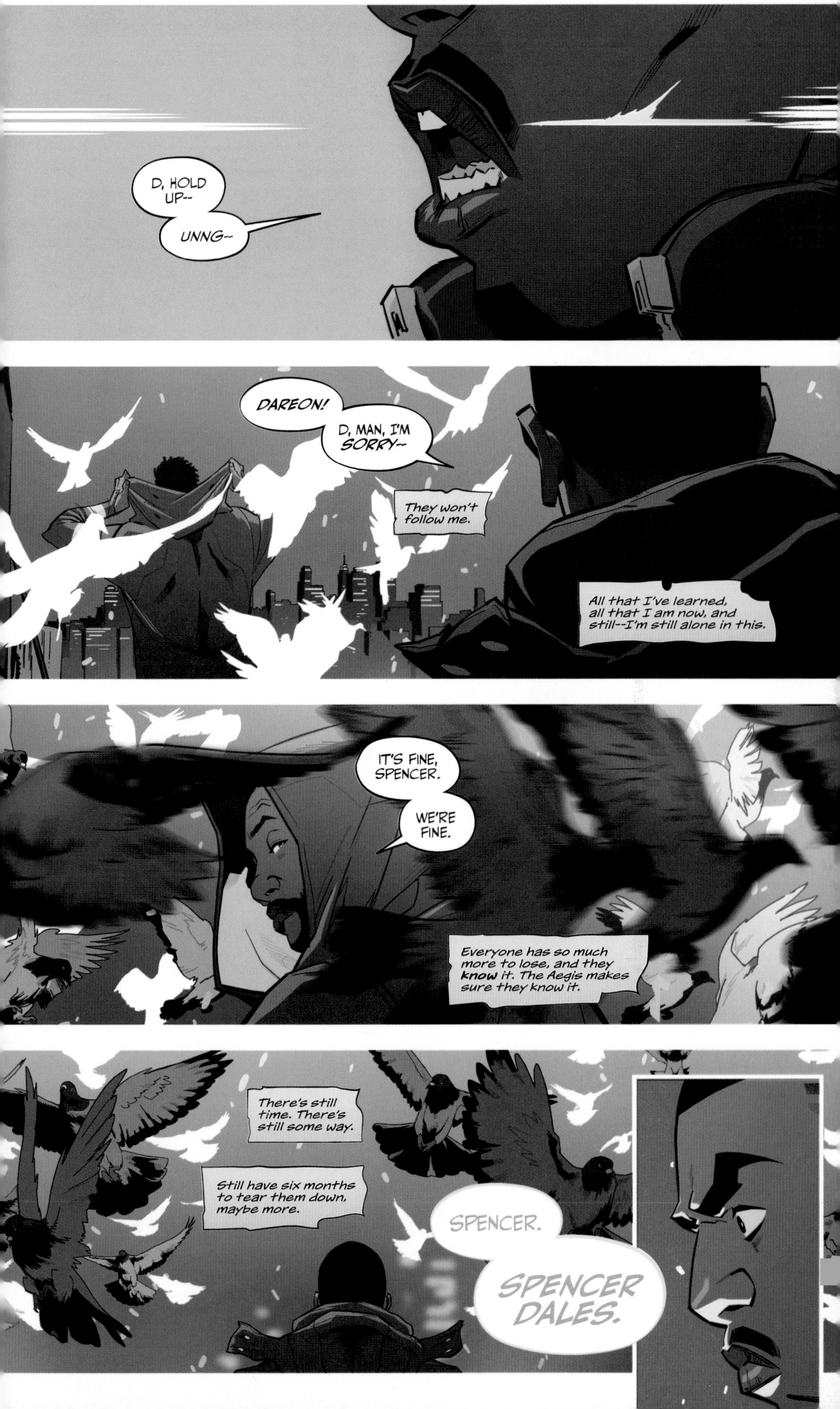
D, HOLD UP--
UNNG--
DAREON!
D, MAN, I'M SORRY--
They won't follow me.
All that I've learned, all that I am now, and still--I'm still alone in this.
IT'S FINE, SPENCER.
WE'RE FINE.
Everyone has so much more to lose, and they **know** it. The Aegis makes sure they know it.
There's still time. There's still some way.
Still have six months to tear them down, maybe more.
SPENCER.
SPENCER DALES.

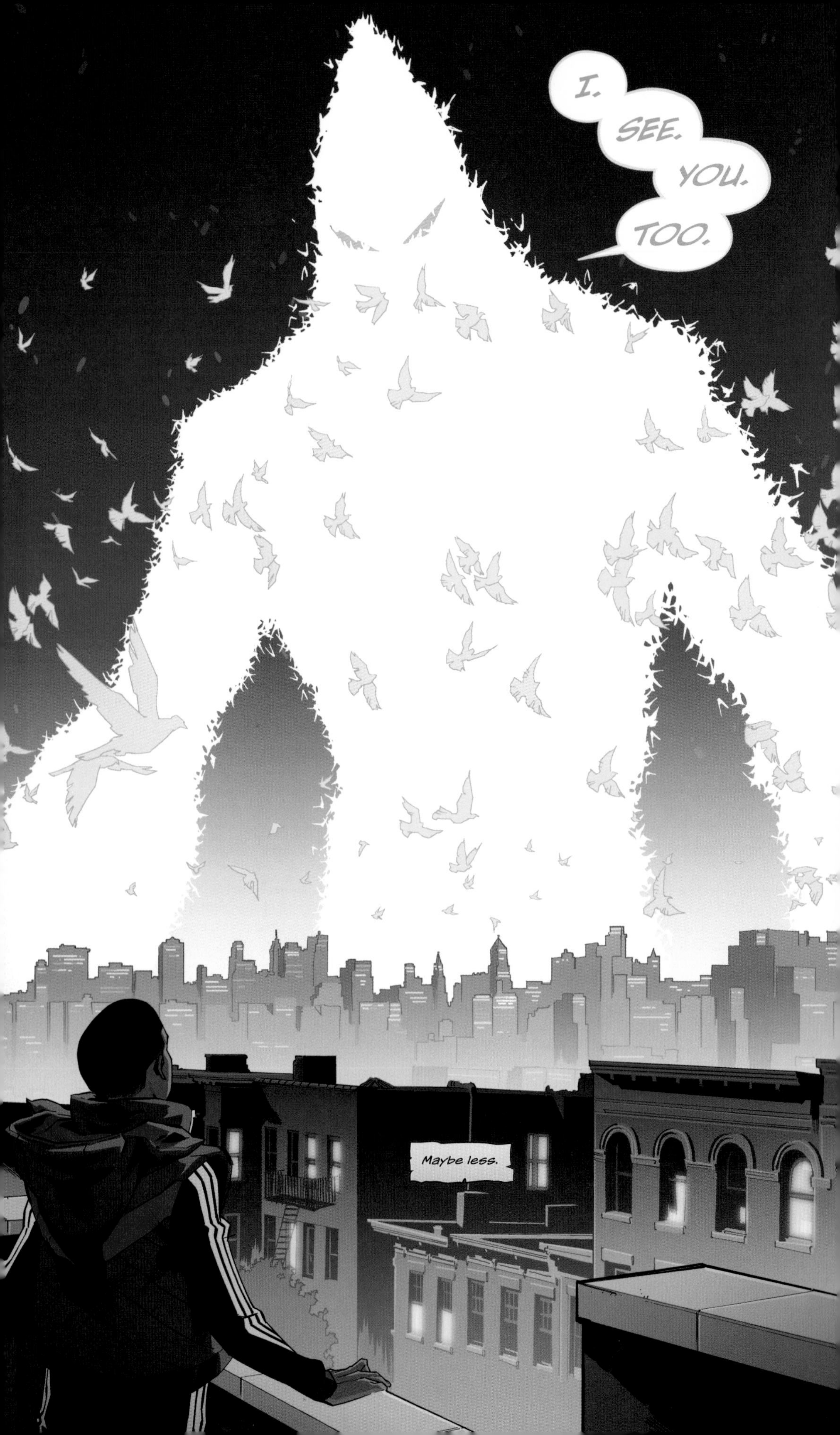
I.
SEE.
YOU.
TOO.
Maybe less.

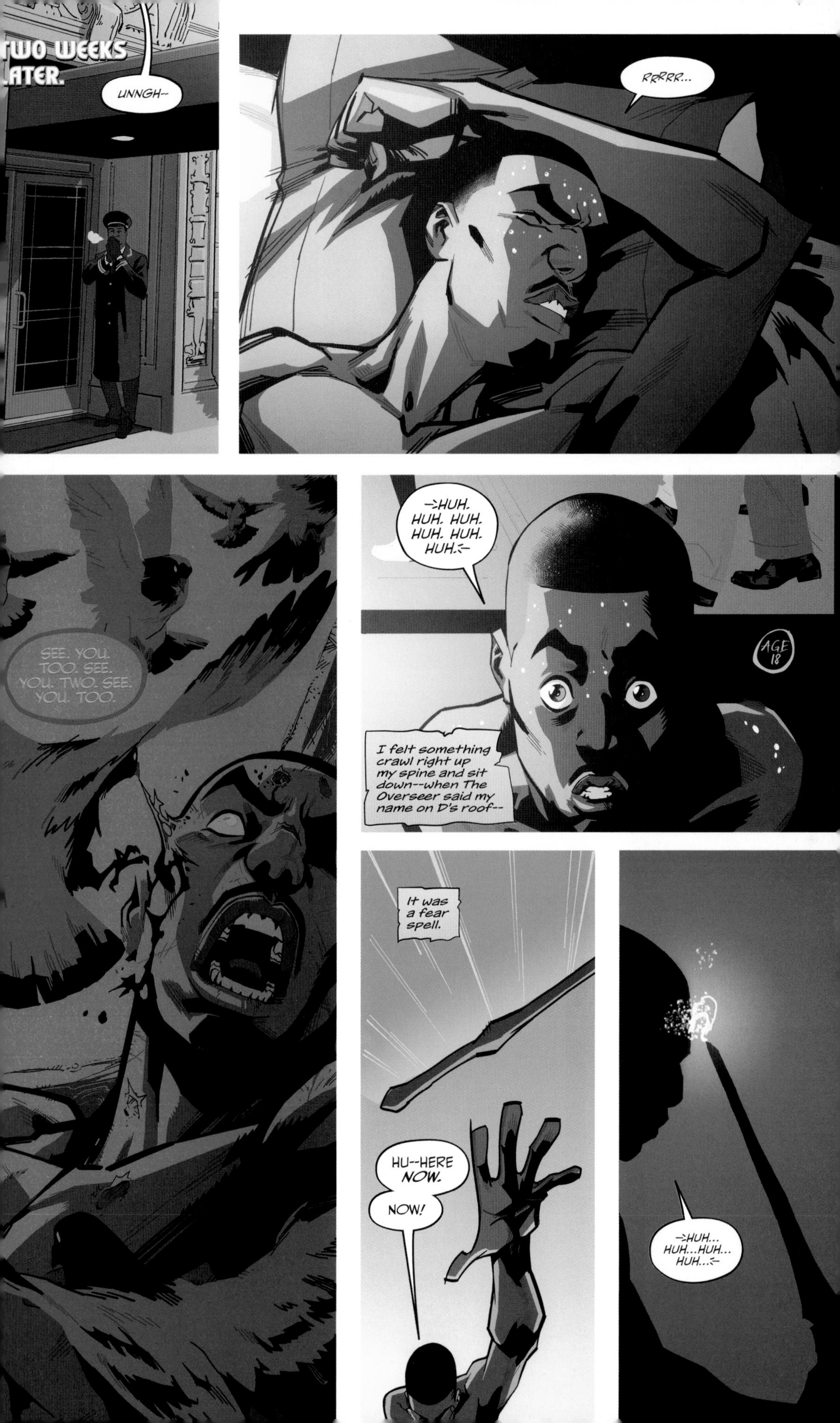
TWO WEEKS LATER.
UNNGH--
RRRRR...
SEE. YOU. TOO. SEE. YOU. TWO. SEE. YOU. TOO.
--HUH. HUH. HUH. HUH. HUH. HUH.--
AGE 18
I felt something crawl right up my spine and sit down--when The Overseer said my name on D's roof--
It was a fear spell.
HU--HERE NOW.
NOW!
--HUH... HUH...HUH... HUH...--

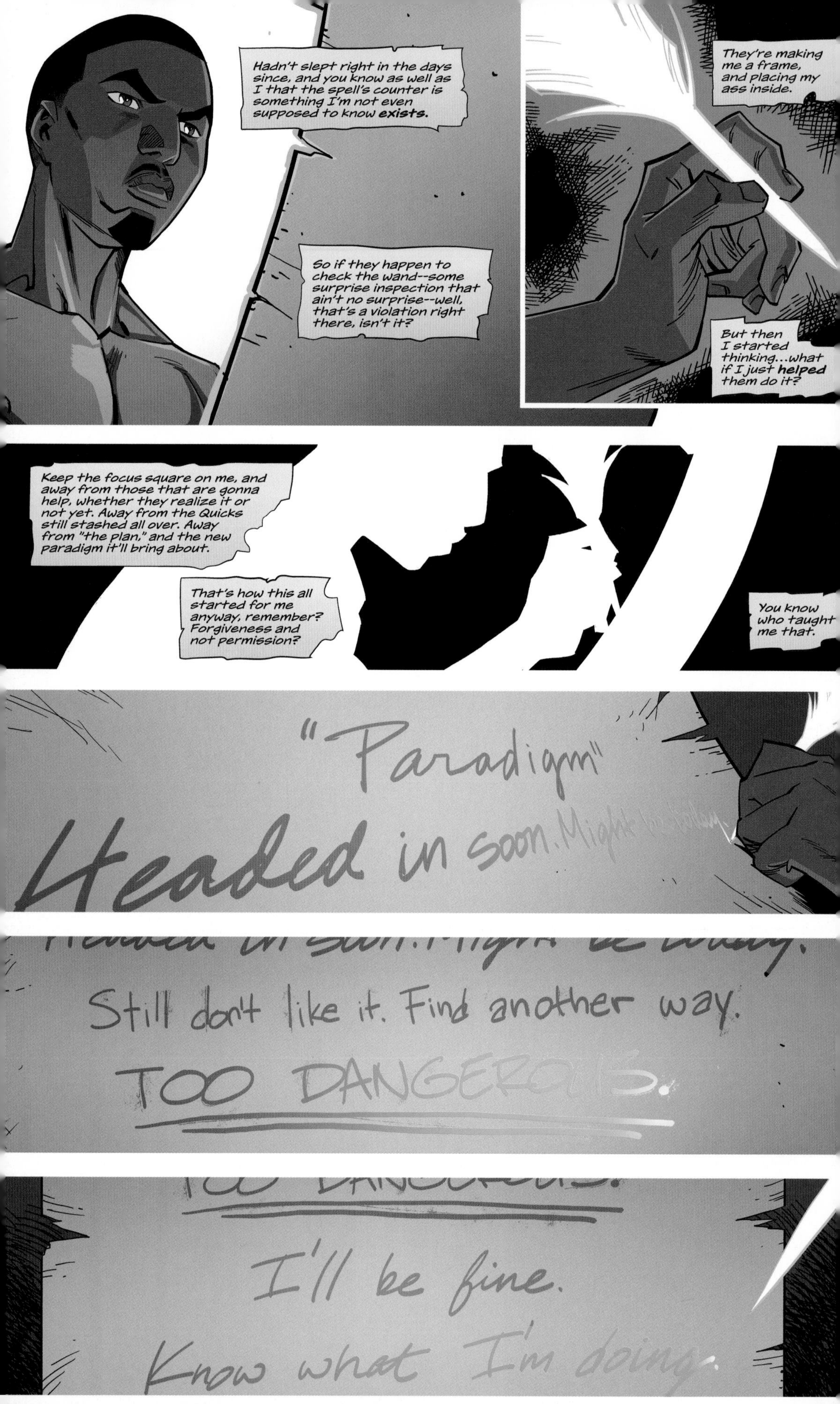

Hadn't slept right in the days since, and you know as well as I that the spell's counter is something I'm not even supposed to know **exists.**
So if they happen to check the wand--some surprise inspection that ain't no surprise--well, that's a violation right there, isn't it?
They're making me a frame, and placing my ass inside.
But then I started thinking...what if I just **helped** them do it?
Keep the focus square on me, and away from those that are gonna help, whether they realize it or not yet. Away from the Quicks still stashed all over. Away from "the plan," and the new paradigm it'll bring about.
That's how this all started for me anyway, remember? Forgiveness and not permission?
You know who taught me that.
"Paradigm"
Headed in soon.
Still don't like it. Find another way.
TOO DANGEROUS.
I'll be fine.
Know what I'm doing.

ATER.

THE COLUMN, SECURE WING.
INTERROGATION ROOM #312.

Man, I do hate those rooms though...

Like everything about The Aegis, they're relics from an earlier time--a reminder that so many look like us left places *just* like this--

With our lives **changed.** Stolen away. For nothing.

And that's what they want us to know--to *feel* every single time we have one of these "reviews". That it's not promised we'll walk back through those doors free.

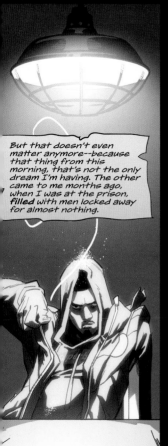

But that doesn't even matter anymore--because that thing from this morning, that's not the only dream I'm having. The other came to me months ago, when I was at the prison, *filled* with men locked away for almost nothing.

There was a sea of lights, and so many more of those wrong doors, but there was something else there, too, and I caught sight of it--something unmistakable. **Undeniable.**

Maybe he can see me. Maybe.

But I know what I saw.

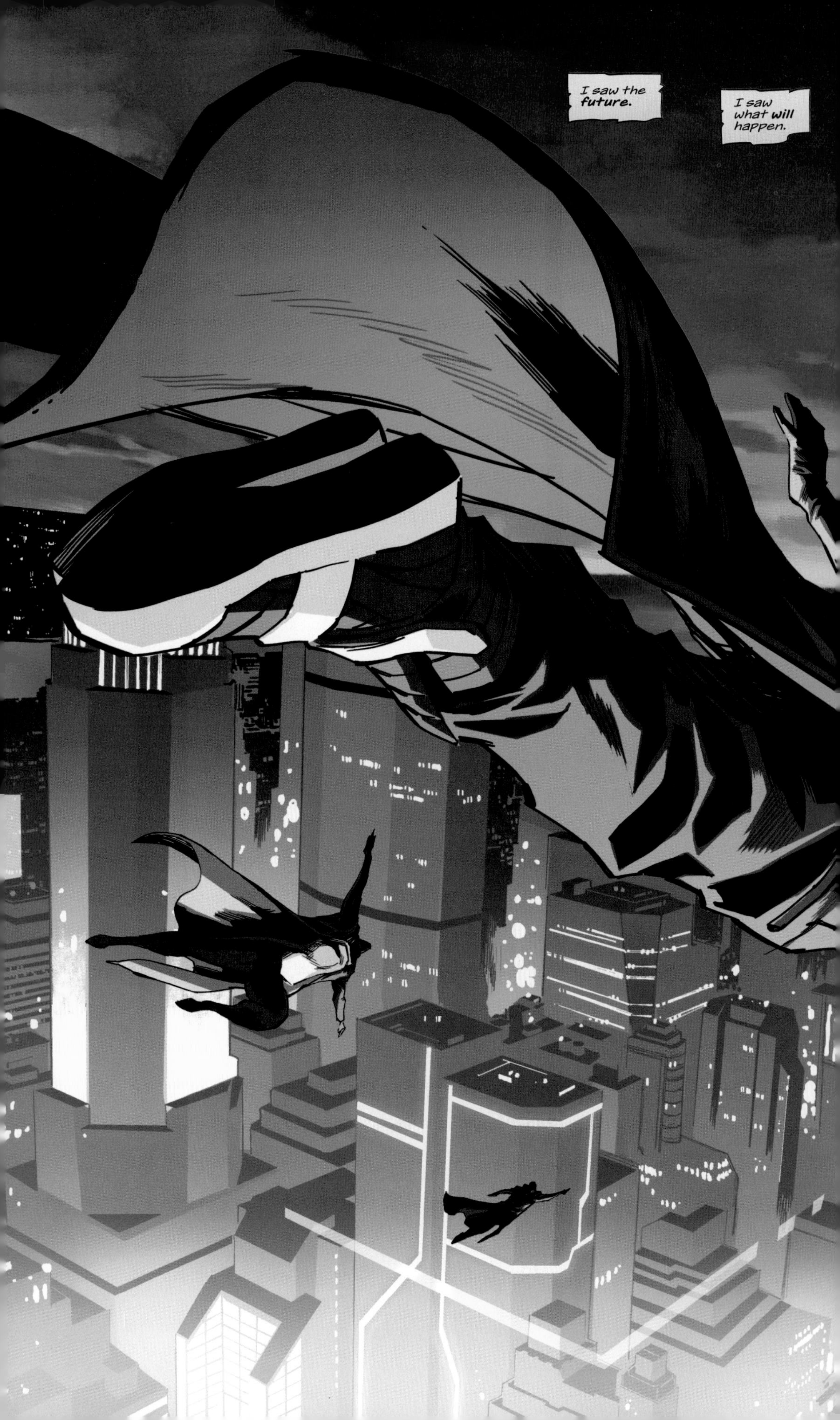
I saw the future.
I saw what will happen.

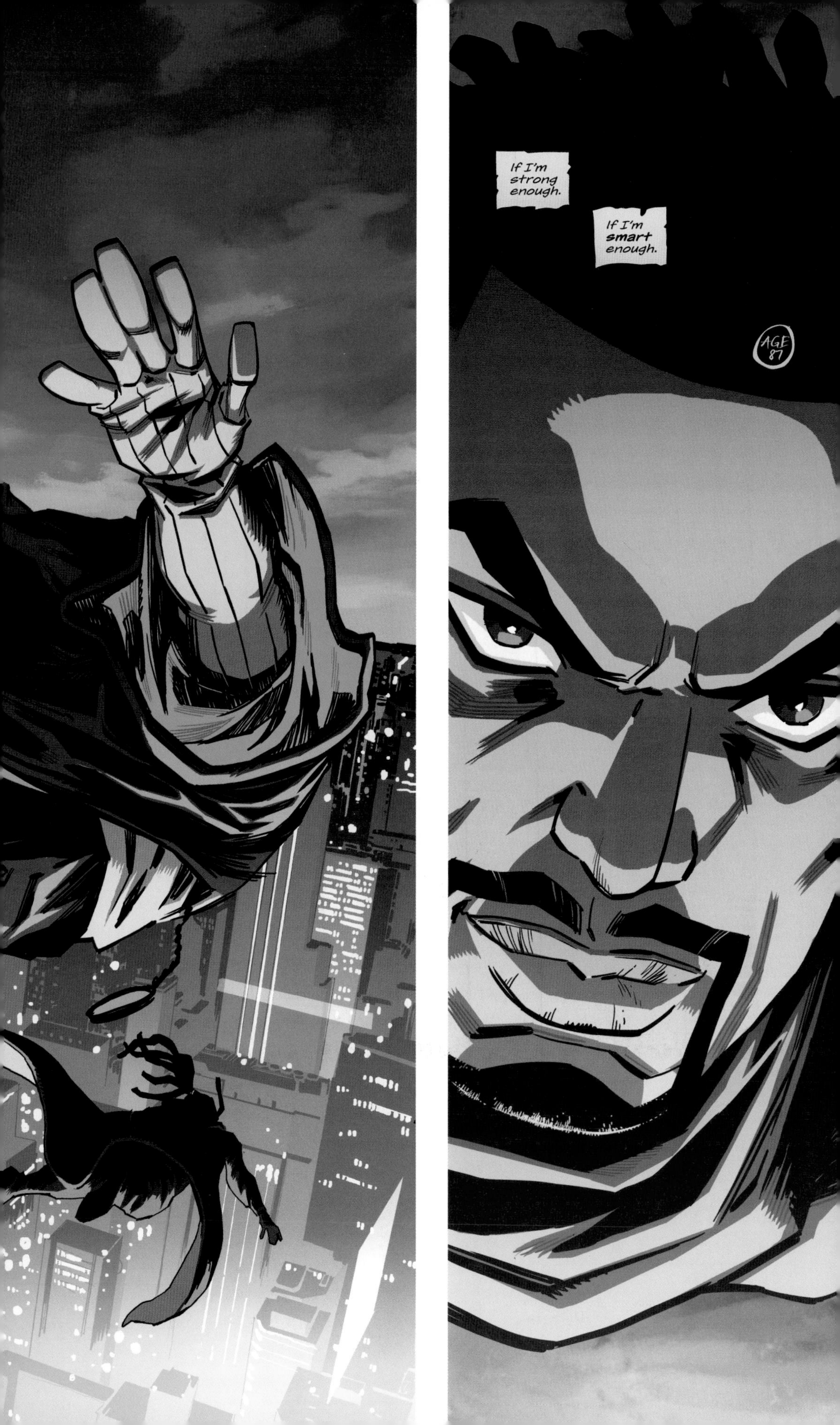
If I'm strong enough.
If I'm **smart** enough.
AGE 87

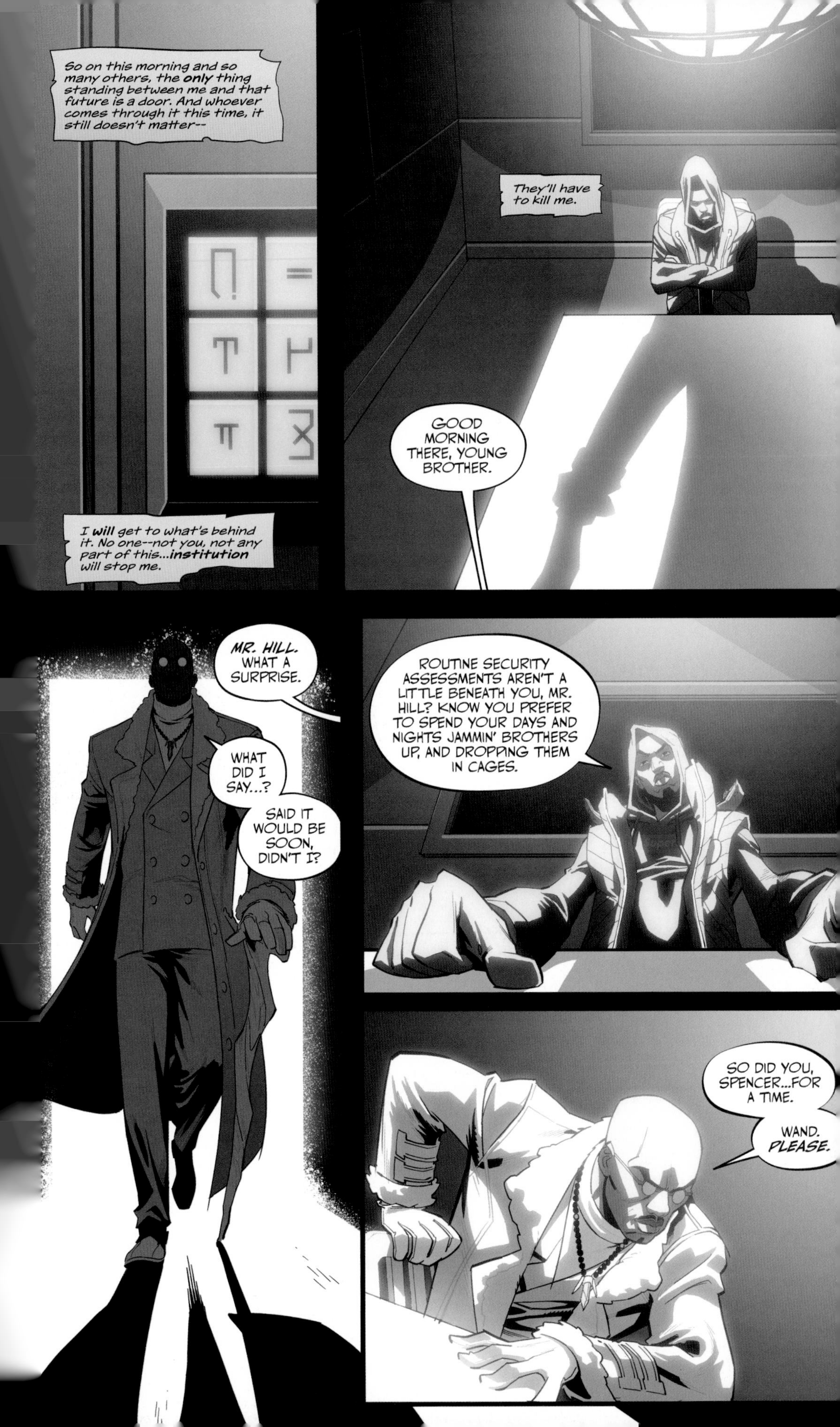

So on this morning and so many others, the only thing standing between me and that future is a door. And whoever comes through it this time, it still doesn't matter--
They'll have to kill me.
I will get to what's behind it. No one--not you, not any part of this...institution will stop me.
GOOD MORNING THERE, YOUNG BROTHER.
MR. HILL. WHAT A SURPRISE.
ROUTINE SECURITY ASSESSMENTS AREN'T A LITTLE BENEATH YOU, MR. HILL? KNOW YOU PREFER TO SPEND YOUR DAYS AND NIGHTS JAMMIN' BROTHERS UP, AND DROPPING THEM IN CAGES.
WHAT DID I SAY...?
SAID IT WOULD BE SOON, DIDN'T I?
SO DID YOU, SPENCER...FOR A TIME.
WAND. PLEASE.

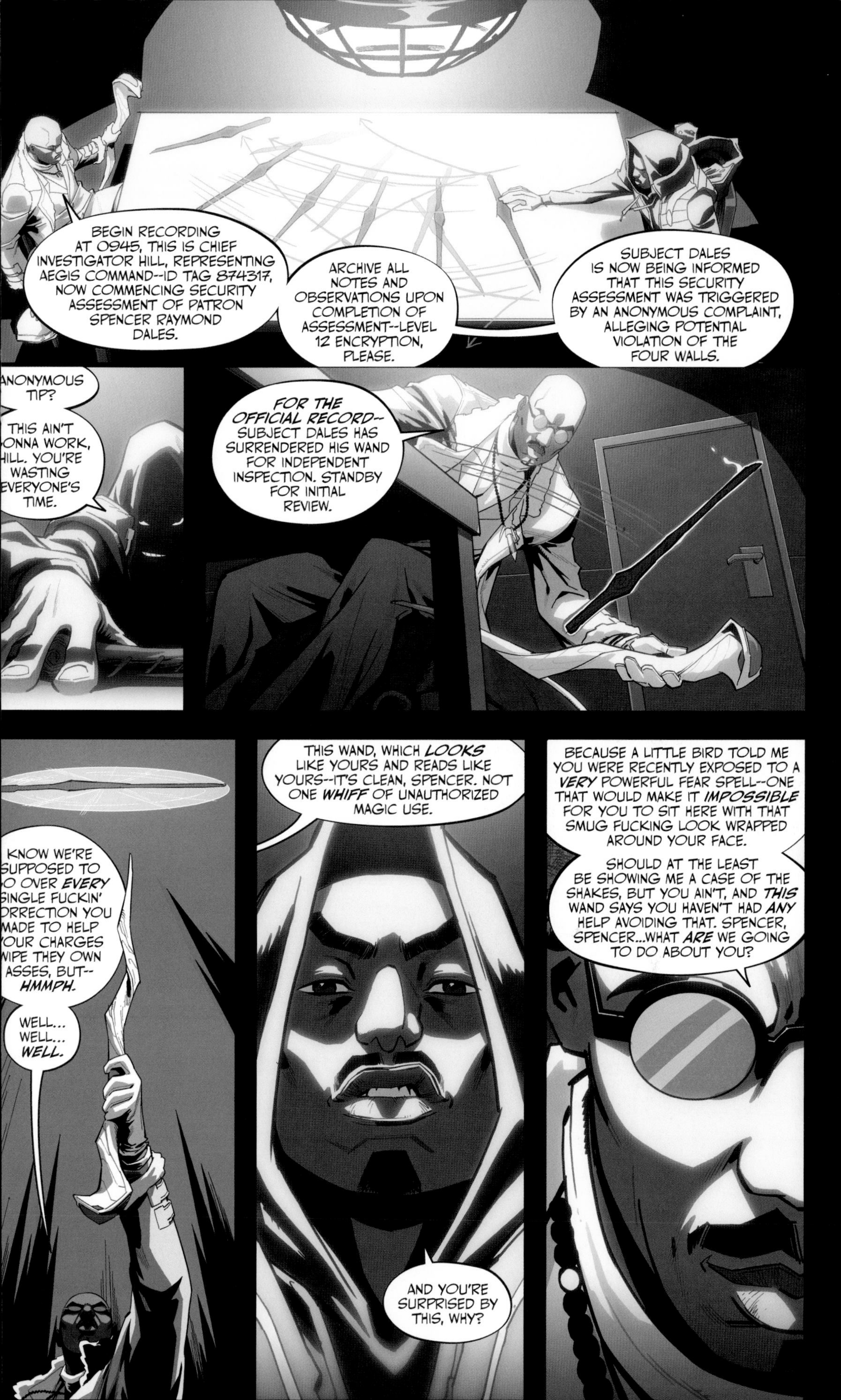
BEGIN RECORDING AT 0945, THIS IS CHIEF INVESTIGATOR HILL, REPRESENTING AEGIS COMMAND--ID TAG 874317, NOW COMMENCING SECURITY ASSESSMENT OF PATRON SPENCER RAYMOND DALES.
ARCHIVE ALL NOTES AND OBSERVATIONS UPON COMPLETION OF ASSESSMENT--LEVEL 12 ENCRYPTION, PLEASE.
SUBJECT DALES IS NOW BEING INFORMED THAT THIS SECURITY ASSESSMENT WAS TRIGGERED BY AN ANONYMOUS COMPLAINT, ALLEGING POTENTIAL VIOLATION OF THE FOUR WALLS.
ANONYMOUS TIP?
THIS AIN'T GONNA WORK, HILL. YOU'RE WASTING EVERYONE'S TIME.
FOR THE OFFICIAL RECORD-- SUBJECT DALES HAS SURRENDERED HIS WAND FOR INDEPENDENT INSPECTION. STANDBY FOR INITIAL REVIEW.
KNOW WE'RE SUPPOSED TO GO OVER *EVERY* SINGLE FUCKIN' CORRECTION YOU MADE TO HELP YOUR CHARGES WIPE THEY OWN ASSES, BUT-- *HMMPH.*
WELL... WELL... *WELL.*
THIS WAND, WHICH *LOOKS* LIKE YOURS AND READS LIKE YOURS--IT'S CLEAN, SPENCER. NOT ONE *WHIFF* OF UNAUTHORIZED MAGIC USE.
AND YOU'RE SURPRISED BY THIS, WHY?
BECAUSE A LITTLE BIRD TOLD ME YOU WERE RECENTLY EXPOSED TO A *VERY* POWERFUL FEAR SPELL--ONE THAT WOULD MAKE IT *IMPOSSIBLE* FOR YOU TO SIT HERE WITH THAT SMUG FUCKING LOOK WRAPPED AROUND YOUR FACE.
SHOULD AT THE LEAST BE SHOWING ME A CASE OF THE SHAKES, BUT YOU AIN'T, AND *THIS* WAND SAYS YOU HAVEN'T HAD *ANY* HELP AVOIDING THAT. SPENCER, SPENCER...WHAT *ARE* WE GOING TO DO ABOUT YOU?

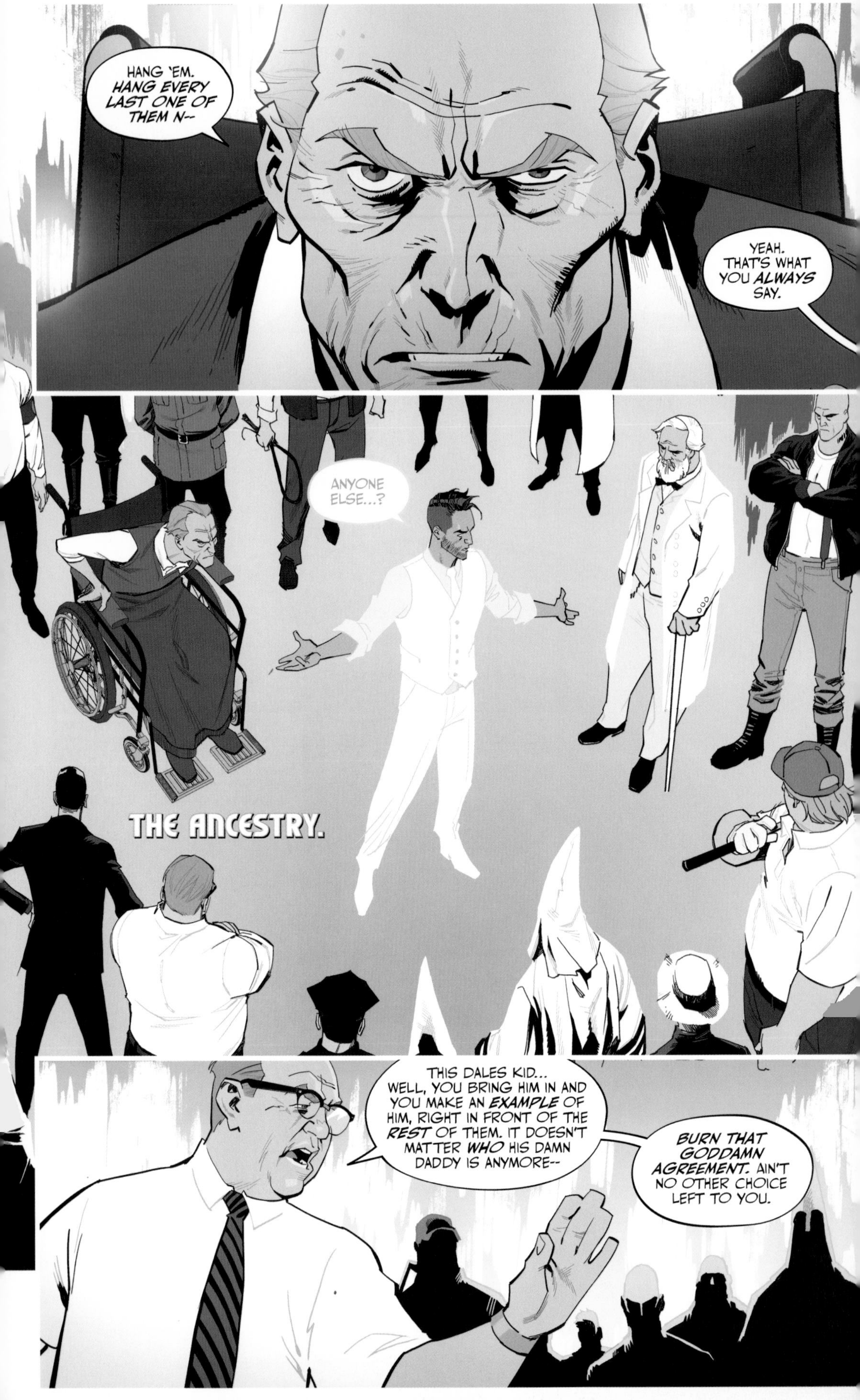
HANG 'EM. HANG EVERY LAST ONE OF THEM N--
YEAH. THAT'S WHAT YOU ALWAYS SAY.
ANYONE ELSE...?
THE ANCESTRY.
THIS DALES KID... WELL, YOU BRING HIM IN AND YOU MAKE AN EXAMPLE OF HIM, RIGHT IN FRONT OF THE REST OF THEM. IT DOESN'T MATTER WHO HIS DAMN DADDY IS ANYMORE--
BURN THAT GODDAMN AGREEMENT. AIN'T NO OTHER CHOICE LEFT TO YOU.

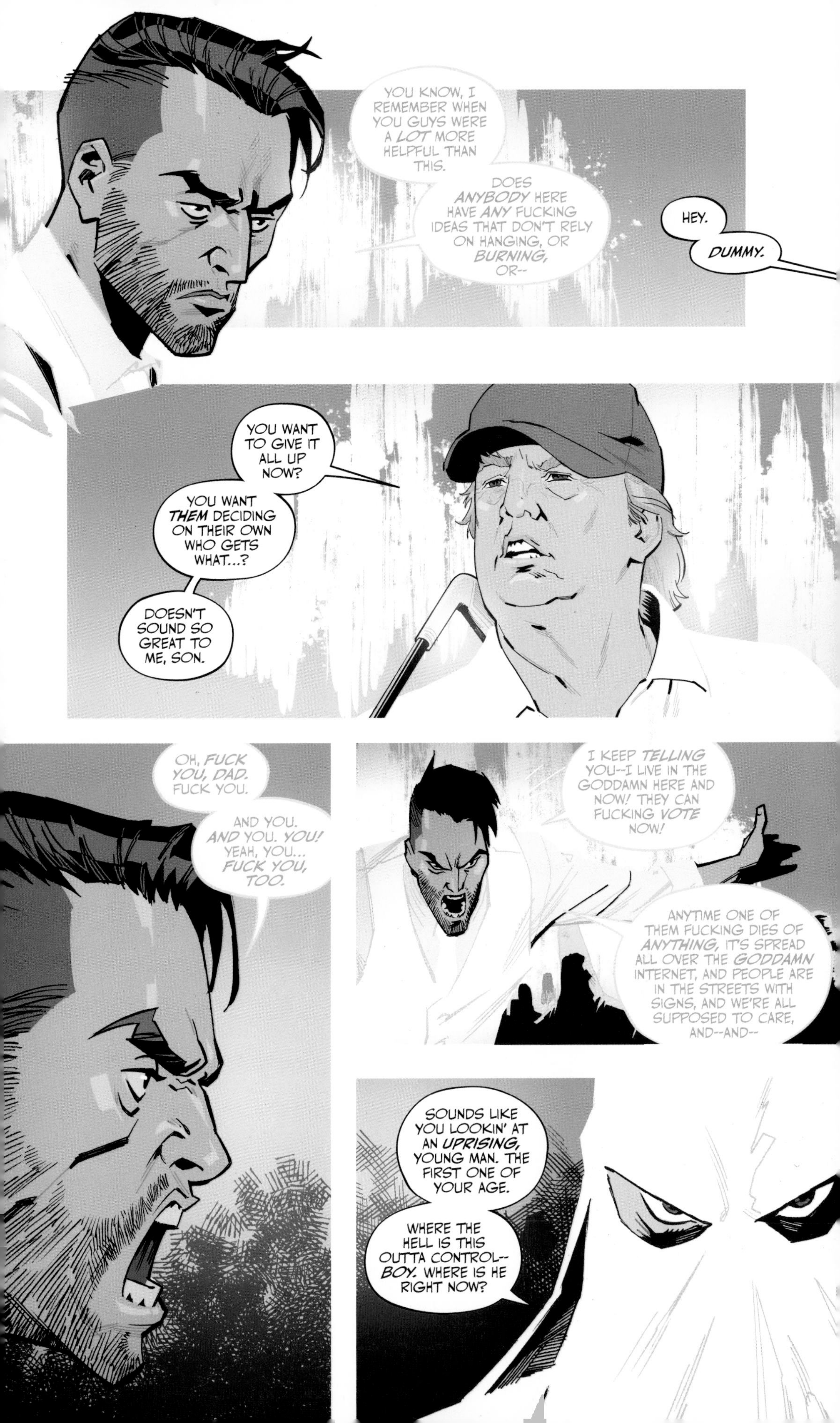
YOU KNOW, I REMEMBER WHEN YOU GUYS WERE A LOT MORE HELPFUL THAN THIS.
DOES ANYBODY HERE HAVE ANY FUCKING IDEAS THAT DON'T RELY ON HANGING, OR BURNING, OR--
HEY.
DUMMY.
YOU WANT TO GIVE IT ALL UP NOW?
YOU WANT THEM DECIDING ON THEIR OWN WHO GETS WHAT...?
DOESN'T SOUND SO GREAT TO ME, SON.
OH, FUCK YOU, DAD. FUCK YOU.
AND YOU. AND YOU. YOU! YEAH, YOU... FUCK YOU, TOO.
I KEEP TELLING YOU--I LIVE IN THE GODDAMN HERE AND NOW! THEY CAN FUCKING VOTE NOW!
ANYTIME ONE OF THEM FUCKING DIES OF ANYTHING, IT'S SPREAD ALL OVER THE GODDAMN INTERNET, AND PEOPLE ARE IN THE STREETS WITH SIGNS, AND WE'RE ALL SUPPOSED TO CARE, AND--AND--
SOUNDS LIKE YOU LOOKIN' AT AN UPRISING, YOUNG MAN. THE FIRST ONE OF YOUR AGE.
WHERE THE HELL IS THIS OUTTA CONTROL--BOY. WHERE IS HE RIGHT NOW?

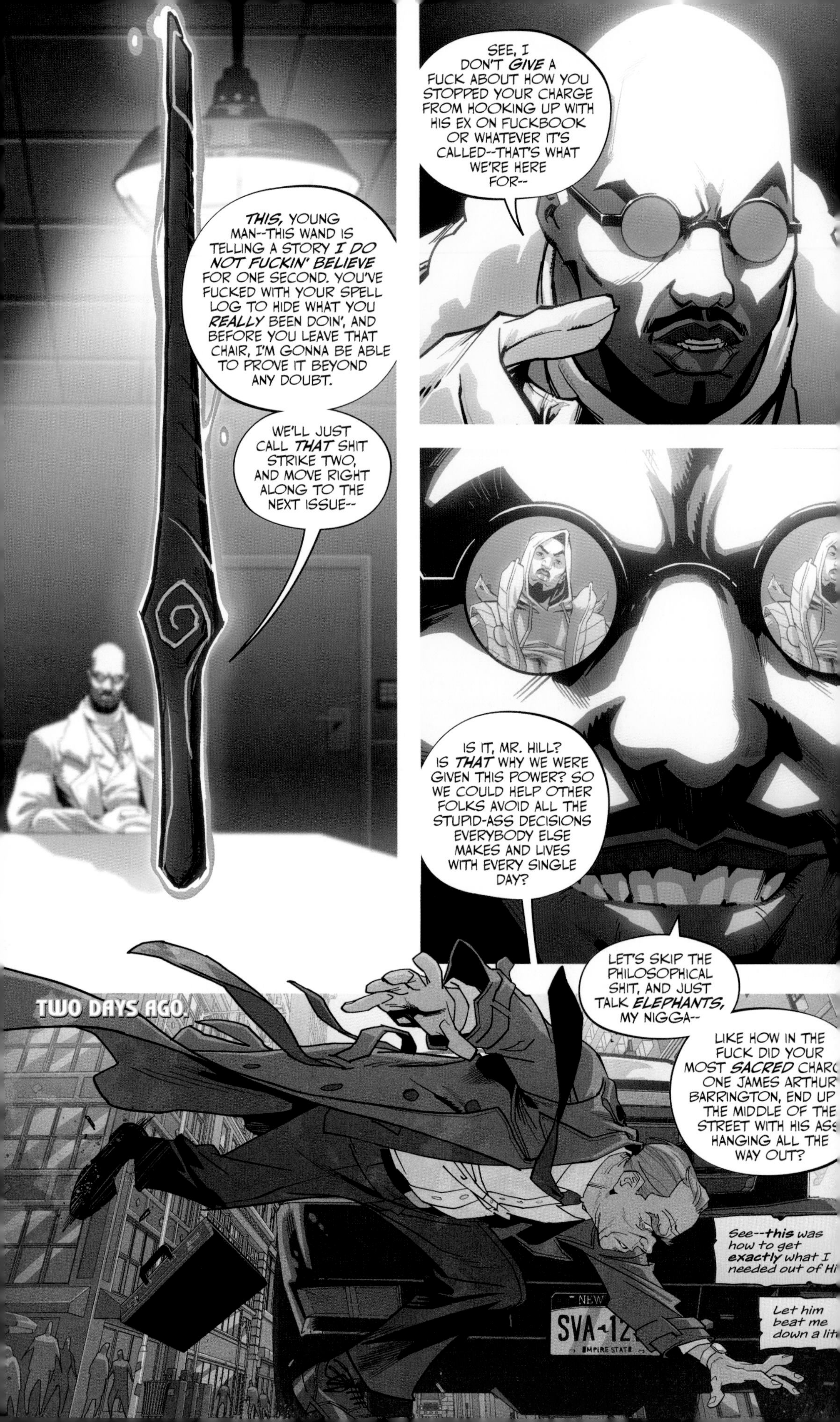

THIS, YOUNG MAN--THIS WAND IS TELLING A STORY I DO NOT FUCKIN' BELIEVE FOR ONE SECOND. YOU'VE FUCKED WITH YOUR SPELL LOG TO HIDE WHAT YOU REALLY BEEN DOIN', AND BEFORE YOU LEAVE THAT CHAIR, I'M GONNA BE ABLE TO PROVE IT BEYOND ANY DOUBT.
WE'LL JUST CALL THAT SHIT STRIKE TWO, AND MOVE RIGHT ALONG TO THE NEXT ISSUE--
SEE, I DON'T GIVE A FUCK ABOUT HOW YOU STOPPED YOUR CHARGE FROM HOOKING UP WITH HIS EX ON FUCKBOOK OR WHATEVER IT'S CALLED--THAT'S WHAT WE'RE HERE FOR--
IS IT, MR. HILL? IS THAT WHY WE WERE GIVEN THIS POWER? SO WE COULD HELP OTHER FOLKS AVOID ALL THE STUPID-ASS DECISIONS EVERYBODY ELSE MAKES AND LIVES WITH EVERY SINGLE DAY?
LET'S SKIP THE PHILOSOPHICAL SHIT, AND JUST TALK ELEPHANTS, MY NIGGA--
LIKE HOW IN THE FUCK DID YOUR MOST SACRED CHARG ONE JAMES ARTHUR BARRINGTON, END UP THE MIDDLE OF THE STREET WITH HIS ASS HANGING ALL THE WAY OUT?
TWO DAYS AGO.
See--this was how to get exactly what I needed out of Hi
Let him beat me down a lit
NEW
SVA-12
EMPIRE STATE

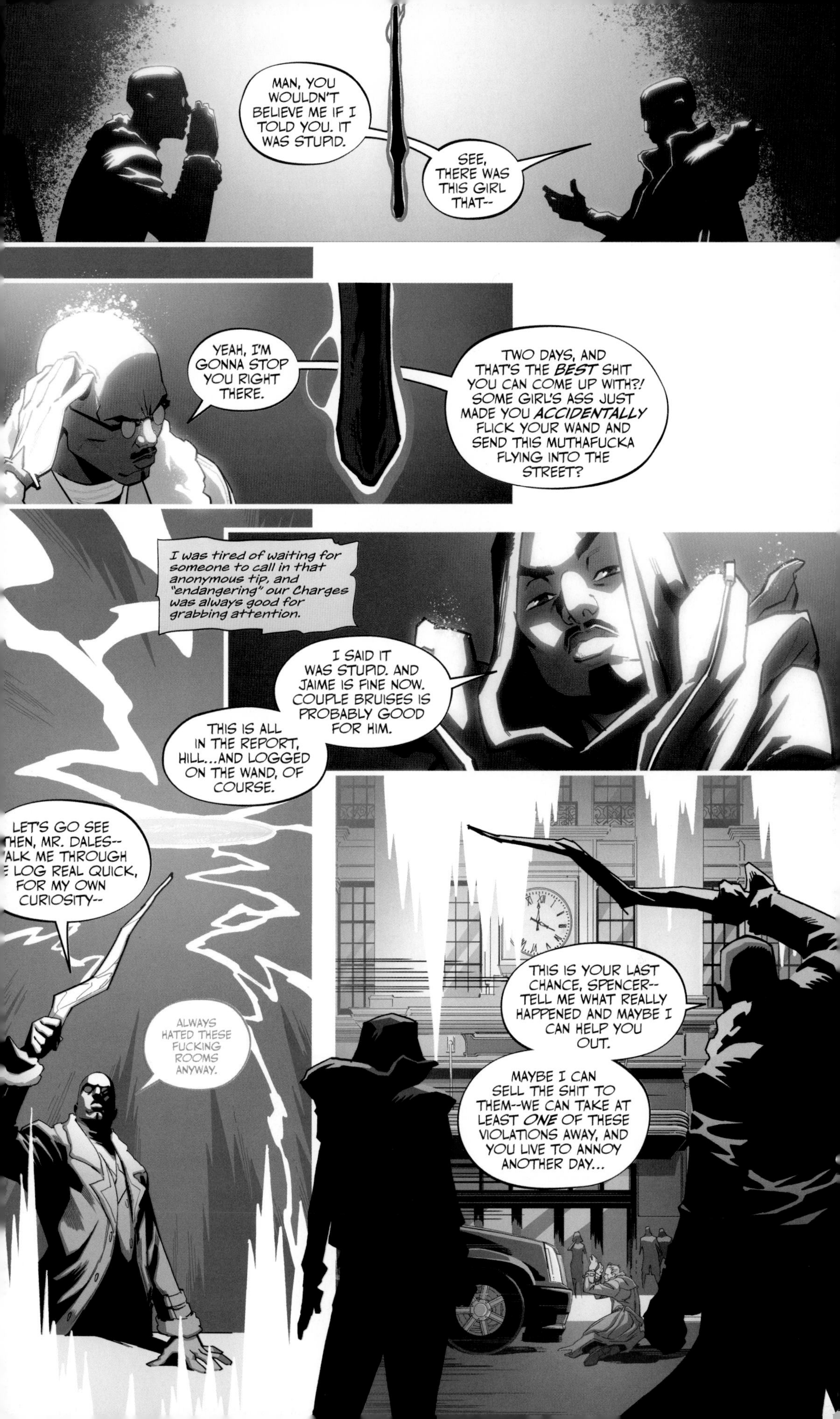
MAN, YOU WOULDN'T BELIEVE ME IF I TOLD YOU. IT WAS STUPID.
SEE, THERE WAS THIS GIRL THAT--
YEAH, I'M GONNA STOP YOU RIGHT THERE.
TWO DAYS, AND THAT'S THE *BEST* SHIT YOU CAN COME UP WITH?! SOME GIRL'S ASS JUST MADE YOU *ACCIDENTALLY* FLICK YOUR WAND AND SEND THIS MUTHAFUCKA FLYING INTO THE STREET?
I was tired of waiting for someone to call in that anonymous tip, and "endangering" our Charges was always good for grabbing attention.
I SAID IT WAS STUPID. AND JAIME IS FINE NOW. COUPLE BRUISES IS PROBABLY GOOD FOR HIM.
THIS IS ALL IN THE REPORT, HILL...AND LOGGED ON THE WAND, OF COURSE.
LET'S GO SEE THEN, MR. DALES-- WALK ME THROUGH THE LOG REAL QUICK, FOR MY OWN CURIOSITY--
ALWAYS HATED THESE FUCKING ROOMS ANYWAY.
THIS IS YOUR LAST CHANCE, SPENCER-- TELL ME WHAT REALLY HAPPENED AND MAYBE I CAN HELP YOU OUT.
MAYBE I CAN SELL THE SHIT TO THEM--WE CAN TAKE AT LEAST *ONE* OF THESE VIOLATIONS AWAY, AND YOU LIVE TO ANNOY ANOTHER DAY...

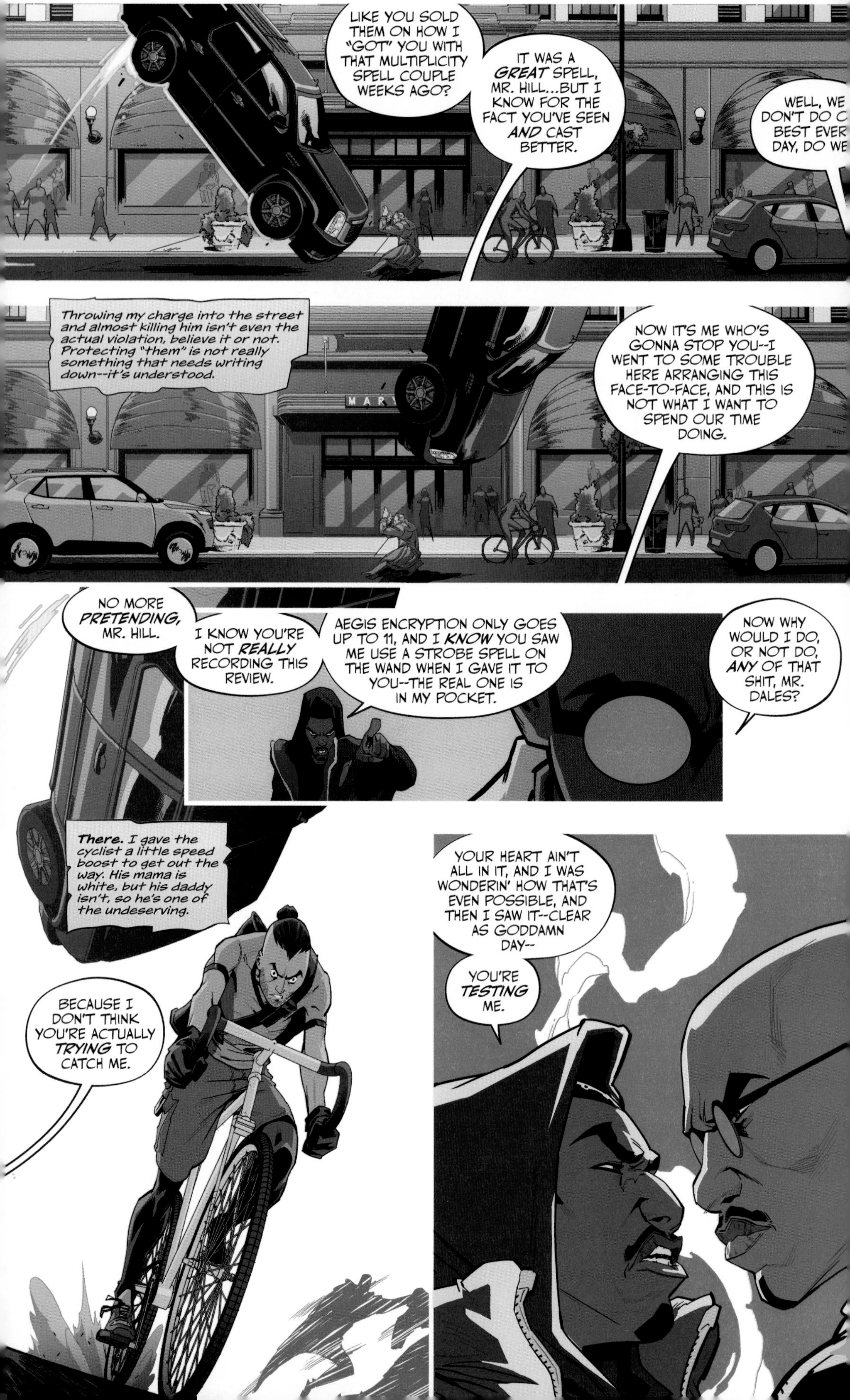
LIKE YOU SOLD THEM ON HOW I "GOT" YOU WITH THAT MULTIPLICITY SPELL COUPLE WEEKS AGO?
IT WAS A GREAT SPELL, MR. HILL...BUT I KNOW FOR THE FACT YOU'VE SEEN AND CAST BETTER.
WELL, WE DON'T DO O BEST EVER DAY, DO WE
Throwing my charge into the street and almost killing him isn't even the actual violation, believe it or not. Protecting "them" is not really something that needs writing down--it's understood.
NOW IT'S ME WHO'S GONNA STOP YOU--I WENT TO SOME TROUBLE HERE ARRANGING THIS FACE-TO-FACE, AND THIS IS NOT WHAT I WANT TO SPEND OUR TIME DOING.
NO MORE PRETENDING, MR. HILL.
I KNOW YOU'RE NOT REALLY RECORDING THIS REVIEW.
AEGIS ENCRYPTION ONLY GOES UP TO 11, AND I KNOW YOU SAW ME USE A STROBE SPELL ON THE WAND WHEN I GAVE IT TO YOU--THE REAL ONE IS IN MY POCKET.
NOW WHY WOULD I DO, OR NOT DO, ANY OF THAT SHIT, MR. DALES?
There. I gave the cyclist a little speed boost to get out the way. His mama is white, but his daddy isn't, so he's one of the undeserving.
BECAUSE I DON'T THINK YOU'RE ACTUALLY TRYING TO CATCH ME.
YOUR HEART AIN'T ALL IN IT, AND I WAS WONDERIN' HOW THAT'S EVEN POSSIBLE, AND THEN I SAW IT--CLEAR AS GODDAMN DAY--
YOU'RE TESTING ME.

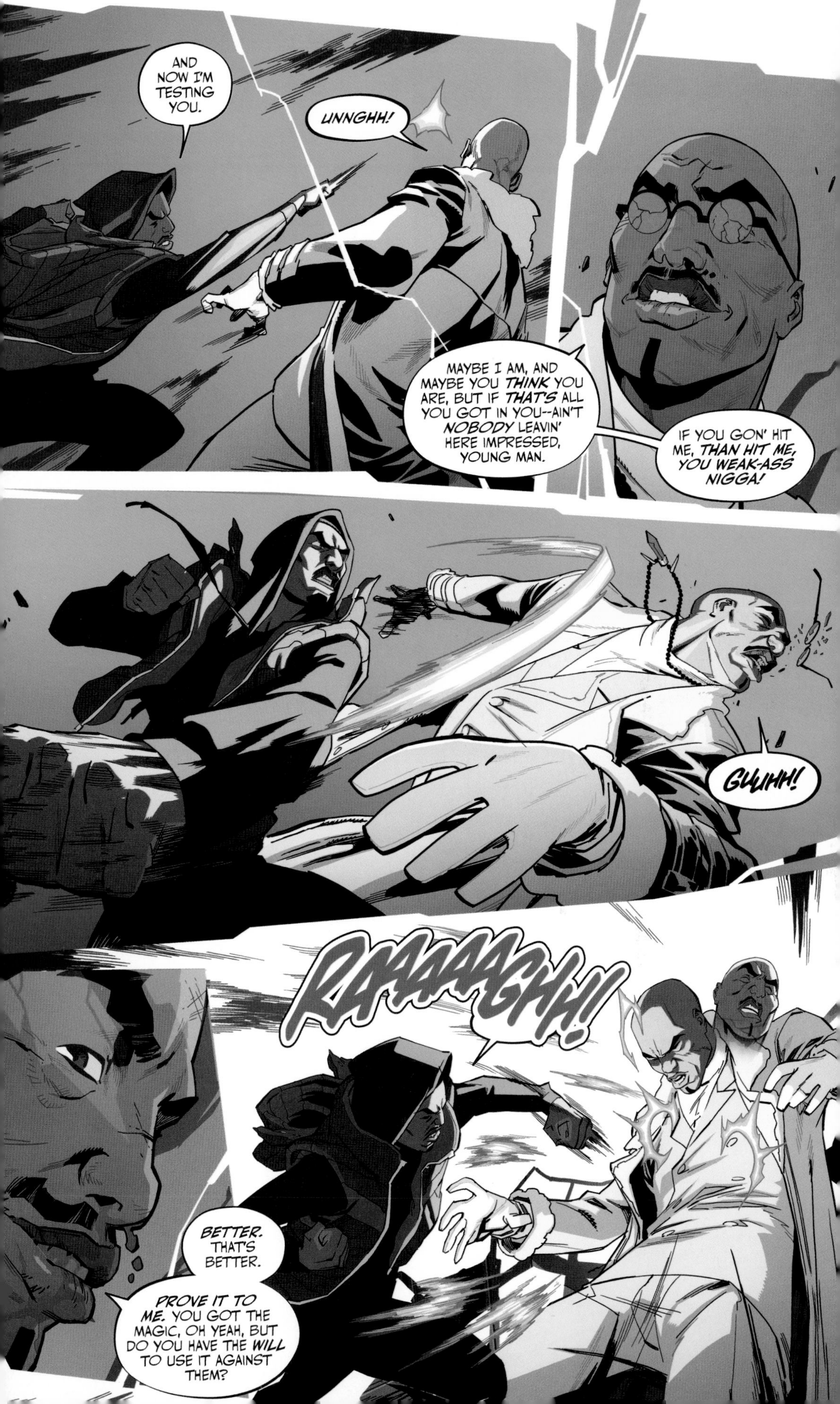
AND NOW I'M TESTING YOU.
UNNGHH!
MAYBE I AM, AND MAYBE YOU THINK YOU ARE, BUT IF THAT'S ALL YOU GOT IN YOU--AIN'T NOBODY LEAVIN' HERE IMPRESSED, YOUNG MAN.
IF YOU GON' HIT ME, THAN HIT ME, YOU WEAK-ASS NIGGA!
GUUHH!
RAAAAAGHH!!
BETTER. THAT'S BETTER.
PROVE IT TO ME. YOU GOT THE MAGIC, OH YEAH, BUT DO YOU HAVE THE WILL TO USE IT AGAINST THEM?

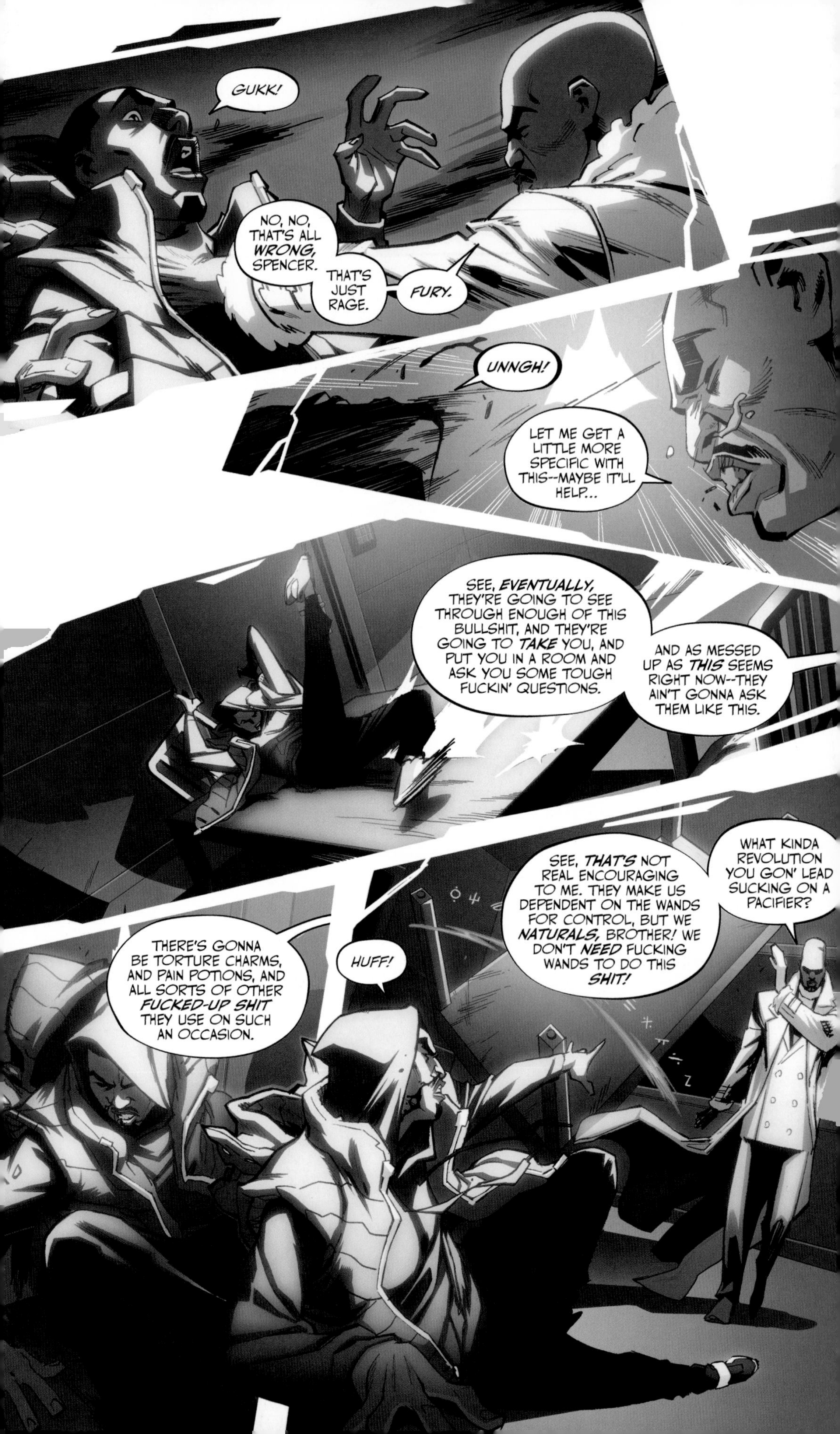
GUKK!
NO, NO, THAT'S ALL WRONG, SPENCER.
THAT'S JUST RAGE.
FURY.
UNNGH!
LET ME GET A LITTLE MORE SPECIFIC WITH THIS--MAYBE IT'LL HELP...
SEE, EVENTUALLY, THEY'RE GOING TO SEE THROUGH ENOUGH OF THIS BULLSHIT, AND THEY'RE GOING TO TAKE YOU, AND PUT YOU IN A ROOM AND ASK YOU SOME TOUGH FUCKIN' QUESTIONS.
AND AS MESSED UP AS THIS SEEMS RIGHT NOW--THEY AIN'T GONNA ASK THEM LIKE THIS.
THERE'S GONNA BE TORTURE CHARMS, AND PAIN POTIONS, AND ALL SORTS OF OTHER FUCKED-UP SHIT THEY USE ON SUCH AN OCCASION.
HUFF!
SEE, THAT'S NOT REAL ENCOURAGING TO ME. THEY MAKE US DEPENDENT ON THE WANDS FOR CONTROL, BUT WE NATURALS, BROTHER! WE DON'T NEED FUCKING WANDS TO DO THIS SHIT!
WHAT KINDA REVOLUTION YOU GON' LEAD SUCKING ON A PACIFIER?

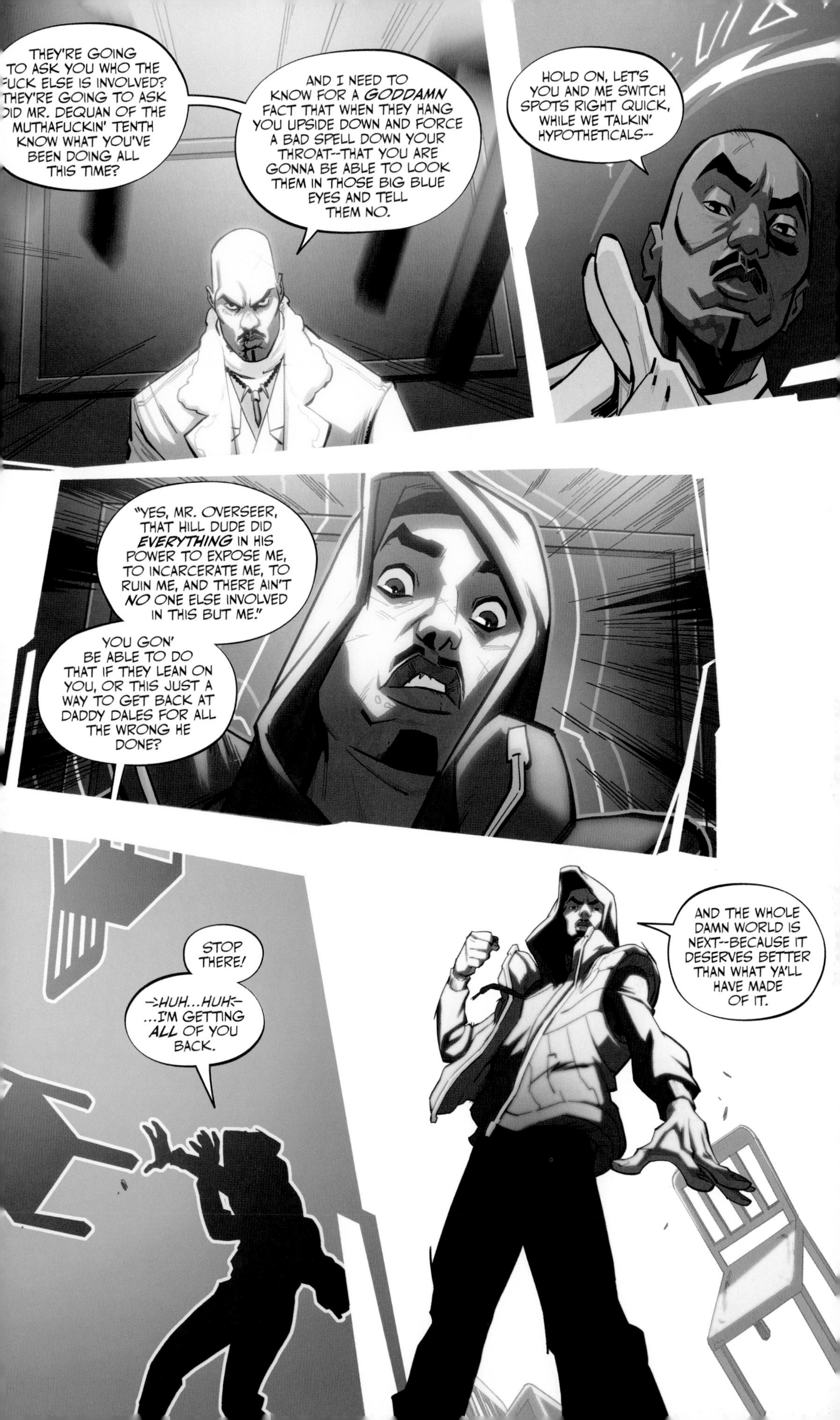
THEY'RE GOING TO ASK YOU WHO THE FUCK ELSE IS INVOLVED? THEY'RE GOING TO ASK DID MR. DEQUAN OF THE MUTHAFUCKIN' TENTH KNOW WHAT YOU'VE BEEN DOING ALL THIS TIME?
AND I NEED TO KNOW FOR A *GODDAMN* FACT THAT WHEN THEY HANG YOU UPSIDE DOWN AND FORCE A BAD SPELL DOWN YOUR THROAT--THAT YOU ARE GONNA BE ABLE TO LOOK THEM IN THOSE BIG BLUE EYES AND TELL THEM NO.
HOLD ON, LET'S YOU AND ME SWITCH SPOTS RIGHT QUICK, WHILE WE TALKIN' HYPOTHETICALS--
"YES, MR. OVERSEER, THAT HILL DUDE DID *EVERYTHING* IN HIS POWER TO EXPOSE ME, TO INCARCERATE ME, TO RUIN ME, AND THERE AIN'T *NO* ONE ELSE INVOLVED IN THIS BUT ME."
YOU GON' BE ABLE TO DO THAT IF THEY LEAN ON YOU, OR THIS JUST A WAY TO GET BACK AT DADDY DALES FOR ALL THE WRONG HE DONE?
STOP THERE!
HUH...HUH...I'M GETTING *ALL* OF YOU BACK.
AND THE WHOLE DAMN WORLD IS NEXT--BECAUSE IT DESERVES BETTER THAN WHAT YA'LL HAVE MADE OF IT.

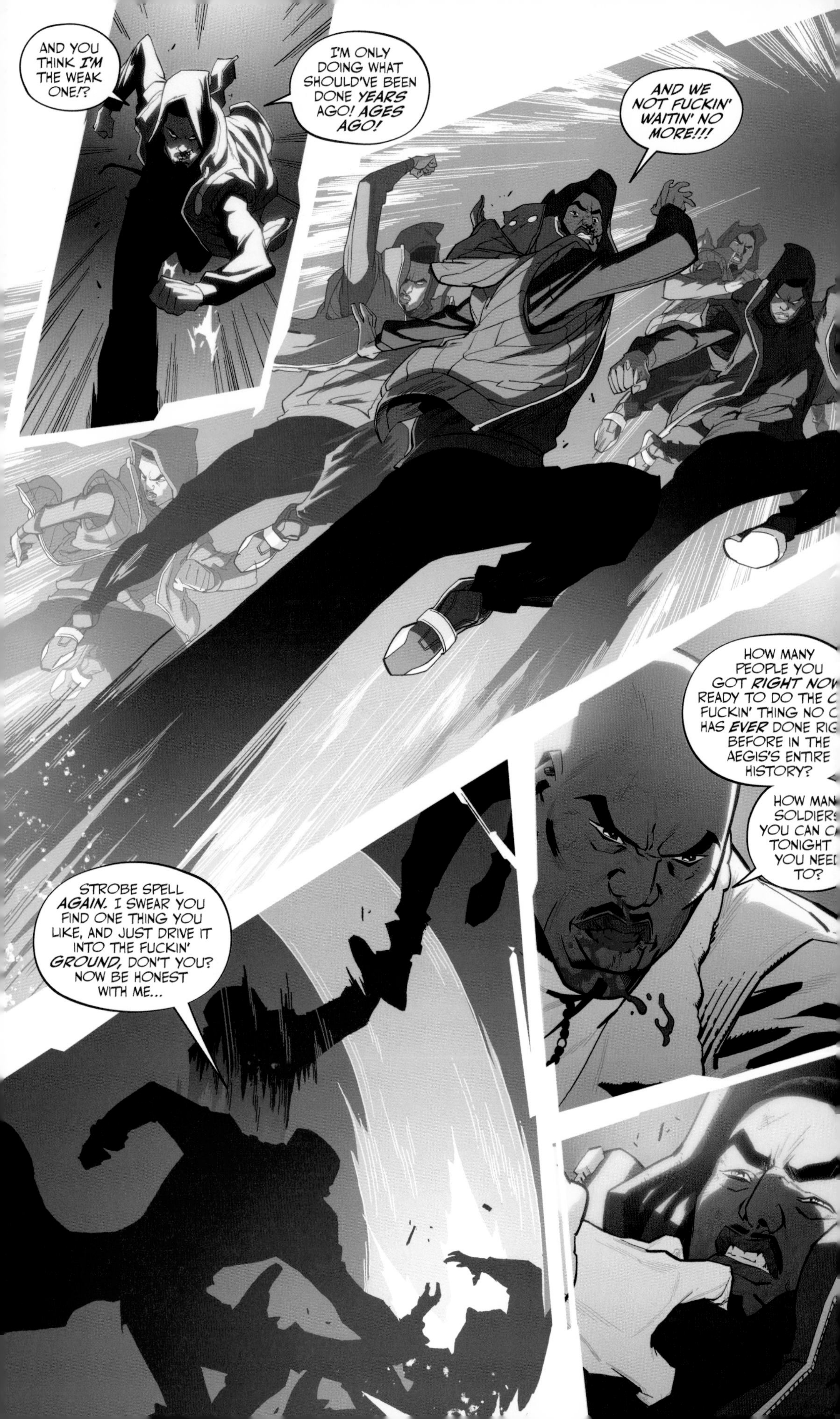

AND YOU THINK *I'M* THE WEAK ONE!?
I'M ONLY DOING WHAT SHOULD'VE BEEN DONE *YEARS* AGO! *AGES AGO!*
AND WE NOT FUCKIN' WAITIN' NO MORE!!!
HOW MANY PEOPLE YOU GOT *RIGHT NOW* READY TO DO THE FUCKIN' THING NO HAS *EVER* DONE BEFORE IN THE AEGIS'S ENTIRE HISTORY?
HOW MAN SOLDIERS YOU CAN TONIGHT YOU NEE TO?
STROBE SPELL *AGAIN.* I SWEAR YOU FIND ONE THING YOU LIKE, AND JUST DRIVE IT INTO THE FUCKIN' *GROUND,* DON'T YOU? NOW BE HONEST WITH ME...

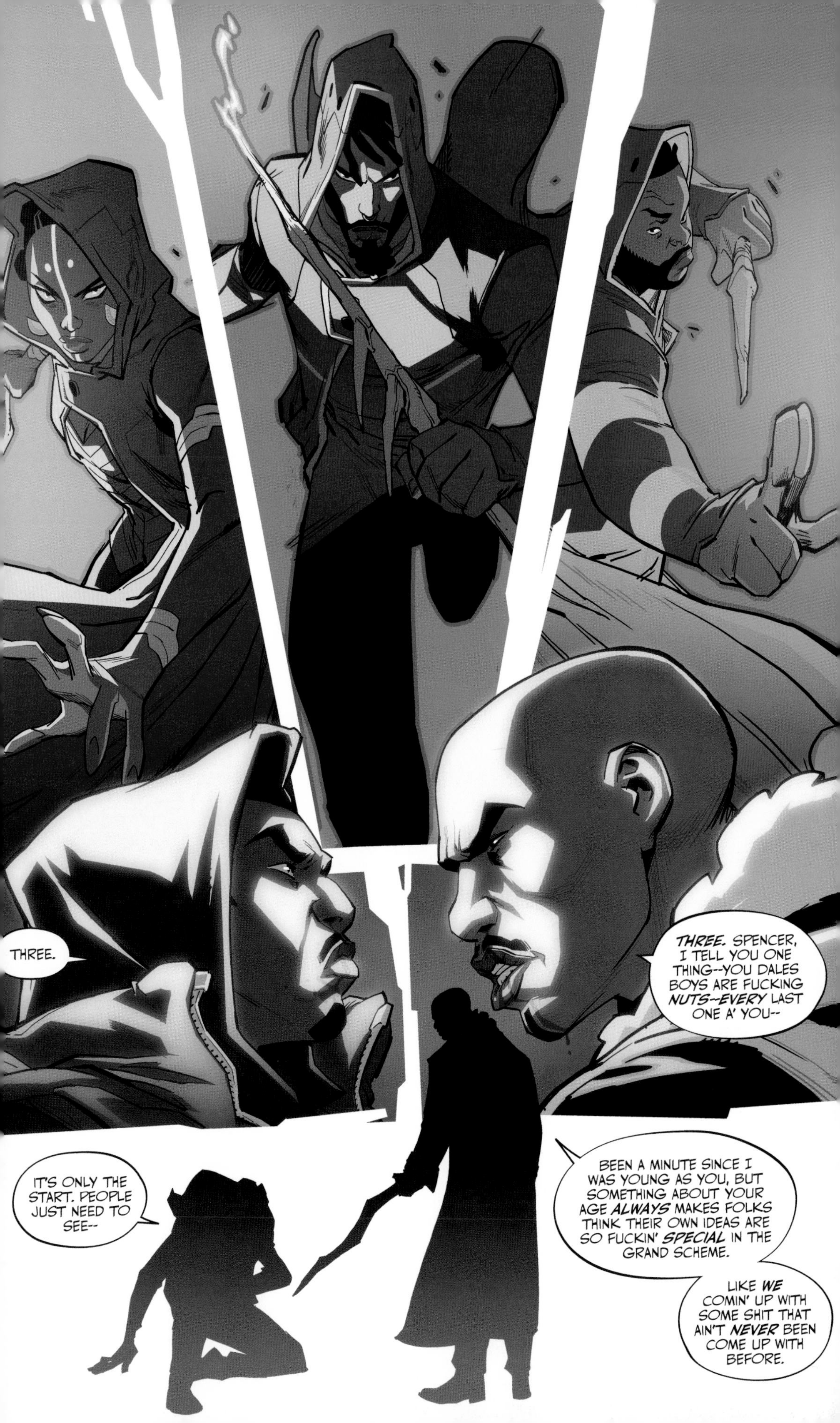
THREE.
THREE. SPENCER, I TELL YOU ONE THING--YOU DALES BOYS ARE FUCKING NUTS--EVERY LAST ONE A' YOU--
IT'S ONLY THE START. PEOPLE JUST NEED TO SEE--
BEEN A MINUTE SINCE I WAS YOUNG AS YOU, BUT SOMETHING ABOUT YOUR AGE ALWAYS MAKES FOLKS THINK THEIR OWN IDEAS ARE SO FUCKIN' SPECIAL IN THE GRAND SCHEME.
LIKE WE COMIN' UP WITH SOME SHIT THAT AIN'T NEVER BEEN COME UP WITH BEFORE.

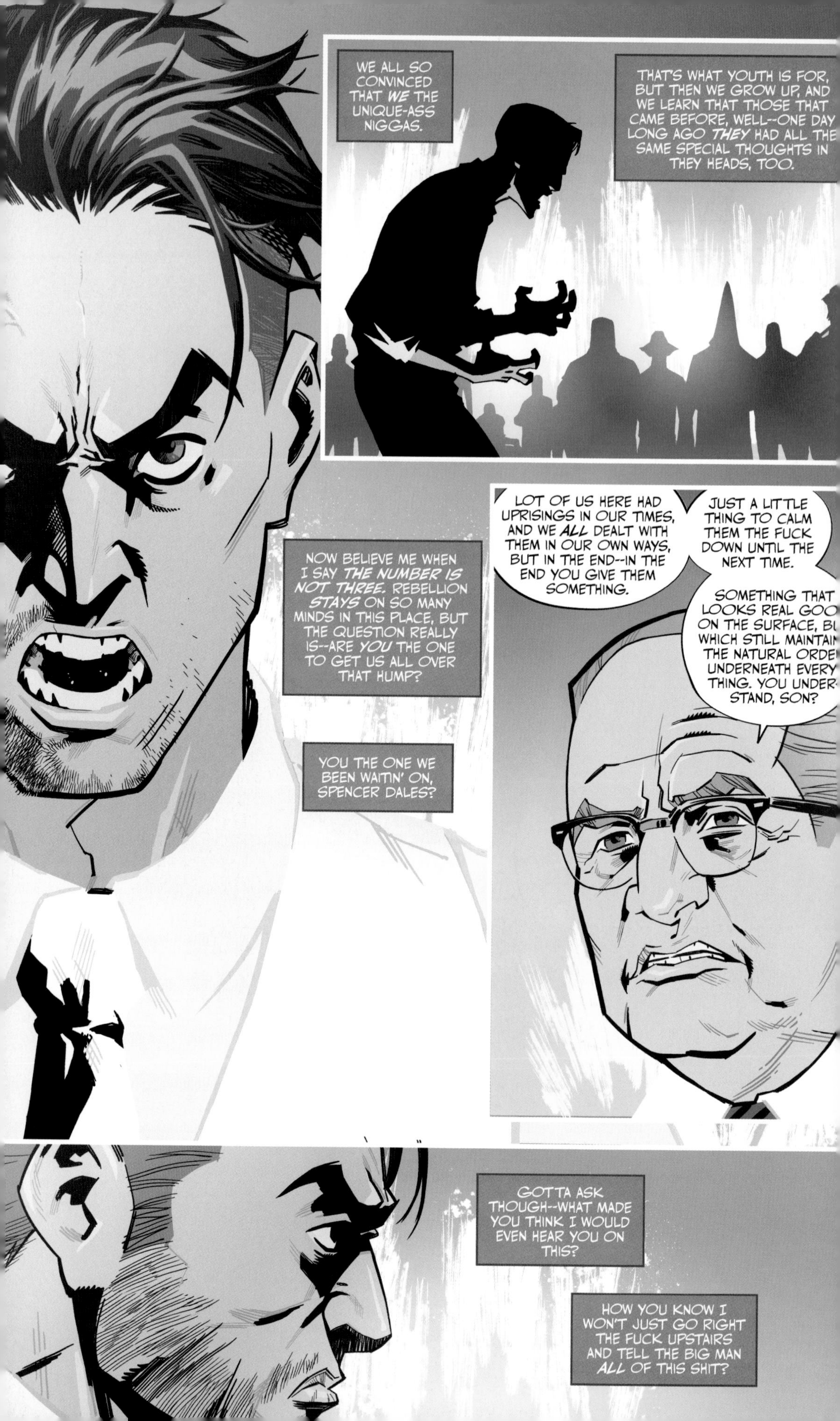
WE ALL SO CONVINCED THAT *WE* THE UNIQUE-ASS NIGGAS.
THAT'S WHAT YOUTH IS FOR, BUT THEN WE GROW UP, AND WE LEARN THAT THOSE THAT CAME BEFORE, WELL--ONE DAY LONG AGO *THEY* HAD ALL THE SAME SPECIAL THOUGHTS IN THEY HEADS, TOO.
NOW BELIEVE ME WHEN I SAY *THE NUMBER IS NOT THREE.* REBELLION *STAYS* ON SO MANY MINDS IN THIS PLACE, BUT THE QUESTION REALLY IS--ARE *YOU* THE ONE TO GET US ALL OVER THAT HUMP?
YOU THE ONE WE BEEN WAITIN' ON, SPENCER DALES?
LOT OF US HERE HAD UPRISINGS IN OUR TIMES, AND WE *ALL* DEALT WITH THEM IN OUR OWN WAYS, BUT IN THE END--IN THE END YOU GIVE THEM SOMETHING.
JUST A LITTLE THING TO CALM THEM THE FUCK DOWN UNTIL THE NEXT TIME.
SOMETHING THAT LOOKS REAL GOO ON THE SURFACE, B WHICH STILL MAINTAI THE NATURAL ORDE UNDERNEATH EVERY THING. YOU UNDER-STAND, SON?
GOTTA ASK THOUGH--WHAT MADE YOU THINK I WOULD EVEN HEAR YOU ON THIS?
HOW YOU KNOW I WON'T JUST GO RIGHT THE FUCK UPSTAIRS AND TELL THE BIG MAN *ALL* OF THIS SHIT?

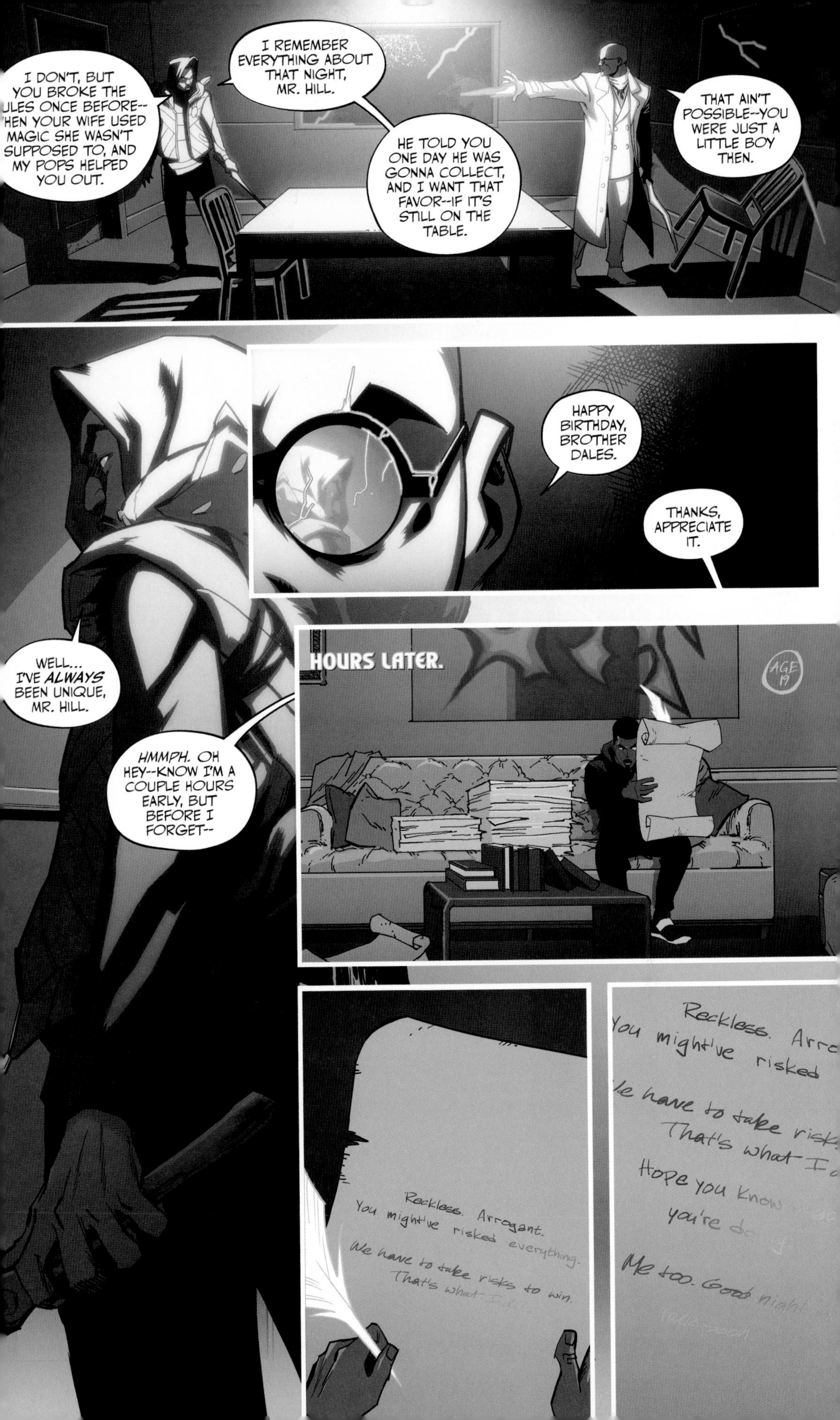
I DON'T, BUT YOU BROKE THE 'ULES ONCE BEFORE-- 'HEN YOUR WIFE USED MAGIC SHE WASN'T SUPPOSED TO, AND MY POPS HELPED YOU OUT.
I REMEMBER EVERYTHING ABOUT THAT NIGHT, MR. HILL.
THAT AIN'T POSSIBLE--YOU WERE JUST A LITTLE BOY THEN.
HE TOLD YOU ONE DAY HE WAS GONNA COLLECT, AND I WANT THAT FAVOR--IF IT'S STILL ON THE TABLE.
WELL... I'VE *ALWAYS* BEEN UNIQUE, MR. HILL.
HAPPY BIRTHDAY, BROTHER DALES.
HMMPH. OH HEY--KNOW I'M A COUPLE HOURS EARLY, BUT BEFORE I FORGET--
THANKS, APPRECIATE IT.
HOURS LATER.
AGE 19
Reckless. Arrogant.
You might've risked everything.
We have to take risks to win.
That's what
Reckless. Arr
You might've risked
le have to take risk
That's what I
Hope you know
you're
Me too. Good night

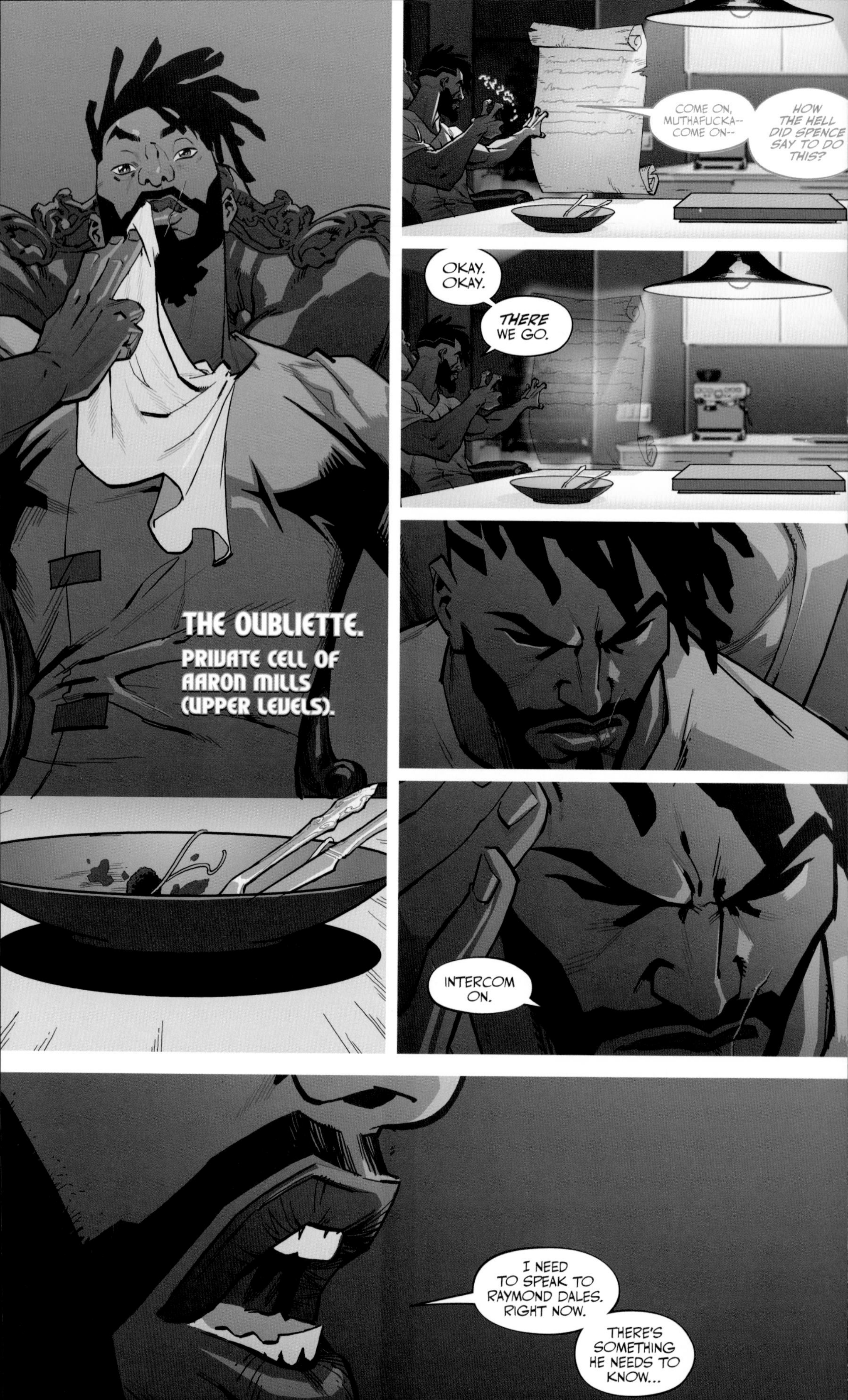
THE OUBLIETTE.
PRIVATE CELL OF AARON MILLS (UPPER LEVELS).
COME ON, MUTHAFUCKA-- COME ON--
HOW THE HELL DID SPENCE SAY TO DO THIS?
OKAY. OKAY.
THERE WE GO.
INTERCOM ON.
I NEED TO SPEAK TO RAYMOND DALES. RIGHT NOW.
THERE'S SOMETHING HE NEEDS TO KNOW...

SUPREMACY
TODAY

SUPREMACY
TOMORROW

SUPREMACY
FOREVER

THE ANCESTRY
FOREVER HONORING
THE GREATEST GIFT GOD GAVE MAN

THE AEGIS

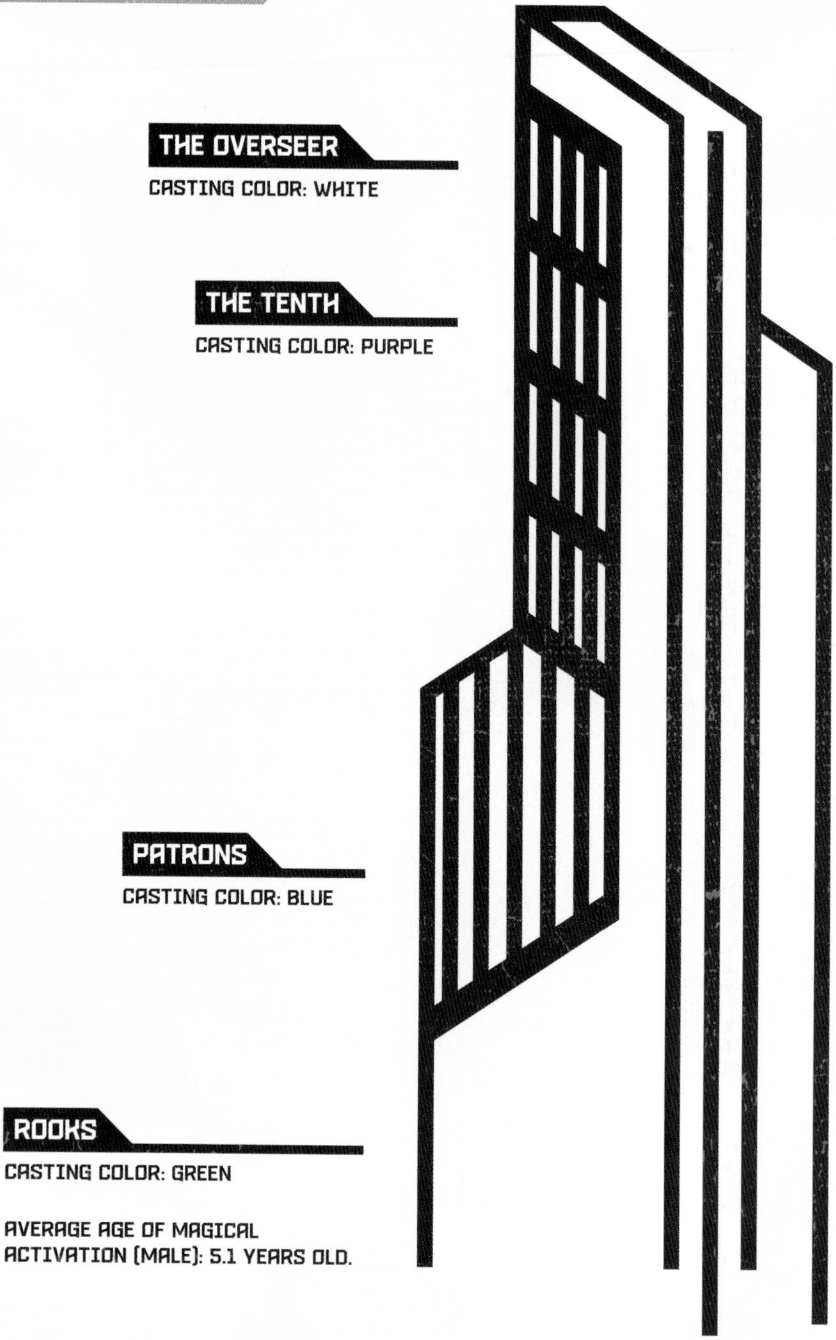
THE OVERSEER
CASTING COLOR: WHITE
THE TENTH
CASTING COLOR: PURPLE
PATRONS
CASTING COLOR: BLUE
ROOKS
CASTING COLOR: GREEN
AVERAGE AGE OF MAGICAL ACTIVATION (MALE): 5.1 YEARS OLD.

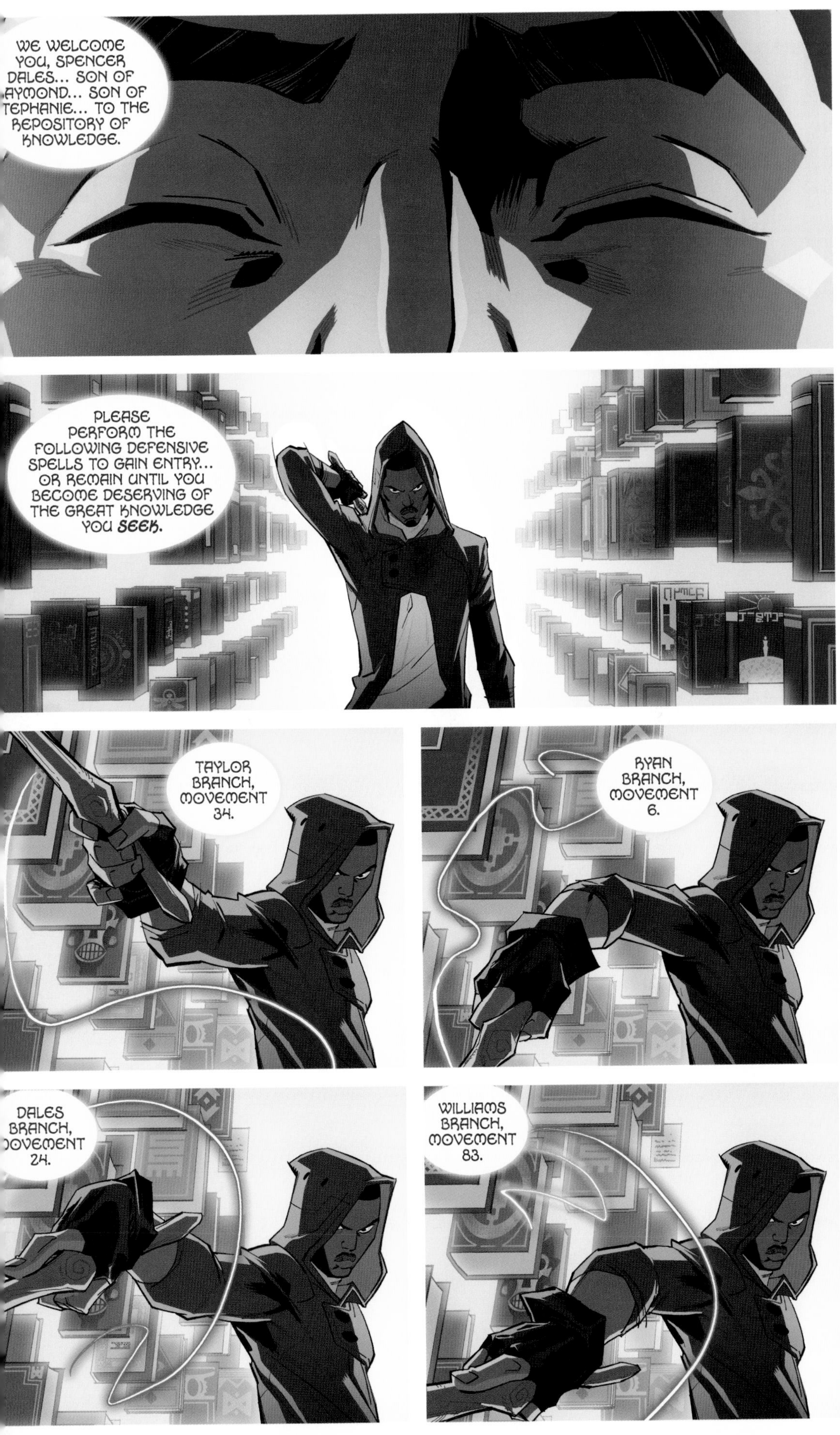

WE WELCOME YOU, SPENCER DALES... SON OF AYMOND... SON OF TEPHANIE... TO THE REPOSITORY OF KNOWLEDGE.
PLEASE PERFORM THE FOLLOWING DEFENSIVE SPELLS TO GAIN ENTRY... OR REMAIN UNTIL YOU BECOME DESERVING OF THE GREAT KNOWLEDGE YOU **SEEK.**
TAYLOR BRANCH, MOVEMENT 34.
RYAN BRANCH, MOVEMENT 6.
DALES BRANCH, OVEMENT 24.
WILLIAMS BRANCH, MOVEMENT 83.

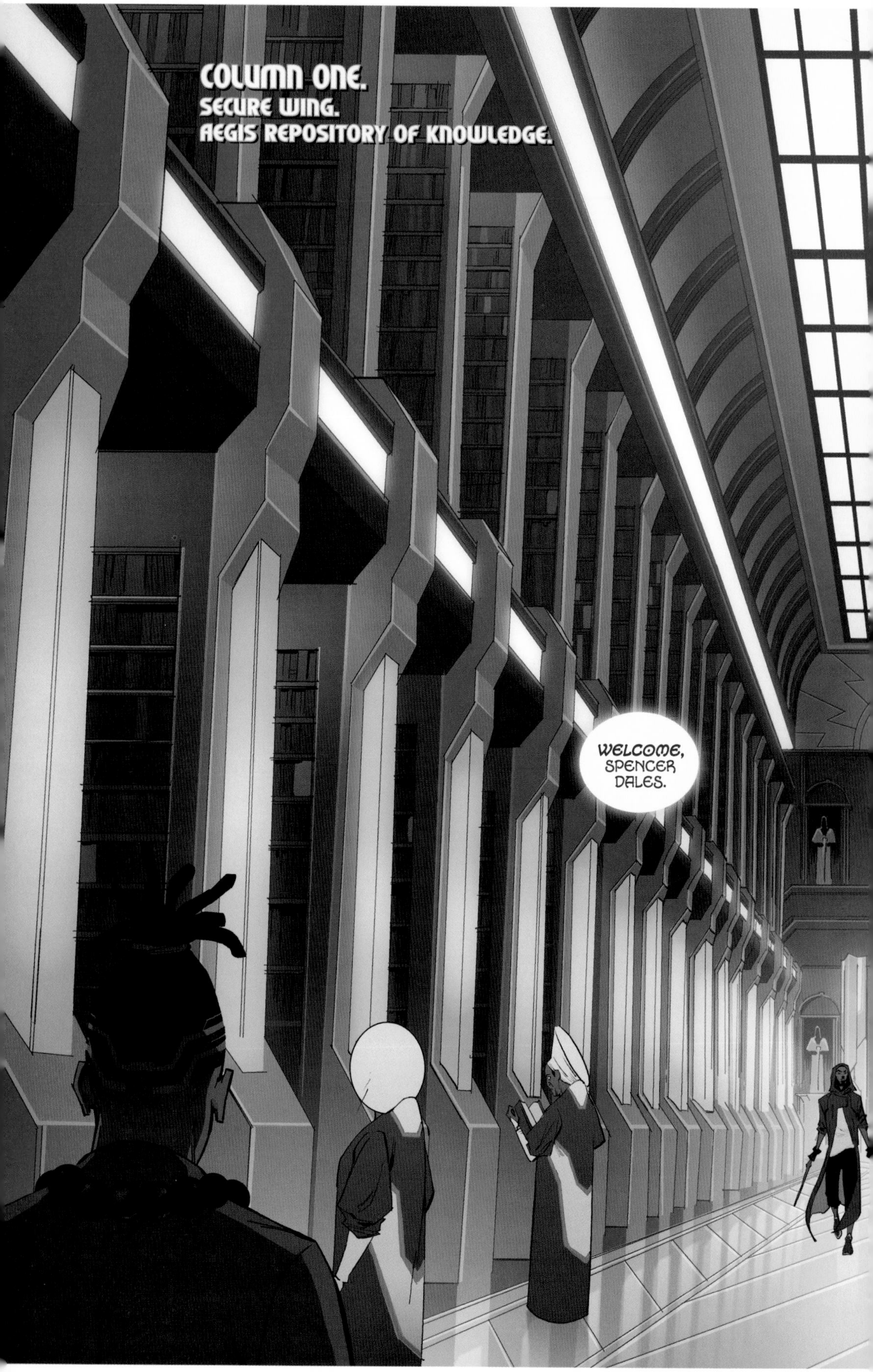
COLUMN ONE.
SECURE WING.
AEGIS REPOSITORY OF KNOWLEDGE.
WELCOME, SPENCER DALES.

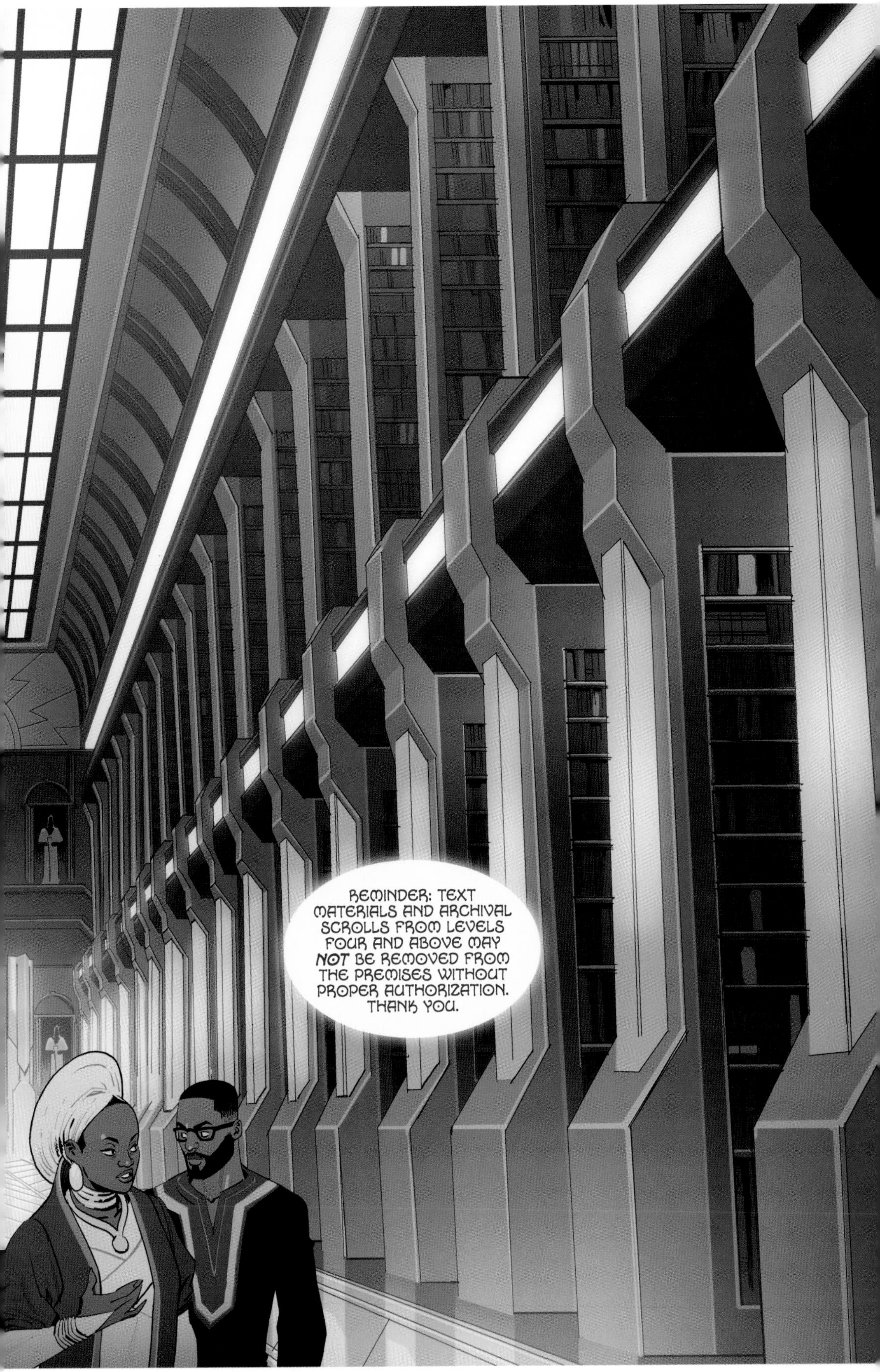
REMINDER: TEXT MATERIALS AND ARCHIVAL SCROLLS FROM LEVELS FOUR AND ABOVE MAY *NOT* BE REMOVED FROM THE PREMISES WITHOUT PROPER AUTHORIZATION. THANK YOU.

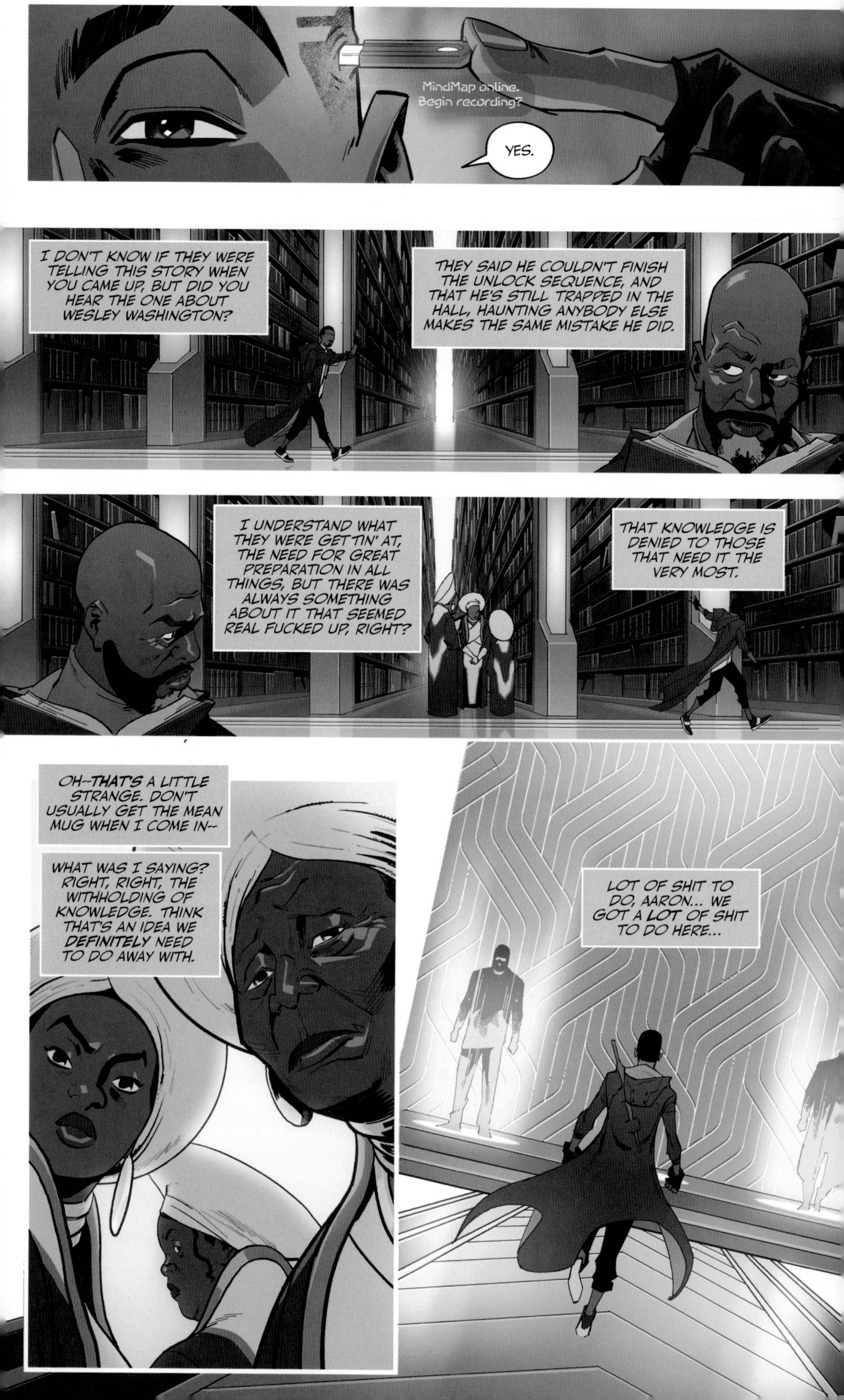
MindMap online.
Begin recording?
YES.
I DON'T KNOW IF THEY WERE TELLING THIS STORY WHEN YOU CAME UP, BUT DID YOU HEAR THE ONE ABOUT WESLEY WASHINGTON?
THEY SAID HE COULDN'T FINISH THE UNLOCK SEQUENCE, AND THAT HE'S STILL TRAPPED IN THE HALL, HAUNTING ANYBODY ELSE MAKES THE SAME MISTAKE HE DID.
I UNDERSTAND WHAT THEY WERE GETTIN' AT, THE NEED FOR GREAT PREPARATION IN ALL THINGS, BUT THERE WAS ALWAYS SOMETHING ABOUT IT THAT SEEMED REAL FUCKED UP, RIGHT?
THAT KNOWLEDGE IS DENIED TO THOSE THAT NEED IT THE VERY MOST.
OH--THAT'S A LITTLE STRANGE. DON'T USUALLY GET THE MEAN MUG WHEN I COME IN--
WHAT WAS I SAYING? RIGHT, RIGHT, THE WITHHOLDING OF KNOWLEDGE. THINK THAT'S AN IDEA WE DEFINITELY NEED TO DO AWAY WITH.
LOT OF SHIT TO DO, AARON... WE GOT A LOT OF SHIT TO DO HERE...

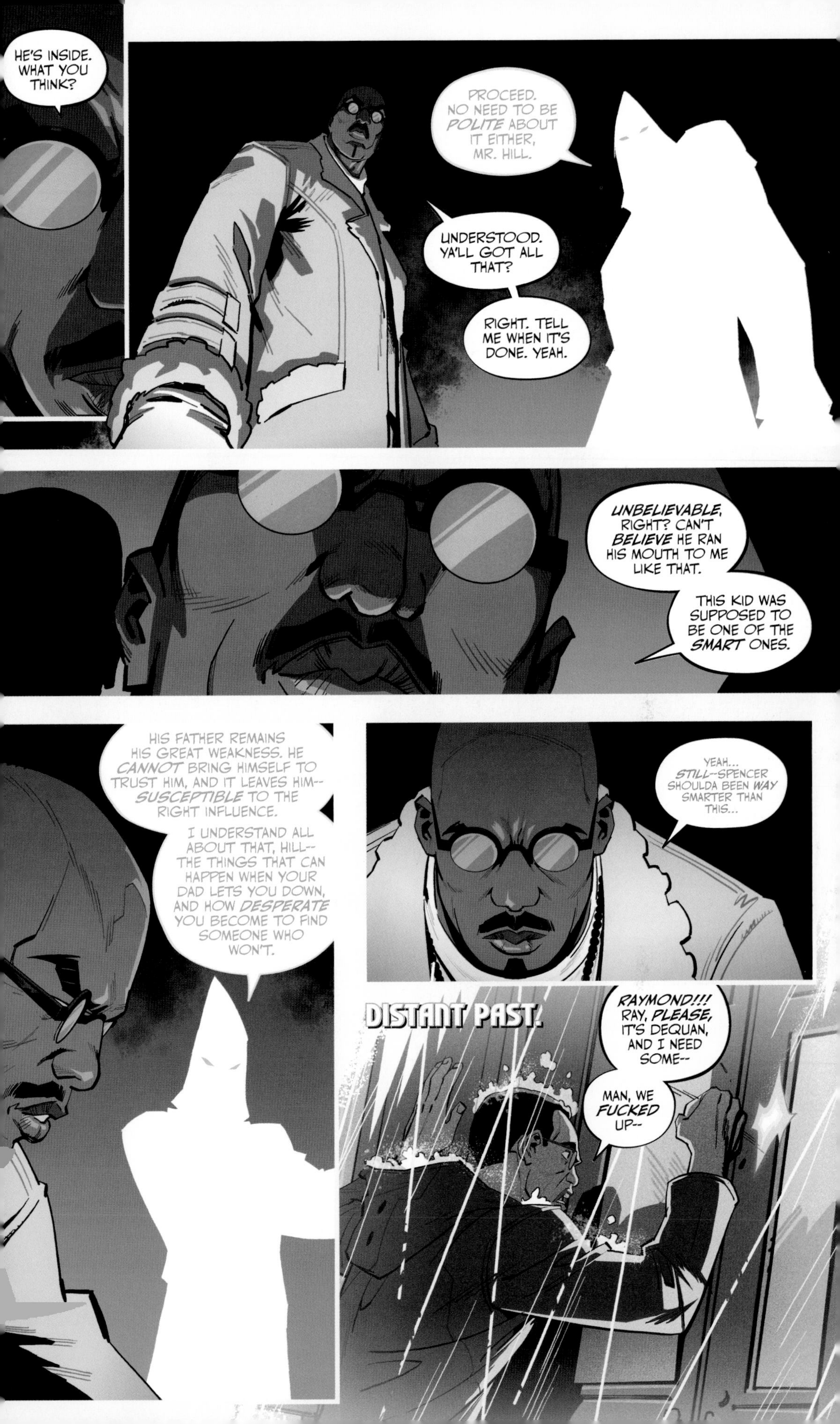
HE'S INSIDE. WHAT YOU THINK?
PROCEED. NO NEED TO BE *POLITE* ABOUT IT EITHER, MR. HILL.
UNDERSTOOD. YA'LL GOT ALL THAT?
RIGHT. TELL ME WHEN IT'S DONE. YEAH.
UNBELIEVABLE, RIGHT? CAN'T *BELIEVE* HE RAN HIS MOUTH TO ME LIKE THAT.
THIS KID WAS SUPPOSED TO BE ONE OF THE *SMART* ONES.
HIS FATHER REMAINS HIS GREAT WEAKNESS. HE *CANNOT* BRING HIMSELF TO TRUST HIM, AND IT LEAVES HIM-- *SUSCEPTIBLE* TO THE RIGHT INFLUENCE.
I UNDERSTAND ALL ABOUT THAT, HILL-- THE THINGS THAT CAN HAPPEN WHEN YOUR DAD LETS YOU DOWN, AND HOW *DESPERATE* YOU BECOME TO FIND SOMEONE WHO WON'T.
YEAH... *STILL*--SPENCER SHOULDA BEEN *WAY* SMARTER THAN THIS...
DISTANT PAST.
RAYMOND!!! RAY, *PLEASE,* IT'S DEQUAN, AND I NEED SOME--
MAN, WE *FUCKED* UP--

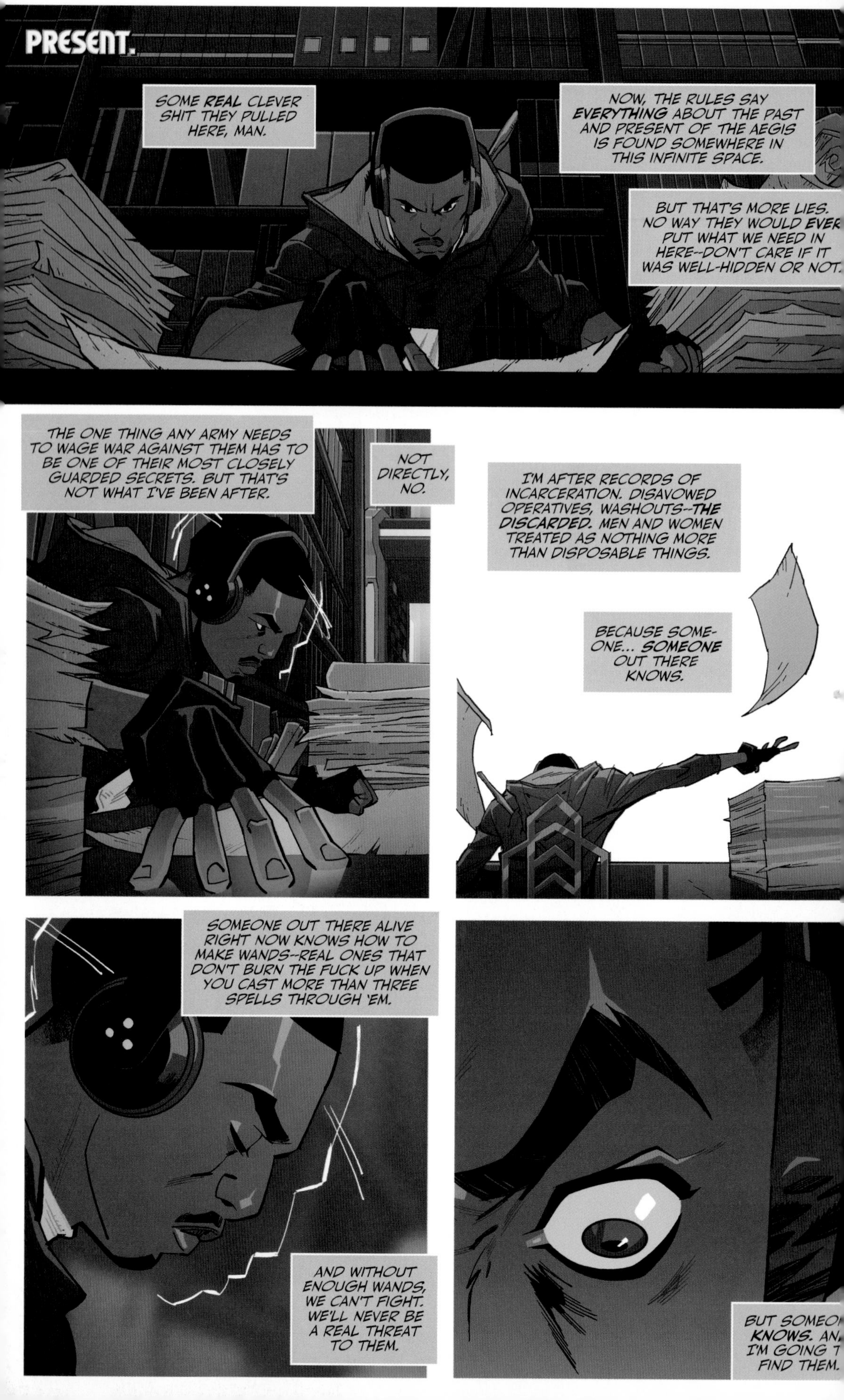
PRESENT.
SOME REAL CLEVER SHIT THEY PULLED HERE, MAN.
NOW, THE RULES SAY EVERYTHING ABOUT THE PAST AND PRESENT OF THE AEGIS IS FOUND SOMEWHERE IN THIS INFINITE SPACE.
BUT THAT'S MORE LIES. NO WAY THEY WOULD EVER PUT WHAT WE NEED IN HERE--DON'T CARE IF IT WAS WELL-HIDDEN OR NOT.
THE ONE THING ANY ARMY NEEDS TO WAGE WAR AGAINST THEM HAS TO BE ONE OF THEIR MOST CLOSELY GUARDED SECRETS. BUT THAT'S NOT WHAT I'VE BEEN AFTER.
NOT DIRECTLY, NO.
I'M AFTER RECORDS OF INCARCERATION. DISAVOWED OPERATIVES, WASHOUTS--THE DISCARDED. MEN AND WOMEN TREATED AS NOTHING MORE THAN DISPOSABLE THINGS.
BECAUSE SOME-ONE... SOMEONE OUT THERE KNOWS.
SOMEONE OUT THERE ALIVE RIGHT NOW KNOWS HOW TO MAKE WANDS--REAL ONES THAT DON'T BURN THE FUCK UP WHEN YOU CAST MORE THAN THREE SPELLS THROUGH 'EM.
AND WITHOUT ENOUGH WANDS, WE CAN'T FIGHT. WE'LL NEVER BE A REAL THREAT TO THEM.
BUT SOMEO KNOWS. AN I'M GOING T FIND THEM.

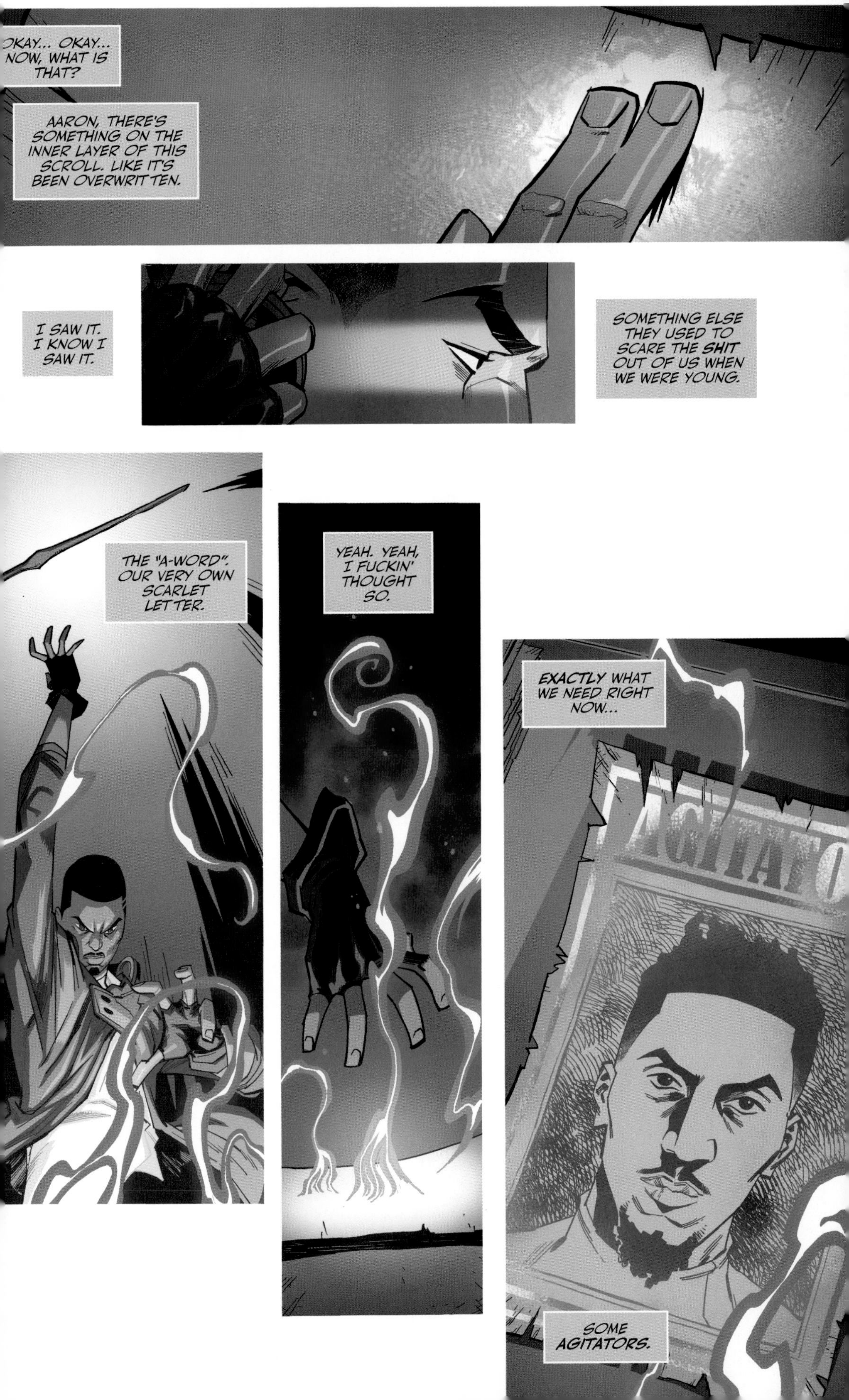

OKAY... OKAY... NOW, WHAT IS THAT?
AARON, THERE'S SOMETHING ON THE INNER LAYER OF THIS SCROLL. LIKE IT'S BEEN OVERWRITTEN.
I SAW IT. I KNOW I SAW IT.
SOMETHING ELSE THEY USED TO SCARE THE SHIT OUT OF US WHEN WE WERE YOUNG.
THE "A-WORD". OUR VERY OWN SCARLET LETTER.
YEAH. YEAH, I FUCKIN' THOUGHT SO.
EXACTLY WHAT WE NEED RIGHT NOW...
AGITATO
SOME AGITATORS.

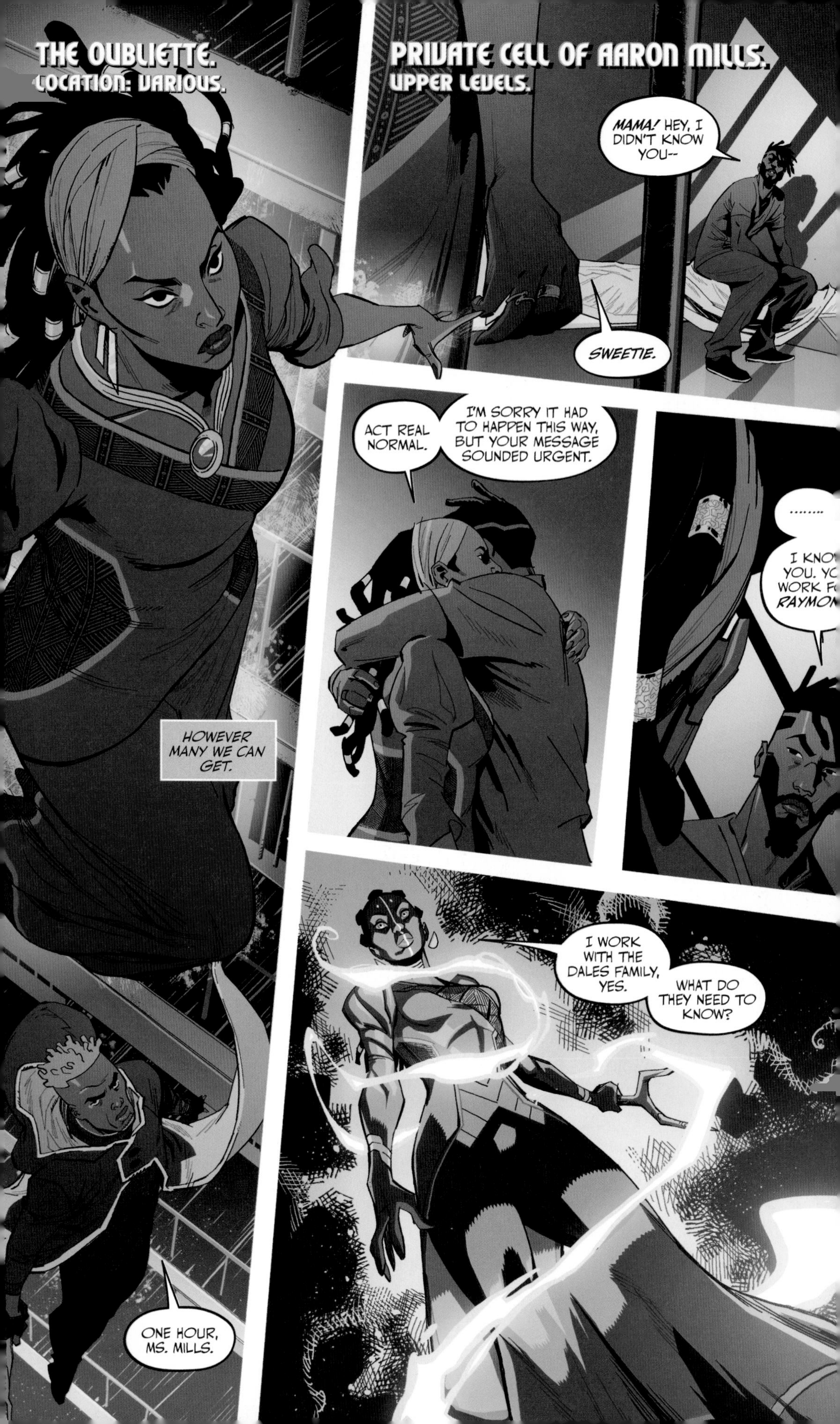
THE OUBLIETTE.
LOCATION: VARIOUS.
HOWEVER MANY WE CAN GET.
ONE HOUR, MS. MILLS.
PRIVATE CELL OF AARON MILLS.
UPPER LEVELS.
MAMA! HEY, I DIDN'T KNOW YOU--
SWEETIE.
ACT REAL NORMAL.
I'M SORRY IT HAD TO HAPPEN THIS WAY, BUT YOUR MESSAGE SOUNDED URGENT.
....
I WORK WITH THE DALES FAMILY, YES.
WHAT DO THEY NEED TO KNOW?

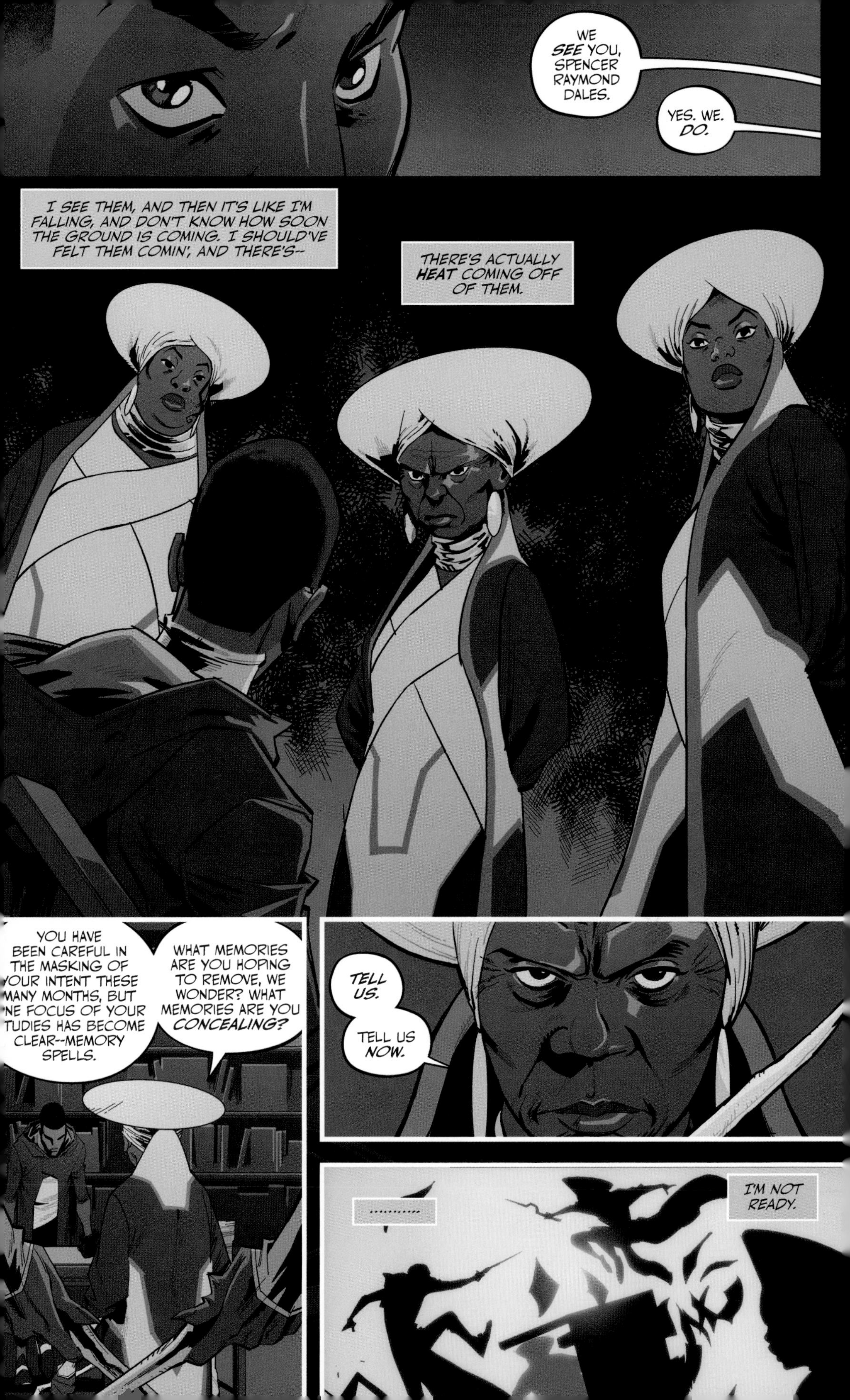
WE SEE YOU, SPENCER RAYMOND DALES.
YES. WE. DO.
I SEE THEM, AND THEN IT'S LIKE I'M FALLING, AND DON'T KNOW HOW SOON THE GROUND IS COMING. I SHOULD'VE FELT THEM COMIN', AND THERE'S--
THERE'S ACTUALLY HEAT COMING OFF OF THEM.
YOU HAVE BEEN CAREFUL IN THE MASKING OF YOUR INTENT THESE MANY MONTHS, BUT NE FOCUS OF YOUR TUDIES HAS BECOME CLEAR--MEMORY SPELLS.
WHAT MEMORIES ARE YOU HOPING TO REMOVE, WE WONDER? WHAT MEMORIES ARE YOU CONCEALING?
TELL US.
TELL US NOW.
....
I'M NOT READY.

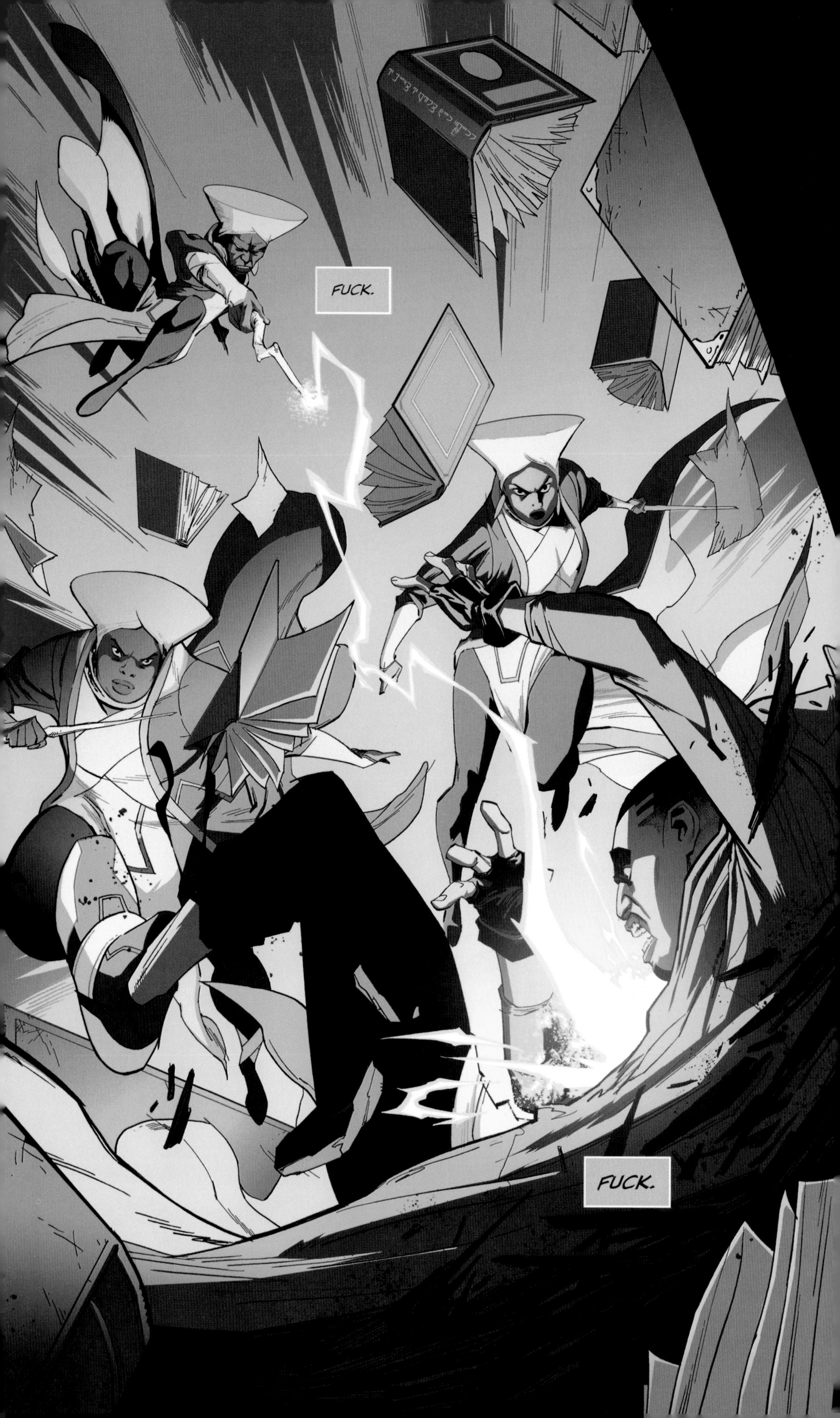
FUCK.
FUCK.

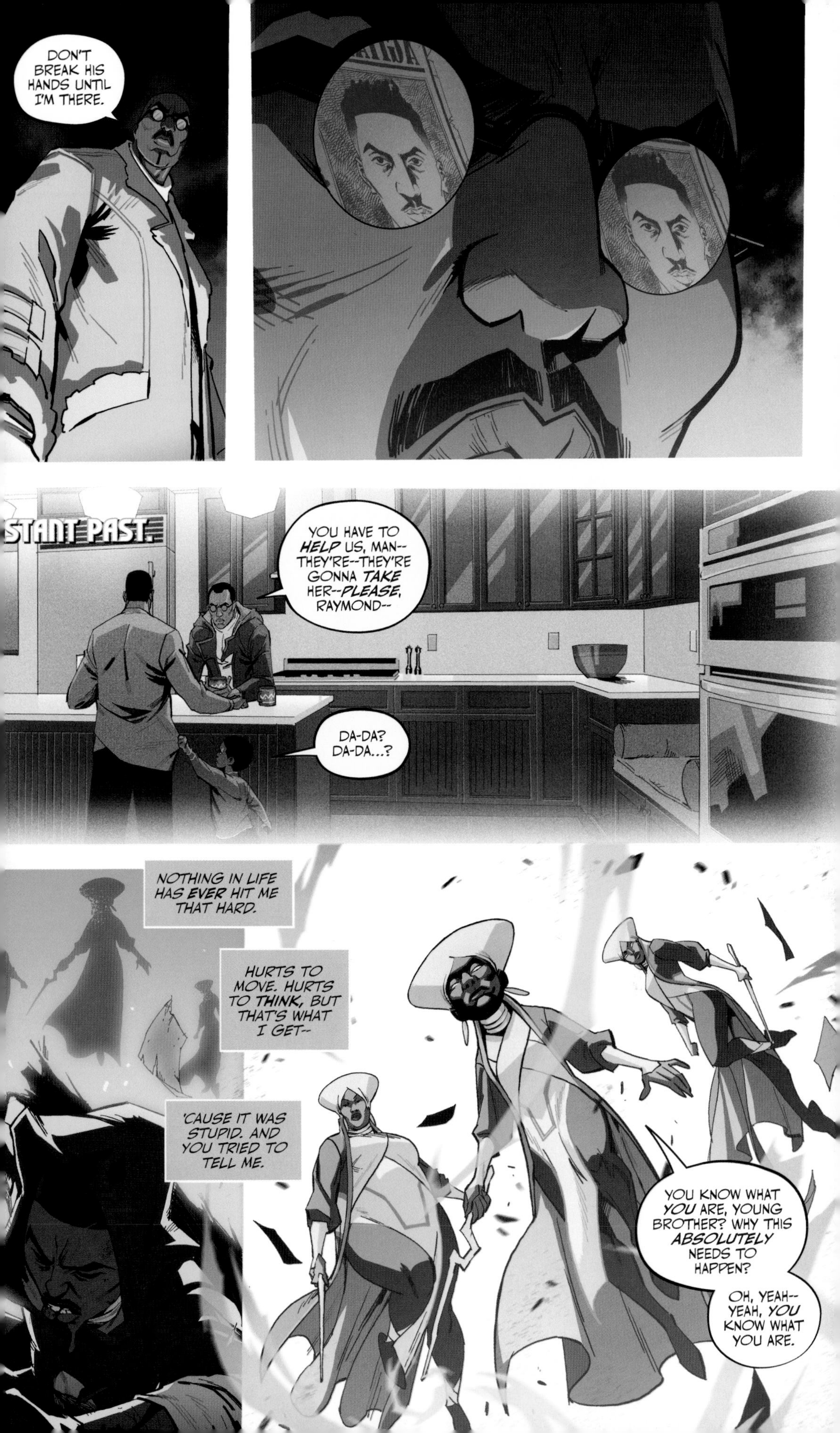
DON'T BREAK HIS HANDS UNTIL I'M THERE.
STANT PAST.
YOU HAVE TO *HELP* US, MAN-- THEY'RE--THEY'RE GONNA *TAKE* HER--*PLEASE,* RAYMOND--
DA-DA? DA-DA...?
NOTHING IN LIFE HAS ***EVER*** *HIT ME THAT HARD.*
HURTS TO MOVE. HURTS TO ***THINK,*** *BUT THAT'S WHAT I GET--*
'CAUSE IT WAS STUPID. AND YOU TRIED TO TELL ME.
YOU KNOW WHAT *YOU* ARE, YOUNG BROTHER? WHY THIS *ABSOLUTELY* NEEDS TO HAPPEN?
OH, YEAH-- YEAH, *YOU* KNOW WHAT YOU ARE.

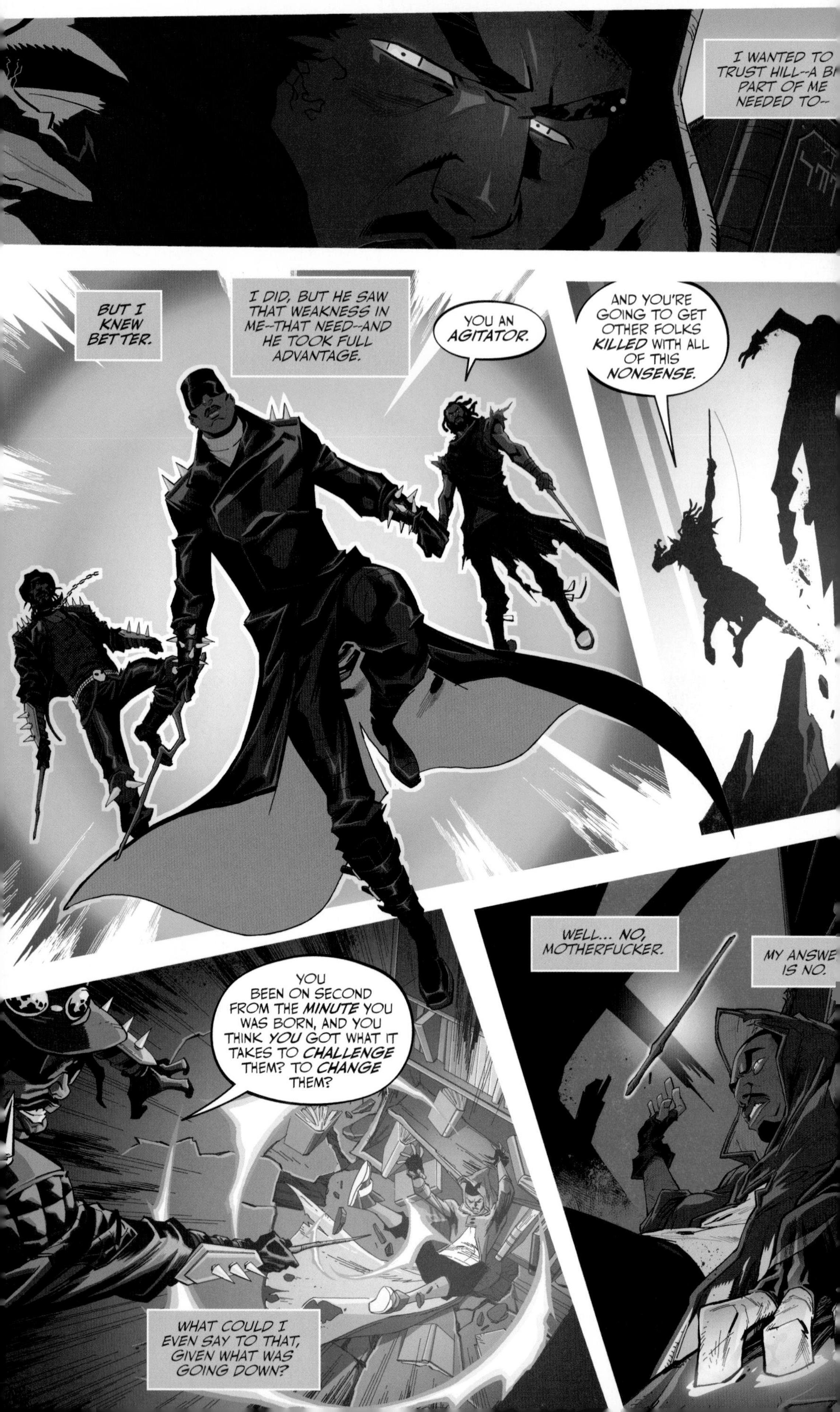

I WANTED TO TRUST HILL--A BI PART OF ME NEEDED TO--
BUT I KNEW BETTER.
I DID, BUT HE SAW THAT WEAKNESS IN ME--THAT NEED--AND HE TOOK FULL ADVANTAGE.
YOU AN AGITATOR.
AND YOU'RE GOING TO GET OTHER FOLKS KILLED WITH ALL OF THIS NONSENSE.
YOU BEEN ON SECOND FROM THE MINUTE YOU WAS BORN, AND YOU THINK YOU GOT WHAT IT TAKES TO CHALLENGE THEM? TO CHANGE THEM?
WHAT COULD I EVEN SAY TO THAT, GIVEN WHAT WAS GOING DOWN?
WELL... NO, MOTHERFUCKER.
MY ANSWE IS NO.

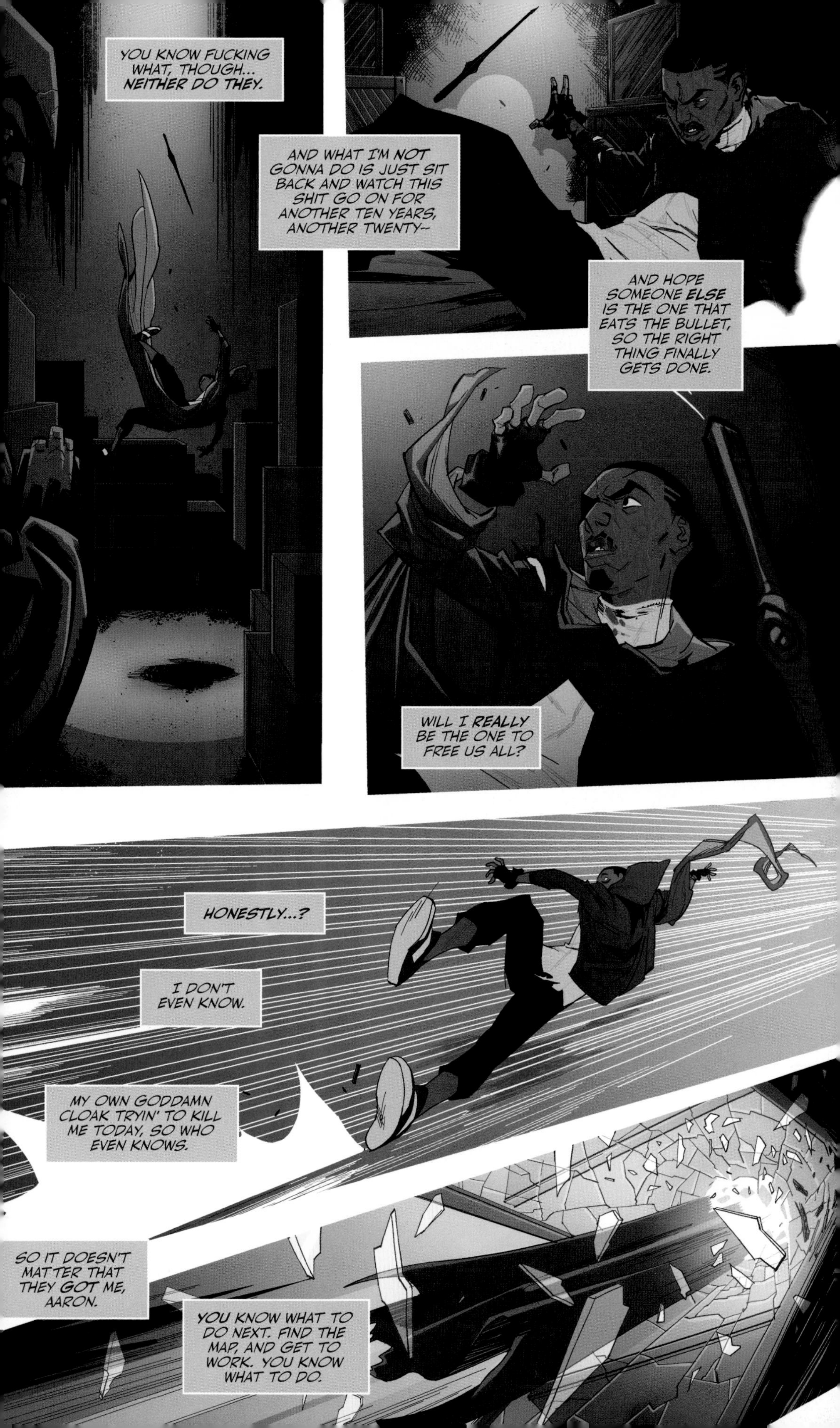

YOU KNOW FUCKING WHAT, THOUGH... NEITHER DO THEY.
AND WHAT I'M NOT GONNA DO IS JUST SIT BACK AND WATCH THIS SHIT GO ON FOR ANOTHER TEN YEARS, ANOTHER TWENTY--
AND HOPE SOMEONE ELSE IS THE ONE THAT EATS THE BULLET, SO THE RIGHT THING FINALLY GETS DONE.
WILL I REALLY BE THE ONE TO FREE US ALL?
HONESTLY...?
I DON'T EVEN KNOW.
MY OWN GODDAMN CLOAK TRYIN' TO KILL ME TODAY, SO WHO EVEN KNOWS.
SO IT DOESN'T MATTER THAT THEY GOT ME, AARON.
YOU KNOW WHAT TO DO NEXT. FIND THE MAP, AND GET TO WORK. YOU KNOW WHAT TO DO.

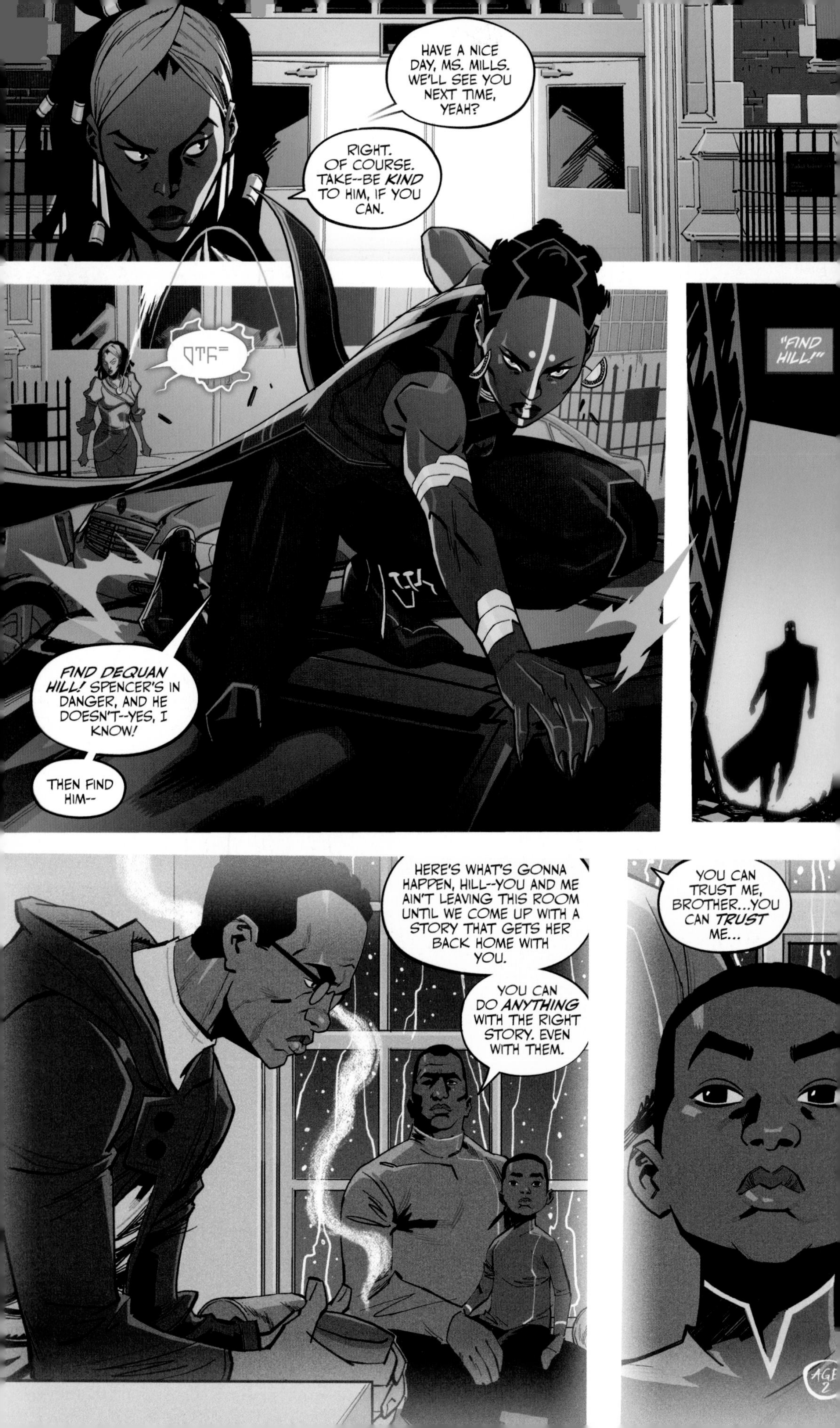
HAVE A NICE DAY, MS. MILLS. WE'LL SEE YOU NEXT TIME, YEAH?
RIGHT. OF COURSE. TAKE--BE KIND TO HIM, IF YOU CAN.
"FIND HILL!"
FIND DEQUAN HILL! SPENCER'S IN DANGER, AND HE DOESN'T--YES, I KNOW!
THEN FIND HIM--
HERE'S WHAT'S GONNA HAPPEN, HILL--YOU AND ME AIN'T LEAVING THIS ROOM UNTIL WE COME UP WITH A STORY THAT GETS HER BACK HOME WITH YOU.
YOU CAN DO ANYTHING WITH THE RIGHT STORY. EVEN WITH THEM.
YOU CAN TRUST ME, BROTHER...YOU CAN TRUST ME...

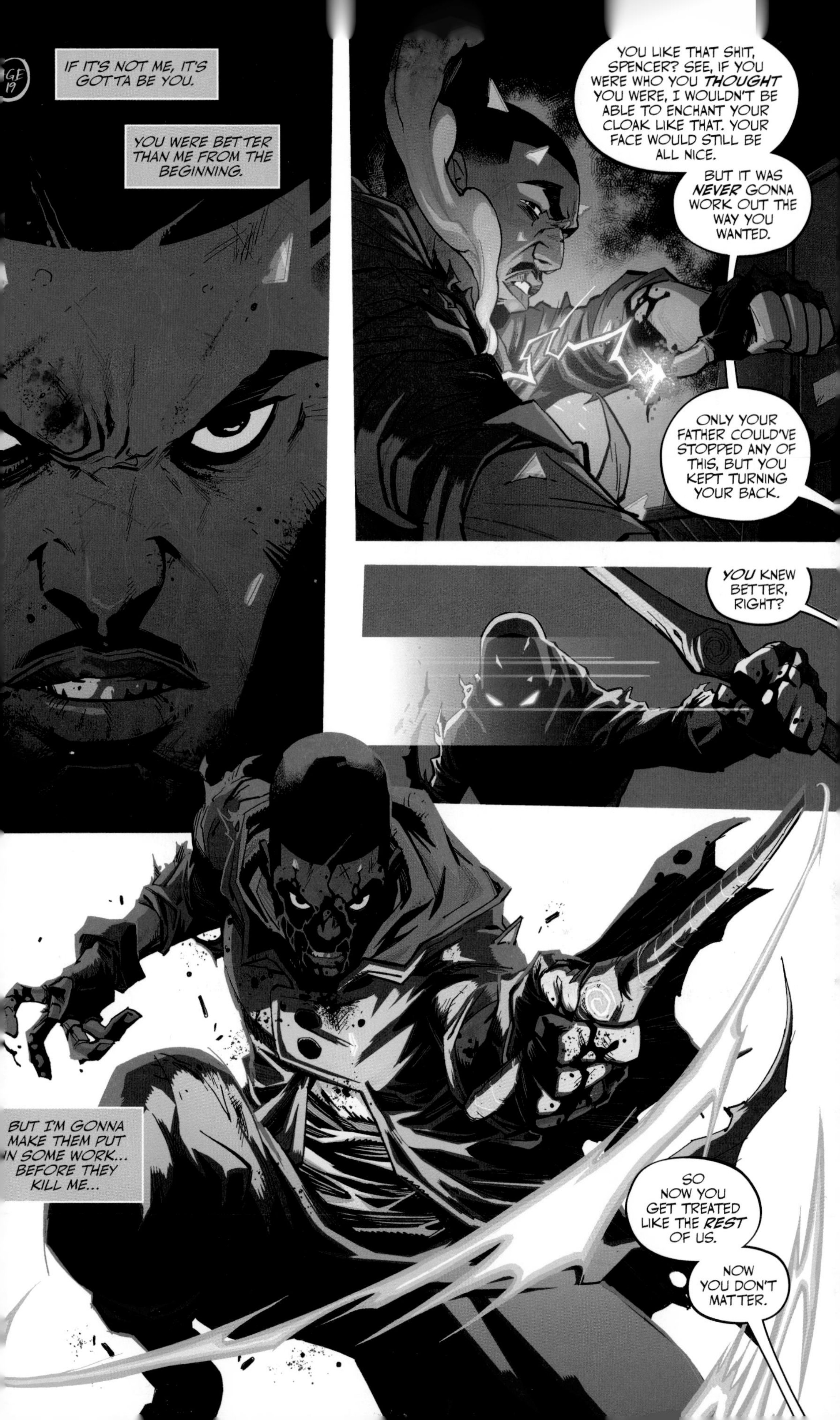
GE
19
IF IT'S NOT ME, IT'S GOTTA BE YOU.
YOU WERE BETTER THAN ME FROM THE BEGINNING.
YOU LIKE THAT SHIT, SPENCER? SEE, IF YOU WERE WHO YOU THOUGHT YOU WERE, I WOULDN'T BE ABLE TO ENCHANT YOUR CLOAK LIKE THAT. YOUR FACE WOULD STILL BE ALL NICE.
BUT IT WAS NEVER GONNA WORK OUT THE WAY YOU WANTED.
ONLY YOUR FATHER COULD'VE STOPPED ANY OF THIS, BUT YOU KEPT TURNING YOUR BACK.
YOU KNEW BETTER, RIGHT?
BUT I'M GONNA MAKE THEM PUT IN SOME WORK... BEFORE THEY KILL ME...
SO NOW YOU GET TREATED LIKE THE REST OF US.
NOW YOU DON'T MATTER.

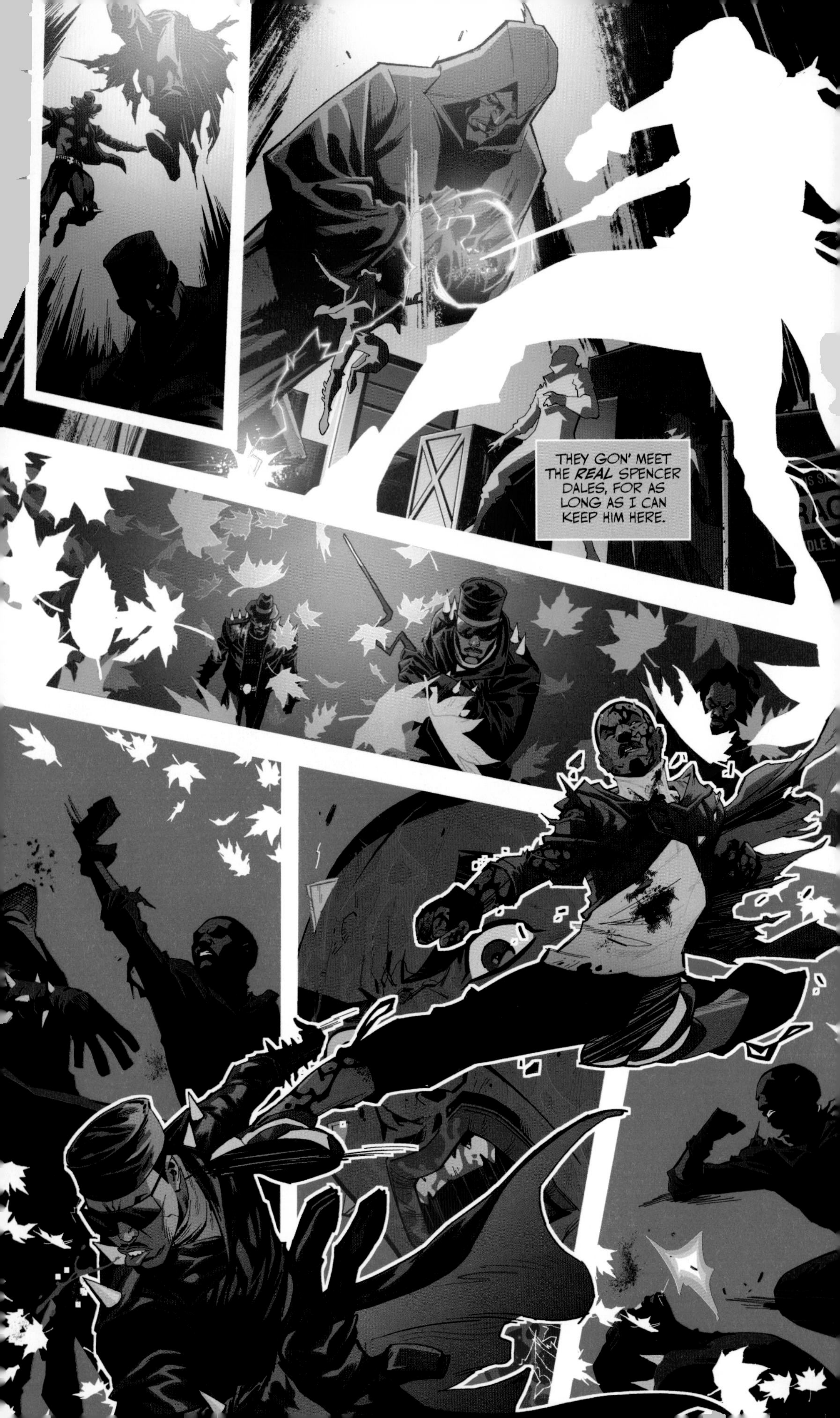
THEY GON' MEET THE REAL SPENCER DALES, FOR AS LONG AS I CAN KEEP HIM HERE.

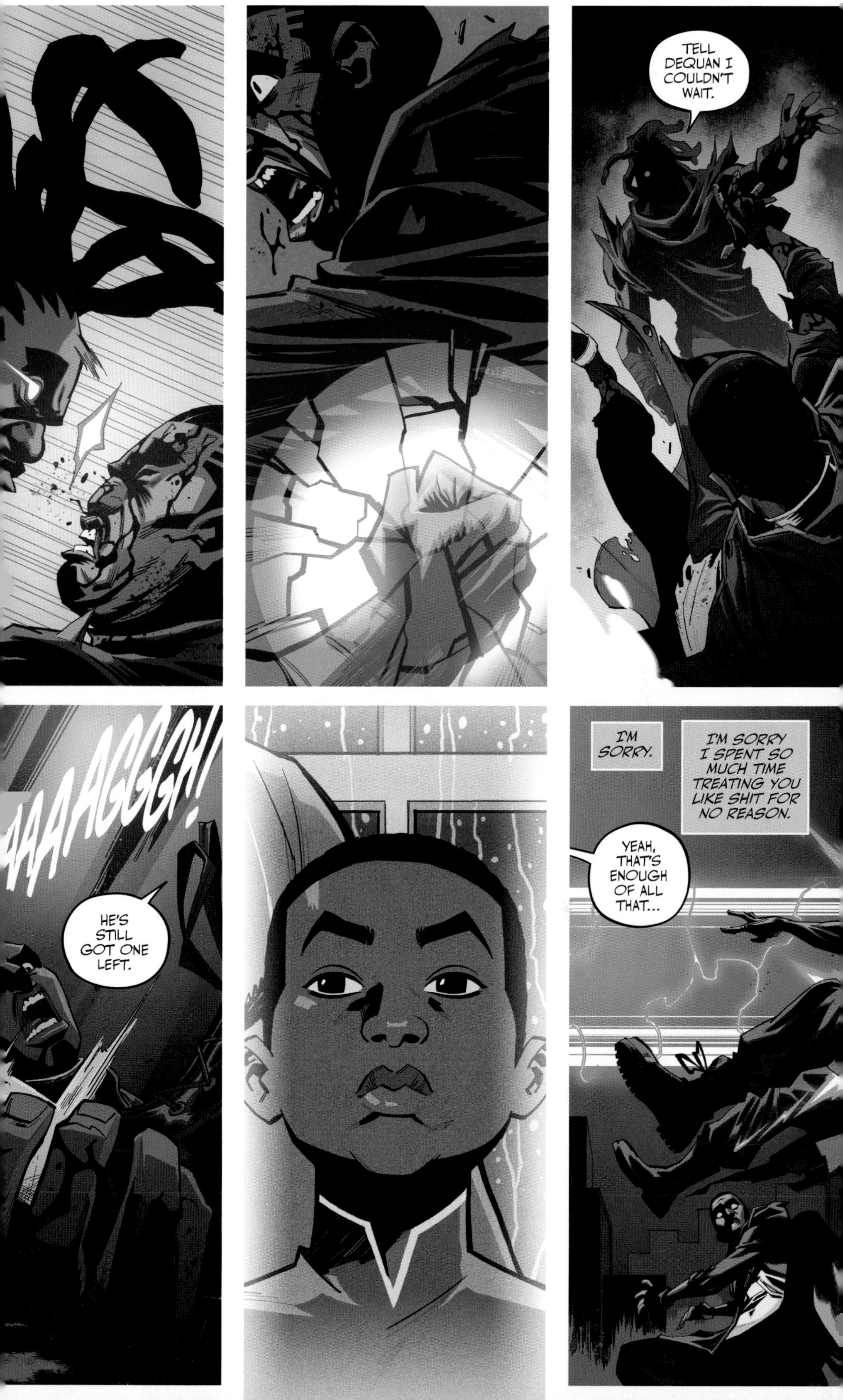

TELL DEQUAN I COULDN'T WAIT.
AAAAGGGH!
HE'S STILL GOT ONE LEFT.
I'M SORRY.
I'M SORRY I SPENT SO MUCH TIME TREATING YOU LIKE SHIT FOR NO REASON.
YEAH, THAT'S ENOUGH OF ALL THAT...

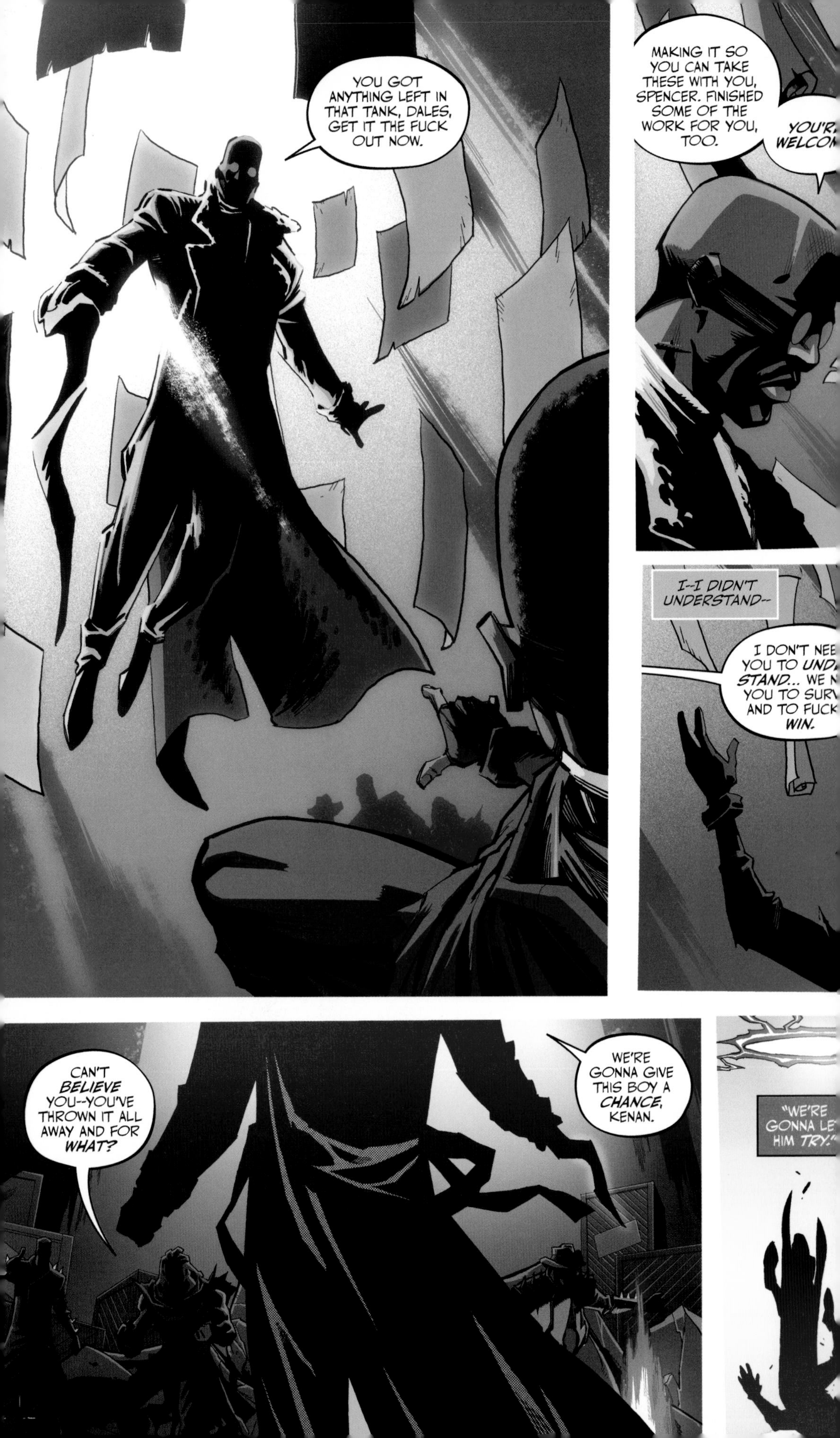
YOU GOT ANYTHING LEFT IN THAT TANK, DALES, GET IT THE FUCK OUT NOW.
MAKING IT SO YOU CAN TAKE THESE WITH YOU, SPENCER. FINISHED SOME OF THE WORK FOR YOU, TOO.
YOU'R WELCO
I--I DIDN'T UNDERSTAND--
I DON'T NEE YOU TO UND STAND... WE N YOU TO SURV AND TO FUCK WIN.
CAN'T BELIEVE YOU--YOU'VE THROWN IT ALL AWAY AND FOR WHAT?
WE'RE GONNA GIVE THIS BOY A CHANCE, KENAN.
"WE'RE GONNA LE HIM TRY."

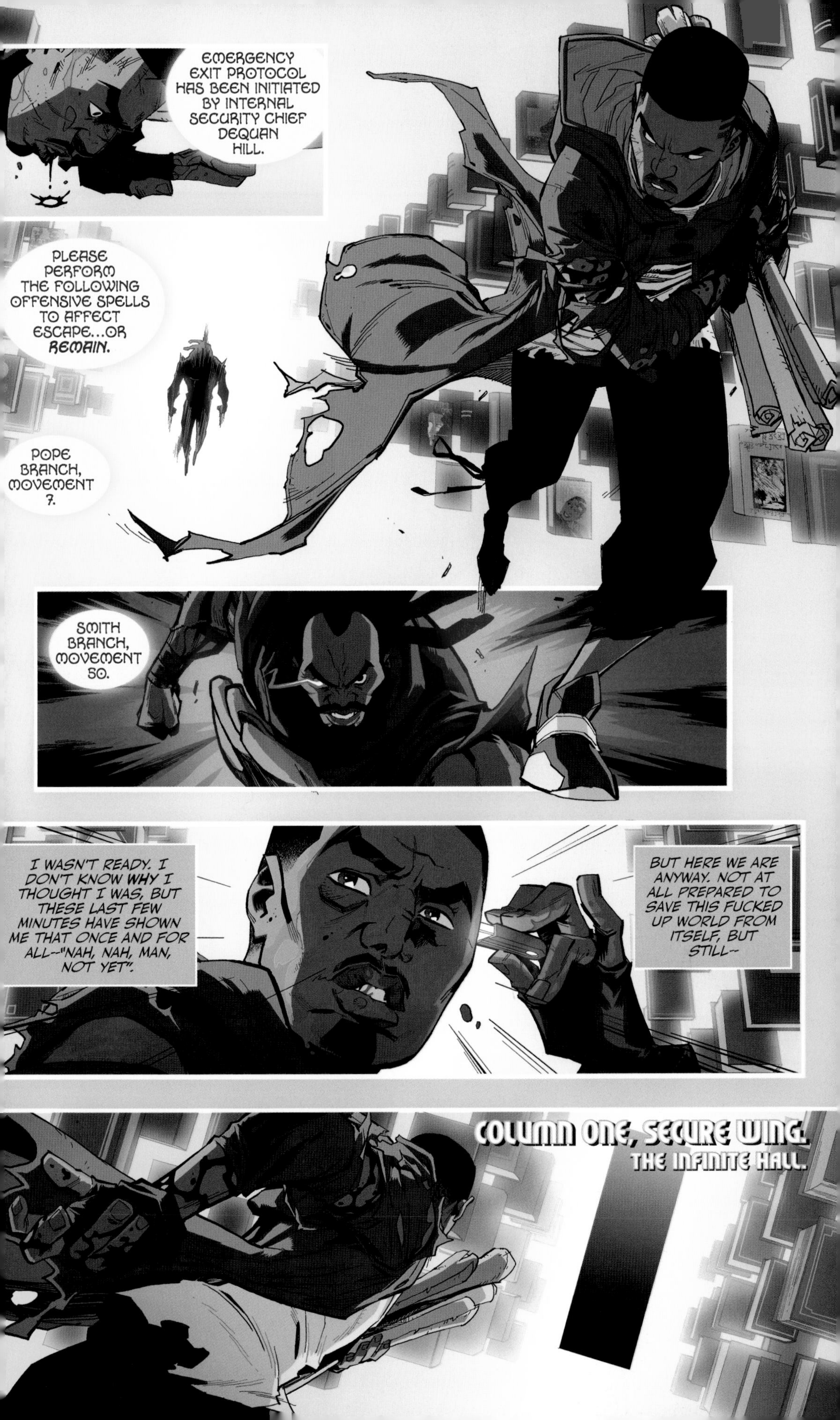
EMERGENCY EXIT PROTOCOL HAS BEEN INITIATED BY INTERNAL SECURITY CHIEF DEQUAN HILL.
PLEASE PERFORM THE FOLLOWING OFFENSIVE SPELLS TO AFFECT ESCAPE...OR REMAIN.
POPE BRANCH, MOVEMENT 7.
SMITH BRANCH, MOVEMENT 50.
I WASN'T READY. I DON'T KNOW WHY I THOUGHT I WAS, BUT THESE LAST FEW MINUTES HAVE SHOWN ME THAT ONCE AND FOR ALL--"NAH, NAH, MAN, NOT YET".
BUT HERE WE ARE ANYWAY. NOT AT ALL PREPARED TO SAVE THIS FUCKED UP WORLD FROM ITSELF, BUT STILL--
COLUMN ONE, SECURE WING.
THE INFINITE HALL.

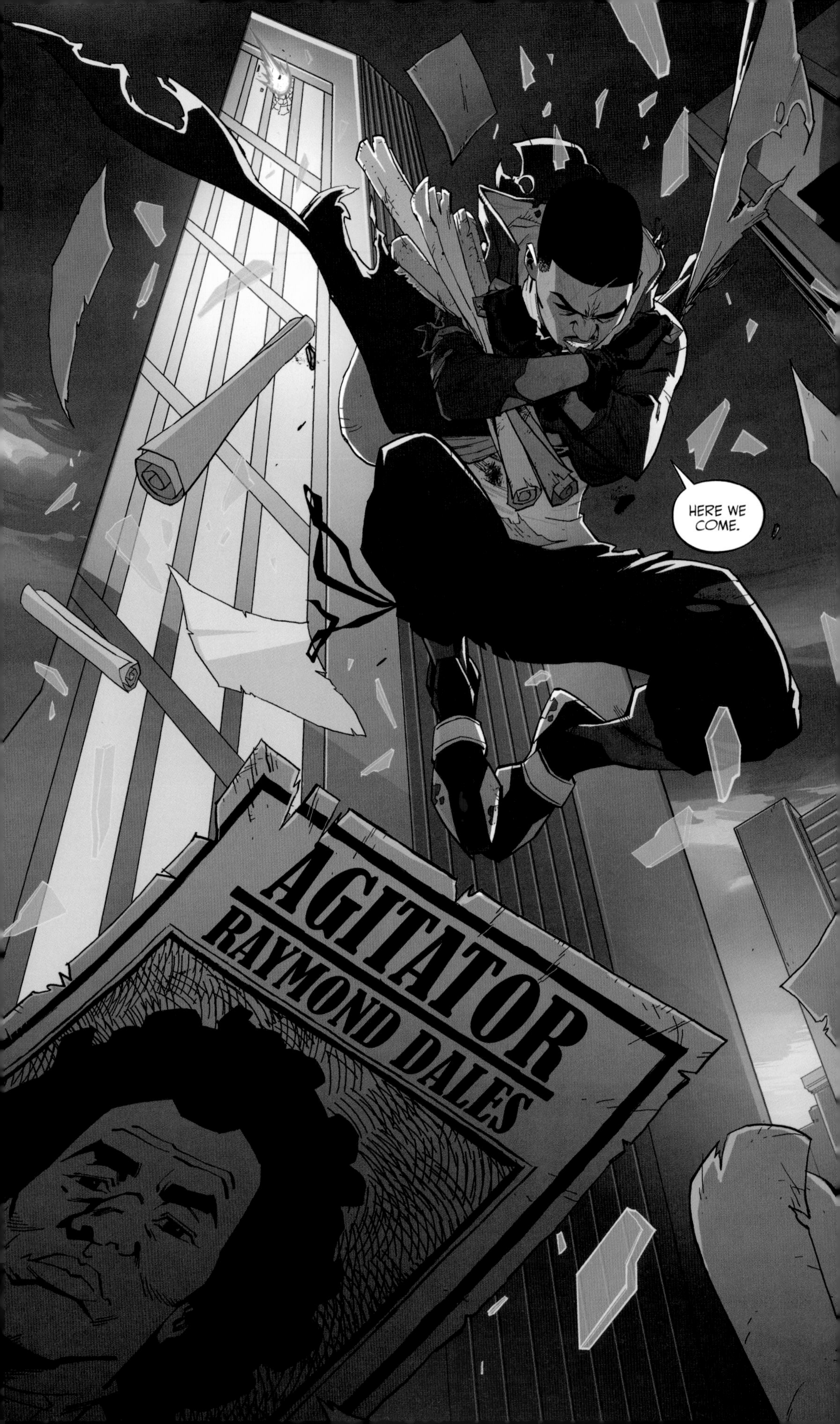
HERE WE COME.
AGITATOR
RAYMOND DALES

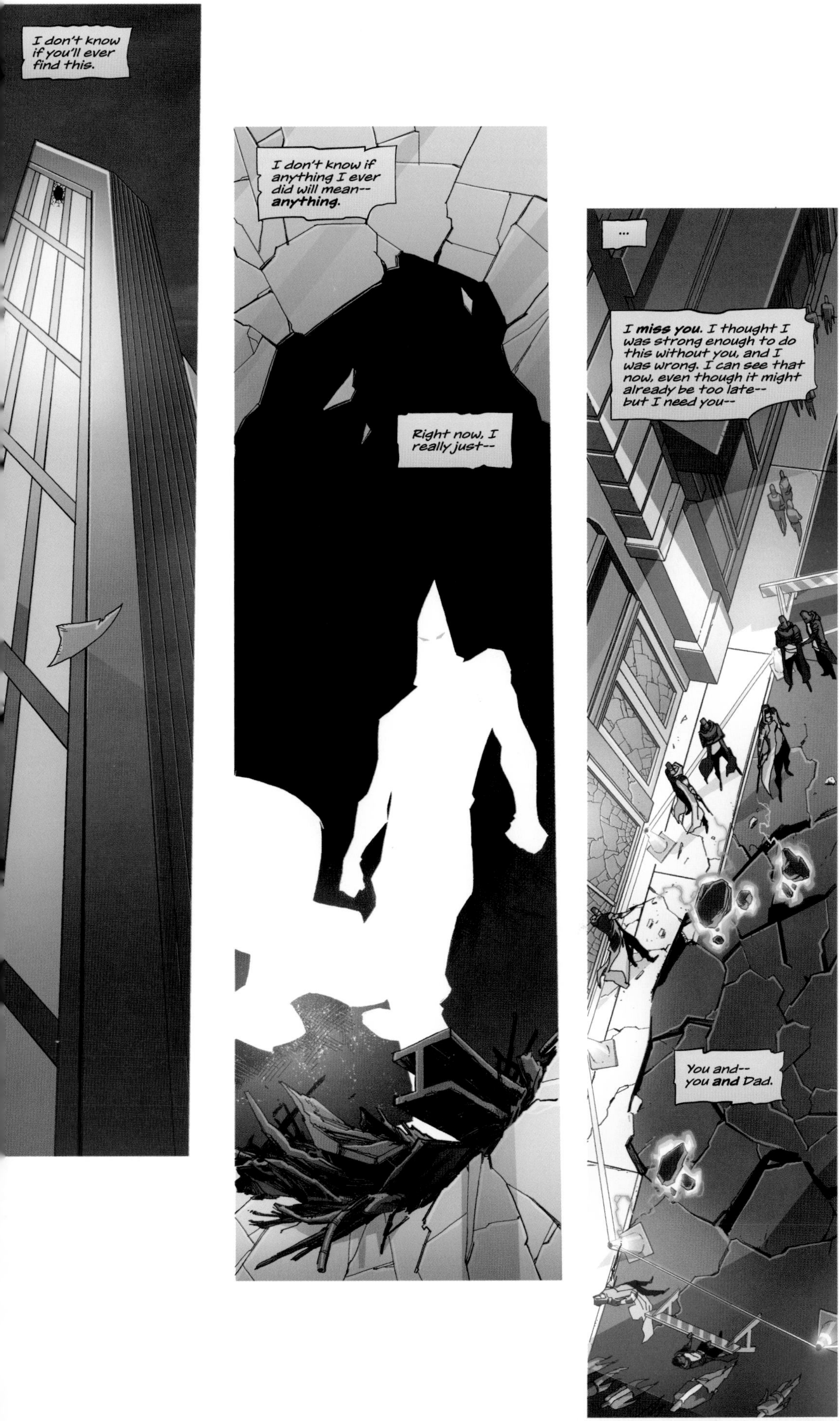
I don't know if you'll ever find this.
I don't know if anything I ever did will mean-- **anything**.
Right now, I really just--
...
I **miss you**. I thought I was strong enough to do this without you, and I was wrong. I can see that now, even though it might already be too late-- but I need you--
You and-- you **and** Dad.

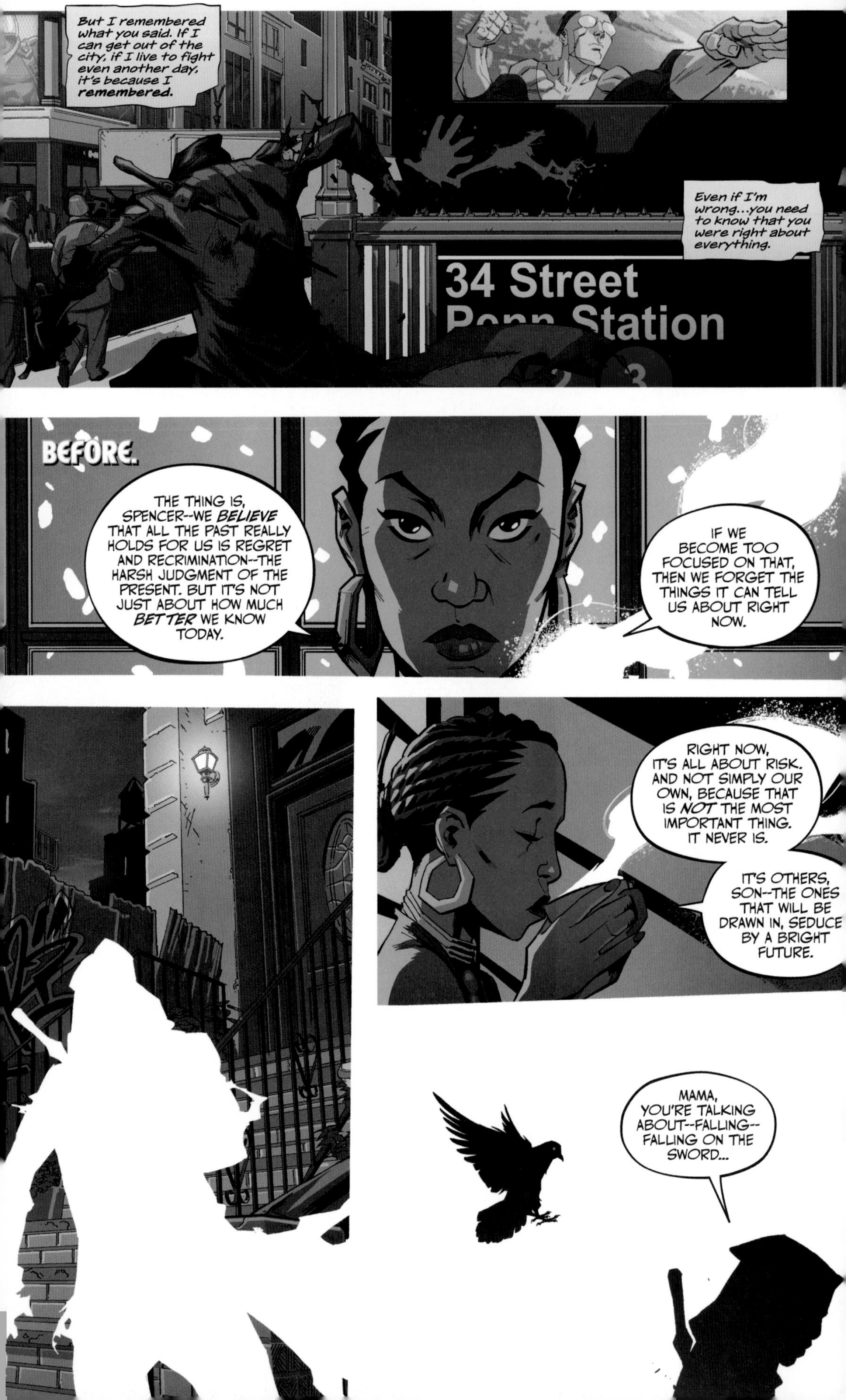

But I remembered what you said. If I can get out of the city, if I live to fight even another day, it's because I remembered.
Even if I'm wrong...you need to know that you were right about everything.
34 Street
Penn Station
BEFORE.
THE THING IS, SPENCER--WE BELIEVE THAT ALL THE PAST REALLY HOLDS FOR US IS REGRET AND RECRIMINATION--THE HARSH JUDGMENT OF THE PRESENT. BUT IT'S NOT JUST ABOUT HOW MUCH BETTER WE KNOW TODAY.
IF WE BECOME TOO FOCUSED ON THAT, THEN WE FORGET THE THINGS IT CAN TELL US ABOUT RIGHT NOW.
RIGHT NOW, IT'S ALL ABOUT RISK. AND NOT SIMPLY OUR OWN, BECAUSE THAT IS NOT THE MOST IMPORTANT THING. IT NEVER IS.
IT'S OTHERS, SON--THE ONES THAT WILL BE DRAWN IN, SEDUCE BY A BRIGHT FUTURE.
MAMA, YOU'RE TALKING ABOUT--FALLING--FALLING ON THE SWORD...

I'M TALKING ABOUT, EATING THE SWORD, UNTIL THERE'S NOTHING LEFT. AND IF YOU'RE NOT *WILLING*--IF THERE'S A PART OF YOU NOT SECRETLY *WELCOMING* THAT RESPONSIBILITY?

THEN, SPENCER....*YOU ACK THE FUCK DOWN*...UNTIL YOU DO.

HEY, GIRL.

DON'T--DON'T WORRY--JUST BEEN A REAL WEIRD DAY--

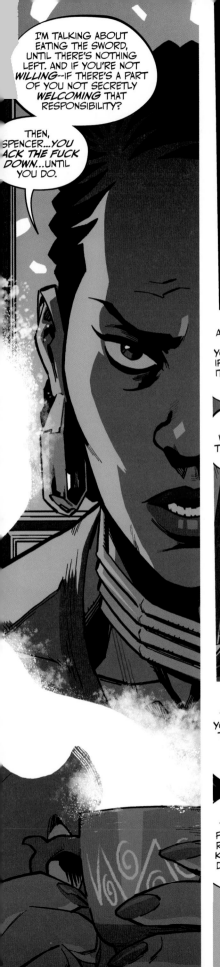

AND THEN YOU *WAIT.* FOR THE REST OF YOUR *NATURAL* LIFE, IF THAT'S HOW LONG IT TAKES. *FOREVER*, SPENCER. PAST FOREVER.

BECAUSE THERE ARE WORSE THINGS THAN DEATH, THAN HUMILIATION.

JUST GIVE ME A SECOND-- NEED SOME DISTANCE FROM YOUR PLACE.

THEY'LL TRACE ME-- SHOULDN'T HAVE COME--

LEADING OTHERS TO THAT FATE--BECAUSE YOU *DIDN'T* THINK THINGS THROUGH. BECAUSE YOU DIDN'T CONSIDER THE WORST, BEFORE YOU CONSIDERED *ANYTHING* ELSE.

UNTIL YOU CAN STARE THAT RIGHT IN ITS FACE...YOU'RE *NOT* READY. YOU *DON'T* KNOW WHAT YOU'RE DOING. YOU *CAN'T* PAY ALL COSTS.

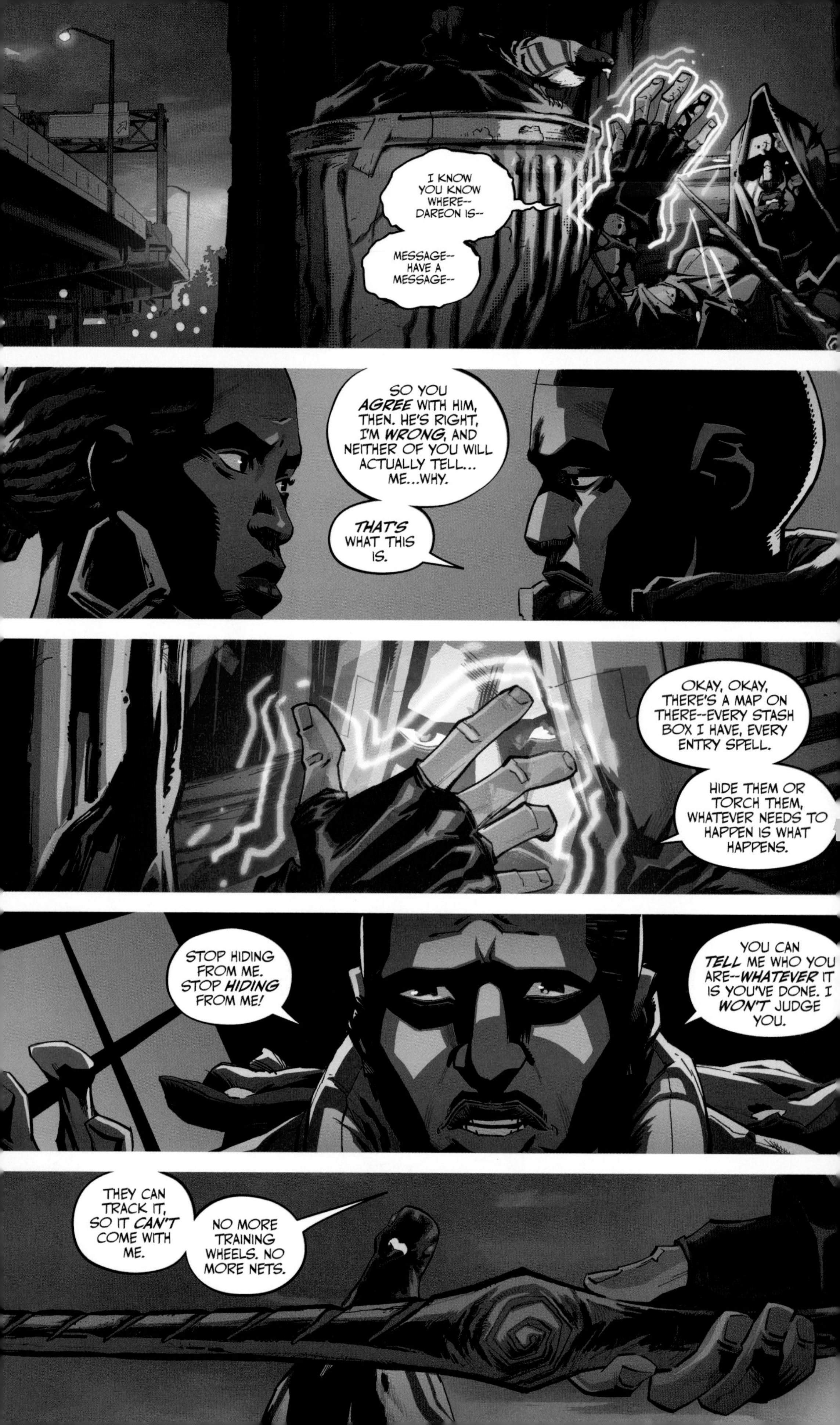
I KNOW YOU KNOW WHERE-- DAREON IS--
MESSAGE-- HAVE A MESSAGE--
SO YOU AGREE WITH HIM, THEN. HE'S RIGHT, I'M WRONG, AND NEITHER OF YOU WILL ACTUALLY TELL... ME...WHY.
THAT'S WHAT THIS IS.
OKAY, OKAY, THERE'S A MAP ON THERE--EVERY STASH BOX I HAVE, EVERY ENTRY SPELL.
HIDE THEM OR TORCH THEM, WHATEVER NEEDS TO HAPPEN IS WHAT HAPPENS.
STOP HIDING FROM ME. STOP HIDING FROM ME!
YOU CAN TELL ME WHO YOU ARE--WHATEVER IT IS YOU'VE DONE. I WON'T JUDGE YOU.
THEY CAN TRACK IT, SO IT CAN'T COME WITH ME.
NO MORE TRAINING WHEELS. NO MORE NETS.

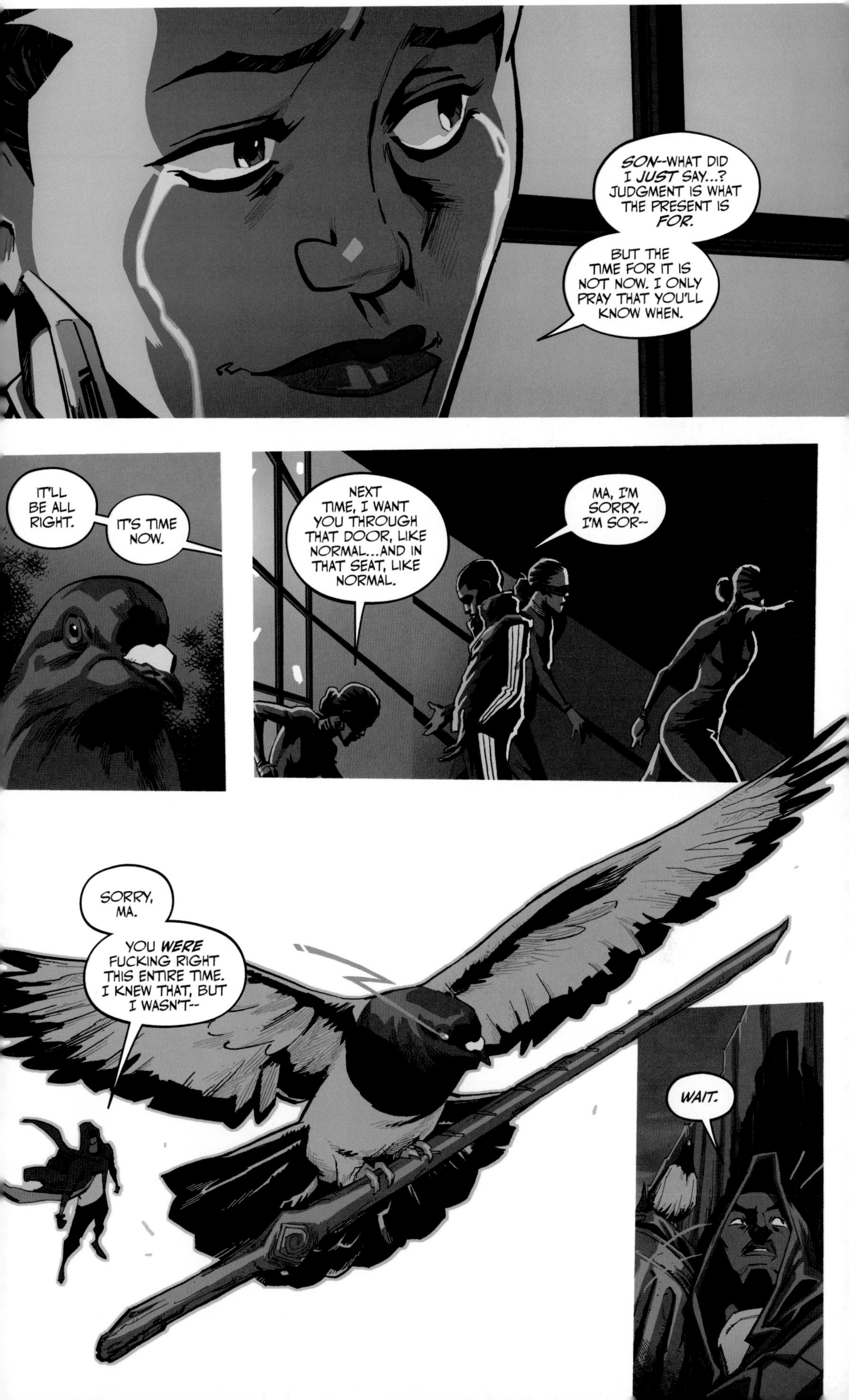
SON--WHAT DID I JUST SAY...? JUDGMENT IS WHAT THE PRESENT IS FOR.
BUT THE TIME FOR IT IS NOT NOW. I ONLY PRAY THAT YOU'LL KNOW WHEN.
IT'LL BE ALL RIGHT.
IT'S TIME NOW.
NEXT TIME, I WANT YOU THROUGH THAT DOOR, LIKE NORMAL...AND IN THAT SEAT, LIKE NORMAL.
MA, I'M SORRY. I'M SOR--
SORRY, MA.
YOU WERE FUCKING RIGHT THIS ENTIRE TIME. I KNEW THAT, BUT I WASN'T--
WAIT.

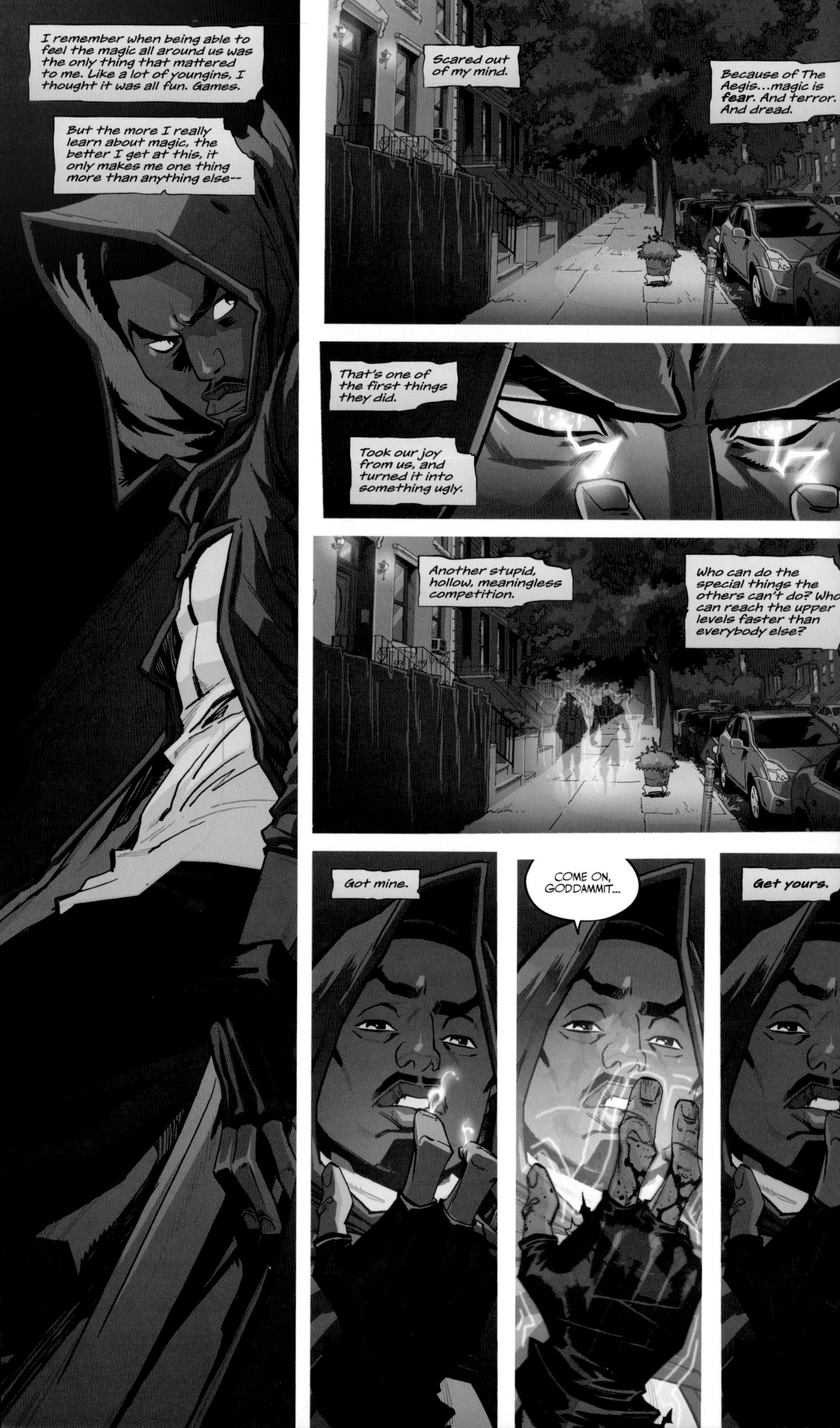
I remember when being able to feel the magic all around us was the only thing that mattered to me. Like a lot of youngins, I thought it was all fun. Games.
But the more I really learn about magic, the better I get at this, it only makes me one thing more than anything else--
Scared out of my mind.
Because of The Aegis...magic is fear. And terror. And dread.
That's one of the first things they did.
Took our joy from us, and turned it into something ugly.
Another stupid, hollow, meaningless competition.
Who can do the special things the others can't do? Who can reach the upper levels faster than everybody else?
Got mine.
COME ON, GODDAMMIT...
Get yours.

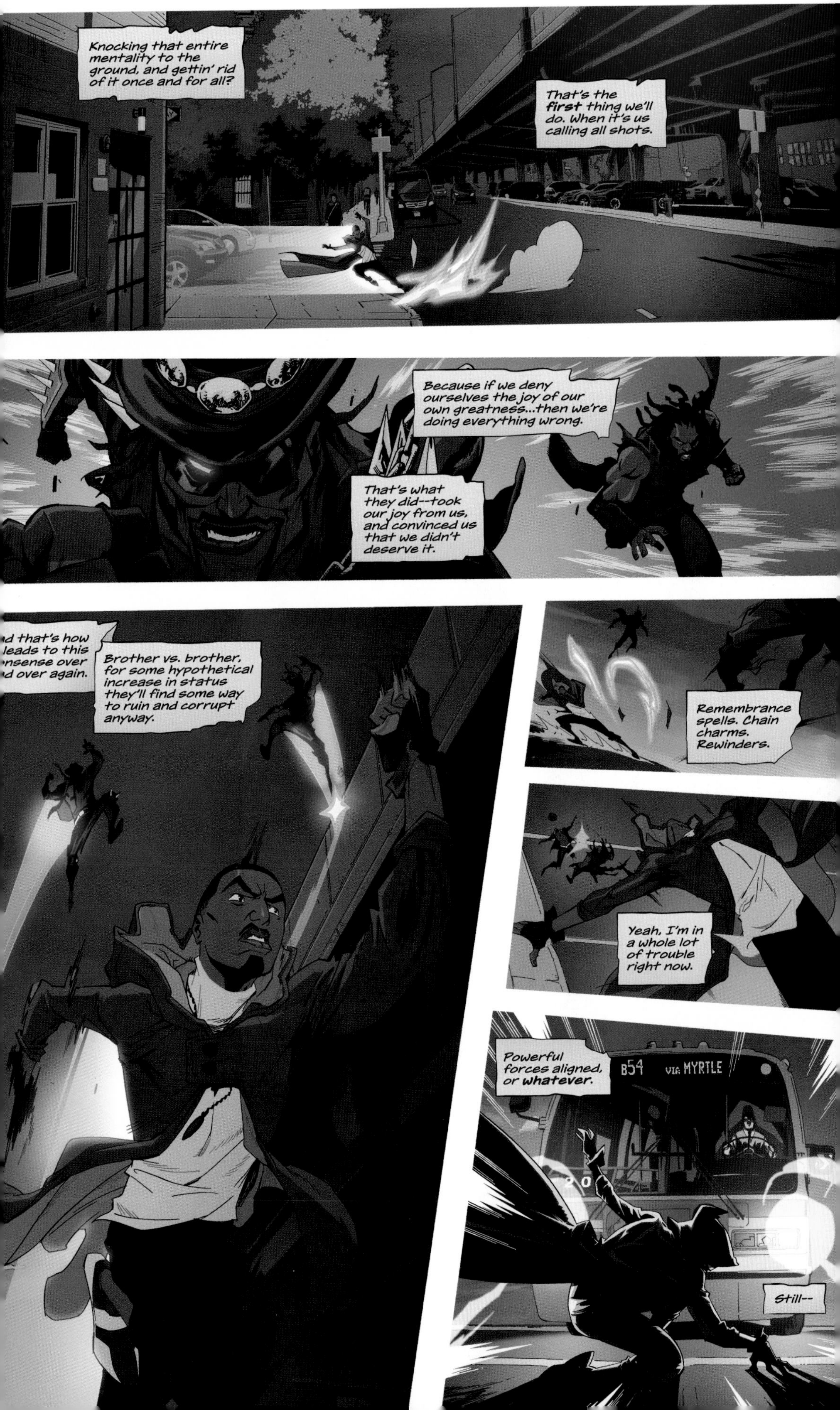
Knocking that entire mentality to the ground, and gettin' rid of it once and for all?
That's the **first** thing we'll do. When it's us calling all shots.
Because if we deny ourselves the joy of our own greatness...then we're doing everything wrong.
That's what they did--took our joy from us, and convinced us that we didn't deserve it.
d that's how leads to this nsense over d over again.
Brother vs. brother, for some hypothetical increase in status they'll find some way to ruin and corrupt anyway.
Remembrance spells. Chain charms. Rewinders.
Yeah, I'm in a whole lot of trouble right now.
Powerful forces aligned, or **whatever**.
B54 VIA MYRTLE
Still--

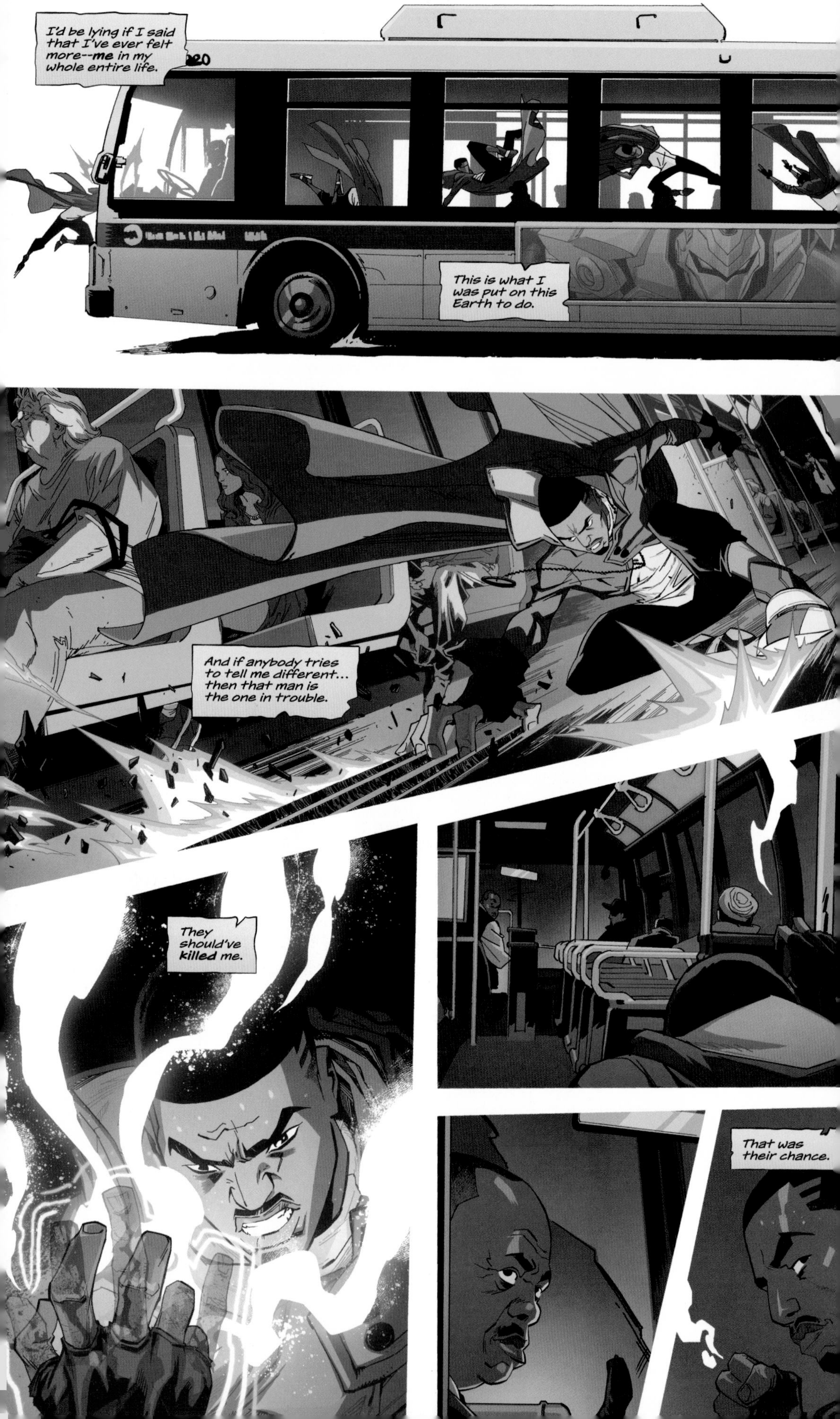
I'd be lying if I said that I've ever felt more--**me** in my whole entire life.
This is what I was put on this Earth to do.
And if anybody tries to tell me different... then that man is the one in trouble.
They should've **killed** me.
That was their chance.

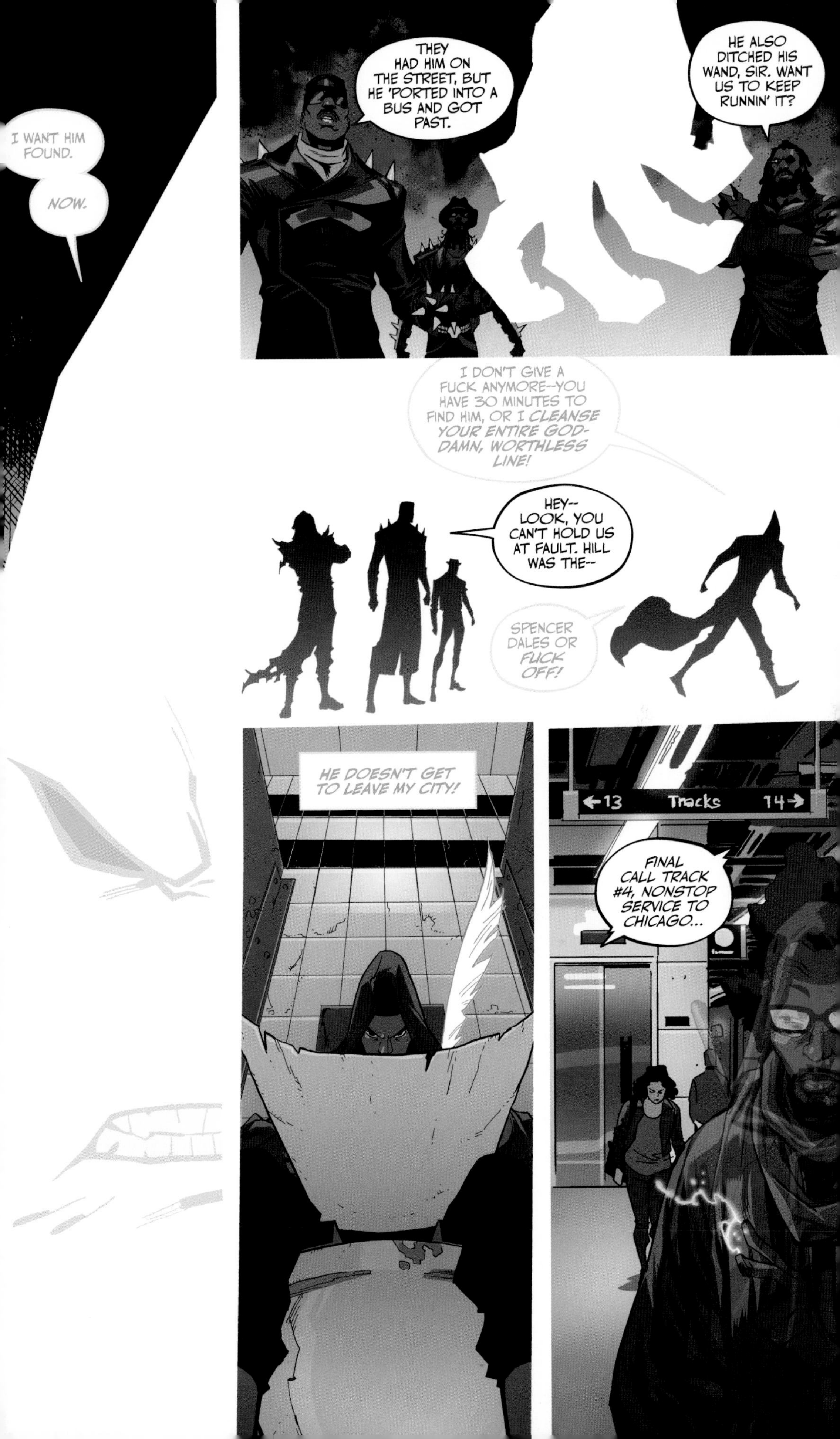
I WANT HIM FOUND.
NOW.
THEY HAD HIM ON THE STREET, BUT HE 'PORTED INTO A BUS AND GOT PAST.
HE ALSO DITCHED HIS WAND, SIR. WANT US TO KEEP RUNNIN' IT?
I DON'T GIVE A FUCK ANYMORE--YOU HAVE 30 MINUTES TO FIND HIM, OR I CLEANSE YOUR ENTIRE GOD-DAMN, WORTHLESS LINE!
HEY-- LOOK, YOU CAN'T HOLD US AT FAULT. HILL WAS THE--
SPENCER DALES OR FUCK OFF!
HE DOESN'T GET TO LEAVE MY CITY!
←13 Tracks 14→
FINAL CALL TRACK #4, NONSTOP SERVICE TO CHICAGO...

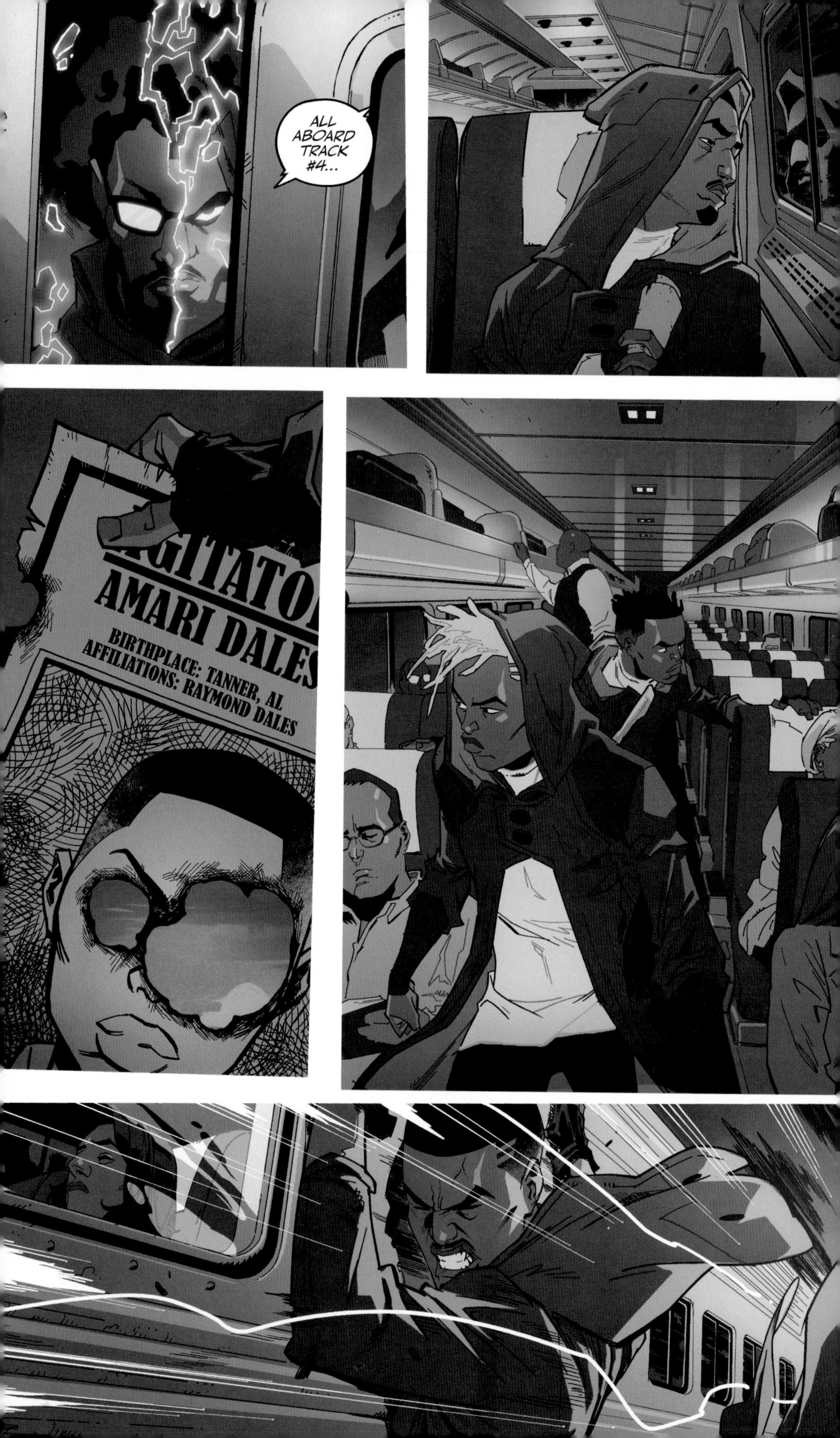
ALL ABOARD TRACK #4...
AGITATOR
AMARI DALES
BIRTHPLACE: TANNER, AL
AFFILIATIONS: RAYMOND DALES

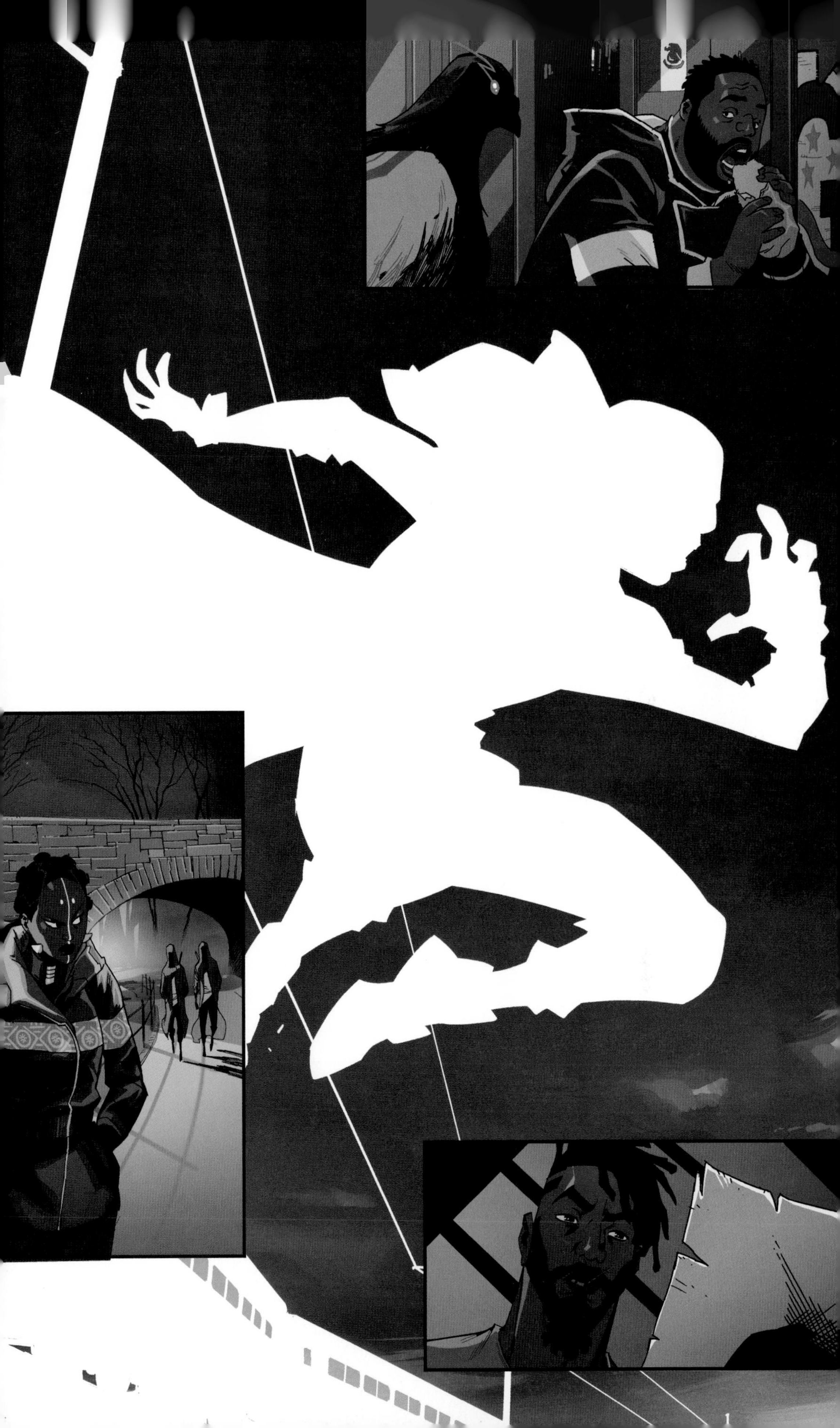

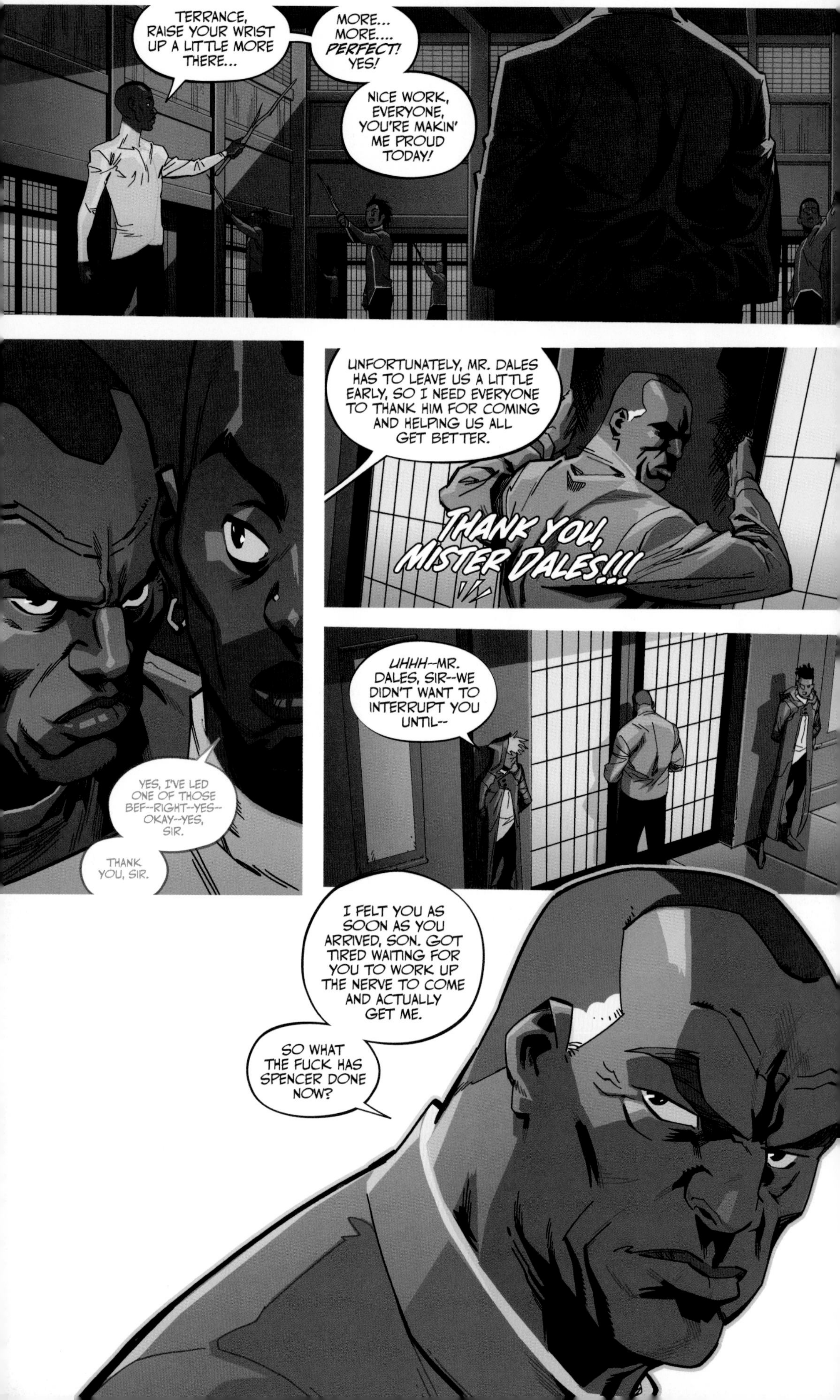
TERRANCE, RAISE YOUR WRIST UP A LITTLE MORE THERE...
MORE... MORE.... PERFECT! YES!
NICE WORK, EVERYONE, YOU'RE MAKIN' ME PROUD TODAY!
YES, I'VE LED ONE OF THOSE BEF--RIGHT--YES--OKAY--YES, SIR.
THANK YOU, SIR.
UNFORTUNATELY, MR. DALES HAS TO LEAVE US A LITTLE EARLY, SO I NEED EVERYONE TO THANK HIM FOR COMING AND HELPING US ALL GET BETTER.
THANK YOU, MISTER DALES!!!
UHHH--MR. DALES, SIR--WE DIDN'T WANT TO INTERRUPT YOU UNTIL--
I FELT YOU AS SOON AS YOU ARRIVED, SON. GOT TIRED WAITING FOR YOU TO WORK UP THE NERVE TO COME AND ACTUALLY GET ME.
SO WHAT THE FUCK HAS SPENCER DONE NOW?

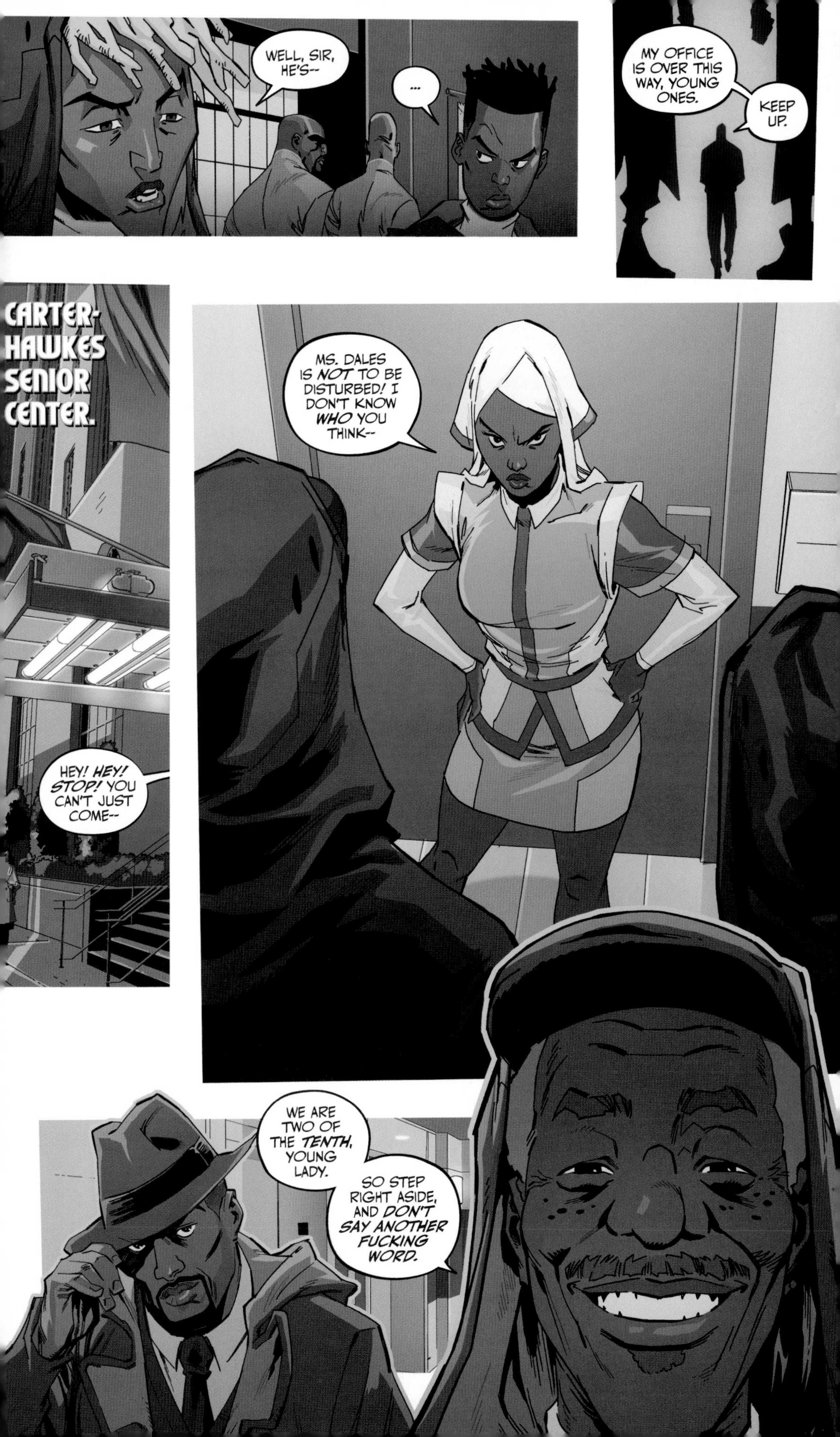
WELL, SIR, HE'S--
...
MY OFFICE IS OVER THIS WAY, YOUNG ONES.
KEEP UP.
CARTER-HAWKES SENIOR CENTER.
HEY! HEY! STOP! YOU CAN'T JUST COME--
MS. DALES IS NOT TO BE DISTURBED! I DON'T KNOW WHO YOU THINK--
WE ARE TWO OF THE TENTH, YOUNG LADY.
SO STEP RIGHT ASIDE, AND DON'T SAY ANOTHER FUCKING WORD.

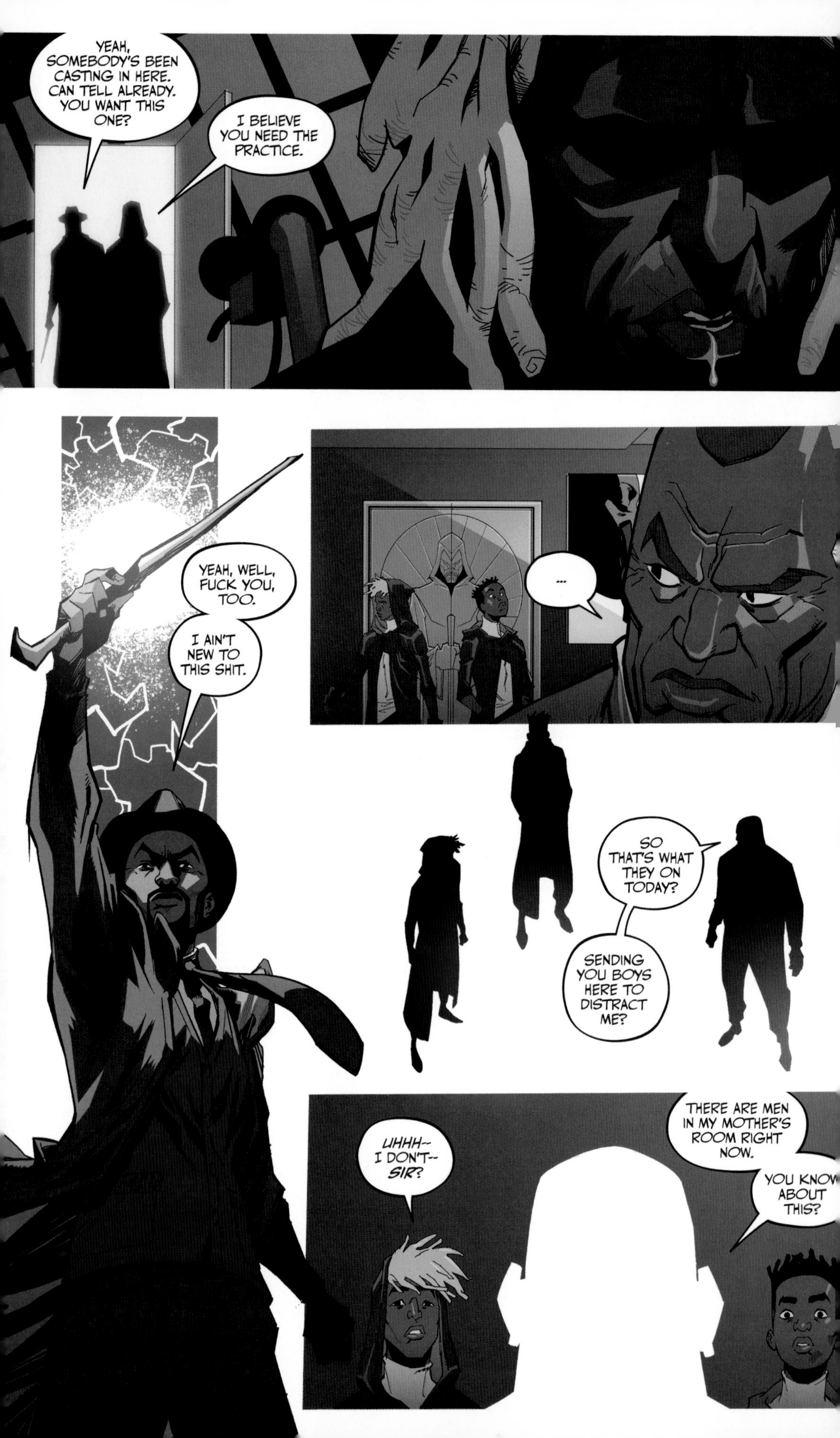
YEAH, SOMEBODY'S BEEN CASTING IN HERE. CAN TELL ALREADY. YOU WANT THIS ONE?
I BELIEVE YOU NEED THE PRACTICE.
YEAH, WELL, FUCK YOU, TOO.
I AIN'T NEW TO THIS SHIT.
...
SO THAT'S WHAT THEY ON TODAY?
SENDING YOU BOYS HERE TO DISTRACT ME?
THERE ARE MEN IN MY MOTHER'S ROOM RIGHT NOW.
YOU KNOW ABOUT THIS?
UHHH-- I DON'T-- SIR?

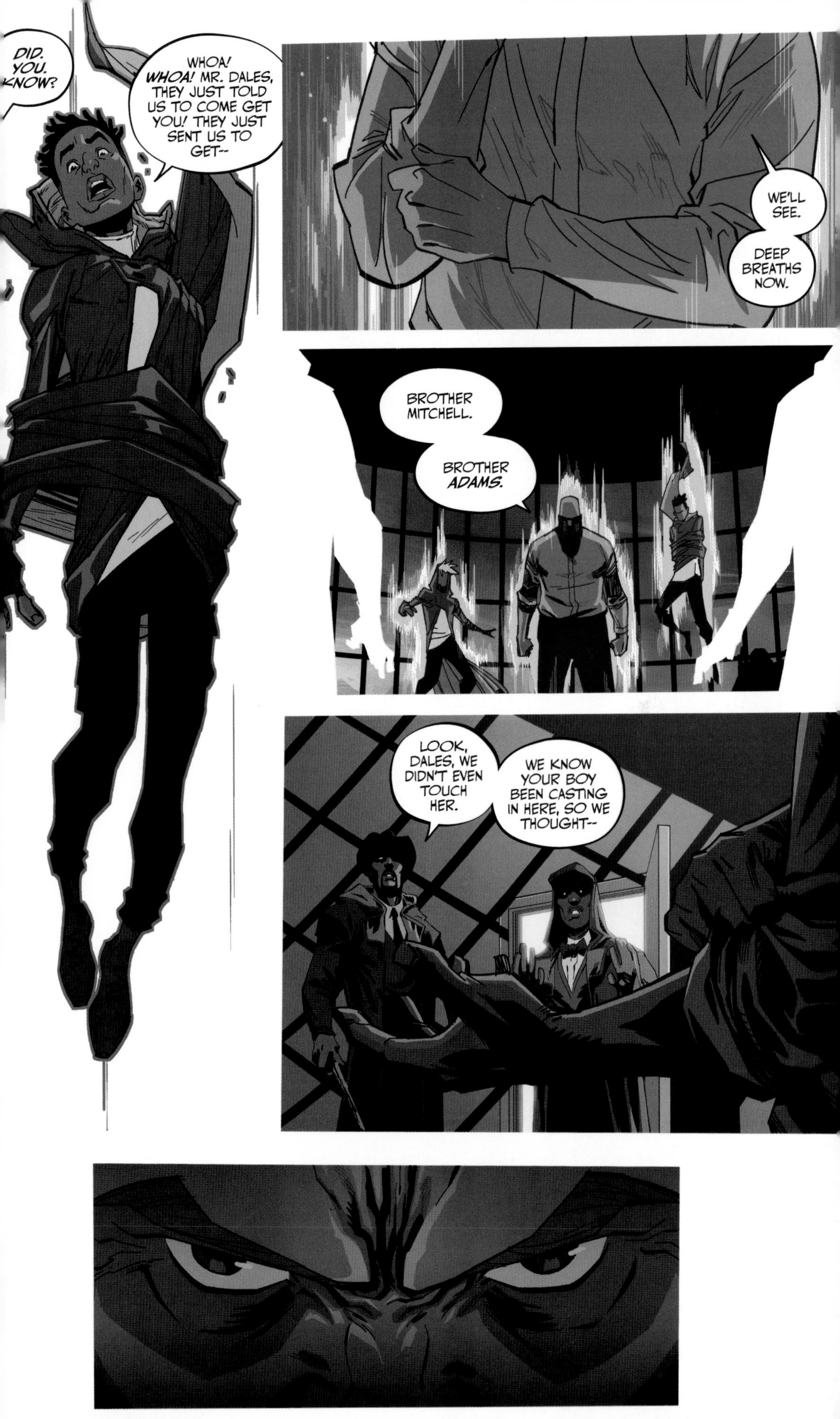
DID. YOU. KNOW?
WHOA! WHOA! MR. DALES, THEY JUST TOLD US TO COME GET YOU! THEY JUST SENT US TO GET--
WE'LL SEE.
DEEP BREATHS NOW.
BROTHER MITCHELL.
BROTHER ADAMS.
LOOK, DALES, WE DIDN'T EVEN TOUCH HER.
WE KNOW YOUR BOY BEEN CASTING IN HERE, SO WE THOUGHT--

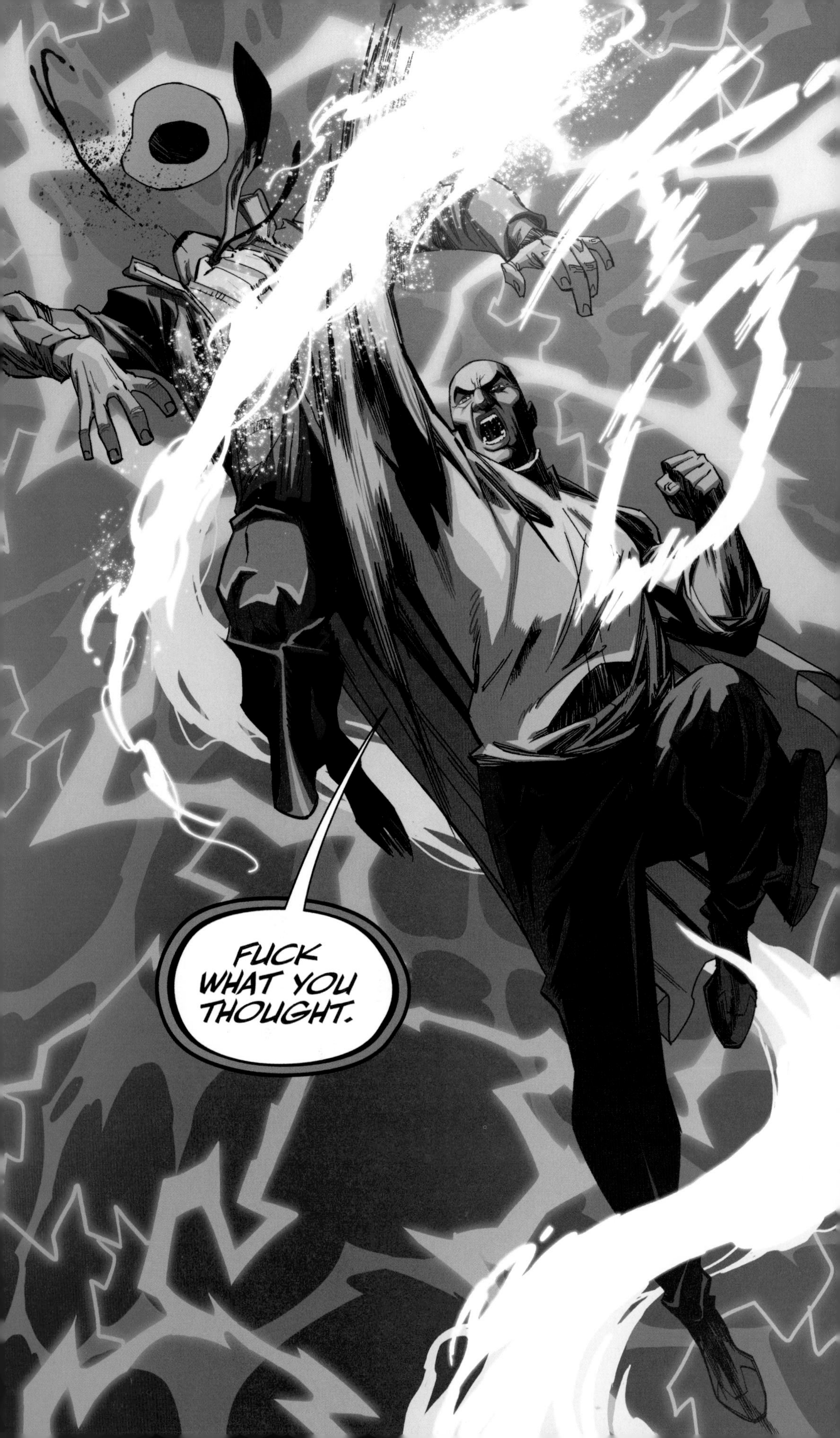
FUCK WHAT YOU THOUGHT.

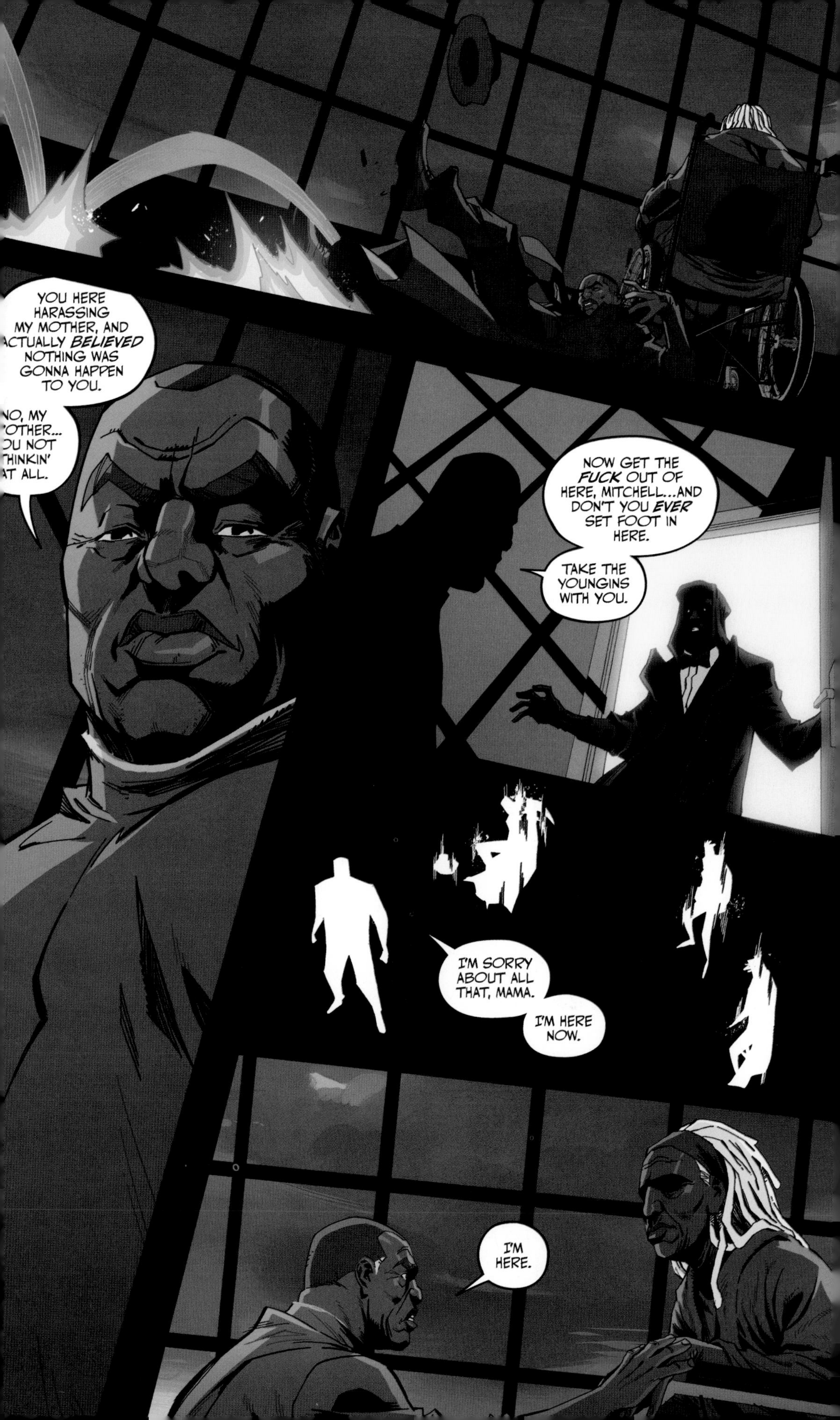
YOU HERE HARASSING MY MOTHER, AND ACTUALLY BELIEVED NOTHING WAS GONNA HAPPEN TO YOU.
NO, MY ...OTHER... ...OU NOT THINKIN' ...AT ALL.
NOW GET THE FUCK OUT OF HERE, MITCHELL...AND DON'T YOU EVER SET FOOT IN HERE.
TAKE THE YOUNGINS WITH YOU.
I'M SORRY ABOUT ALL THAT, MAMA.
I'M HERE NOW.
I'M HERE.

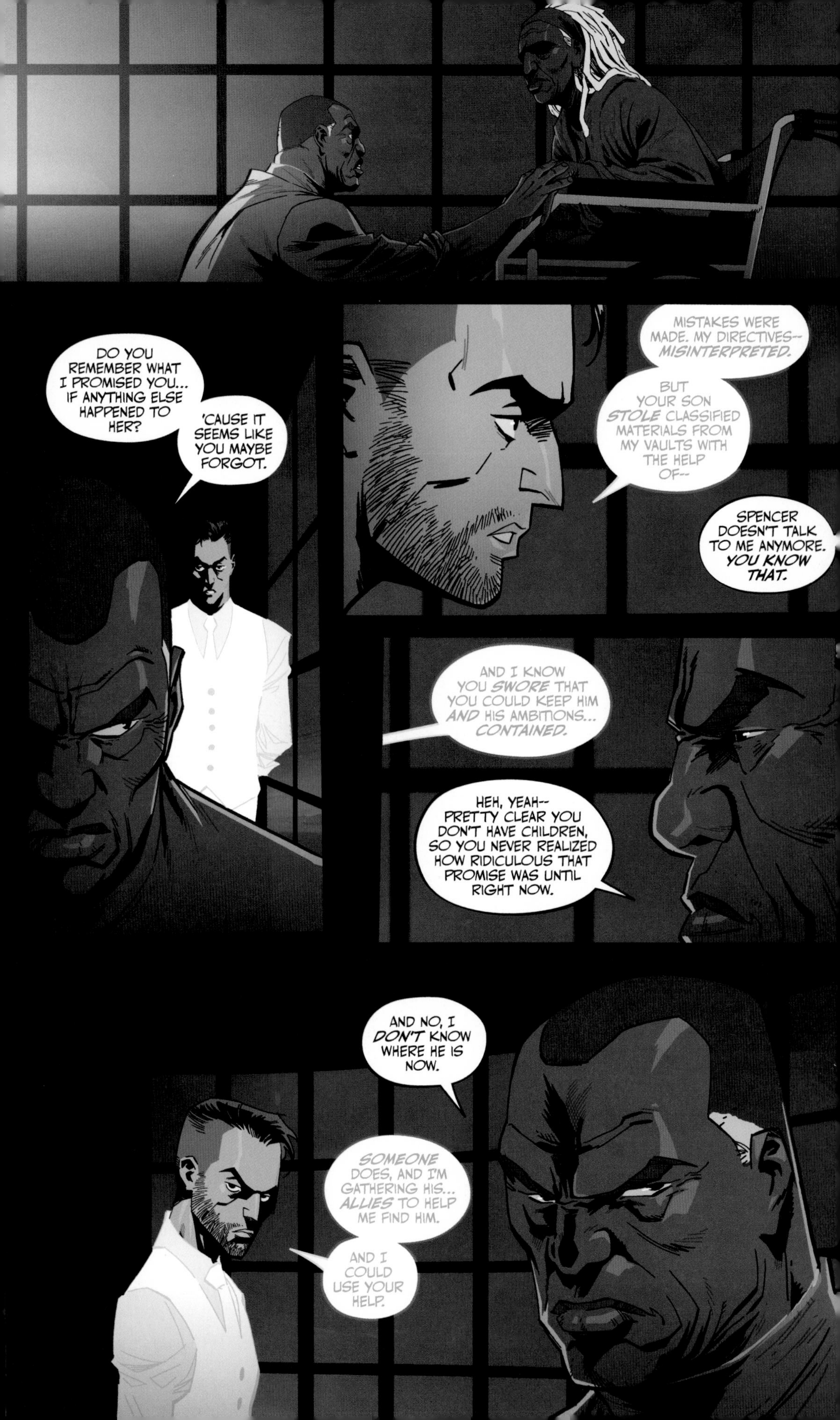
DO YOU REMEMBER WHAT I PROMISED YOU... IF ANYTHING ELSE HAPPENED TO HER?
'CAUSE IT SEEMS LIKE YOU MAYBE FORGOT.
MISTAKES WERE MADE. MY DIRECTIVES-- MISINTERPRETED.
BUT YOUR SON STOLE CLASSIFIED MATERIALS FROM MY VAULTS WITH THE HELP OF--
SPENCER DOESN'T TALK TO ME ANYMORE. YOU KNOW THAT.
AND I KNOW YOU SWORE THAT YOU COULD KEEP HIM AND HIS AMBITIONS... CONTAINED.
HEH, YEAH-- PRETTY CLEAR YOU DON'T HAVE CHILDREN, SO YOU NEVER REALIZED HOW RIDICULOUS THAT PROMISE WAS UNTIL RIGHT NOW.
AND NO, I DON'T KNOW WHERE HE IS NOW.
SOMEONE DOES, AND I'M GATHERING HIS... ALLIES TO HELP ME FIND HIM.
AND I COULD USE YOUR HELP.

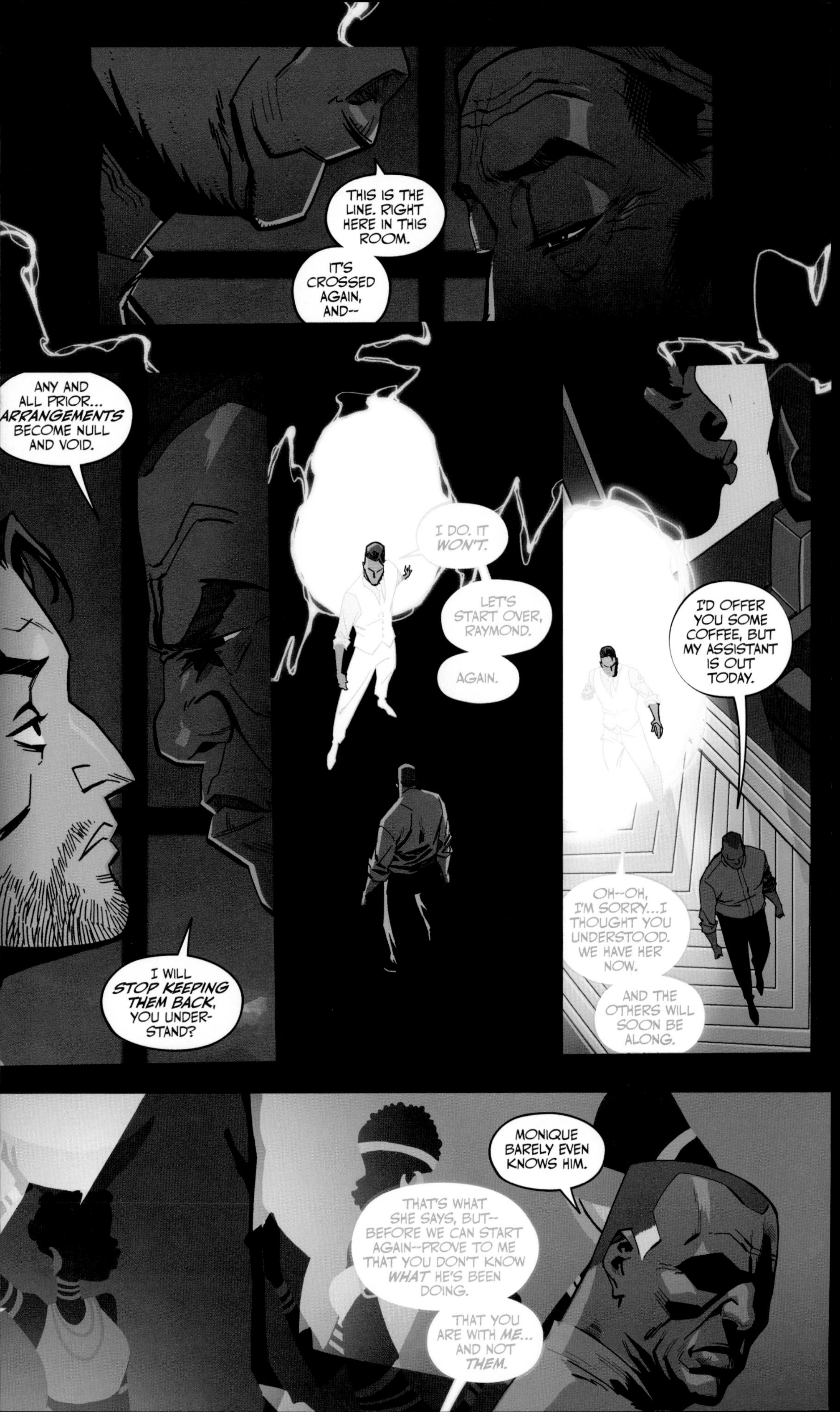
THIS IS THE LINE. RIGHT HERE IN THIS ROOM.
IT'S CROSSED AGAIN, AND--
ANY AND ALL PRIOR... ARRANGEMENTS BECOME NULL AND VOID.
I WILL STOP KEEPING THEM BACK, YOU UNDERSTAND?
I DO. IT WON'T.
LET'S START OVER, RAYMOND.
AGAIN.
I'D OFFER YOU SOME COFFEE, BUT MY ASSISTANT IS OUT TODAY.
OH--OH, I'M SORRY...I THOUGHT YOU UNDERSTOOD. WE HAVE HER NOW.
AND THE OTHERS WILL SOON BE ALONG.
MONIQUE BARELY EVEN KNOWS HIM.
THAT'S WHAT SHE SAYS, BUT-- BEFORE WE CAN START AGAIN--PROVE TO ME THAT YOU DON'T KNOW WHAT HE'S BEEN DOING.
THAT YOU ARE WITH ME... AND NOT THEM.

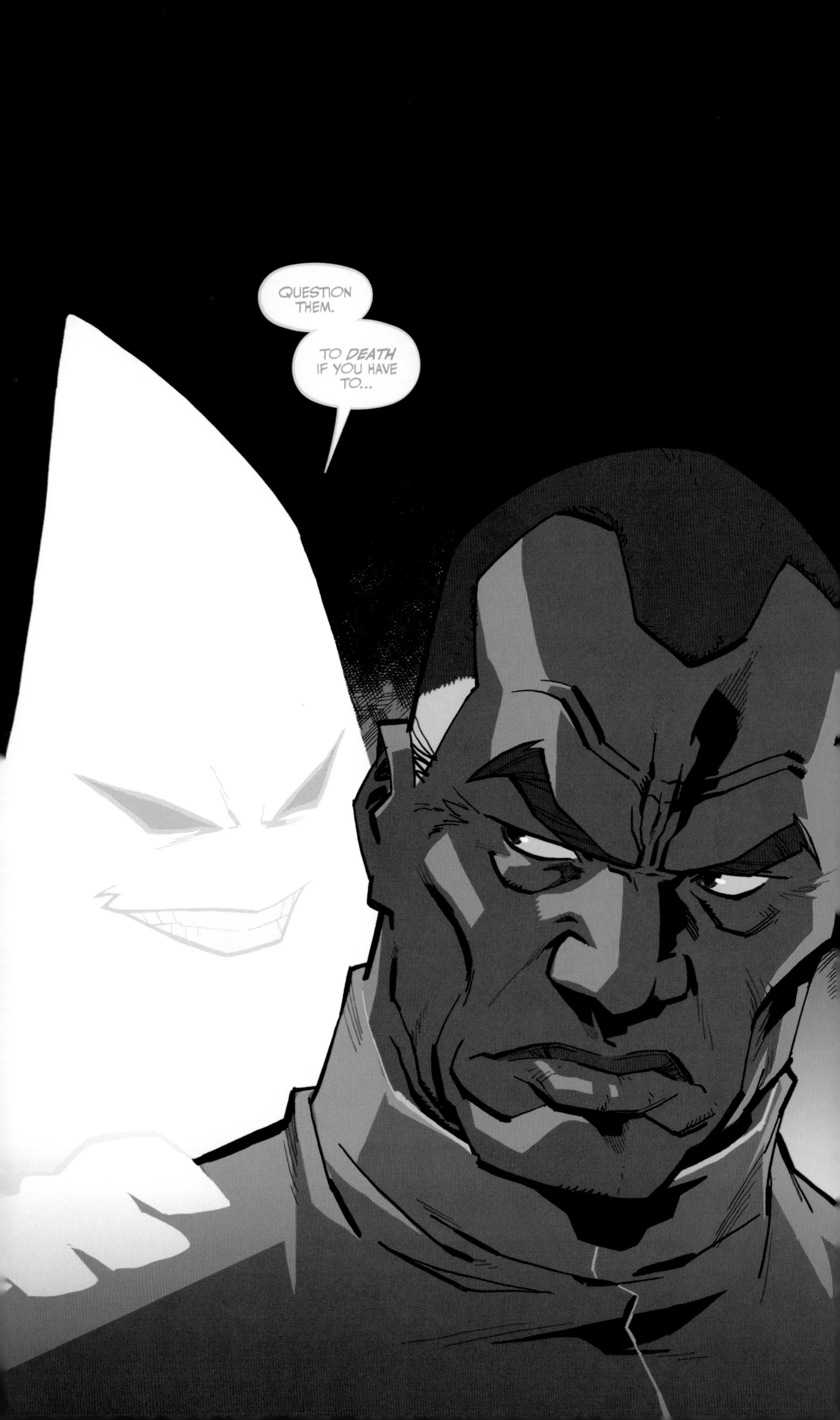
QUESTION THEM.
TO *DEATH* IF YOU HAVE TO...

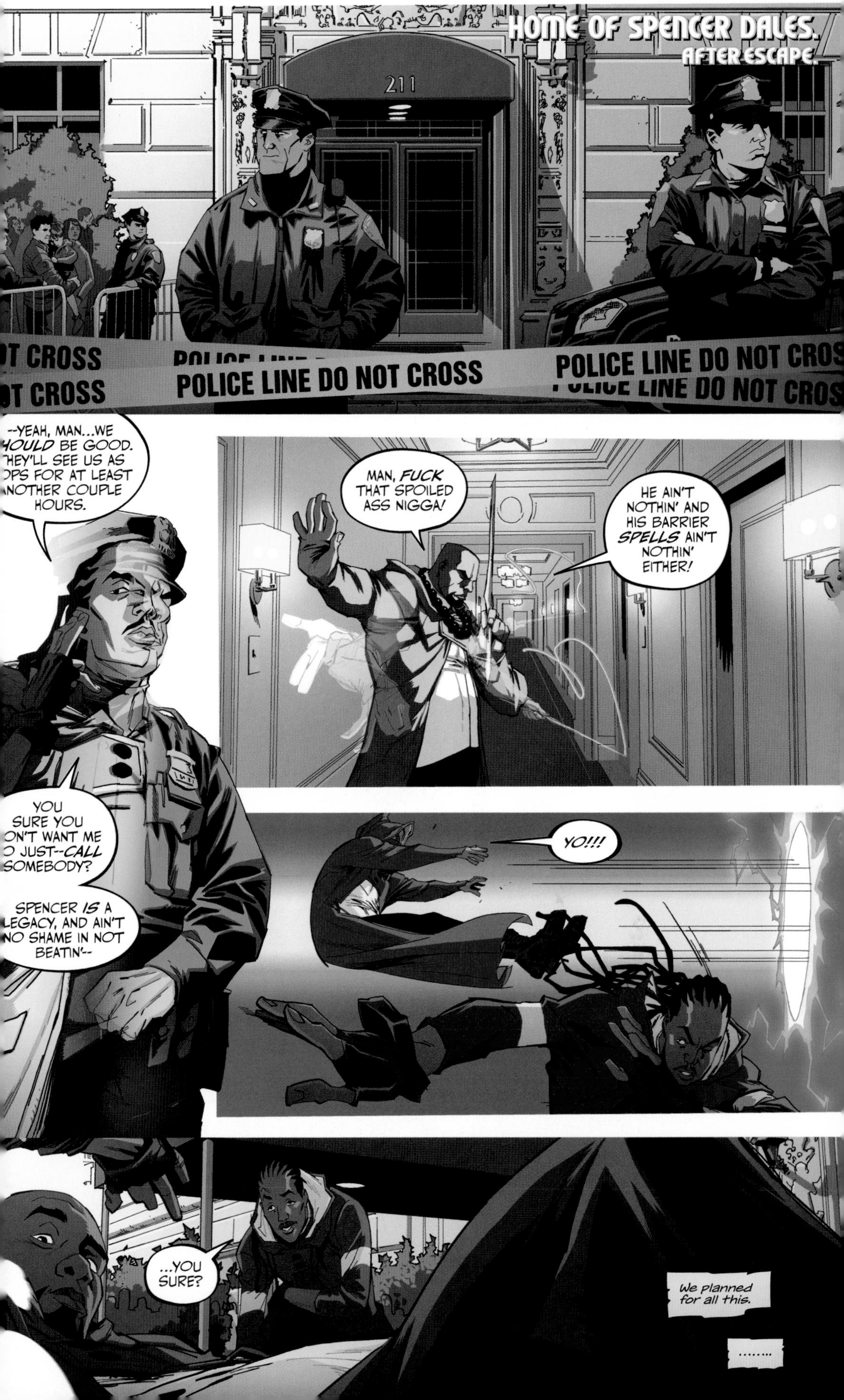
HOME OF SPENCER DALES.
AFTER ESCAPE.
211
POLICE LINE DO NOT CROSS
--YEAH, MAN...WE HOULD BE GOOD. HEY'LL SEE US AS OPS FOR AT LEAST NOTHER COUPLE HOURS.
MAN, FUCK THAT SPOILED ASS NIGGA!
HE AIN'T NOTHIN' AND HIS BARRIER SPELLS AIN'T NOTHIN' EITHER!
YOU SURE YOU ON'T WANT ME O JUST--CALL SOMEBODY?
SPENCER IS A LEGACY, AND AIN'T NO SHAME IN NOT BEATIN'--
YO!!!
...YOU SURE?
We planned for all this.
....

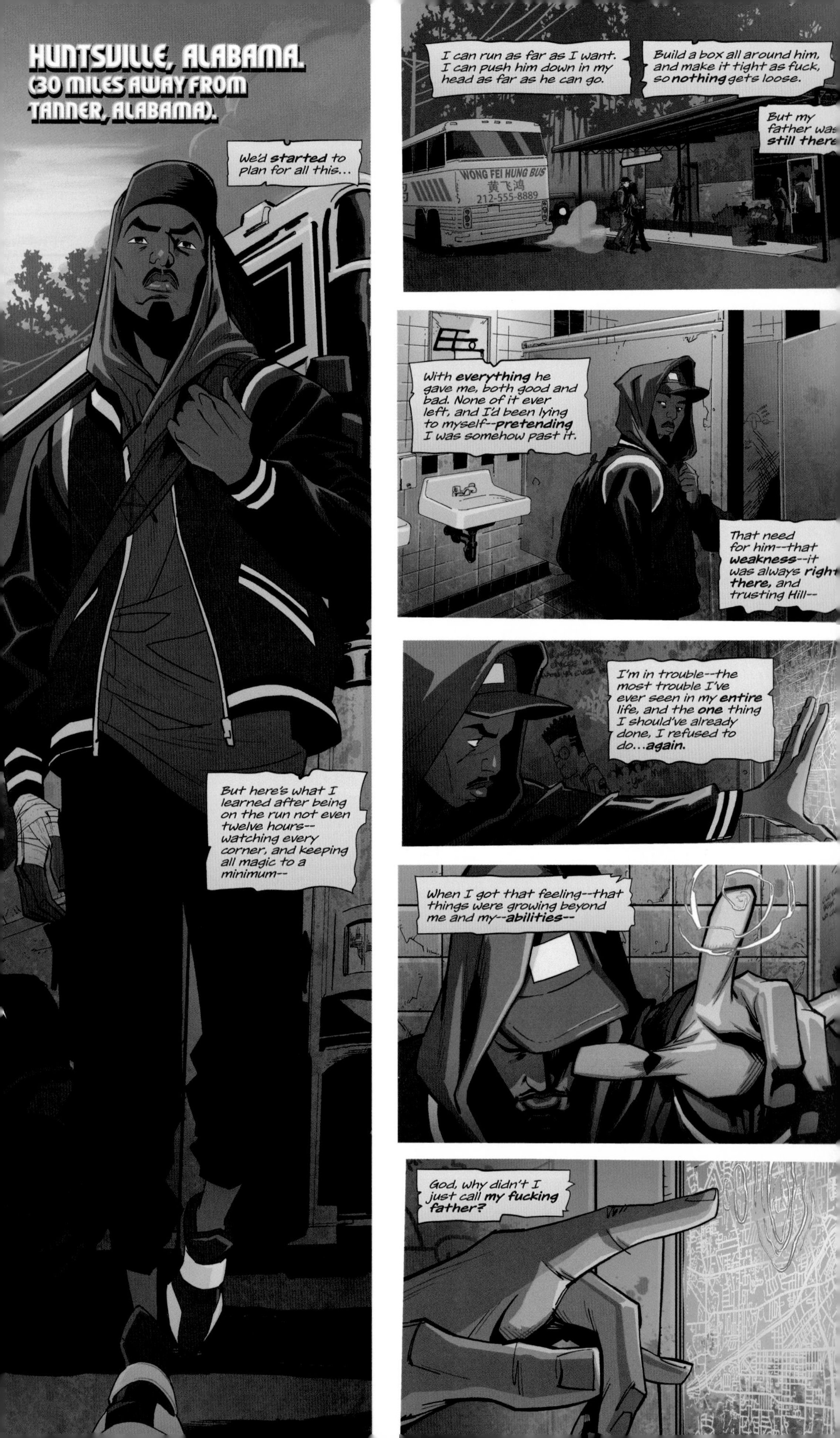
HUNTSVILLE, ALABAMA. (30 MILES AWAY FROM TANNER, ALABAMA).
We'd started to plan for all this...
But here's what I learned after being on the run not even twelve hours--watching every corner, and keeping all magic to a minimum--
I can run as far as I want. I can push him down in my head as far as he can go.
Build a box all around him, and make it tight as fuck, so nothing gets loose.
But my father was still there
WONG FEI HUNG BUS
黄飞鸿
212-555-8889
With everything he gave me, both good and bad. None of it ever left, and I'd been lying to myself--pretending I was somehow past it.
That need for him--that weakness--it was always right there, and trusting Hill--
I'm in trouble--the most trouble I've ever seen in my entire life, and the one thing I should've already done, I refused to do...again.
When I got that feeling--that things were growing beyond me and my--abilities--
God, why didn't I just call my fucking father?

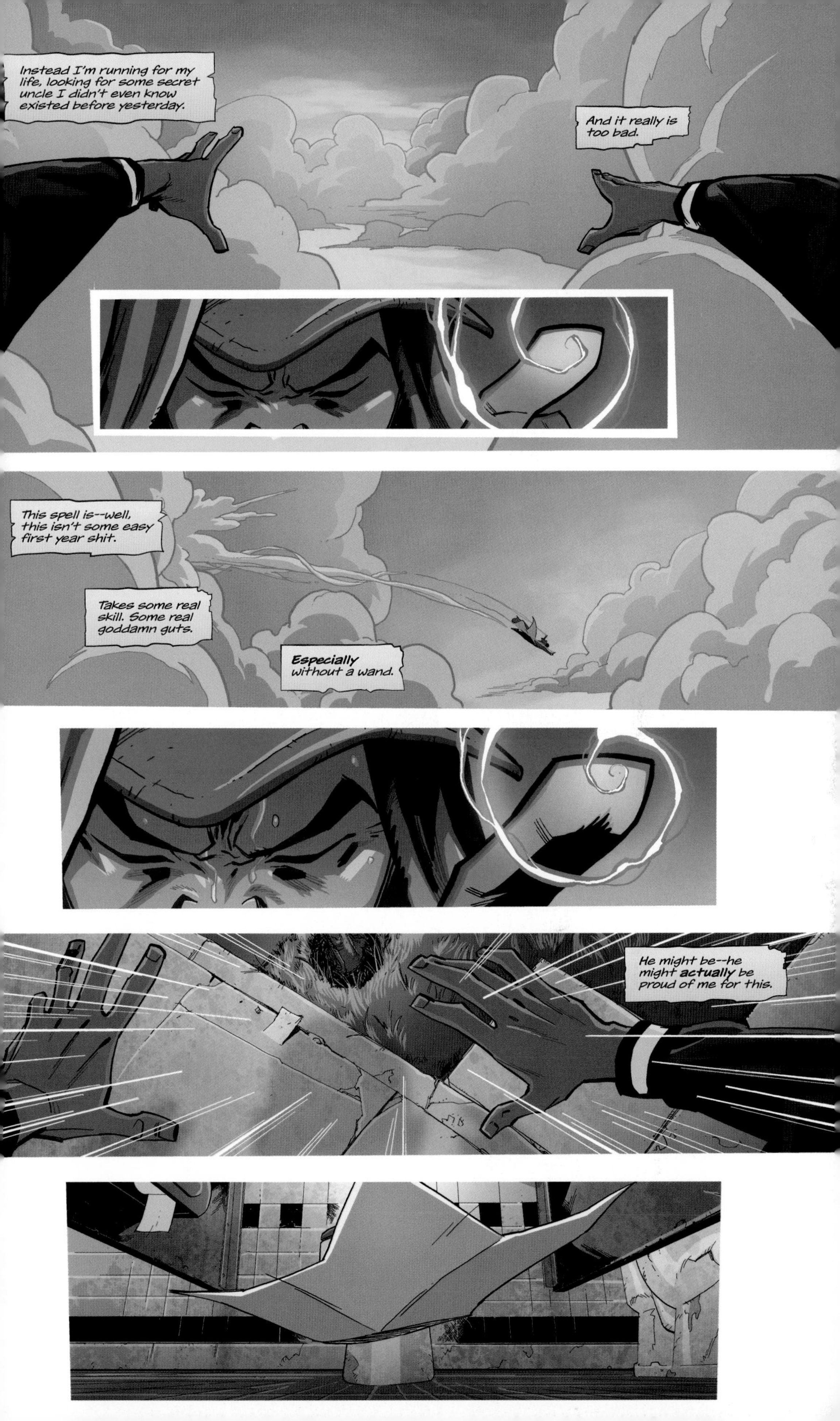
Instead I'm running for my life, looking for some secret uncle I didn't even know existed before yesterday.
And it really is too bad.
This spell is--well, this isn't some easy first year shit.
Takes some real skill. Some real goddamn guts.
Especially without a wand.
He might be--he might **actually** be proud of me for this.

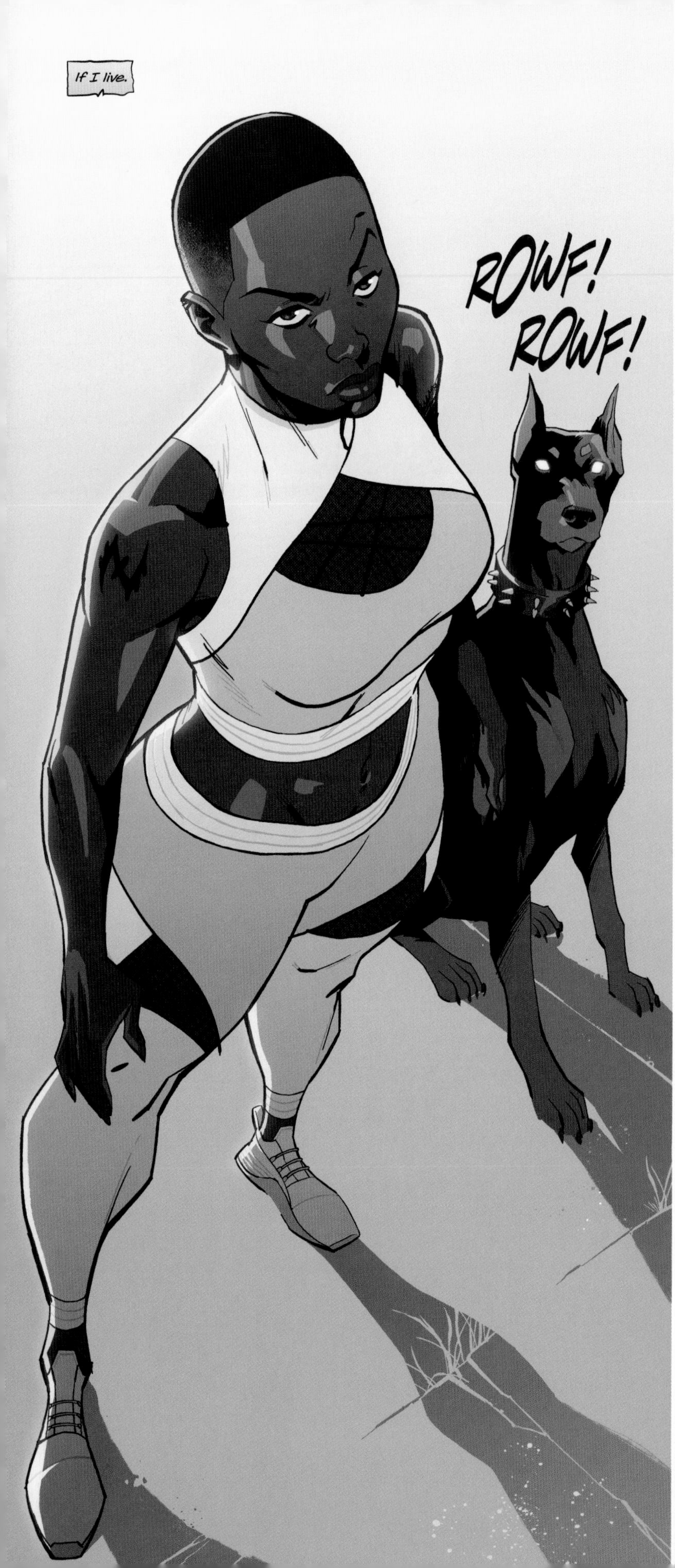
If I live.
ROWF! ROWF!

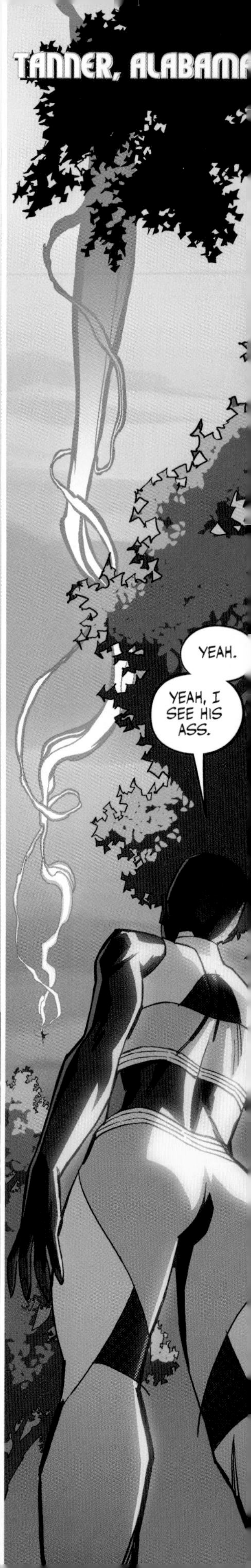
TANNER, ALABAMA
YEAH.
YEAH, I SEE HIS ASS.

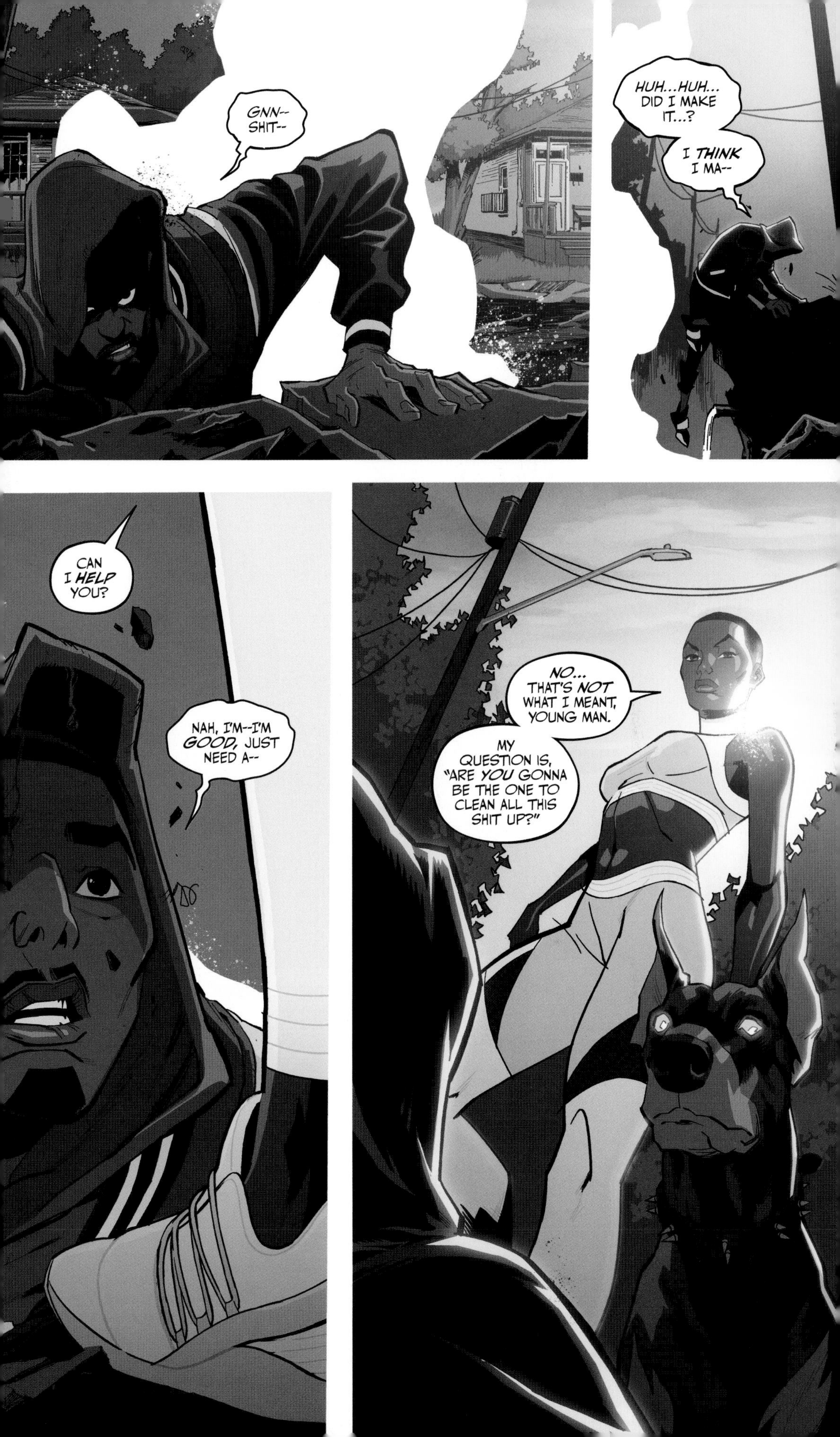

GNN--
SHIT--
HUH...HUH...
DID I MAKE
IT...?
I THINK
I MA--
CAN
I HELP
YOU?
NAH, I'M--I'M
GOOD, JUST
NEED A--
NO...
THAT'S NOT
WHAT I MEANT,
YOUNG MAN.
MY
QUESTION IS,
"ARE YOU GONNA
BE THE ONE TO
CLEAN ALL THIS
SHIT UP?"

OH. YEAH, I--*DAMN*, I MUST'VE--

MY BAD. I DON'T KNOW THESE SPELLS BY HEART YET...

I SWEAR-- YOUNGINS' ALL THE SAME--

PATRON.

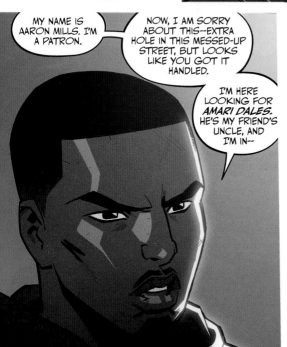

MY NAME IS AARON MILLS. I'M A PATRON.

NOW, I AM SORRY ABOUT THIS--EXTRA HOLE IN THIS MESSED-UP STREET, BUT LOOKS LIKE YOU GOT IT HANDLED.

I'M HERE LOOKING FOR *AMARI DALES.* HE'S MY FRIEND'S UNCLE, AND I'M IN--

SHE'S YOUR FRIEND'S *AUNT,* AND SOUNDS LIKE A *REAL* GOOD FRIEND IF YOU DIDN'T EVEN KNOW THAT.

WAS ON MY WAY SOMEWHERE WHEN YOU DROPPED OUT THE SKY, AND SCHEDULE IS TIGHT TODAY. OH, AND JUST SO WE SET *WHATEVER* THIS IS GONNA BE ON THE RIGHT FOOT--

THIS AARON MILLS WHOSE NAME YOU TOOK, AND TRYING TO PASS IT OFF AS YOUR OWN?

WHATEVER YOU DID TO HIM TO GET IT...YOU NOT GONNA DO THAT TO *ME,* UNDERSTAND?

AND IF THE EXPLANATION AIN'T SOMETHING I LIKE, YOU IN SOM *DEEP* TROUBLE, YOUNG PATRON...

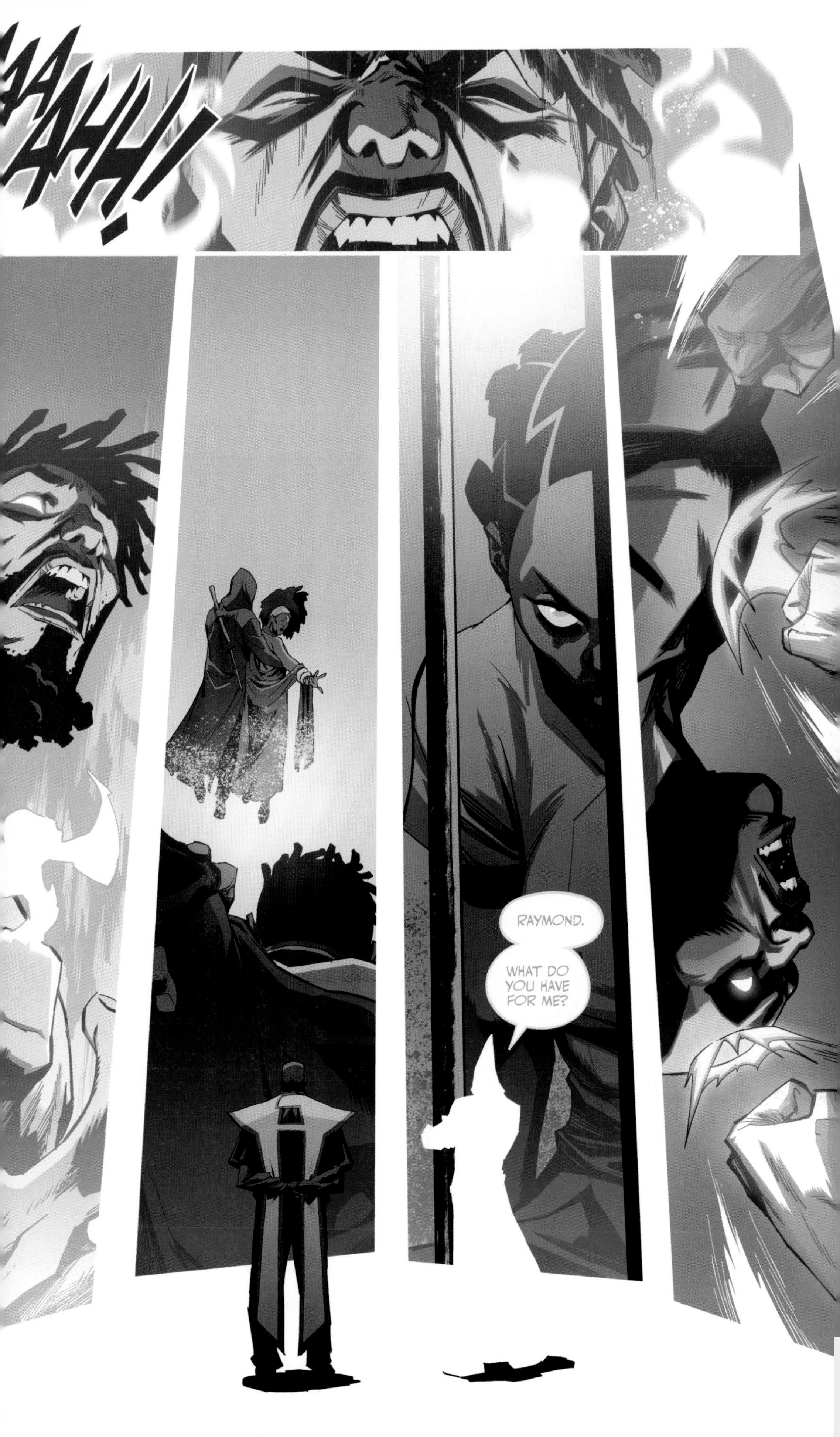
AAAHH!!
RAYMOND.
WHAT DO YOU HAVE FOR ME?

AARON...SON-- I NEED YOU TO FOCUS NOW. THINK REAL HARD, AND TELL ME *WHERE* HE IS.

BEFORE IT'S OUT OF EVERYONE'S HANDS...

HE WAS RIGHT-- HE WAS *RIGHT* ABOUT YOU THIS WHOLE TIME--

BEFORE YOU ASK, YOUR MOTHER IS JUST FINE. WE KNOW ALL ABOUT HER-- UNFORTUNATE PAST, AND WE NOT HERE TO SEE ALL THAT HARD WORK COME UNDONE.

BUT YOUR PLACE? WELL, THAT'S GETTING TORN APART BY FORENSICS NOW, AND ANY SPELL IN THERE THAT AIN'T *SUPPOSED* TO BE IS GONNA BE A *BIG* PROBLEM FOR YOU.

I--HE WANTED TO, BUT I WOULDN'T LET HIM--SPENCER WANTED TO TAKE DOWN THE REMEMBRANCE SPELL...SAID IT WAS WRONG...LIKE THAT EVER MADE A DIFFERENCE...

MR. DALES--WHAT IN THE HELL ARE YOU--

THIS IS YOUR FAULT, MONIQUE. I *ASKED* YOU TO KEEP AN EYE ON HIM--KEEP SOMETHING LIKE THIS FROM HAPPENING.

WHAT...? YOU CAN'T BE--ARE YOU *SERIOUS* WITH--

I AM, LITTLE GIRL. I TRUSTED YOU WITH MY *FAMILY,* AND YOU WENT OFF AND JUST DID--*WHAT- EVER.* GUESS MAYBE I WAS WRONG ABOUT YOU.

YOU--YOU KNOW WHY I HELPED HI HUH...HUGH YOU KNOW

I DON'T, MAN. I *REALLY* DON'T, BUT UNLESS YOU WANT TO LOSE EVERYTHING ELSE YOU GOT LEFT--GIVE ME SOMETHING I CAN GIVE THEM.

THANK YOU, DEQUAN. JUST HANG ON UNTIL I CAN GET YOU OUT OF HERE.

THINK ABOUT YOUR *WIFE,* HILL. THINK ABOUT YOUR *OWN* SONS...AND WHAT *THEY* STAND TO LOSE.

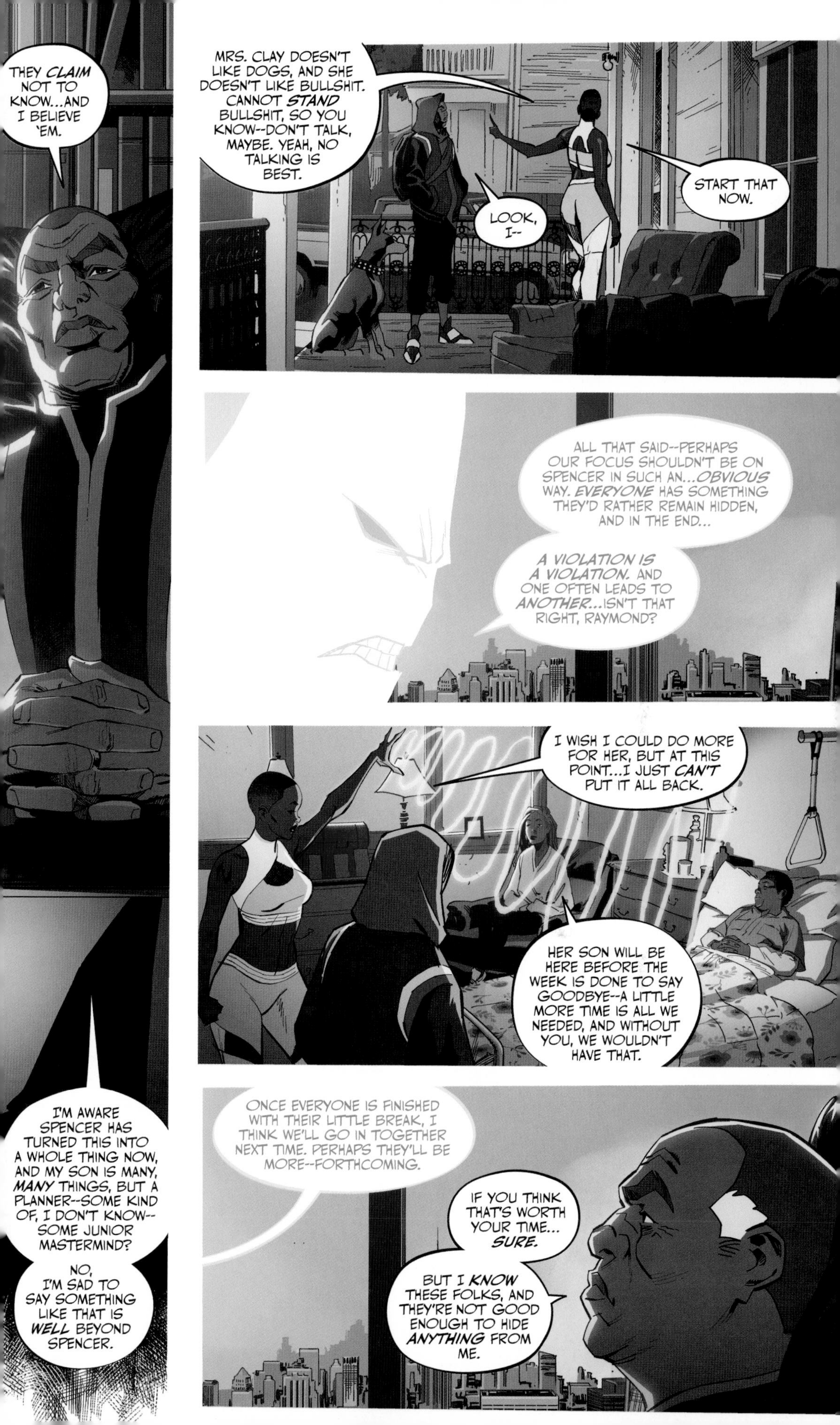
THEY CLAIM NOT TO KNOW...AND I BELIEVE 'EM.
MRS. CLAY DOESN'T LIKE DOGS, AND SHE DOESN'T LIKE BULLSHIT. CANNOT STAND BULLSHIT, SO YOU KNOW--DON'T TALK, MAYBE. YEAH, NO TALKING IS BEST.
LOOK, I--
START THAT NOW.
ALL THAT SAID--PERHAPS OUR FOCUS SHOULDN'T BE ON SPENCER IN SUCH AN...OBVIOUS WAY. EVERYONE HAS SOMETHING THEY'D RATHER REMAIN HIDDEN, AND IN THE END...
A VIOLATION IS A VIOLATION. AND ONE OFTEN LEADS TO ANOTHER...ISN'T THAT RIGHT, RAYMOND?
I WISH I COULD DO MORE FOR HER, BUT AT THIS POINT...I JUST CAN'T PUT IT ALL BACK.
HER SON WILL BE HERE BEFORE THE WEEK IS DONE TO SAY GOODBYE--A LITTLE MORE TIME IS ALL WE NEEDED, AND WITHOUT YOU, WE WOULDN'T HAVE THAT.
I'M AWARE SPENCER HAS TURNED THIS INTO A WHOLE THING NOW, AND MY SON IS MANY, MANY THINGS, BUT A PLANNER--SOME KIND OF, I DON'T KNOW--SOME JUNIOR MASTERMIND?
NO, I'M SAD TO SAY SOMETHING LIKE THAT IS WELL BEYOND SPENCER.
ONCE EVERYONE IS FINISHED WITH THEIR LITTLE BREAK, I THINK WE'LL GO IN TOGETHER NEXT TIME. PERHAPS THEY'LL BE MORE--FORTHCOMING.
IF YOU THINK THAT'S WORTH YOUR TIME... SURE.
BUT I KNOW THESE FOLKS, AND THEY'RE NOT GOOD ENOUGH TO HIDE ANYTHING FROM ME.

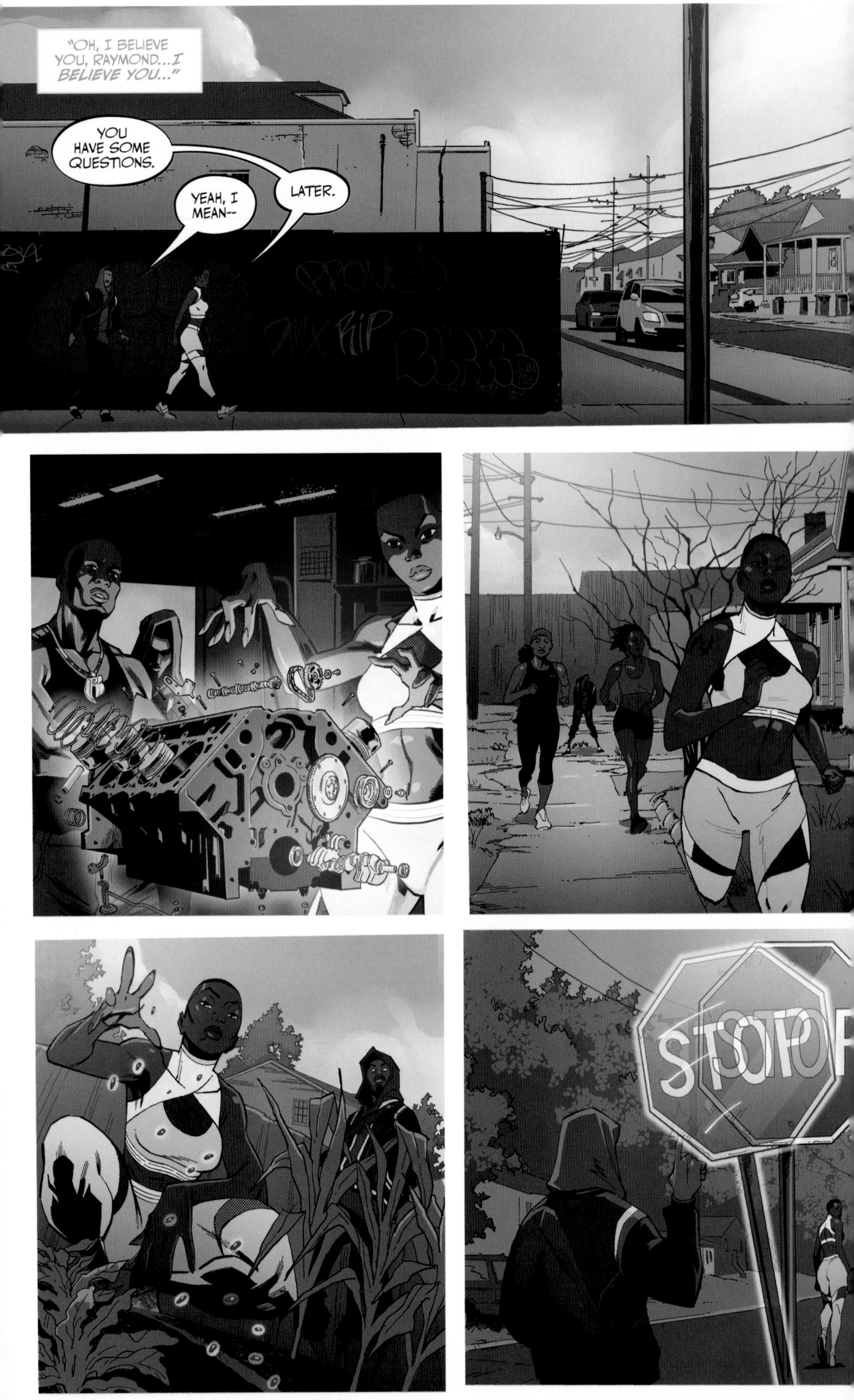
"OH, I BELIEVE YOU, RAYMOND...I BELIEVE YOU..."
YOU HAVE SOME QUESTIONS.
YEAH, I MEAN--
LATER.
STOP

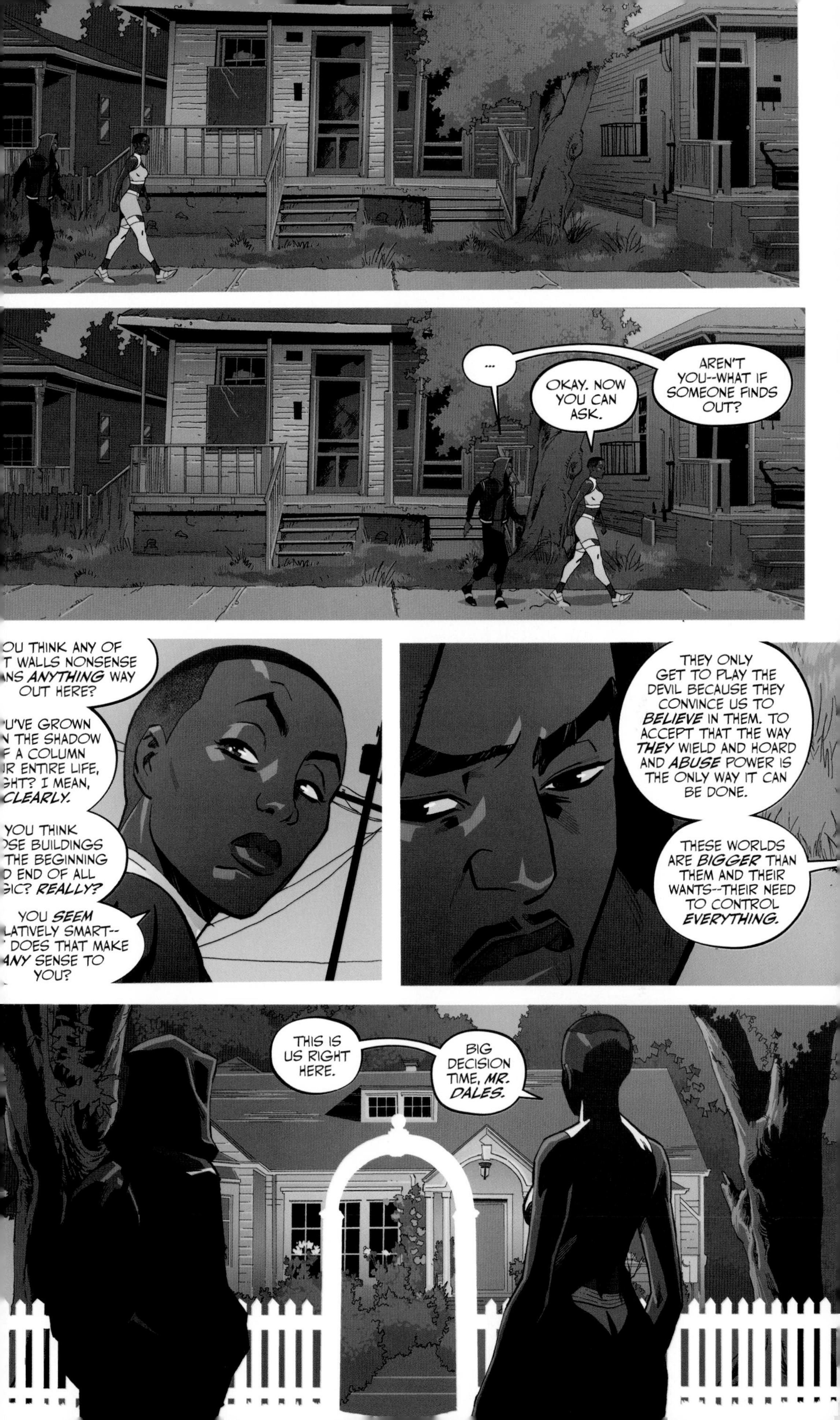
...
ARE'NT YOU--WHAT IF SOMEONE FINDS OUT?
OKAY. NOW YOU CAN ASK.
OU THINK ANY OF T WALLS NONSENSE ANS ANYTHING WAY OUT HERE?
U'VE GROWN N THE SHADOW F A COLUMN R ENTIRE LIFE, GHT? I MEAN, CLEARLY.
YOU THINK OSE BUILDINGS THE BEGINNING D END OF ALL GIC? REALLY?
YOU SEEM LATIVELY SMART-- DOES THAT MAKE ANY SENSE TO YOU?
THEY ONLY GET TO PLAY THE DEVIL BECAUSE THEY CONVINCE US TO BELIEVE IN THEM. TO ACCEPT THAT THE WAY THEY WIELD AND HOARD AND ABUSE POWER IS THE ONLY WAY IT CAN BE DONE.
THESE WORLDS ARE BIGGER THAN THEM AND THEIR WANTS--THEIR NEED TO CONTROL EVERYTHING.
THIS IS US RIGHT HERE.
BIG DECISION TIME, MR. DALES.

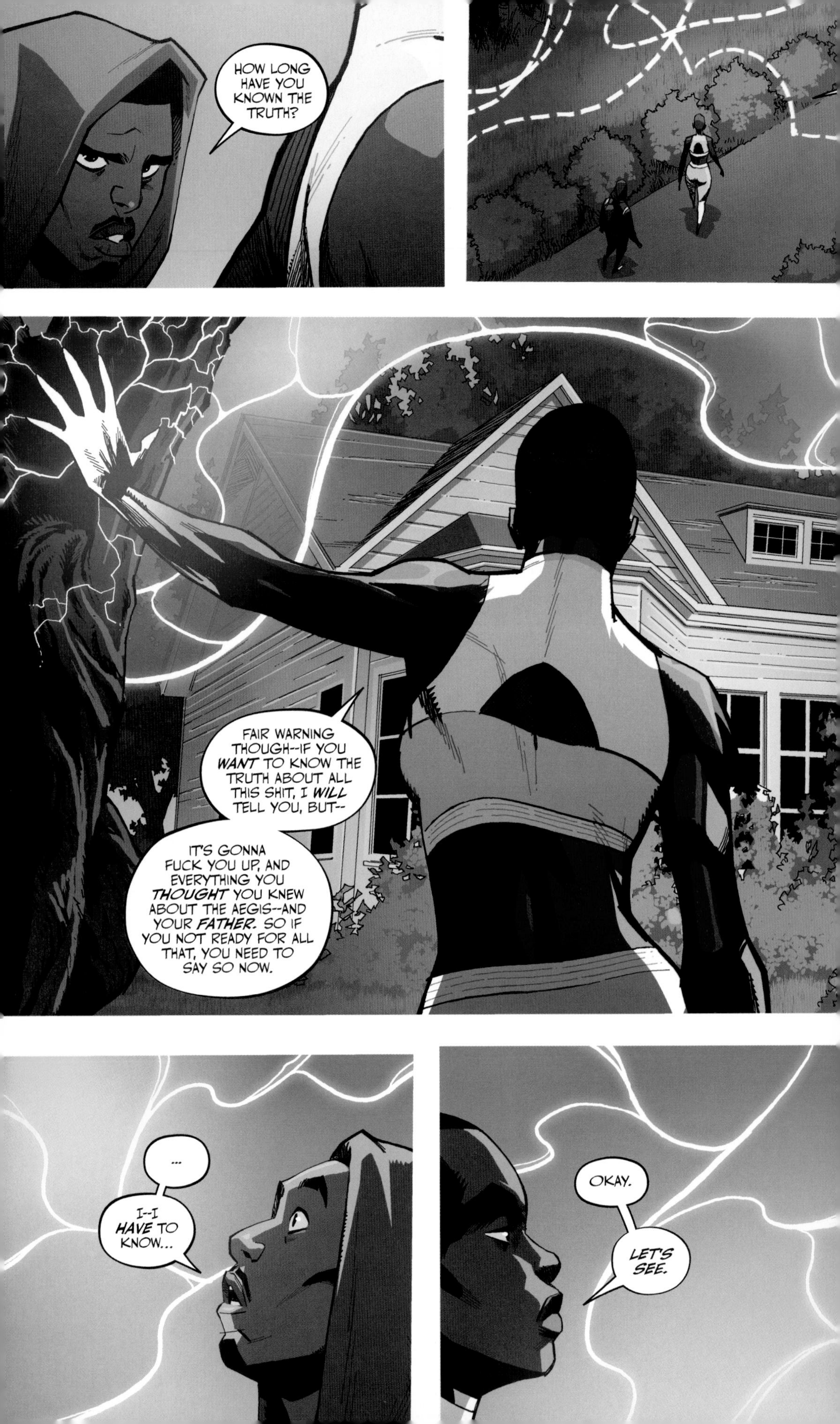
HOW LONG HAVE YOU KNOWN THE TRUTH?
FAIR WARNING THOUGH--IF YOU *WANT* TO KNOW THE TRUTH ABOUT ALL THIS SHIT, I *WILL* TELL YOU, BUT--
IT'S GONNA FUCK YOU UP, AND EVERYTHING YOU *THOUGHT* YOU KNEW ABOUT THE AEGIS--AND YOUR *FATHER*. SO IF YOU NOT READY FOR ALL THAT, YOU NEED TO SAY SO NOW.
...
I--I *HAVE* TO KNOW...
OKAY.
LET'S SEE.

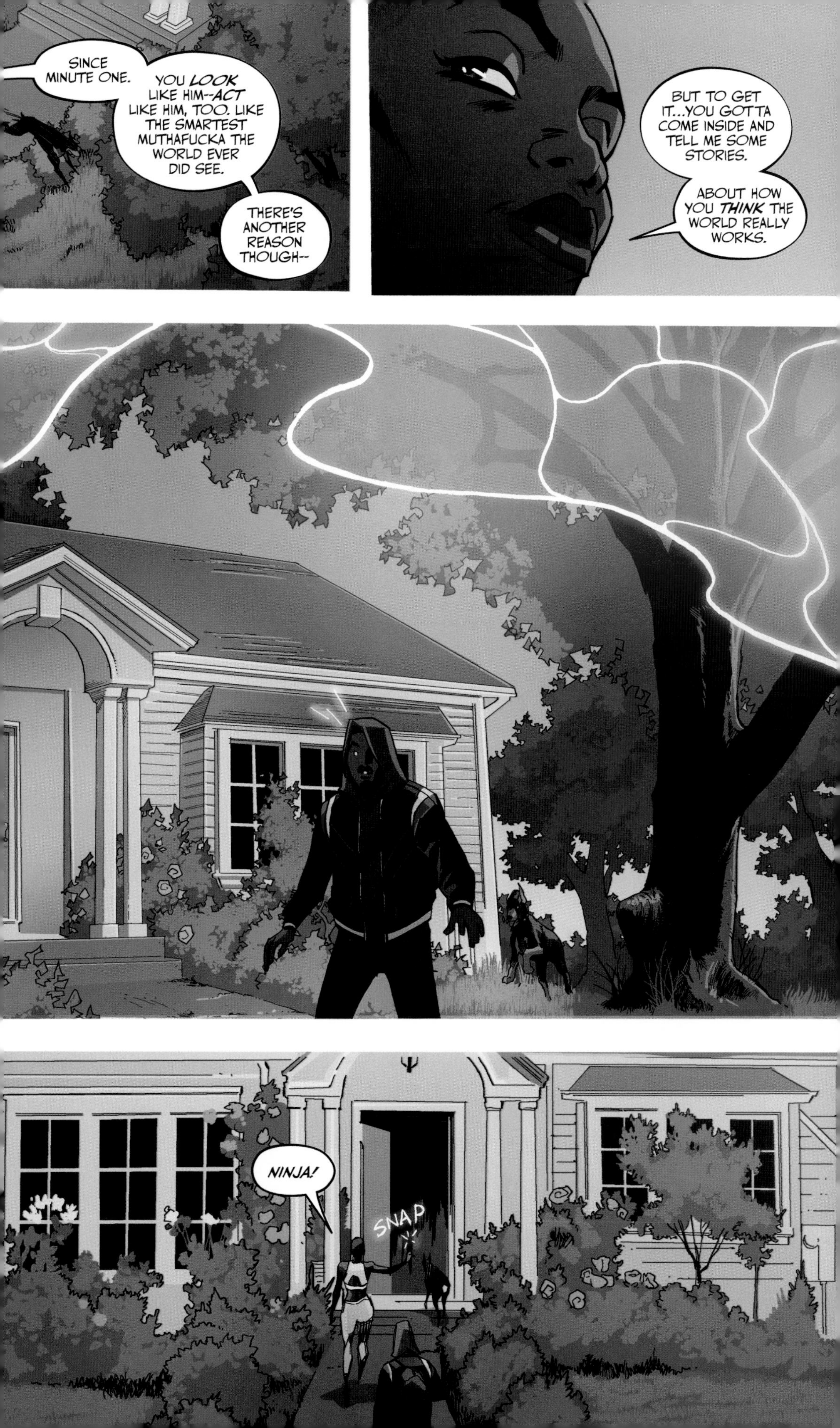
SINCE MINUTE ONE.
YOU *LOOK* LIKE HIM--*ACT* LIKE HIM, TOO. LIKE THE SMARTEST MUTHAFUCKA THE WORLD EVER DID SEE.
THERE'S ANOTHER REASON THOUGH--
BUT TO GET IT...YOU GOTTA COME INSIDE AND TELL ME SOME STORIES.
ABOUT HOW YOU *THINK* THE WORLD REALLY WORKS.
NINJA!
SNAP

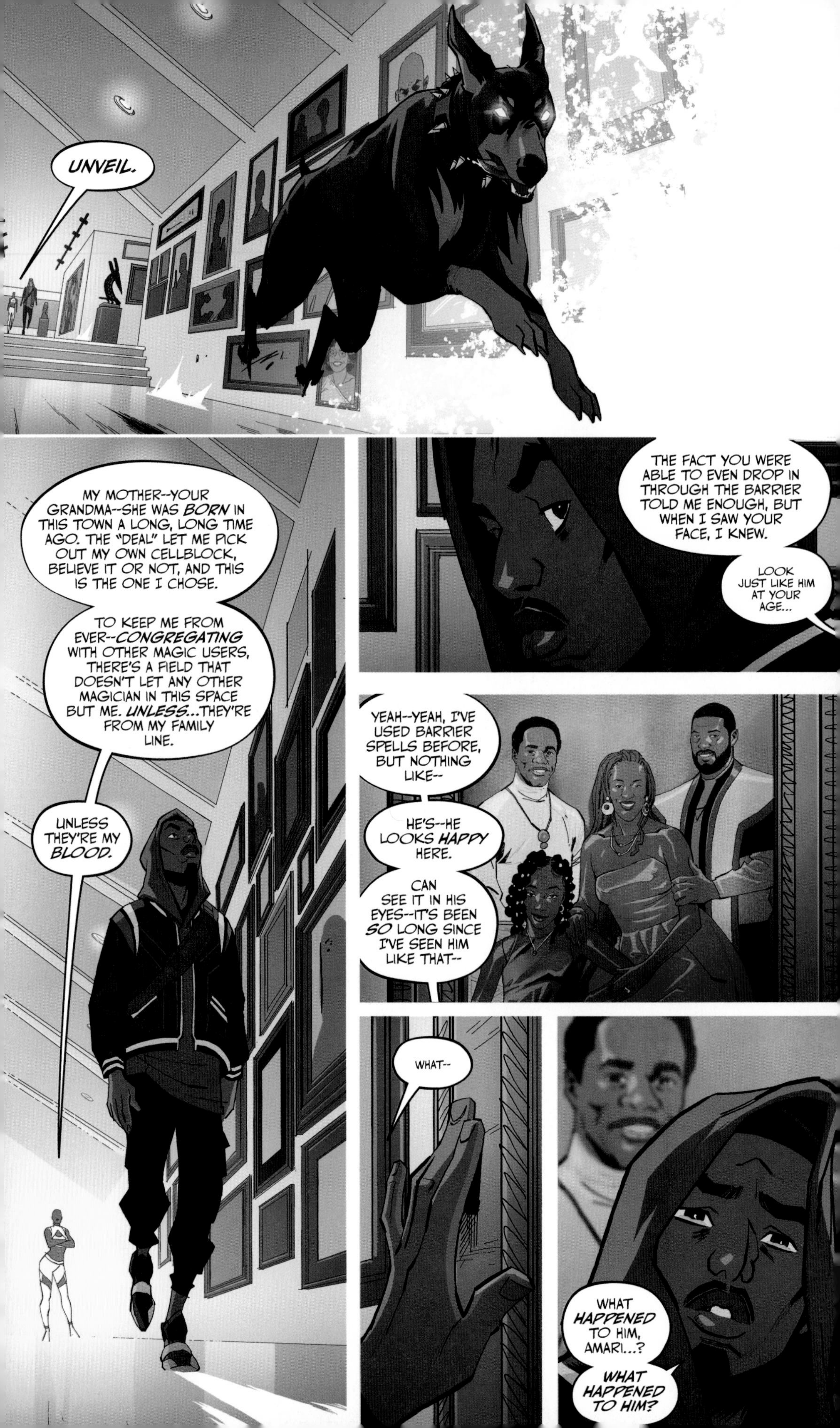
UNVEIL.
MY MOTHER--YOUR GRANDMA--SHE WAS BORN IN THIS TOWN A LONG, LONG TIME AGO. THE "DEAL" LET ME PICK OUT MY OWN CELLBLOCK, BELIEVE IT OR NOT, AND THIS IS THE ONE I CHOSE.
TO KEEP ME FROM EVER--CONGREGATING WITH OTHER MAGIC USERS, THERE'S A FIELD THAT DOESN'T LET ANY OTHER MAGICIAN IN THIS SPACE BUT ME. UNLESS...THEY'RE FROM MY FAMILY LINE.
UNLESS THEY'RE MY BLOOD.
THE FACT YOU WERE ABLE TO EVEN DROP IN THROUGH THE BARRIER TOLD ME ENOUGH, BUT WHEN I SAW YOUR FACE, I KNEW.
LOOK JUST LIKE HIM AT YOUR AGE...
YEAH--YEAH, I'VE USED BARRIER SPELLS BEFORE, BUT NOTHING LIKE--
HE'S--HE LOOKS HAPPY HERE.
CAN SEE IT IN HIS EYES--IT'S BEEN SO LONG SINCE I'VE SEEN HIM LIKE THAT--
WHAT--
WHAT HAPPENED TO HIM, AMARI...?
WHAT HAPPENED TO HIM?

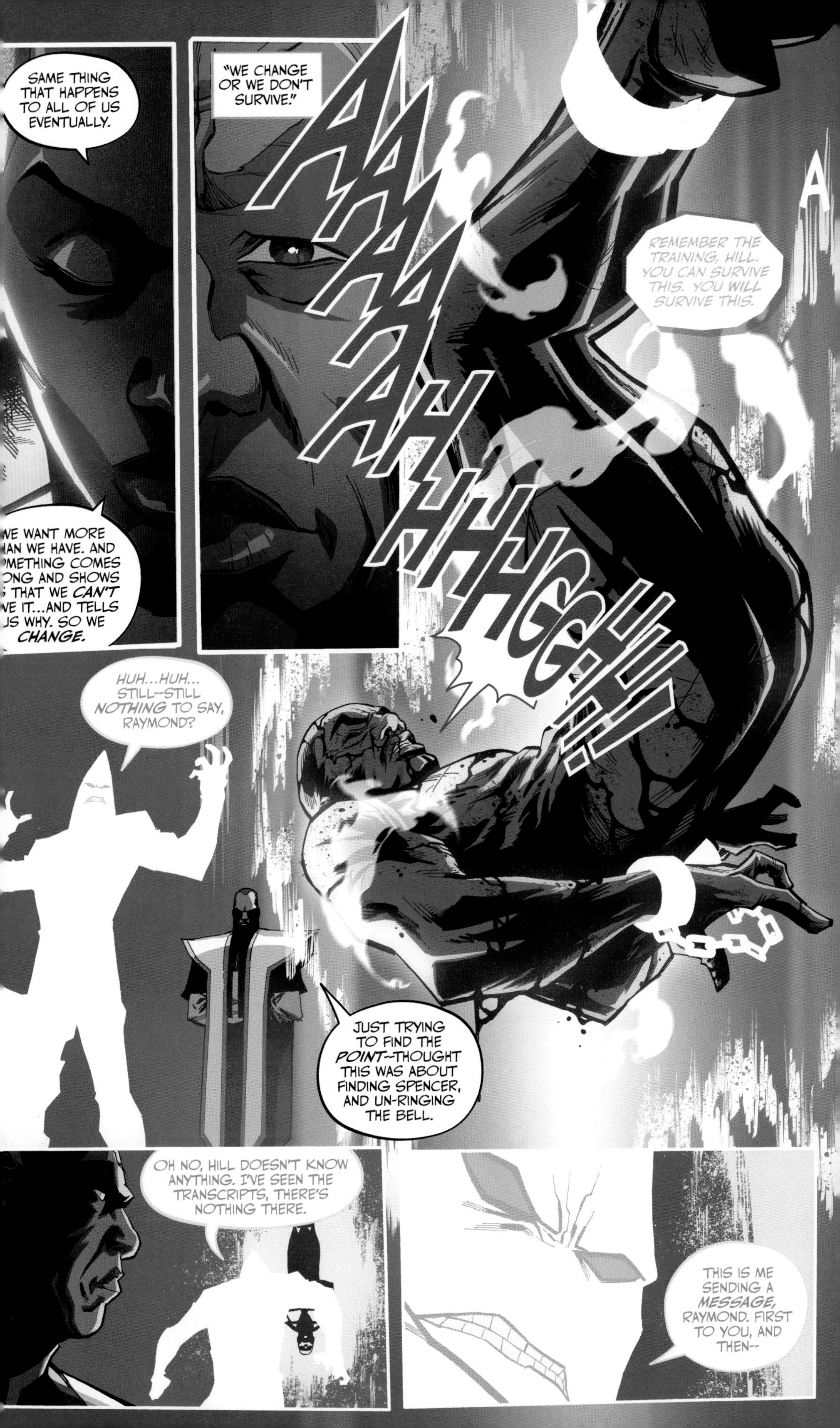
SAME THING THAT HAPPENS TO ALL OF US EVENTUALLY.
"WE CHANGE OR WE DON'T SURVIVE."
WE WANT MORE THAN WE HAVE. AND SOMETHING COMES ALONG AND SHOWS US THAT WE *CAN'T* HAVE IT...AND TELLS US WHY. SO WE *CHANGE.*
AAAAAAAHHHHGGHH!!!
A
REMEMBER THE TRAINING, HILL. YOU CAN SURVIVE THIS. YOU *WILL* SURVIVE THIS.
HUH...HUH... STILL--STILL *NOTHING* TO SAY, RAYMOND?
JUST TRYING TO FIND THE *POINT*--THOUGHT THIS WAS ABOUT FINDING SPENCER, AND UN-RINGING THE BELL.
OH NO, HILL DOESN'T KNOW ANYTHING. I'VE SEEN THE TRANSCRIPTS, THERE'S NOTHING THERE.
THIS IS ME SENDING A *MESSAGE,* RAYMOND. FIRST TO YOU, AND THEN--

--TO BOTH OF *THEM*.

SEE, THIS DOESN'T ALWAYS HAVE TO STAY SO...*CORDIAL.* I AM TRYING TO CONTROL MYSELF HERE, BUT--

THE STRUGGLE IS SO *REAL.*

IT WOULD BE SO MUCH EASIER TO JUST *KILL* YOU, BUT THIS--*THIS* REQUIRES A DEGREE OF SKILL. AND PATIENCE.

AND ABOVE ALL ELSE... *RESTRAINT.*

GRRRAAA

YOU HEAR THAT, DEQUAN? THIS ISN'T EVEN ABOUT YOU.

IT'S... ABOUT... *THEM.* OUR CHILDREN.

AND WE CAN DO FUCKING *ANYTHING* FOR THEM.

WE ALREADY HAVE.

HE SHOULD'V JUST LE THEM *KIL* ME.

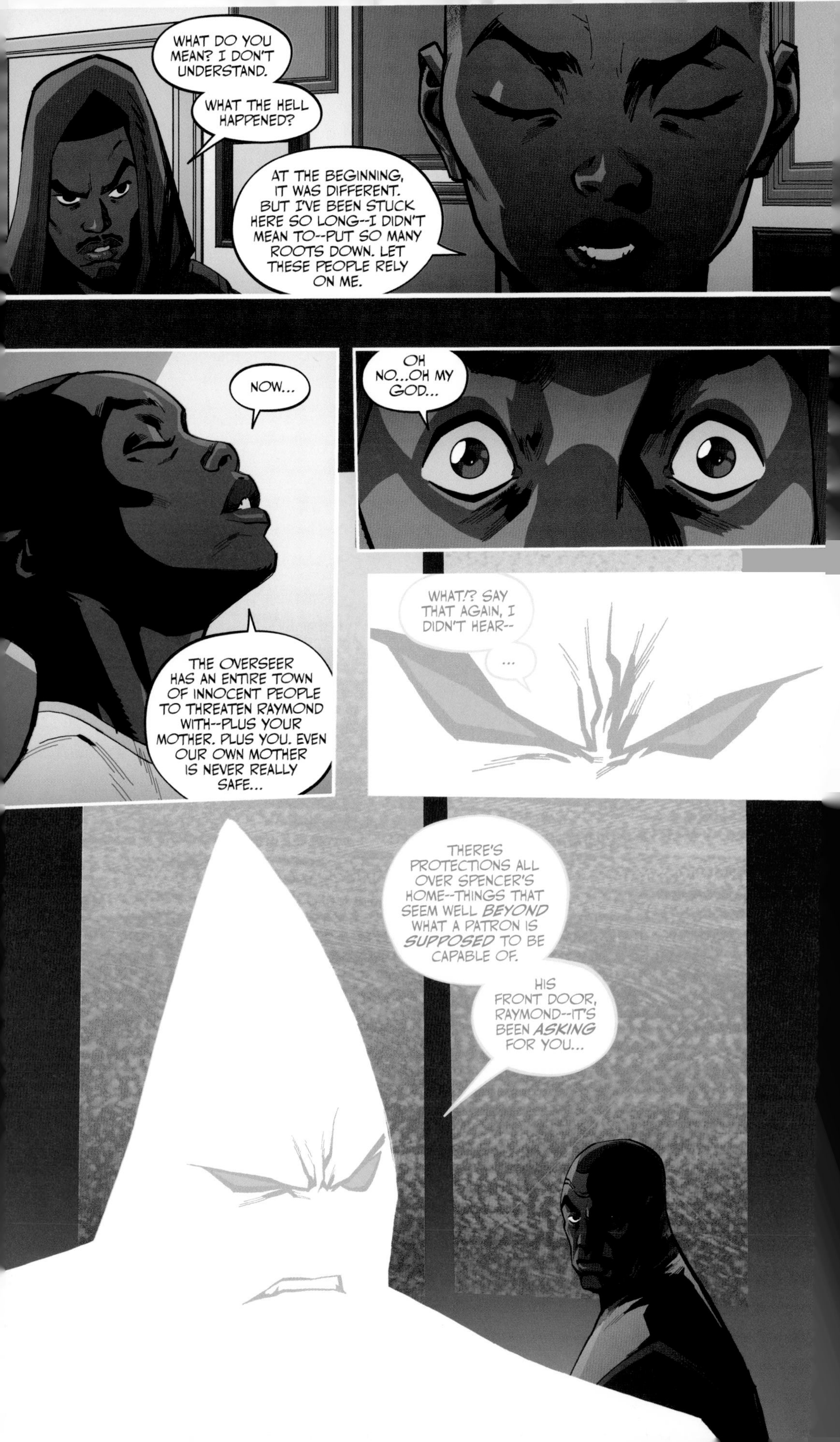
WHAT DO YOU MEAN? I DON'T UNDERSTAND.
WHAT THE HELL HAPPENED?
AT THE BEGINNING, IT WAS DIFFERENT. BUT I'VE BEEN STUCK HERE SO LONG--I DIDN'T MEAN TO--PUT SO MANY ROOTS DOWN. LET THESE PEOPLE RELY ON ME.
NOW...
OH NO...OH MY GOD...
THE OVERSEER HAS AN ENTIRE TOWN OF INNOCENT PEOPLE TO THREATEN RAYMOND WITH--PLUS YOUR MOTHER. PLUS YOU. EVEN OUR OWN MOTHER IS NEVER REALLY SAFE...
WHAT!? SAY THAT AGAIN, I DIDN'T HEAR--
...
THERE'S PROTECTIONS ALL OVER SPENCER'S HOME--THINGS THAT SEEM WELL BEYOND WHAT A PATRON IS SUPPOSED TO BE CAPABLE OF.
HIS FRONT DOOR, RAYMOND--IT'S BEEN ASKING FOR YOU...

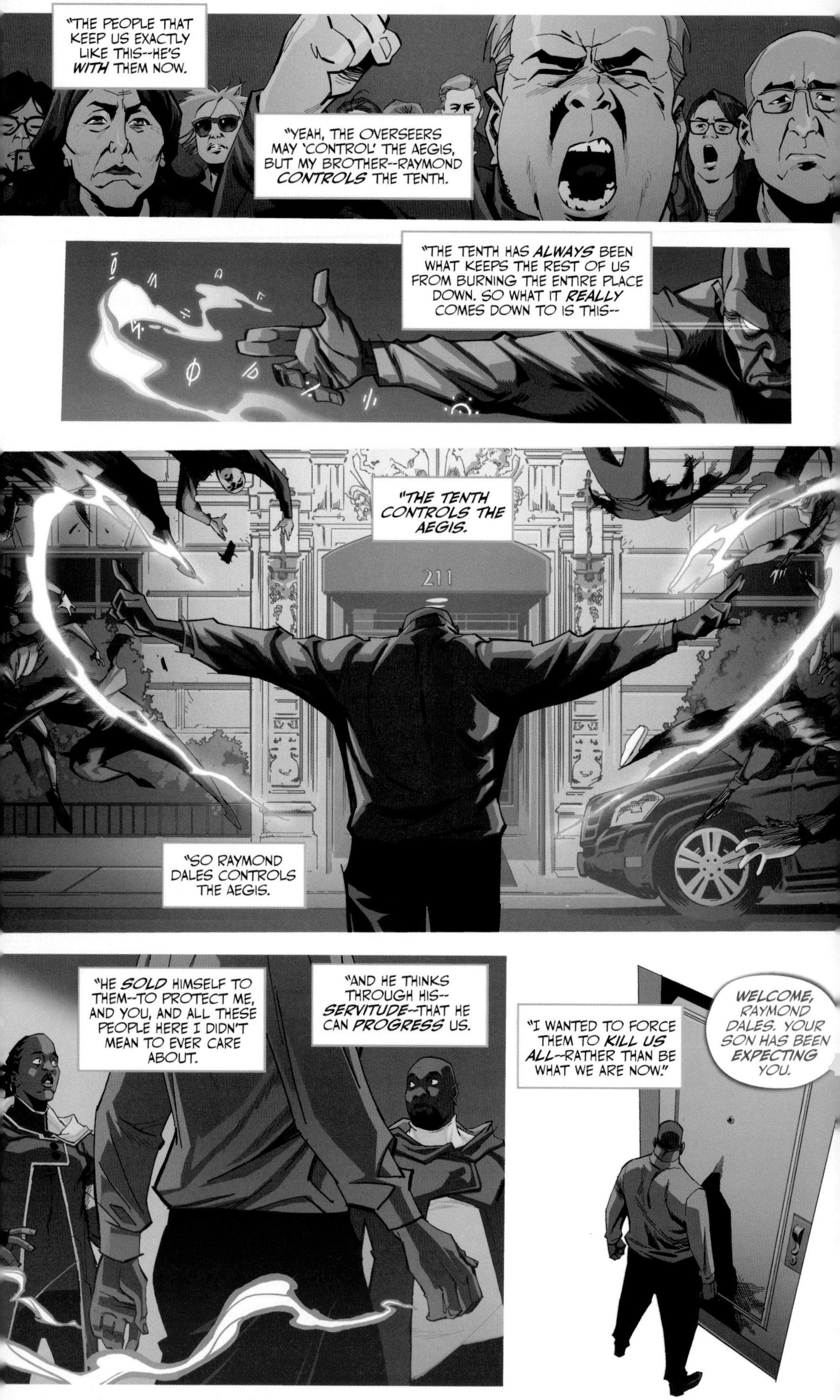
"THE PEOPLE THAT KEEP US EXACTLY LIKE THIS--HE'S *WITH* THEM NOW.
"YEAH, THE OVERSEERS MAY 'CONTROL' THE AEGIS, BUT MY BROTHER--RAYMOND *CONTROLS* THE TENTH.
"THE TENTH HAS *ALWAYS* BEEN WHAT KEEPS THE REST OF US FROM BURNING THE ENTIRE PLACE DOWN. SO WHAT IT *REALLY* COMES DOWN TO IS THIS--
"THE TENTH CONTROLS THE AEGIS.
211
"SO RAYMOND DALES CONTROLS THE AEGIS.
"HE *SOLD* HIMSELF TO THEM--TO PROTECT ME, AND YOU, AND ALL THESE PEOPLE HERE I DIDN'T MEAN TO EVER CARE ABOUT.
"AND HE THINKS THROUGH HIS-- *SERVITUDE*--THAT HE CAN *PROGRESS* US.
"I WANTED TO FORCE THEM TO *KILL US ALL*--RATHER THAN BE WHAT WE ARE NOW."
WELCOME, RAYMOND DALES. YOUR SON HAS BEEN EXPECTING YOU.

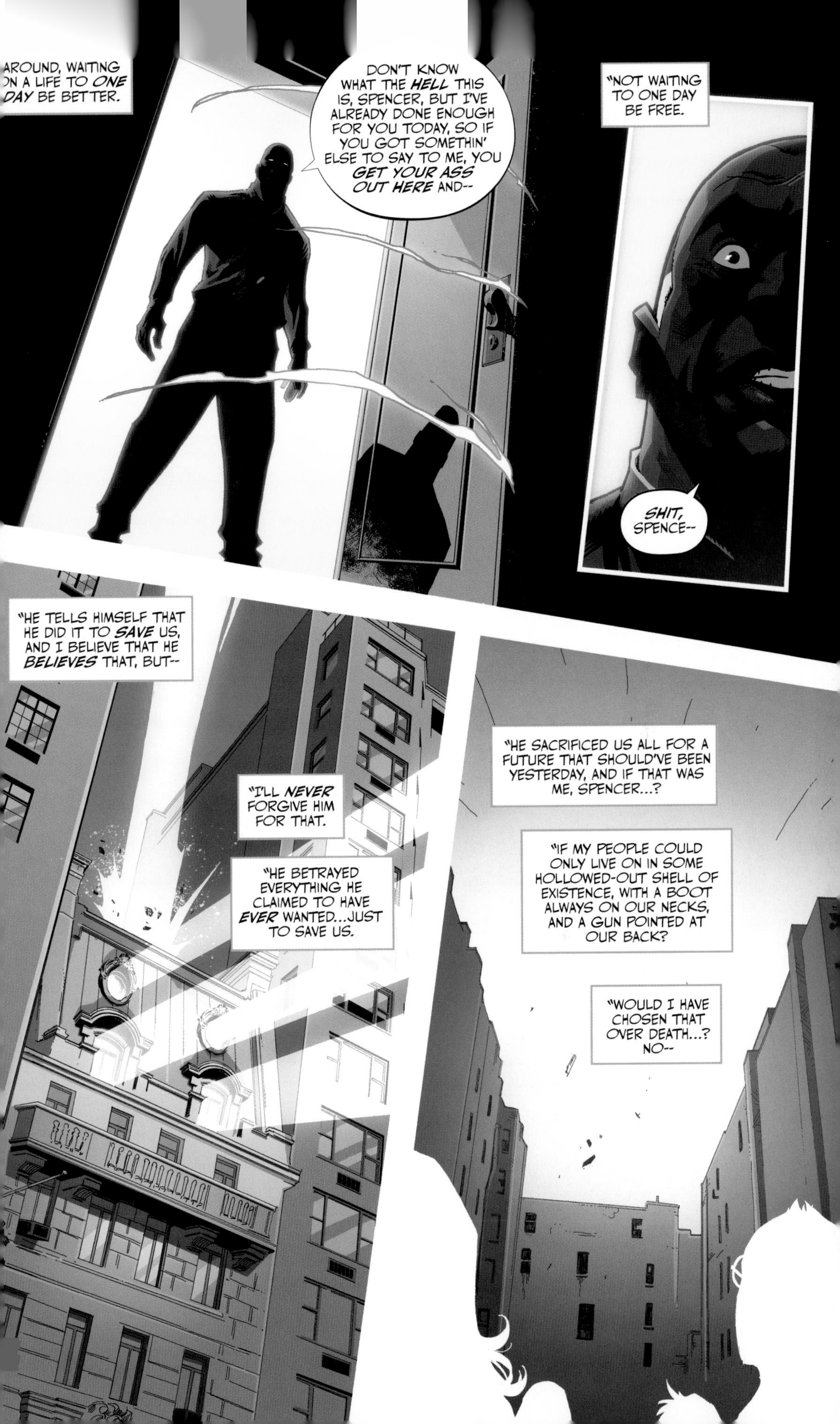
AROUND, WAITING ON A LIFE TO *ONE DAY* BE BETTER.
DON'T KNOW WHAT THE *HELL* THIS IS, SPENCER, BUT I'VE ALREADY DONE ENOUGH FOR YOU TODAY, SO IF YOU GOT SOMETHIN' ELSE TO SAY TO ME, YOU *GET YOUR ASS OUT HERE* AND--
"NOT WAITING TO ONE DAY BE FREE.
SHIT, SPENCE--
"HE TELLS HIMSELF THAT HE DID IT TO *SAVE* US, AND I BELIEVE THAT HE *BELIEVES* THAT, BUT--
"I'LL *NEVER* FORGIVE HIM FOR THAT.
"HE BETRAYED EVERYTHING HE CLAIMED TO HAVE *EVER* WANTED...JUST TO SAVE US.
"HE SACRIFICED US ALL FOR A FUTURE THAT SHOULD'VE BEEN YESTERDAY, AND IF THAT WAS ME, SPENCER...?
"IF MY PEOPLE COULD ONLY LIVE ON IN SOME HOLLOWED-OUT SHELL OF EXISTENCE, WITH A BOOT ALWAYS ON OUR NECKS, AND A GUN POINTED AT OUR BACK?
"WOULD I HAVE CHOSEN THAT OVER DEATH...? NO--

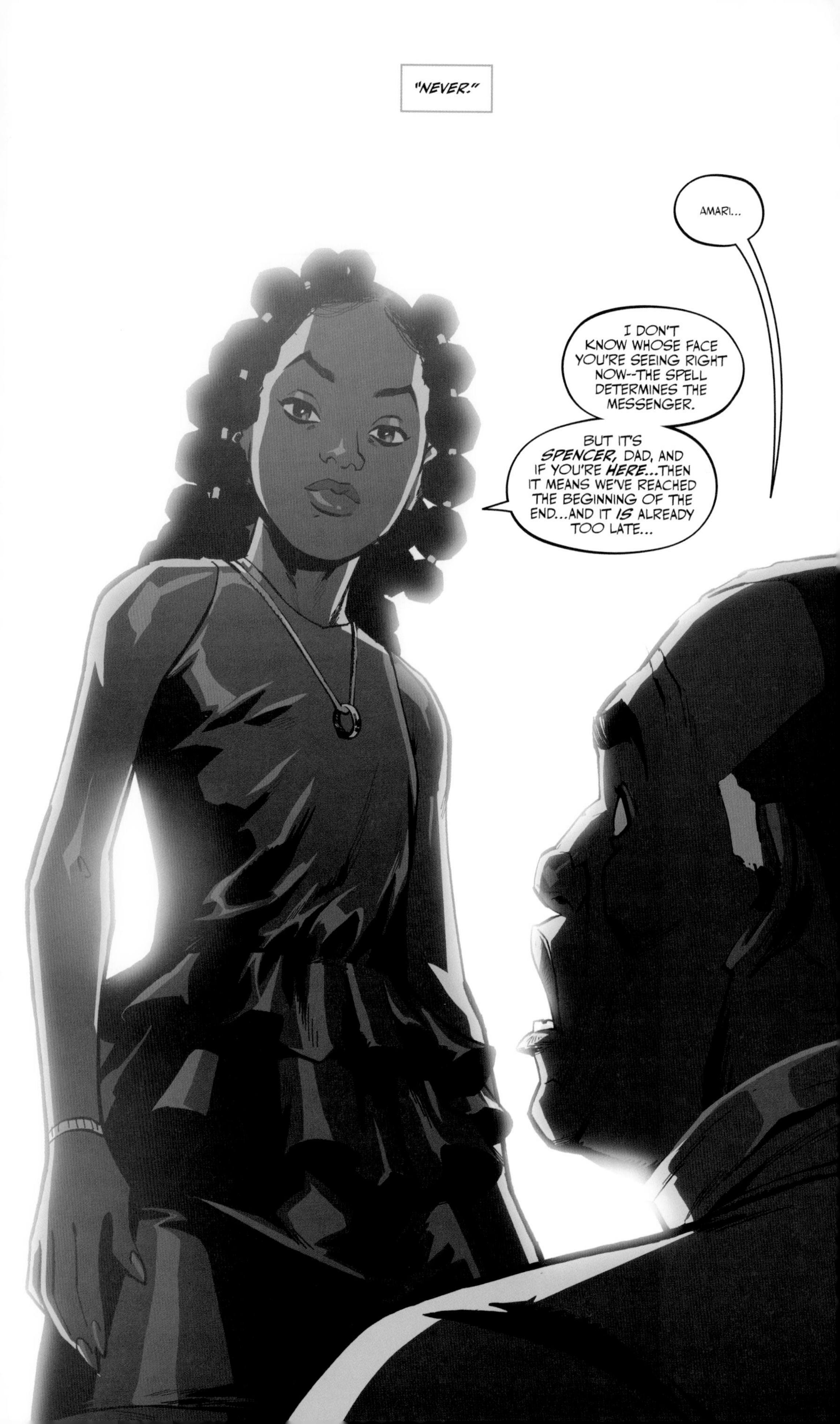
"NEVER."
AMARI...
I DON'T KNOW WHOSE FACE YOU'RE SEEING RIGHT NOW--THE SPELL DETERMINES THE MESSENGER.
BUT IT'S SPENCER, DAD, AND IF YOU'RE HERE...THEN IT MEANS WE'VE REACHED THE BEGINNING OF THE END...AND IT IS ALREADY TOO LATE...

THE FOUR WALLS

I

THE PROTECTION AND DEFENSE OF THE UNDESERVING IS NOT ALLOWED.

II

THE CREATION OF A MAGICIAN'S WAND WITHOUT PERMISSION IS NOT ALLOWED.

III

THE CASTING OF SPELLS WITHOUT AN APPROVED WAND IS NOT ALLOWED.

IV

~~THE USE OF MAGIC BY FEMALES IS NOT ALLOWED.~~

LIES! FUCK THESE LIES!

THE OVERSEER

CASTING COLOR: WHITE

THE TENTH

CASTING COLOR: PURPLE

PATRONS

CASTING COLOR: BLUE

ROOKS

CASTING COLOR: GREEN

AVERAGE AGE OF MAGICAL
ACTIVATION (MALE): 5.1 YEARS OLD.

THE AEGIS

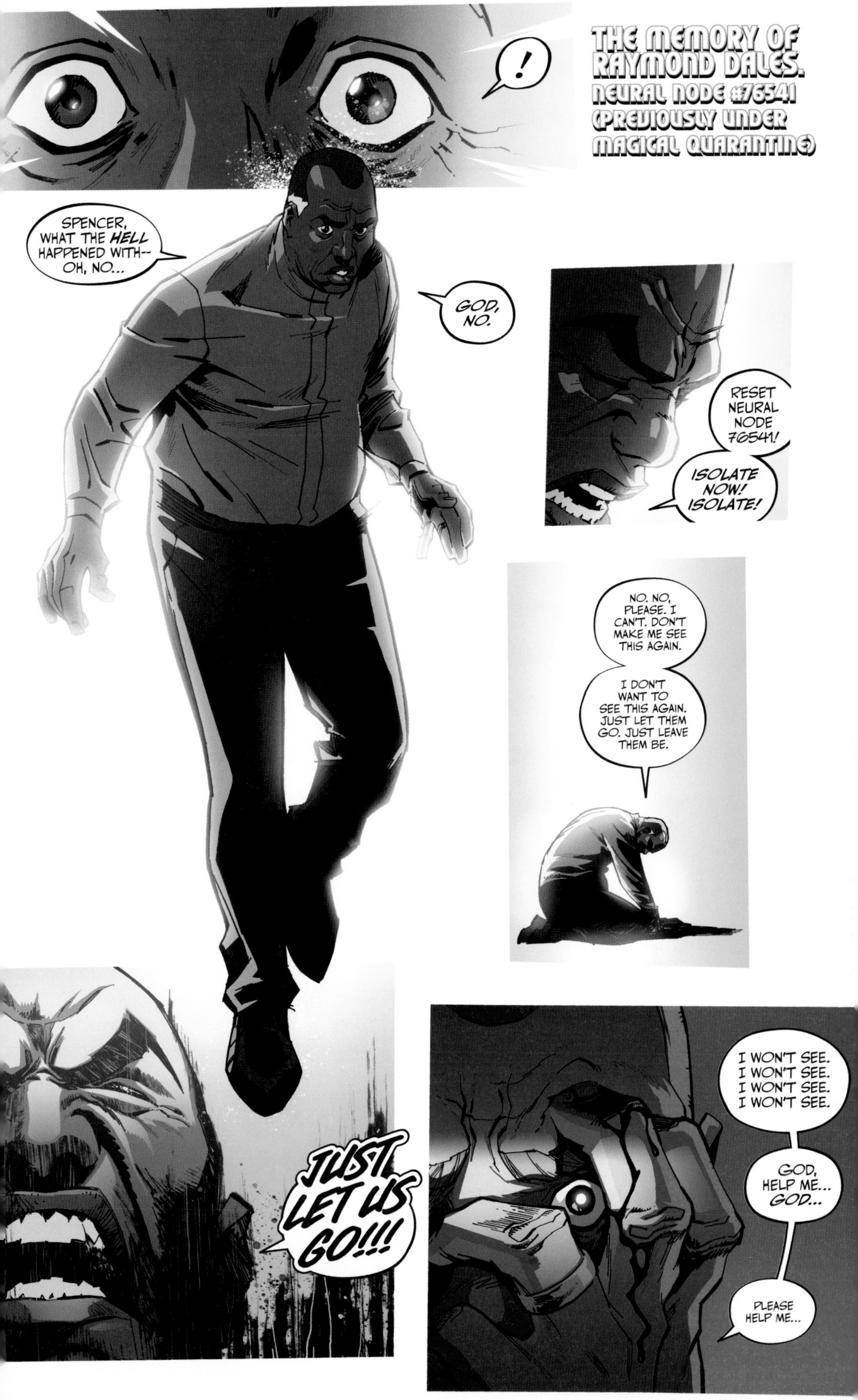
!
THE MEMORY OF RAYMOND DALES.
NEURAL NODE #76541 (PREVIOUSLY UNDER MAGICAL QUARANTINE)
SPENCER, WHAT THE HELL HAPPENED WITH-- OH, NO...
GOD, NO.
RESET NEURAL NODE 76541!
ISOLATE NOW! ISOLATE!
NO. NO, PLEASE. I CAN'T. DON'T MAKE ME SEE THIS AGAIN.
I DON'T WANT TO SEE THIS AGAIN. JUST LET THEM GO. JUST LEAVE THEM BE.
JUST LET US GO!!!
I WON'T SEE. I WON'T SEE. I WON'T SEE. I WON'T SEE.
GOD, HELP ME... GOD...
PLEASE HELP ME...

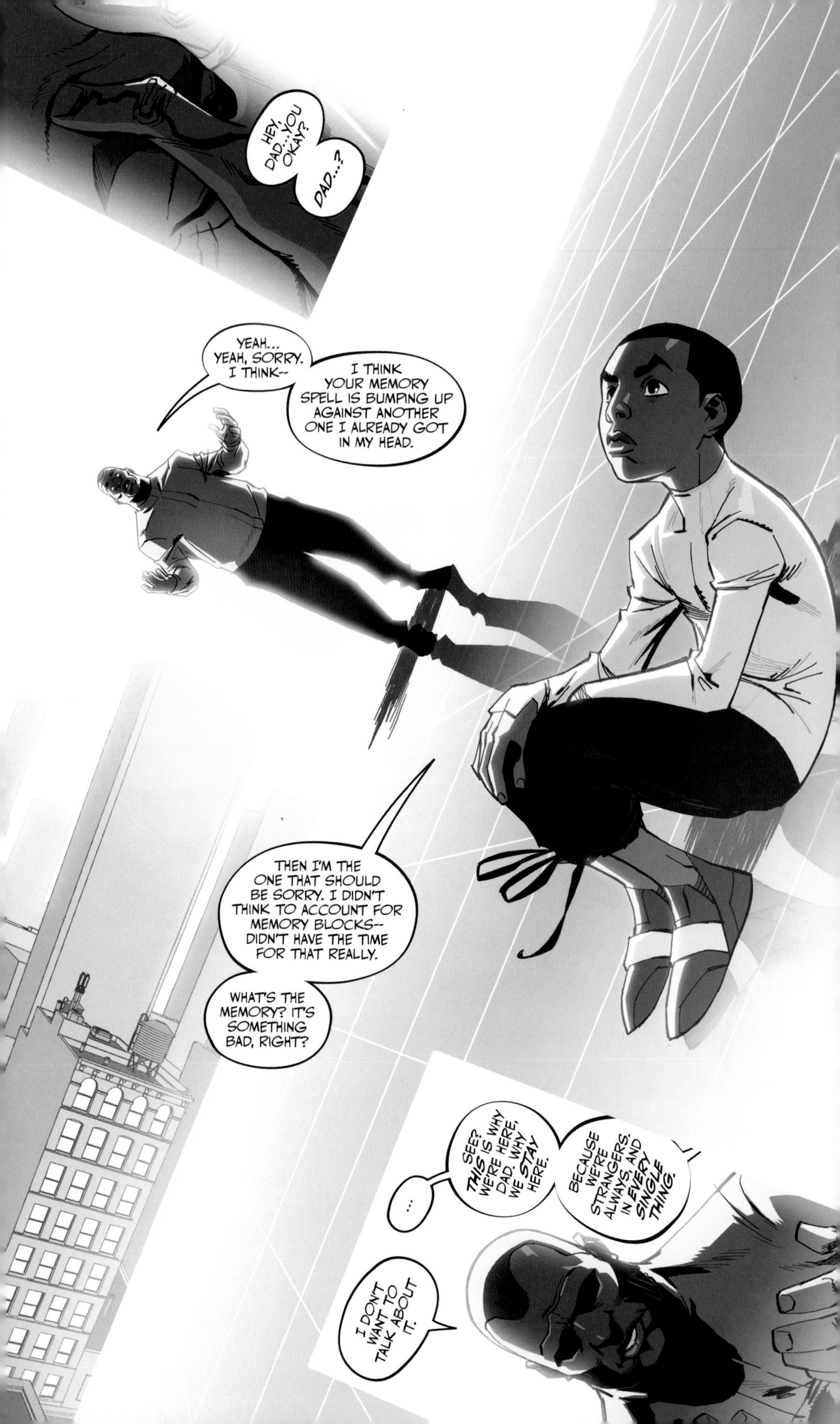
HEY, DAD...YOU OKAY?
DAD...?
YEAH... YEAH, SORRY. I THINK--
I THINK YOUR MEMORY SPELL IS BUMPING UP AGAINST ANOTHER ONE I ALREADY GOT IN MY HEAD.
THEN I'M THE ONE THAT SHOULD BE SORRY. I DIDN'T THINK TO ACCOUNT FOR MEMORY BLOCKS-- DIDN'T HAVE THE TIME FOR THAT REALLY.
WHAT'S THE MEMORY? IT'S SOMETHING BAD, RIGHT?
SEE? THIS IS WHY WE'RE HERE, DAD. WHY WE STAY HERE.
BECAUSE WE'RE STRANGERS, ALWAYS, IN EVERY SINGLE THING.
...
I DON'T WANT TO TALK ABOUT IT.

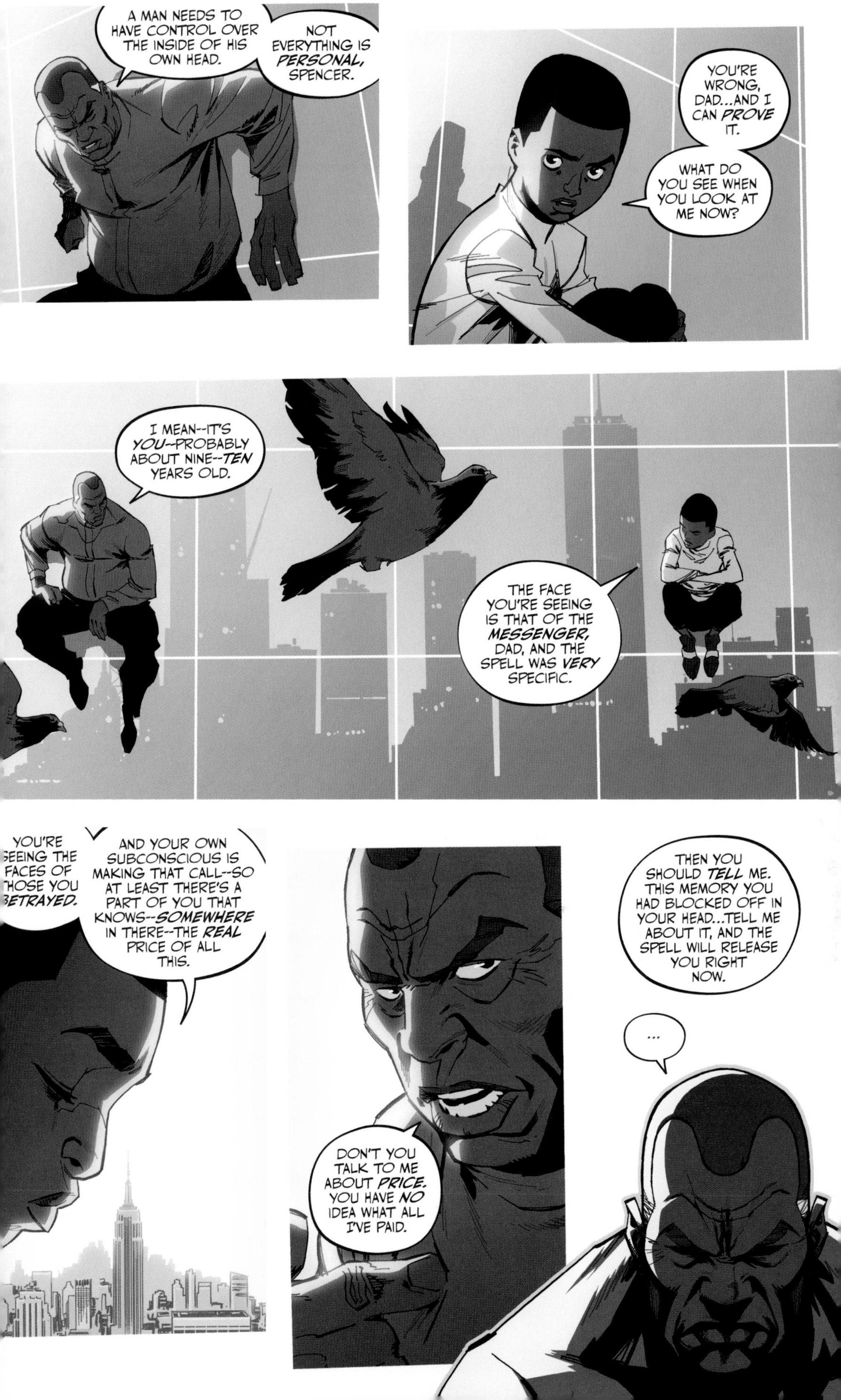
A MAN NEEDS TO HAVE CONTROL OVER THE INSIDE OF HIS OWN HEAD.
NOT EVERYTHING IS *PERSONAL,* SPENCER.
YOU'RE WRONG, DAD...AND I CAN *PROVE* IT.
WHAT DO YOU SEE WHEN YOU LOOK AT ME NOW?
I MEAN--IT'S *YOU*--PROBABLY ABOUT NINE--*TEN* YEARS OLD.
THE FACE YOU'RE SEEING IS THAT OF THE *MESSENGER,* DAD, AND THE SPELL WAS *VERY* SPECIFIC.
YOU'RE SEEING THE FACES OF THOSE YOU *BETRAYED.*
AND YOUR OWN SUBCONSCIOUS IS MAKING THAT CALL--SO AT LEAST THERE'S A PART OF YOU THAT KNOWS--*SOMEWHERE* IN THERE--THE *REAL* PRICE OF ALL THIS.
DON'T YOU TALK TO ME ABOUT *PRICE.* YOU HAVE *NO* IDEA WHAT ALL I'VE PAID.
THEN YOU SHOULD *TELL* ME. THIS MEMORY YOU HAD BLOCKED OFF IN YOUR HEAD...TELL ME ABOUT IT, AND THE SPELL WILL RELEASE YOU RIGHT NOW.
...

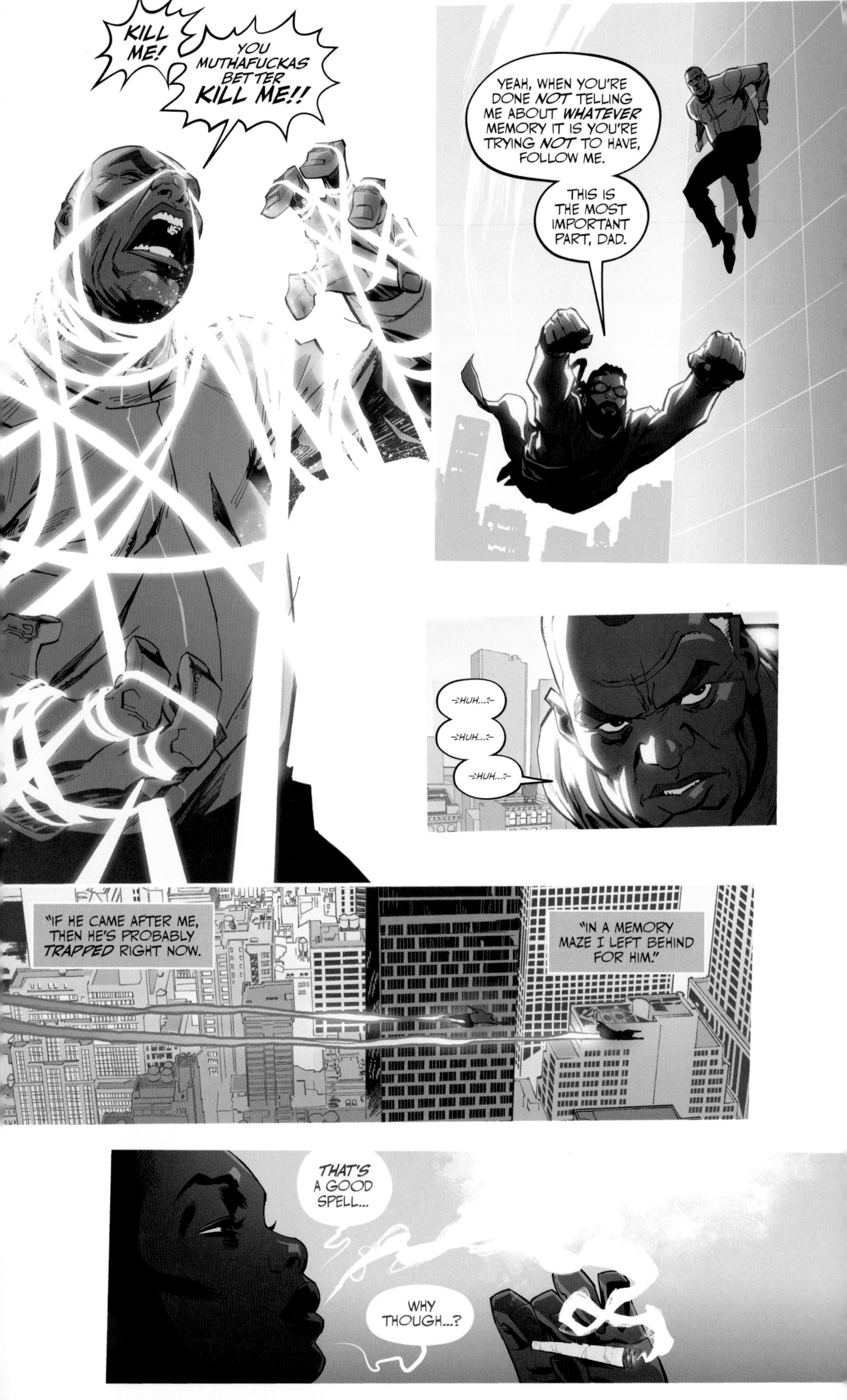
KILL ME!
YOU MUTHAFUCKAS BETTER KILL ME!!
YEAH, WHEN YOU'RE DONE NOT TELLING ME ABOUT WHATEVER MEMORY IT IS YOU'RE TRYING NOT TO HAVE, FOLLOW ME.
THIS IS THE MOST IMPORTANT PART, DAD.
HUH...
HUH...
HUH...
"IF HE CAME AFTER ME, THEN HE'S PROBABLY TRAPPED RIGHT NOW.
"IN A MEMORY MAZE I LEFT BEHIND FOR HIM."
THAT'S A GOOD SPELL...
WHY THOUGH...?

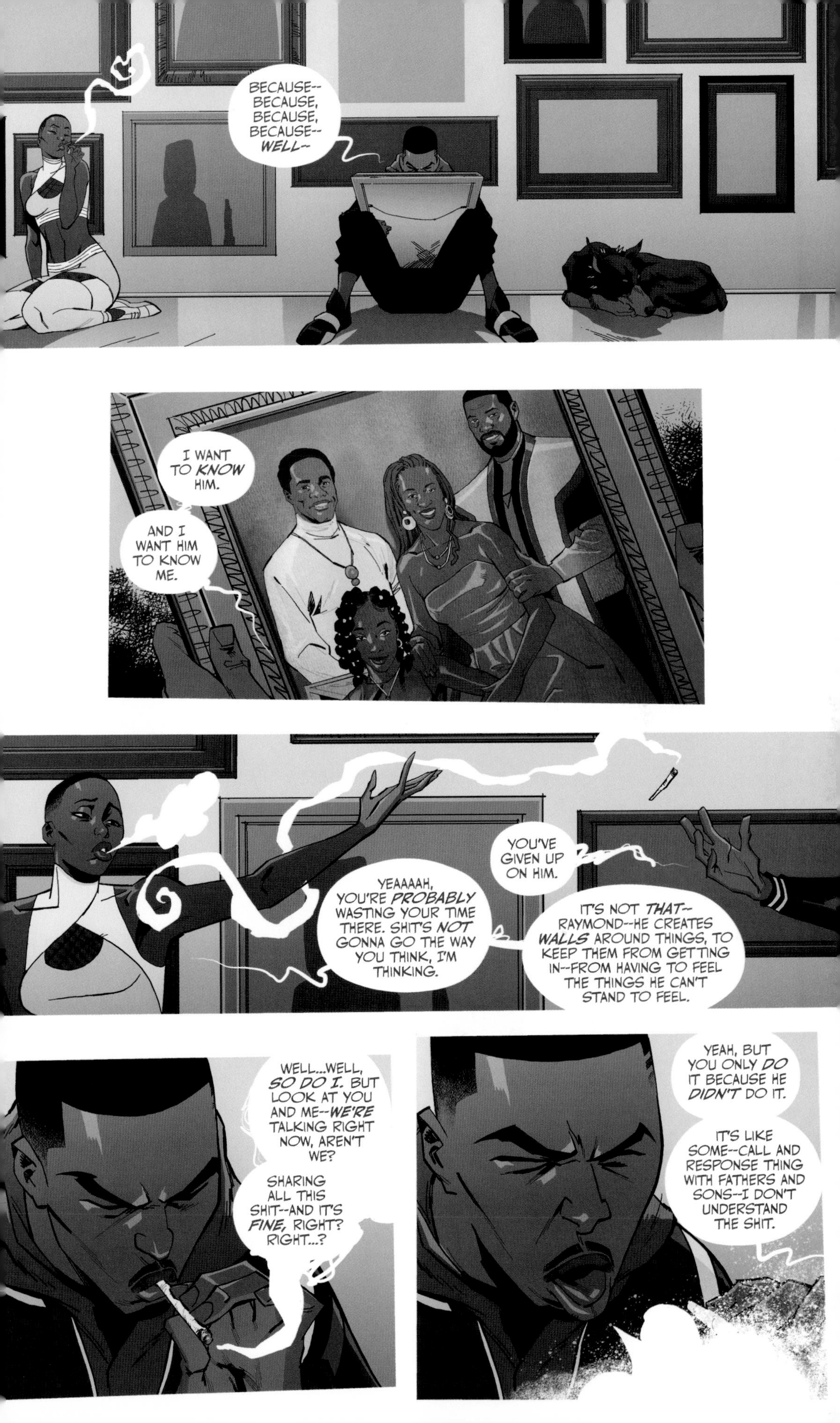
BECAUSE-- BECAUSE, BECAUSE, BECAUSE-- WELL--
I WANT TO KNOW HIM.
AND I WANT HIM TO KNOW ME.
YOU'VE GIVEN UP ON HIM.
YEAAAAH, YOU'RE PROBABLY WASTING YOUR TIME THERE. SHIT'S NOT GONNA GO THE WAY YOU THINK, I'M THINKING.
IT'S NOT THAT-- RAYMOND--HE CREATES WALLS AROUND THINGS, TO KEEP THEM FROM GETTING IN--FROM HAVING TO FEEL THE THINGS HE CAN'T STAND TO FEEL.
WELL...WELL, SO DO I. BUT LOOK AT YOU AND ME--WE'RE TALKING RIGHT NOW, AREN'T WE?
SHARING ALL THIS SHIT--AND IT'S FINE, RIGHT? RIGHT...?
YEAH, BUT YOU ONLY DO IT BECAUSE HE DIDN'T DO IT.
IT'S LIKE SOME--CALL AND RESPONSE THING WITH FATHERS AND SONS--I DON'T UNDERSTAND THE SHIT.

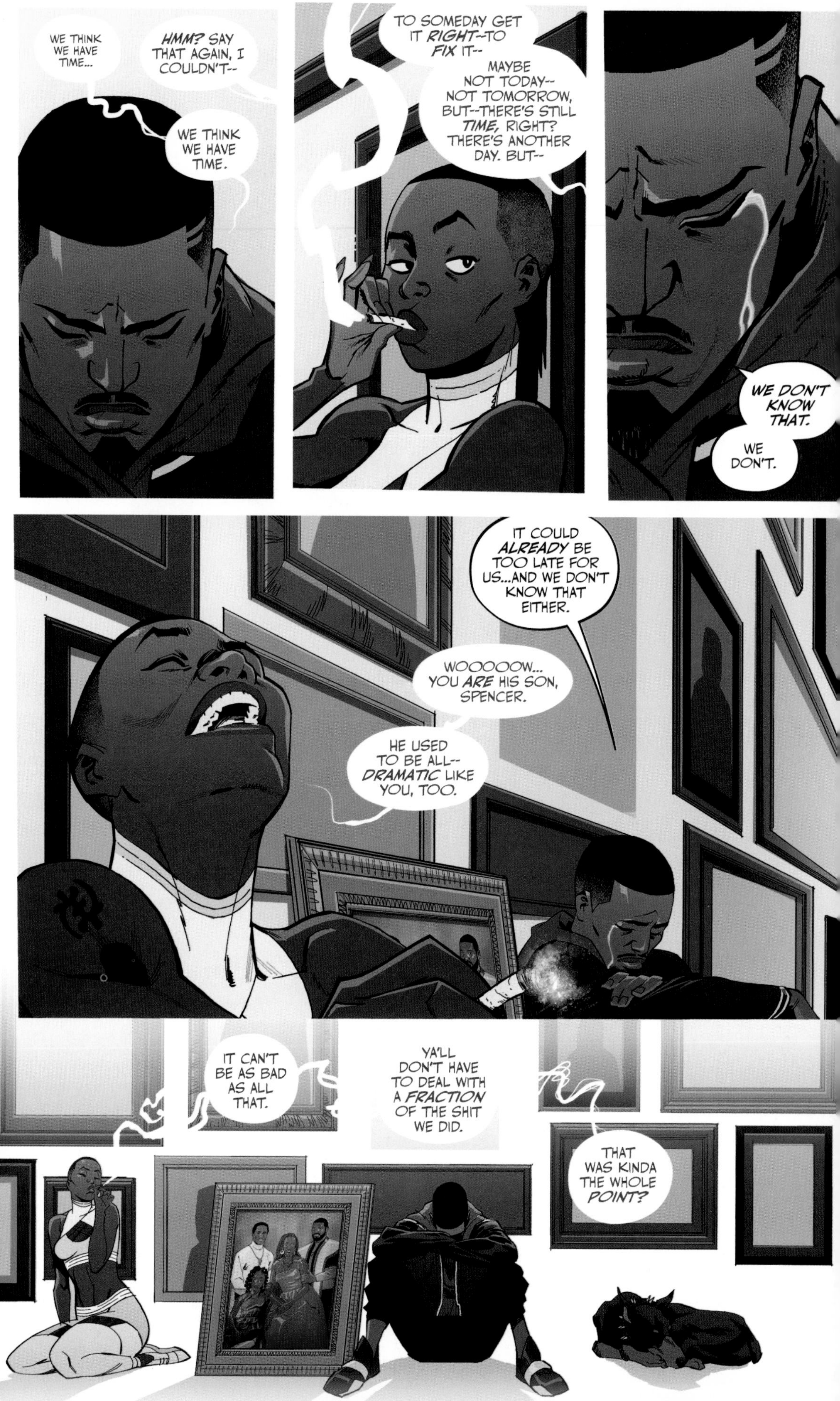
WE THINK WE HAVE TIME...
HMM? SAY THAT AGAIN, I COULDN'T--
WE THINK WE HAVE TIME.
TO SOMEDAY GET IT RIGHT--TO FIX IT--
MAYBE NOT TODAY-- NOT TOMORROW, BUT--THERE'S STILL TIME, RIGHT? THERE'S ANOTHER DAY. BUT--
WE DON'T KNOW THAT.
WE DON'T.
IT COULD ALREADY BE TOO LATE FOR US...AND WE DON'T KNOW THAT EITHER.
WOOOOOW... YOU ARE HIS SON, SPENCER.
HE USED TO BE ALL-- DRAMATIC LIKE YOU, TOO.
IT CAN'T BE AS BAD AS ALL THAT.
YA'LL DON'T HAVE TO DEAL WITH A FRACTION OF THE SHIT WE DID.
THAT WAS KINDA THE WHOLE POINT?

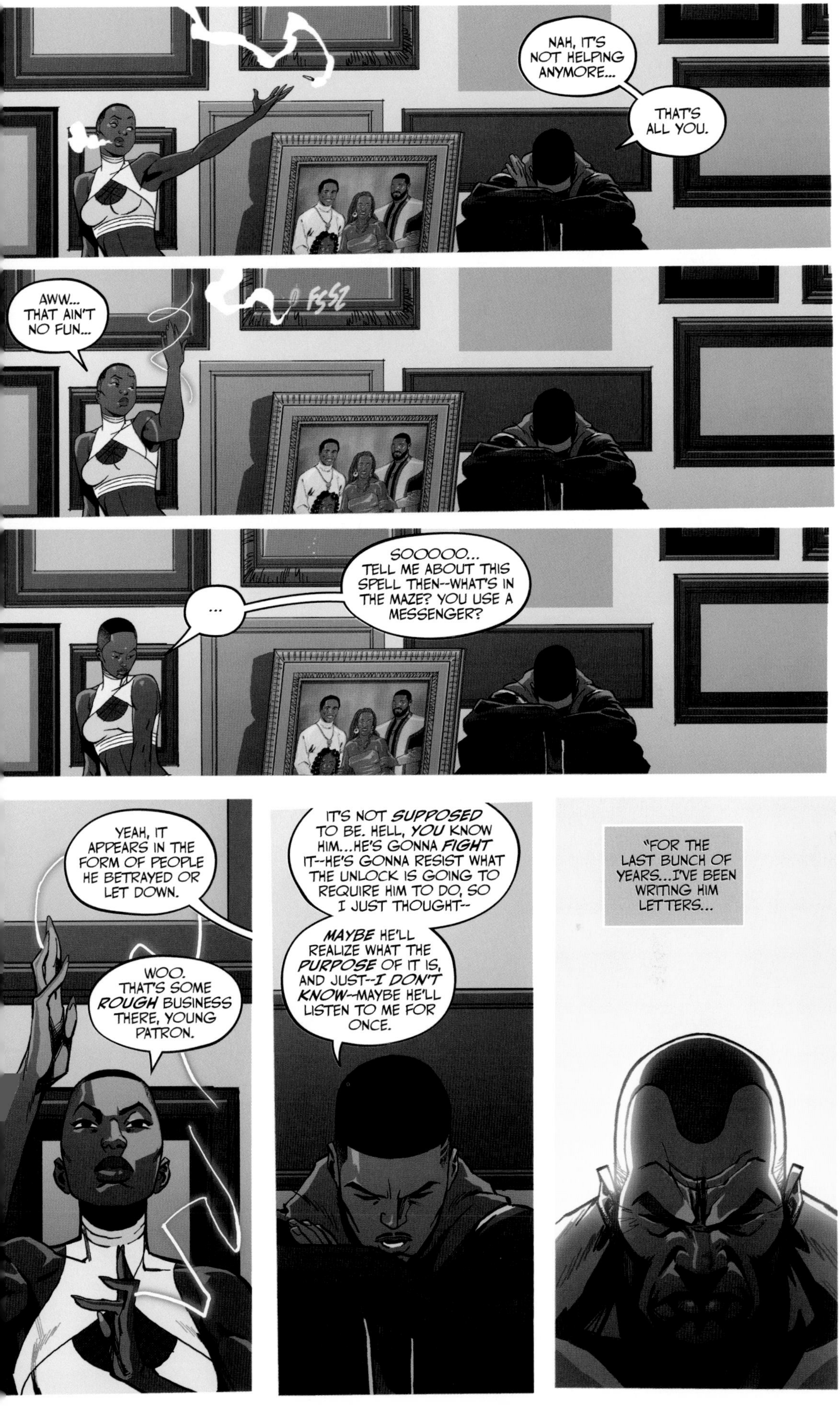
NAH, IT'S NOT HELPING ANYMORE...
THAT'S ALL YOU.
AWW... THAT AIN'T NO FUN...
FSSZ
...
SOOOOO... TELL ME ABOUT THIS SPELL THEN--WHAT'S IN THE MAZE? YOU USE A MESSENGER?
YEAH, IT APPEARS IN THE FORM OF PEOPLE HE BETRAYED OR LET DOWN.
WOO. THAT'S SOME ROUGH BUSINESS THERE, YOUNG PATRON.
IT'S NOT SUPPOSED TO BE. HELL, YOU KNOW HIM...HE'S GONNA FIGHT IT--HE'S GONNA RESIST WHAT THE UNLOCK IS GOING TO REQUIRE HIM TO DO, SO I JUST THOUGHT--
MAYBE HE'LL REALIZE WHAT THE PURPOSE OF IT IS, AND JUST--I DON'T KNOW--MAYBE HE'LL LISTEN TO ME FOR ONCE.
"FOR THE LAST BUNCH OF YEARS...I'VE BEEN WRITING HIM LETTERS...

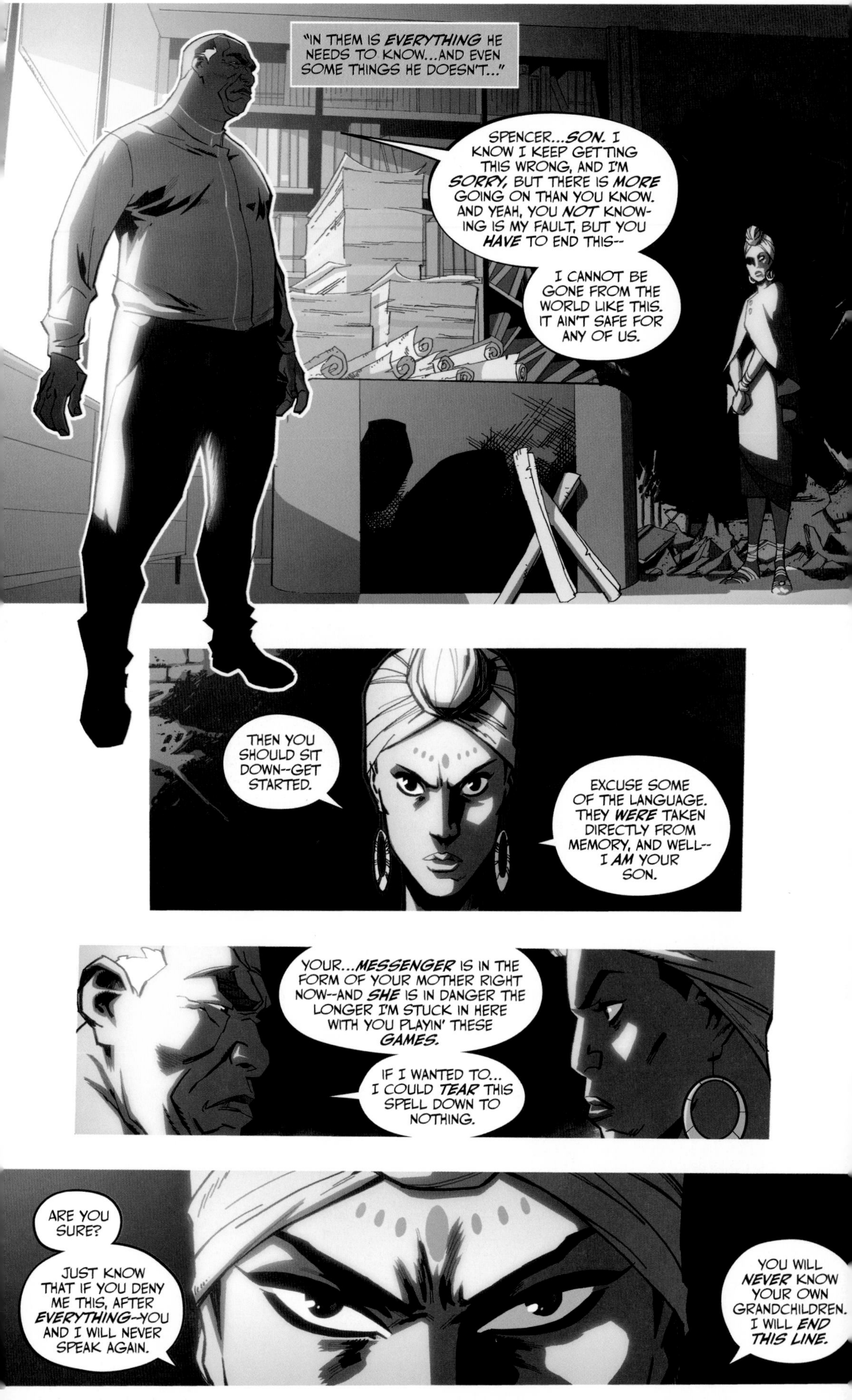
"IN THEM IS EVERYTHING HE NEEDS TO KNOW...AND EVEN SOME THINGS HE DOESN'T..."
SPENCER...SON. I KNOW I KEEP GETTING THIS WRONG, AND I'M SORRY, BUT THERE IS MORE GOING ON THAN YOU KNOW. AND YEAH, YOU NOT KNOWING IS MY FAULT, BUT YOU HAVE TO END THIS--
I CANNOT BE GONE FROM THE WORLD LIKE THIS. IT AIN'T SAFE FOR ANY OF US.
THEN YOU SHOULD SIT DOWN--GET STARTED.
EXCUSE SOME OF THE LANGUAGE. THEY WERE TAKEN DIRECTLY FROM MEMORY, AND WELL-- I AM YOUR SON.
YOUR...MESSENGER IS IN THE FORM OF YOUR MOTHER RIGHT NOW--AND SHE IS IN DANGER THE LONGER I'M STUCK IN HERE WITH YOU PLAYIN' THESE GAMES.
IF I WANTED TO... I COULD TEAR THIS SPELL DOWN TO NOTHING.
ARE YOU SURE?
JUST KNOW THAT IF YOU DENY ME THIS, AFTER EVERYTHING--YOU AND I WILL NEVER SPEAK AGAIN.
YOU WILL NEVER KNOW YOUR OWN GRANDCHILDREN. I WILL END THIS LINE.

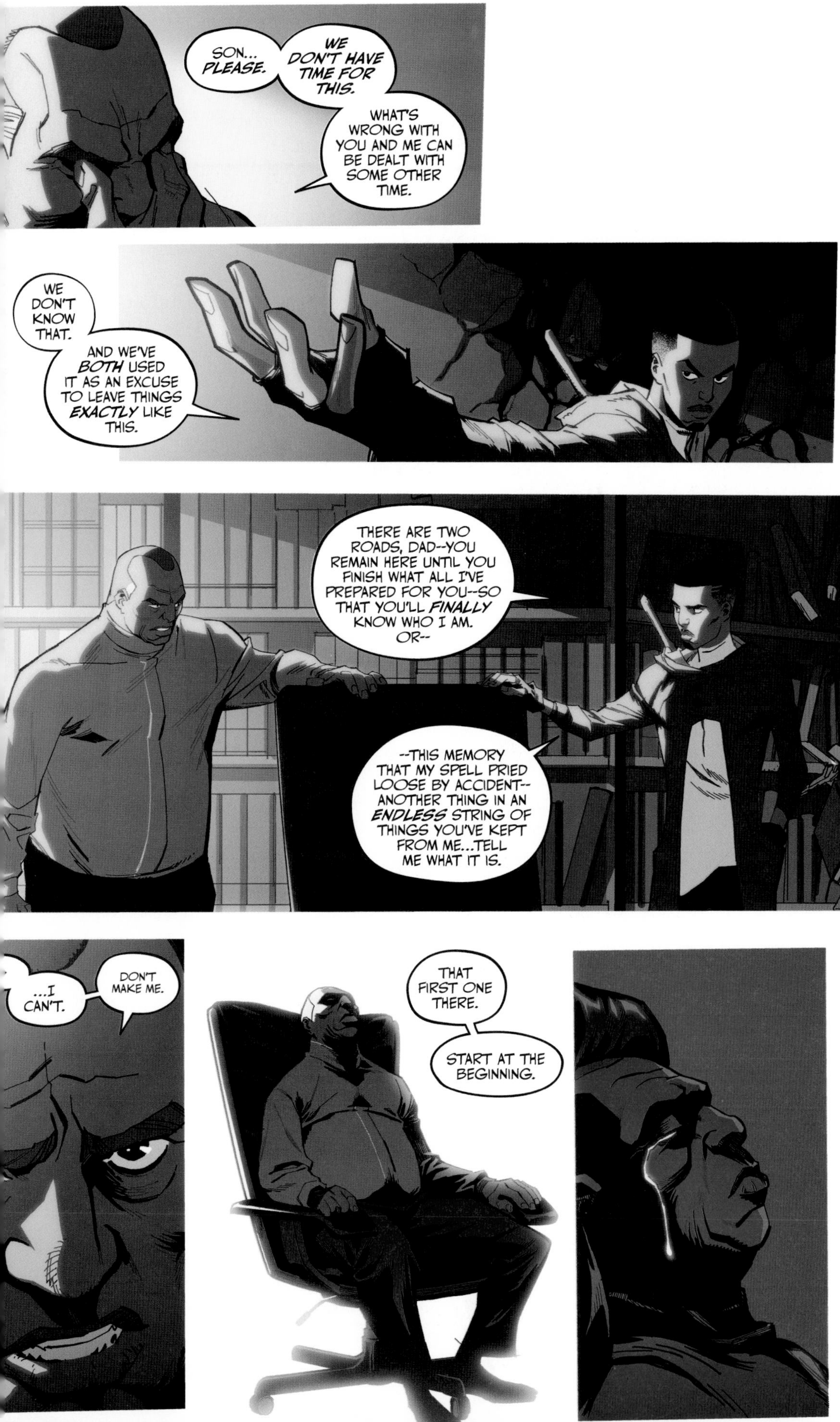
SON... PLEASE.
WE DON'T HAVE TIME FOR THIS.
WHAT'S WRONG WITH YOU AND ME CAN BE DEALT WITH SOME OTHER TIME.
WE DON'T KNOW THAT.
AND WE'VE BOTH USED IT AS AN EXCUSE TO LEAVE THINGS EXACTLY LIKE THIS.
THERE ARE TWO ROADS, DAD--YOU REMAIN HERE UNTIL YOU FINISH WHAT ALL I'VE PREPARED FOR YOU--SO THAT YOU'LL FINALLY KNOW WHO I AM. OR--
--THIS MEMORY THAT MY SPELL PRIED LOOSE BY ACCIDENT--ANOTHER THING IN AN ENDLESS STRING OF THINGS YOU'VE KEPT FROM ME...TELL ME WHAT IT IS.
...I CAN'T.
DON'T MAKE ME.
THAT FIRST ONE THERE.
START AT THE BEGINNING.

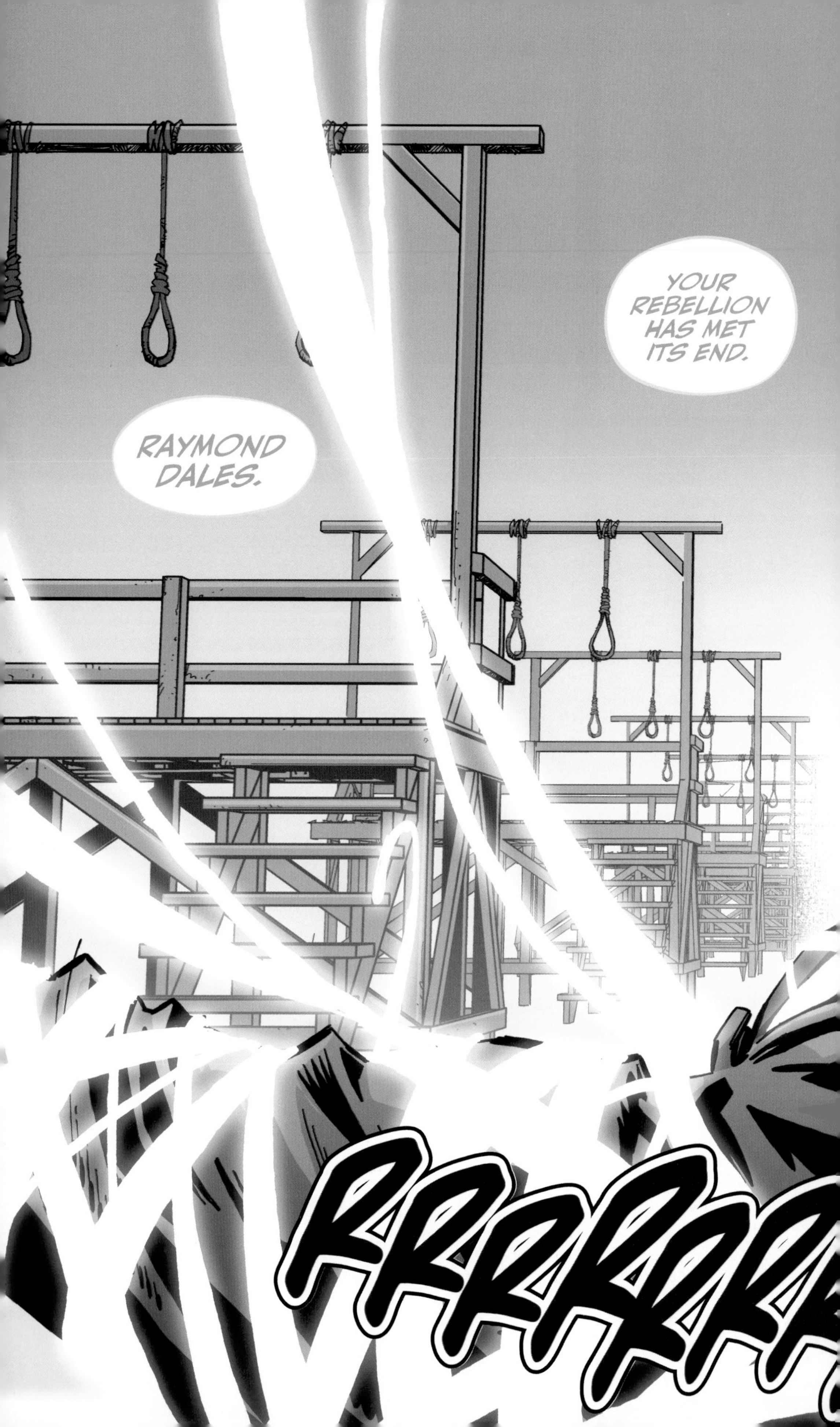
RAYMOND DALES.
YOUR REBELLION HAS MET ITS END.
RRRRRR

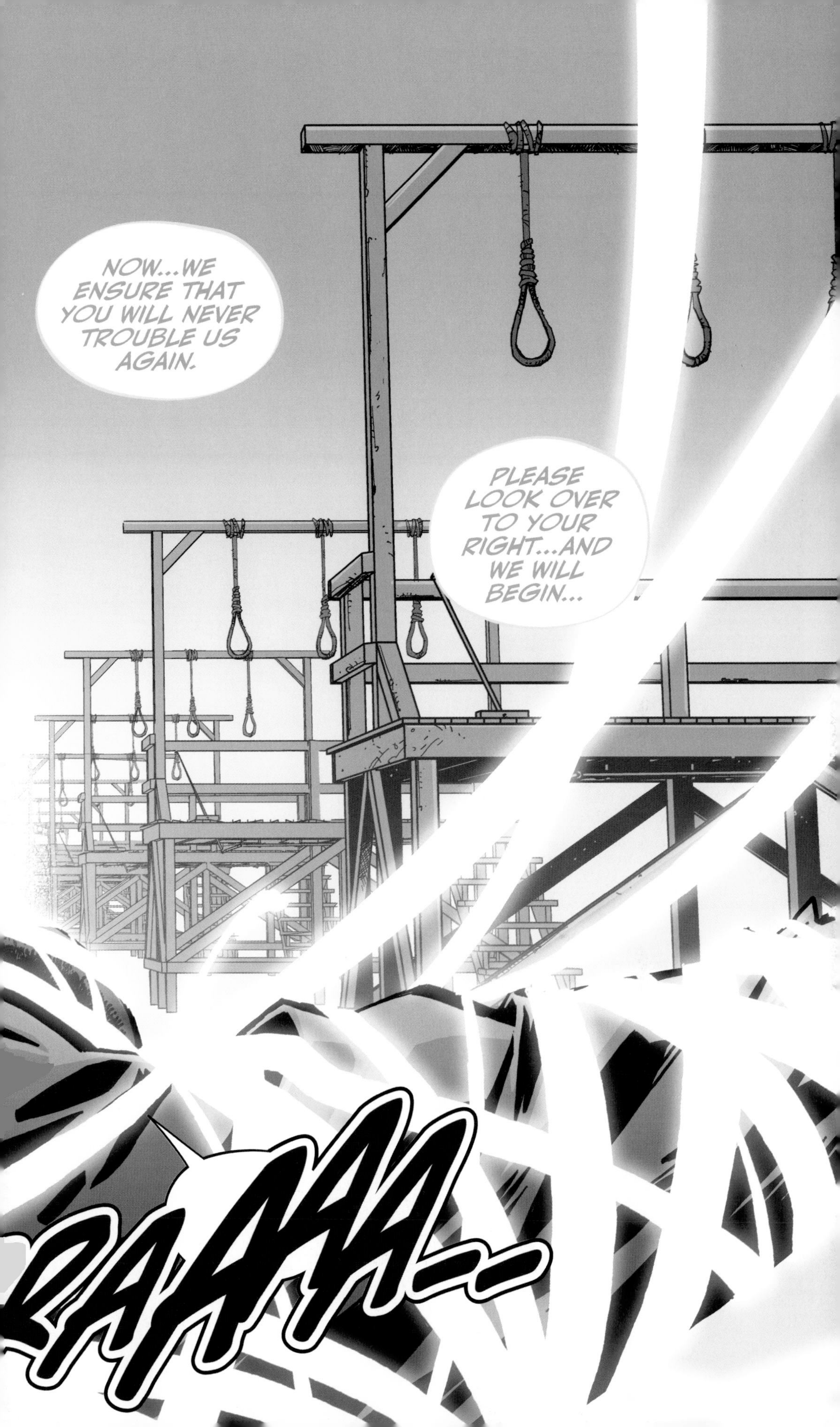
NOW...WE ENSURE THAT YOU WILL NEVER TROUBLE US AGAIN.
PLEASE LOOK OVER TO YOUR RIGHT...AND WE WILL BEGIN...
RAAAA--

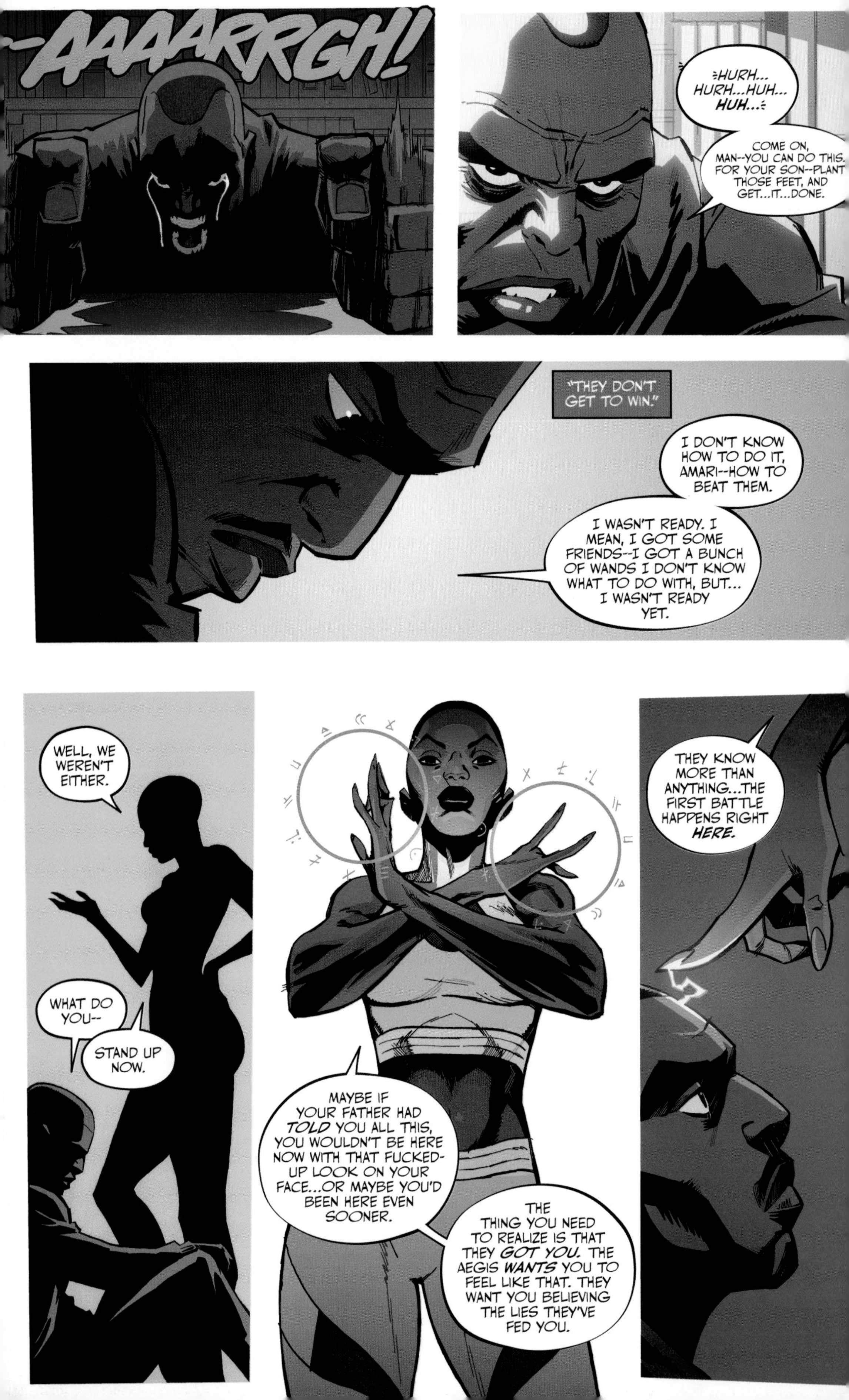

AAAARRGH!
HURH... HURH...HUH... HUH...
COME ON, MAN--YOU CAN DO THIS. FOR YOUR SON--PLANT THOSE FEET, AND GET...IT...DONE.
"THEY DON'T GET TO WIN."
I DON'T KNOW HOW TO DO IT, AMARI--HOW TO BEAT THEM.
I WASN'T READY. I MEAN, I GOT SOME FRIENDS--I GOT A BUNCH OF WANDS I DON'T KNOW WHAT TO DO WITH, BUT... I WASN'T READY YET.
WELL, WE WEREN'T EITHER.
WHAT DO YOU--
STAND UP NOW.
MAYBE IF YOUR FATHER HAD TOLD YOU ALL THIS, YOU WOULDN'T BE HERE NOW WITH THAT FUCKED-UP LOOK ON YOUR FACE...OR MAYBE YOU'D BEEN HERE EVEN SOONER.
THE THING YOU NEED TO REALIZE IS THAT THEY GOT YOU. THE AEGIS WANTS YOU TO FEEL LIKE THAT. THEY WANT YOU BELIEVING THE LIES THEY'VE FED YOU.
THEY KNOW MORE THAN ANYTHING...THE FIRST BATTLE HAPPENS RIGHT HERE.

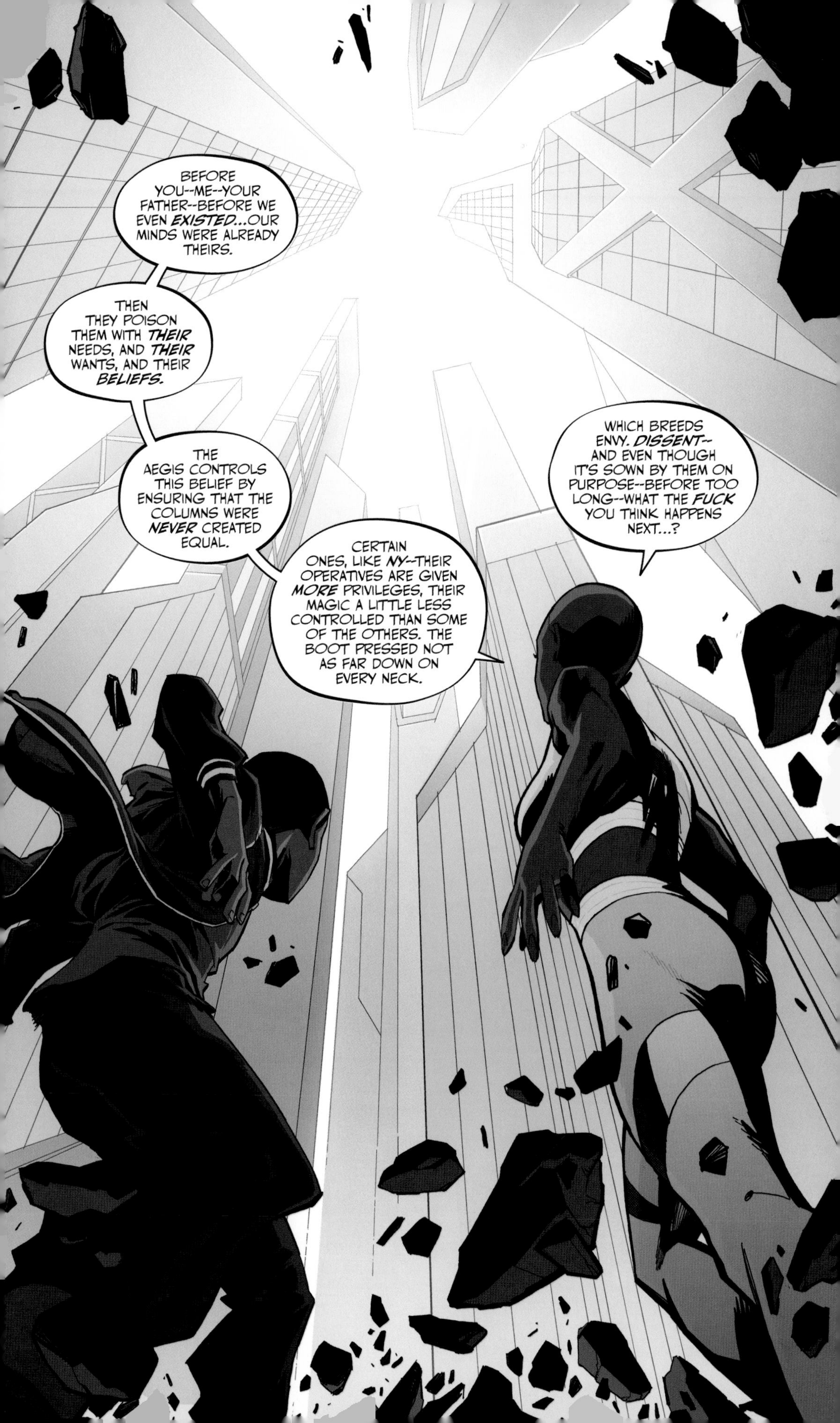
BEFORE YOU--ME--YOUR FATHER--BEFORE WE EVEN *EXISTED*...OUR MINDS WERE ALREADY THEIRS.
THEN THEY POISON THEM WITH *THEIR* NEEDS, AND *THEIR* WANTS, AND THEIR *BELIEFS.*
THE AEGIS CONTROLS THIS BELIEF BY ENSURING THAT THE COLUMNS WERE *NEVER* CREATED EQUAL.
CERTAIN ONES, LIKE *NY*--THEIR OPERATIVES ARE GIVEN *MORE* PRIVILEGES, THEIR MAGIC A LITTLE LESS CONTROLLED THAN SOME OF THE OTHERS. THE BOOT PRESSED NOT AS FAR DOWN ON EVERY NECK.
WHICH BREEDS ENVY. *DISSENT*-- AND EVEN THOUGH IT'S SOWN BY THEM ON PURPOSE--BEFORE TOO LONG--WHAT THE *FUCK* YOU THINK HAPPENS NEXT...?

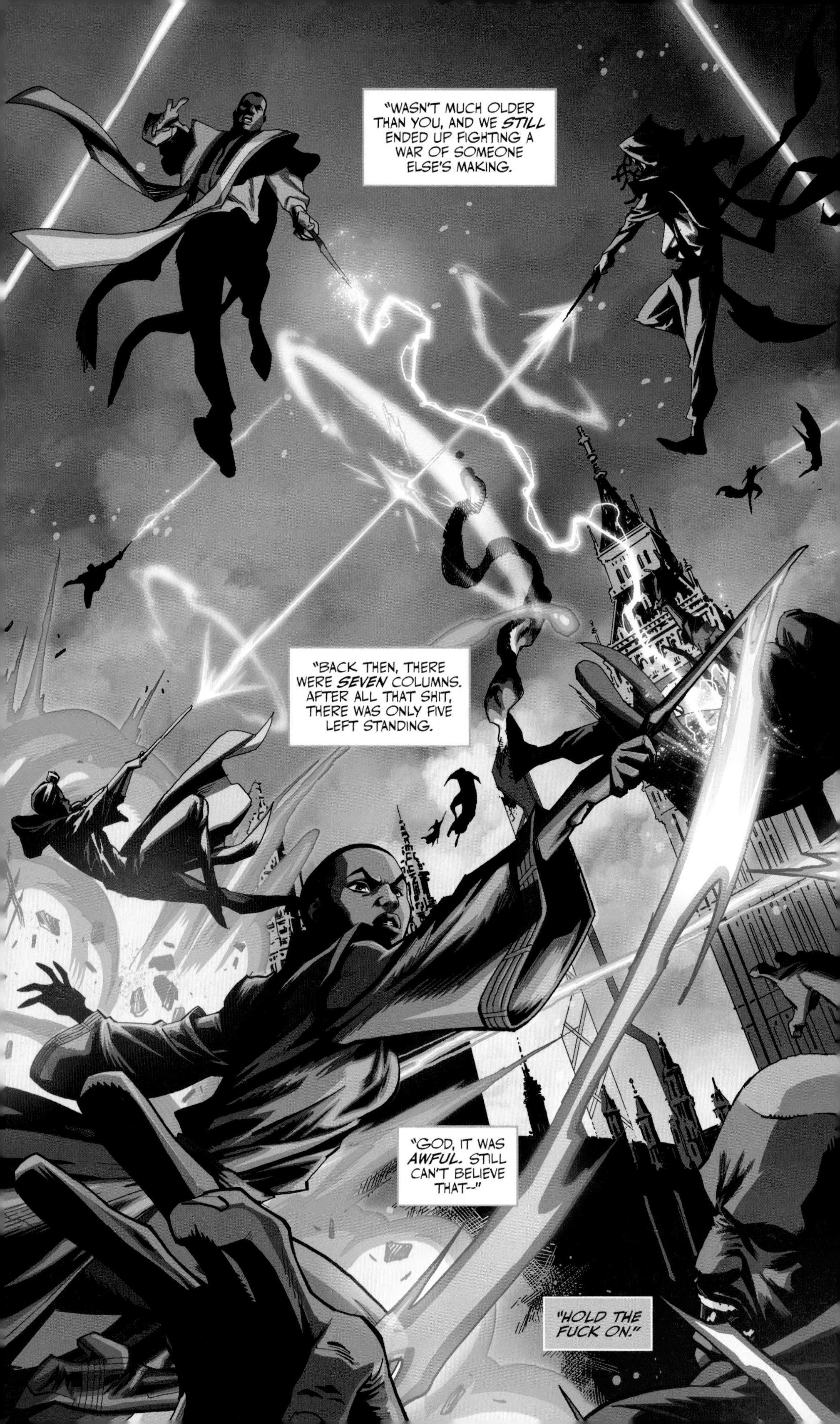
"WASN'T MUCH OLDER THAN YOU, AND WE STILL ENDED UP FIGHTING A WAR OF SOMEONE ELSE'S MAKING.
"BACK THEN, THERE WERE SEVEN COLUMNS. AFTER ALL THAT SHIT, THERE WAS ONLY FIVE LEFT STANDING.
"GOD, IT WAS AWFUL. STILL CAN'T BELIEVE THAT--"
"HOLD THE FUCK ON."

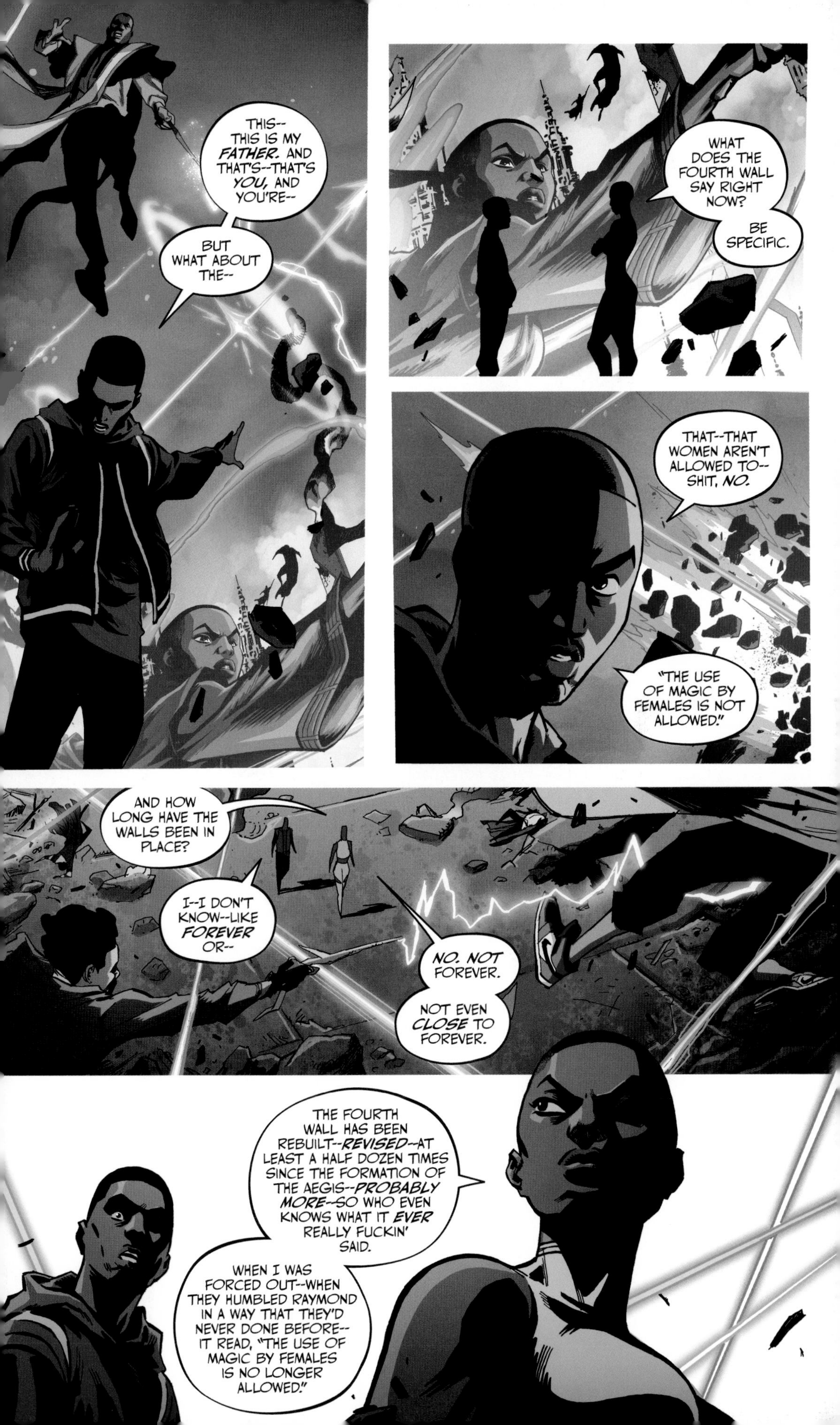
THIS-- THIS IS MY *FATHER.* AND THAT'S--THAT'S *YOU,* AND YOU'RE--
BUT WHAT ABOUT THE--
WHAT DOES THE FOURTH WALL SAY RIGHT NOW?
BE SPECIFIC.
THAT--THAT WOMEN AREN'T ALLOWED TO-- SHIT, *NO.*
"THE USE OF MAGIC BY FEMALES IS NOT ALLOWED."
AND HOW LONG HAVE THE WALLS BEEN IN PLACE?
I--I DON'T KNOW--LIKE *FOREVER* OR--
NO. NOT FOREVER.
NOT EVEN *CLOSE* TO FOREVER.
THE FOURTH WALL HAS BEEN REBUILT--*REVISED*--AT LEAST A HALF DOZEN TIMES SINCE THE FORMATION OF THE AEGIS--*PROBABLY MORE*--SO WHO EVEN KNOWS WHAT IT *EVER* REALLY FUCKIN' SAID.
WHEN I WAS FORCED OUT--WHEN THEY HUMBLED RAYMOND IN A WAY THAT THEY'D NEVER DONE BEFORE-- IT READ, "THE USE OF MAGIC BY FEMALES IS NO LONGER ALLOWED."

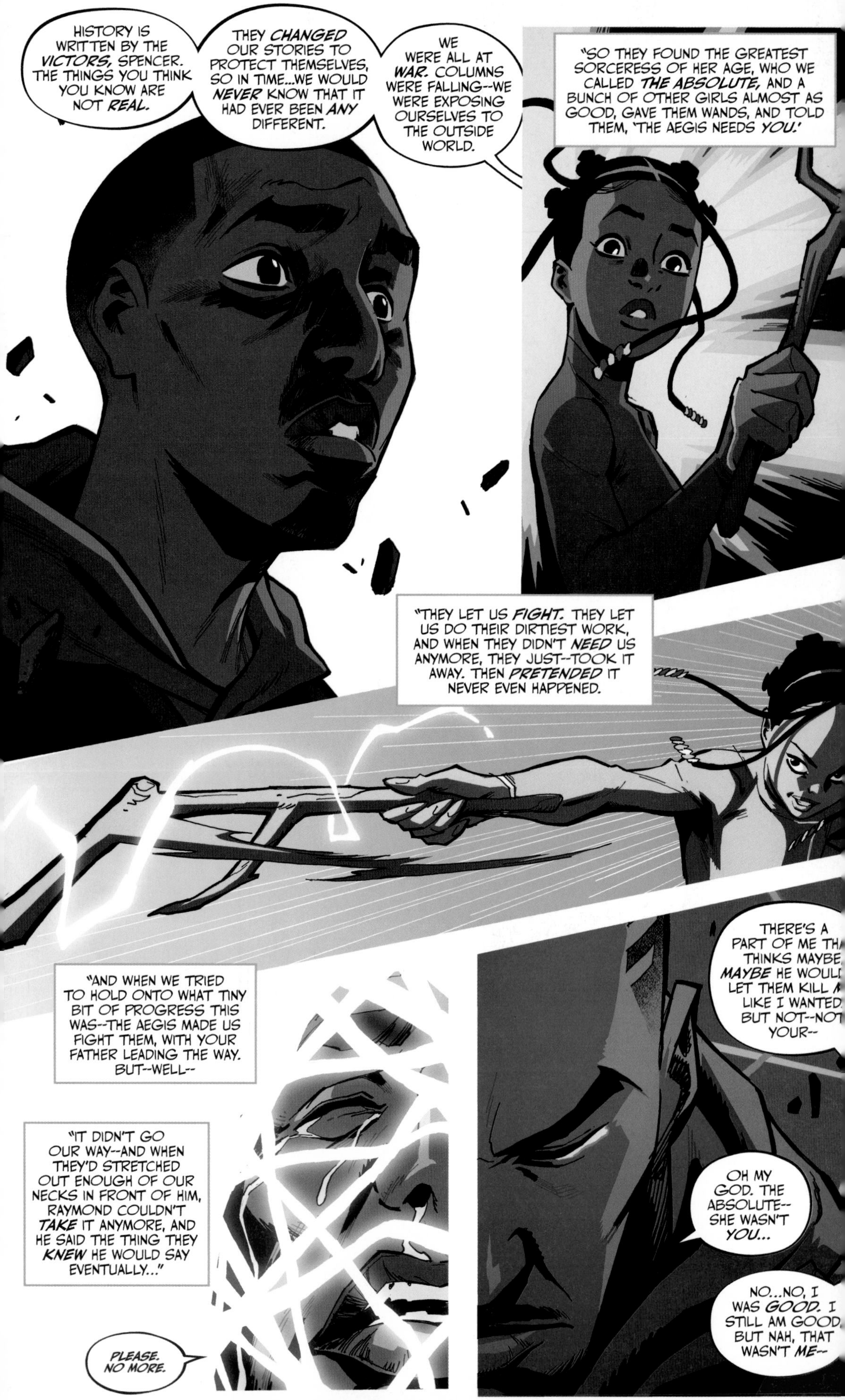

HISTORY IS WRITTEN BY THE VICTORS, SPENCER. THE THINGS YOU THINK YOU KNOW ARE NOT REAL.
THEY CHANGED OUR STORIES TO PROTECT THEMSELVES, SO IN TIME...WE WOULD NEVER KNOW THAT IT HAD EVER BEEN ANY DIFFERENT.
WE WERE ALL AT WAR. COLUMNS WERE FALLING--WE WERE EXPOSING OURSELVES TO THE OUTSIDE WORLD.
"SO THEY FOUND THE GREATEST SORCERESS OF HER AGE, WHO WE CALLED THE ABSOLUTE, AND A BUNCH OF OTHER GIRLS ALMOST AS GOOD, GAVE THEM WANDS, AND TOLD THEM, 'THE AEGIS NEEDS YOU.'
"THEY LET US FIGHT. THEY LET US DO THEIR DIRTIEST WORK, AND WHEN THEY DIDN'T NEED US ANYMORE, THEY JUST--TOOK IT AWAY. THEN PRETENDED IT NEVER EVEN HAPPENED.
"AND WHEN WE TRIED TO HOLD ONTO WHAT TINY BIT OF PROGRESS THIS WAS--THE AEGIS MADE US FIGHT THEM, WITH YOUR FATHER LEADING THE WAY. BUT--WELL--
"IT DIDN'T GO OUR WAY--AND WHEN THEY'D STRETCHED OUT ENOUGH OF OUR NECKS IN FRONT OF HIM, RAYMOND COULDN'T TAKE IT ANYMORE, AND HE SAID THE THING THEY KNEW HE WOULD SAY EVENTUALLY..."
PLEASE. NO MORE.
THERE'S A PART OF ME TH THINKS MAYBE, MAYBE HE WOUL LET THEM KILL LIKE I WANTED BUT NOT--NO YOUR--
OH MY GOD. THE ABSOLUTE-- SHE WASN'T YOU...
NO...NO, I WAS GOOD. I STILL AM GOOD BUT NAH, THAT WASN'T ME--

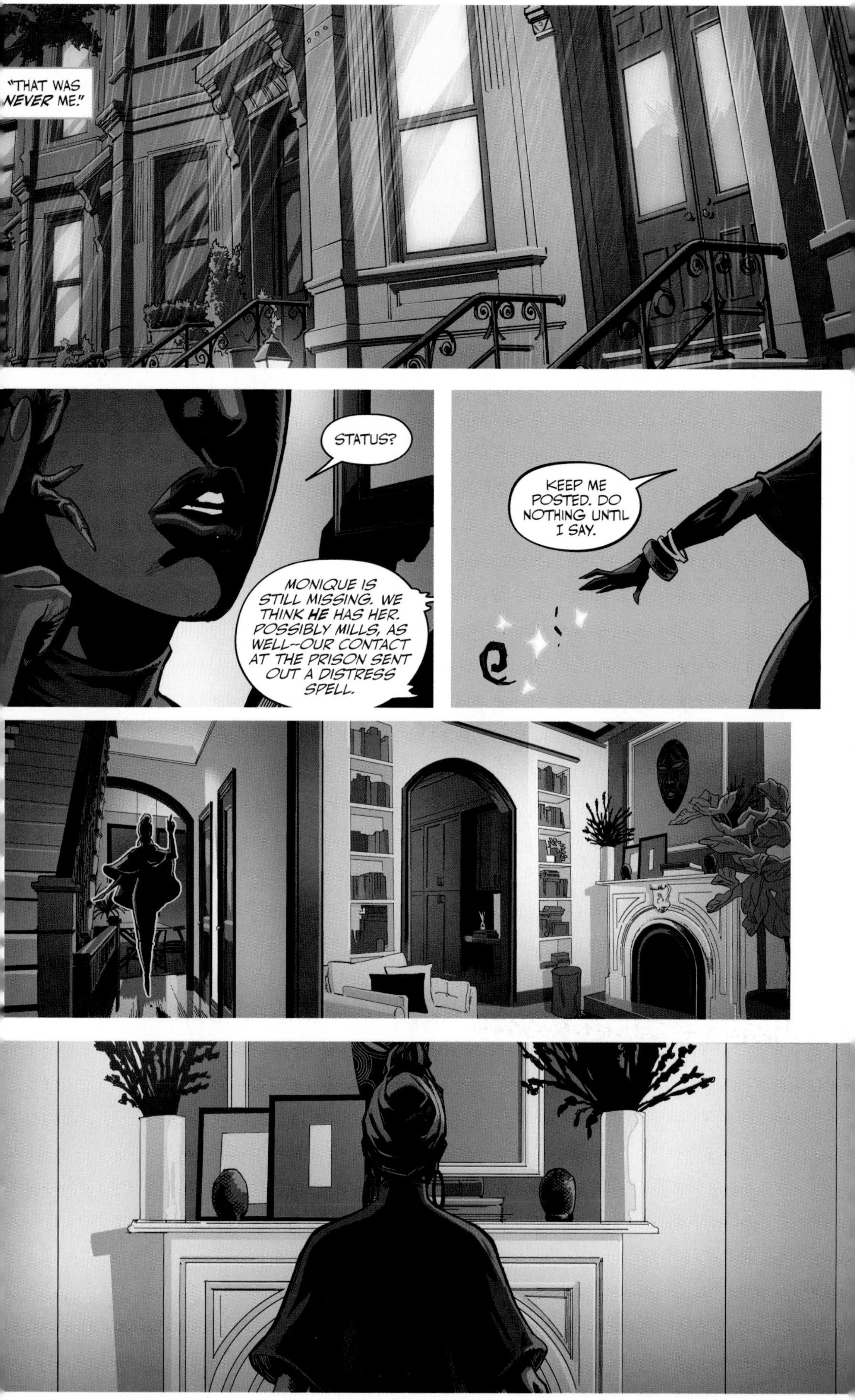
"THAT WAS *NEVER* ME."
STATUS?
MONIQUE IS STILL MISSING. WE THINK **HE** HAS HER. POSSIBLY MILLS, AS WELL--OUR CONTACT AT THE PRISON SENT OUT A DISTRESS SPELL.
KEEP ME POSTED. DO NOTHING UNTIL I SAY.

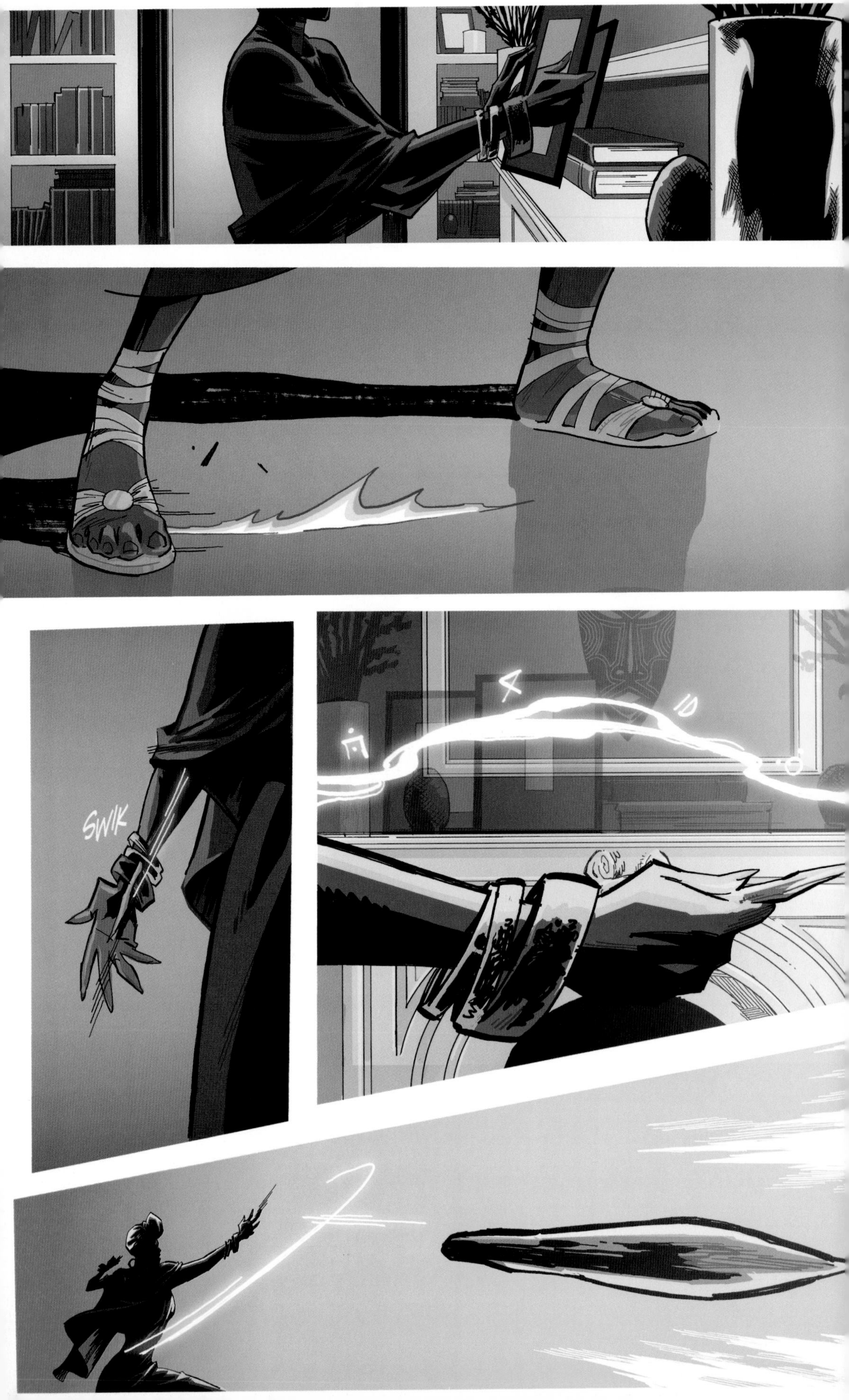
SWIK

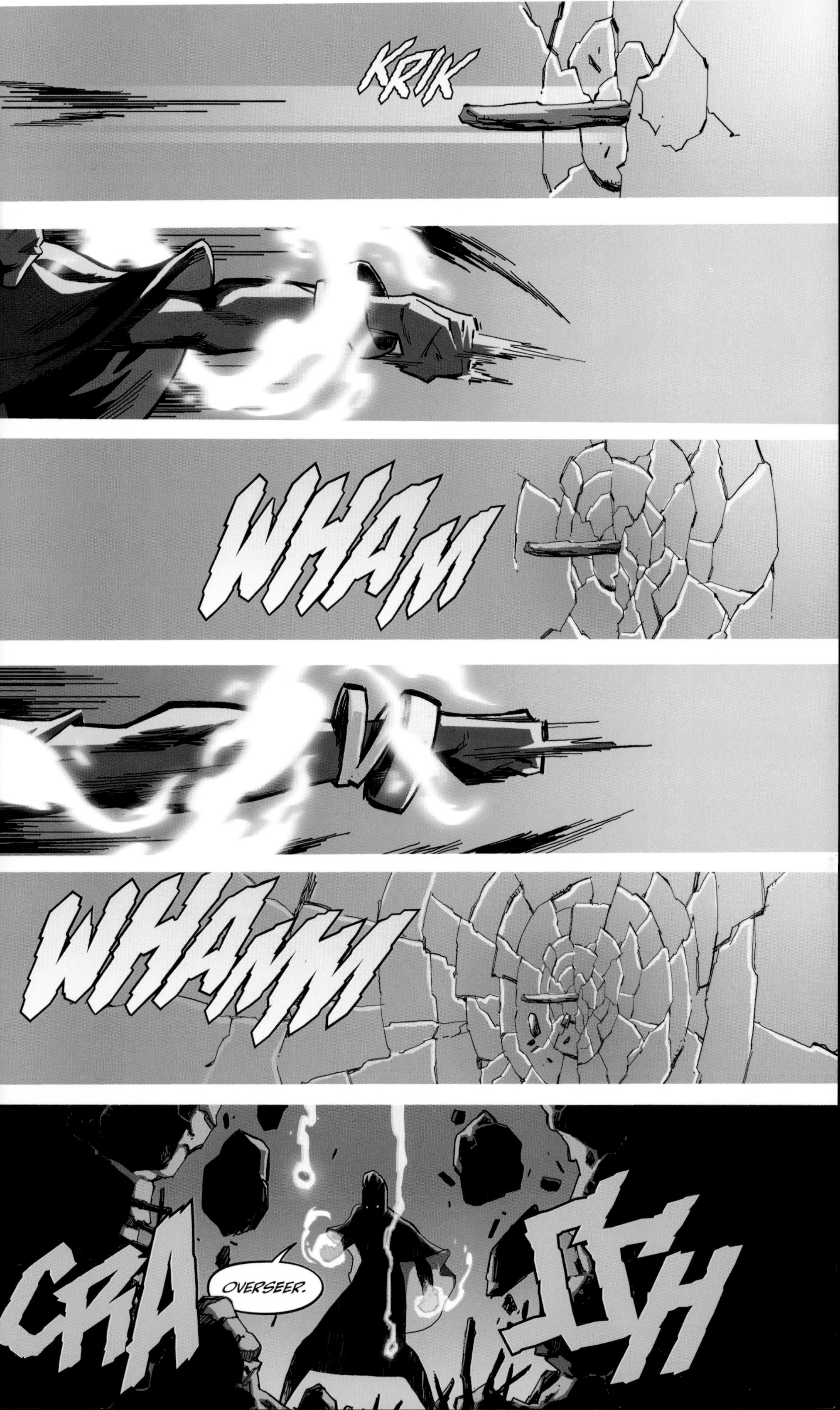
KRIK
WHAM
WHAMM
CRA
OVERSEER.
SSH

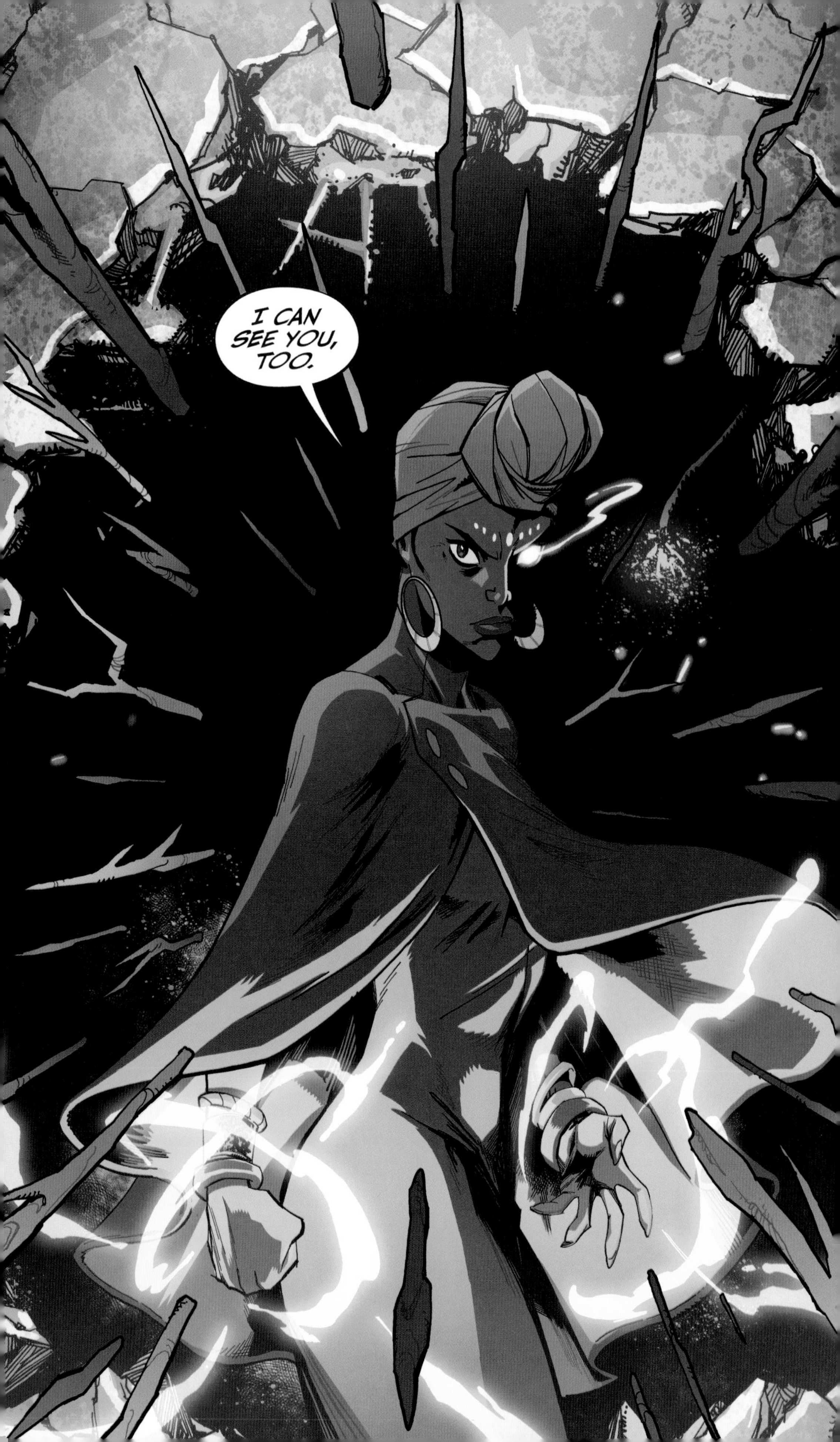
I CAN SEE YOU, TOO.

EXCELLENCE IS REAL

COVER GALLERY

image

SKYBOUND

7

$3.99 US

BRANDON THOMAS • KHARY RANDOLPH • EMILIO LOPEZ

EXCELLENCE™

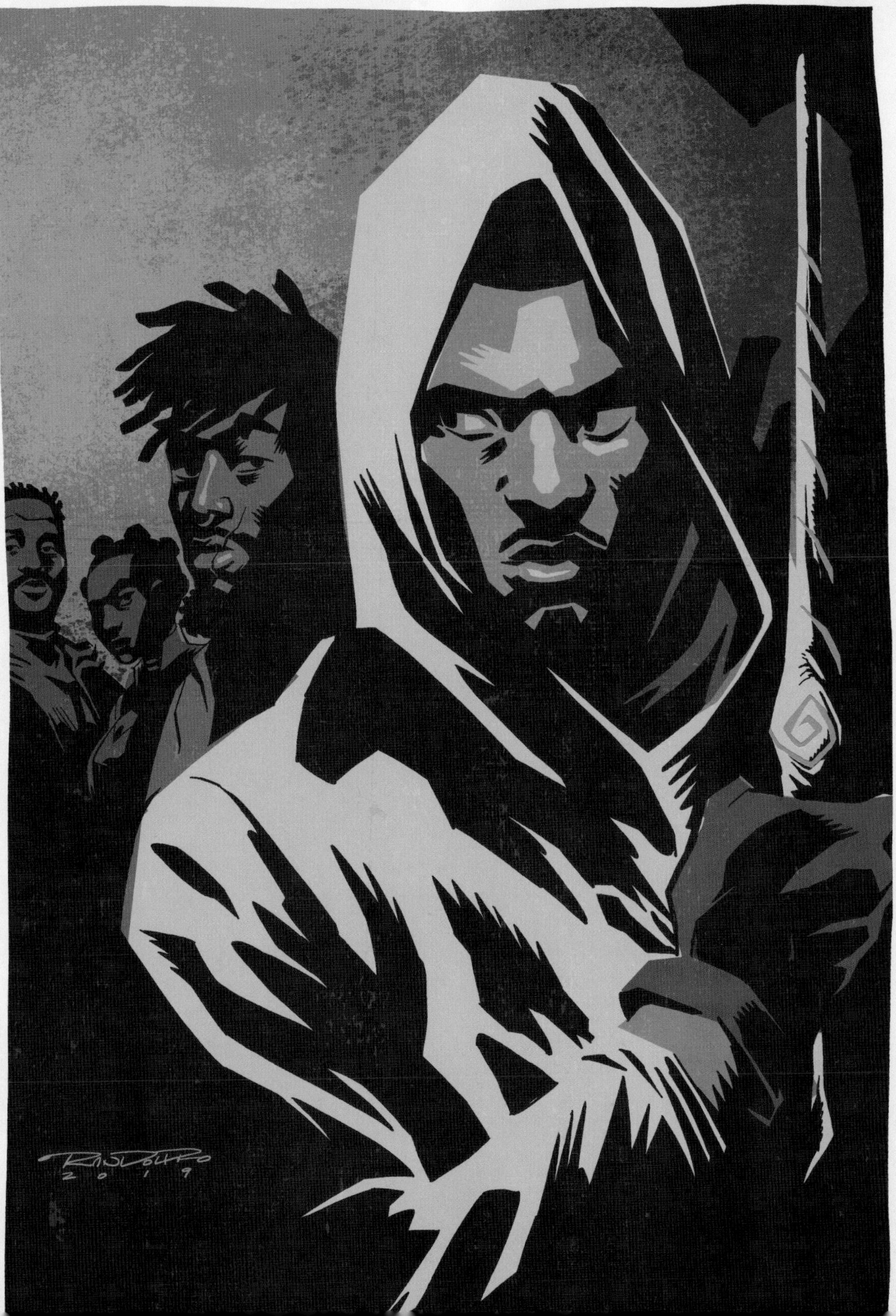

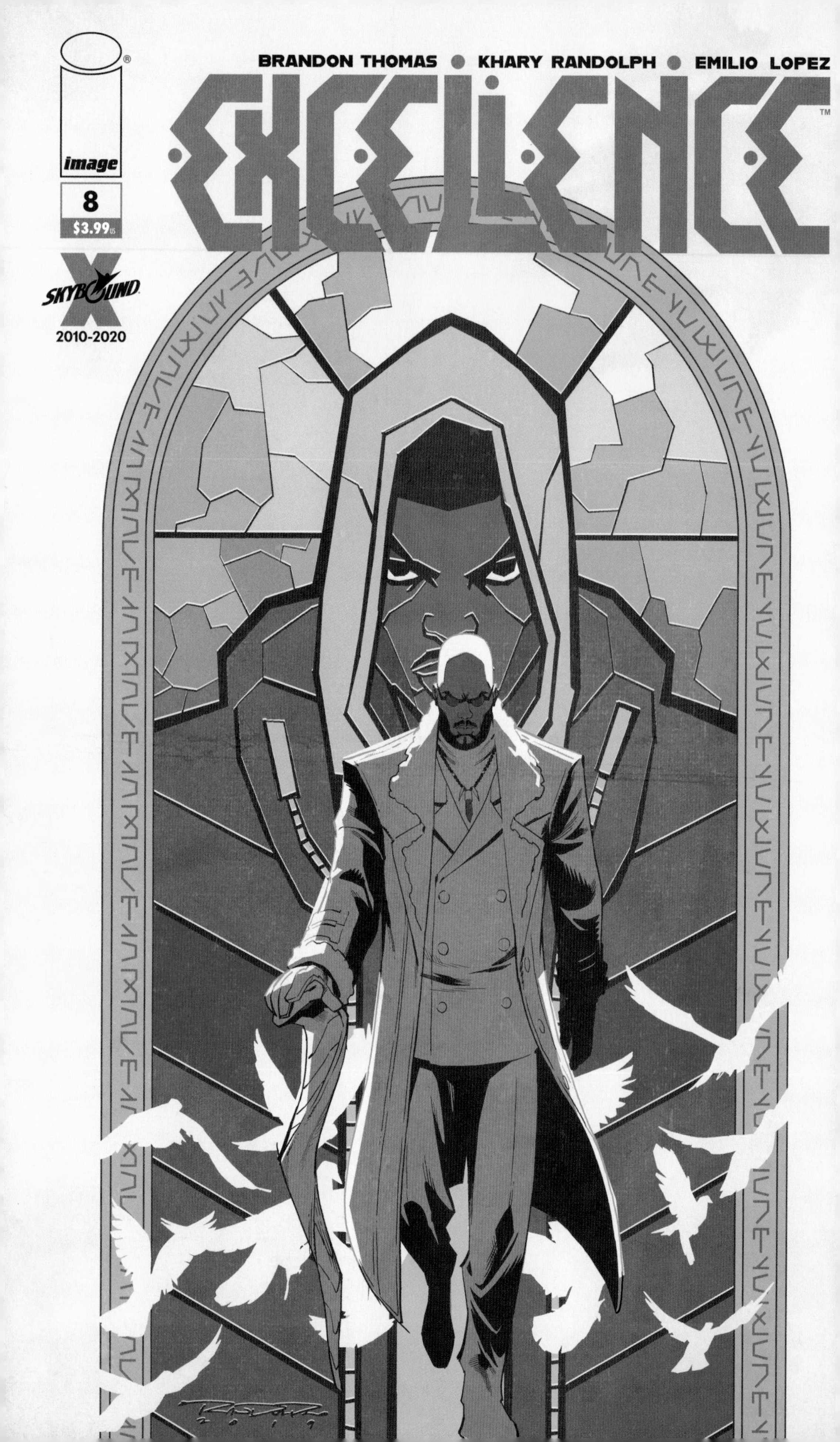
image
8
$3.99 US
SKYBOUND
2010-2020
BRANDON THOMAS • KHARY RANDOLPH • EMILIO LOPEZ
EXCELLENCE™

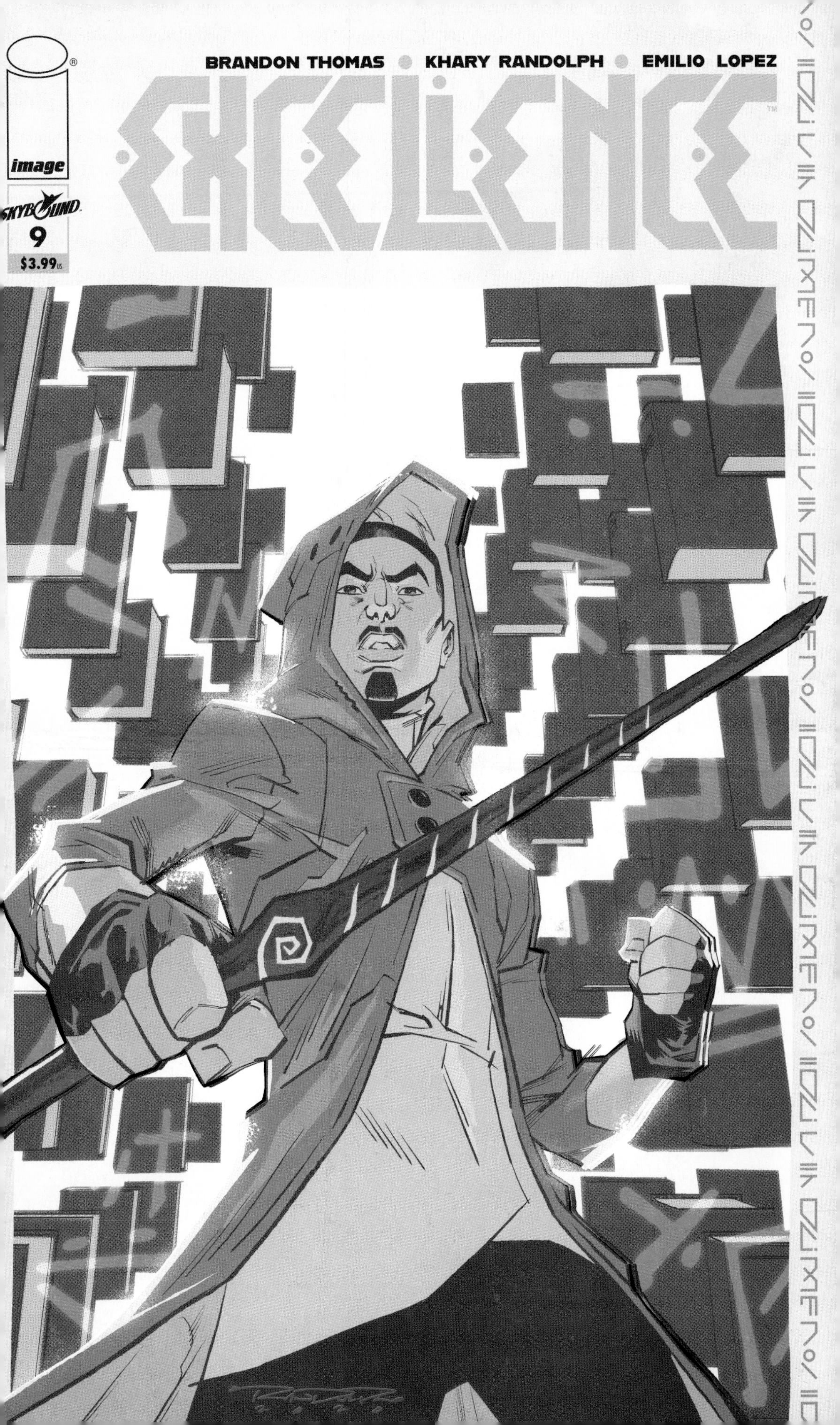
image
SKYBOUND
9
$3.99 US
BRANDON THOMAS • KHARY RANDOLPH • EMILIO LOPEZ
EXCELLENCE™

image

SKYBOUND

10

$3.99 US

BRANDON THOMAS • KHARY RANDOLPH • EMILIO LOPEZ

EXCELLENCE™

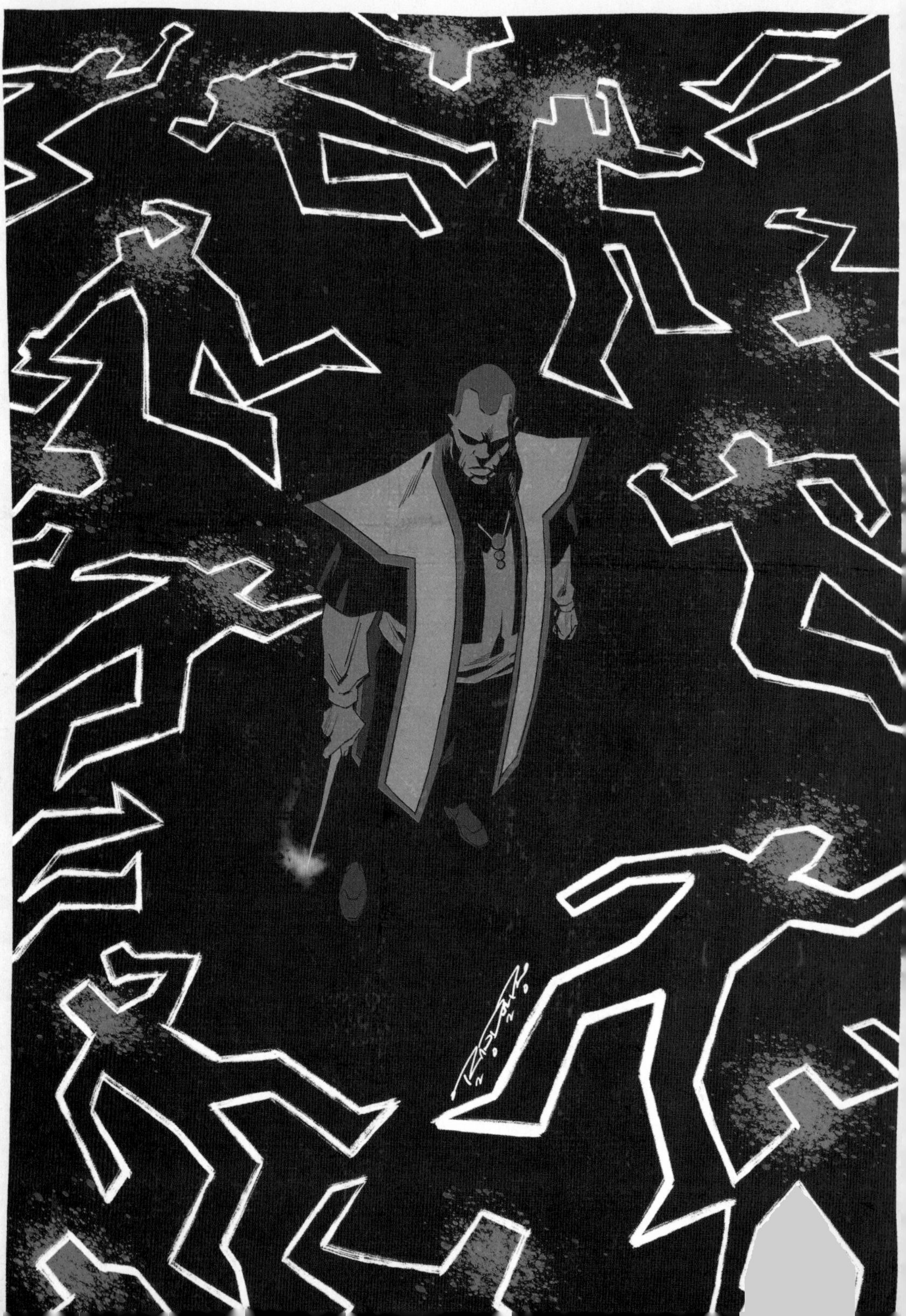

image
SKYBOUND
11
$3.99 US

BRANDON THOMAS • KHARY RANDOLPH • EMILIO LOPEZ

EXCELLENCE™

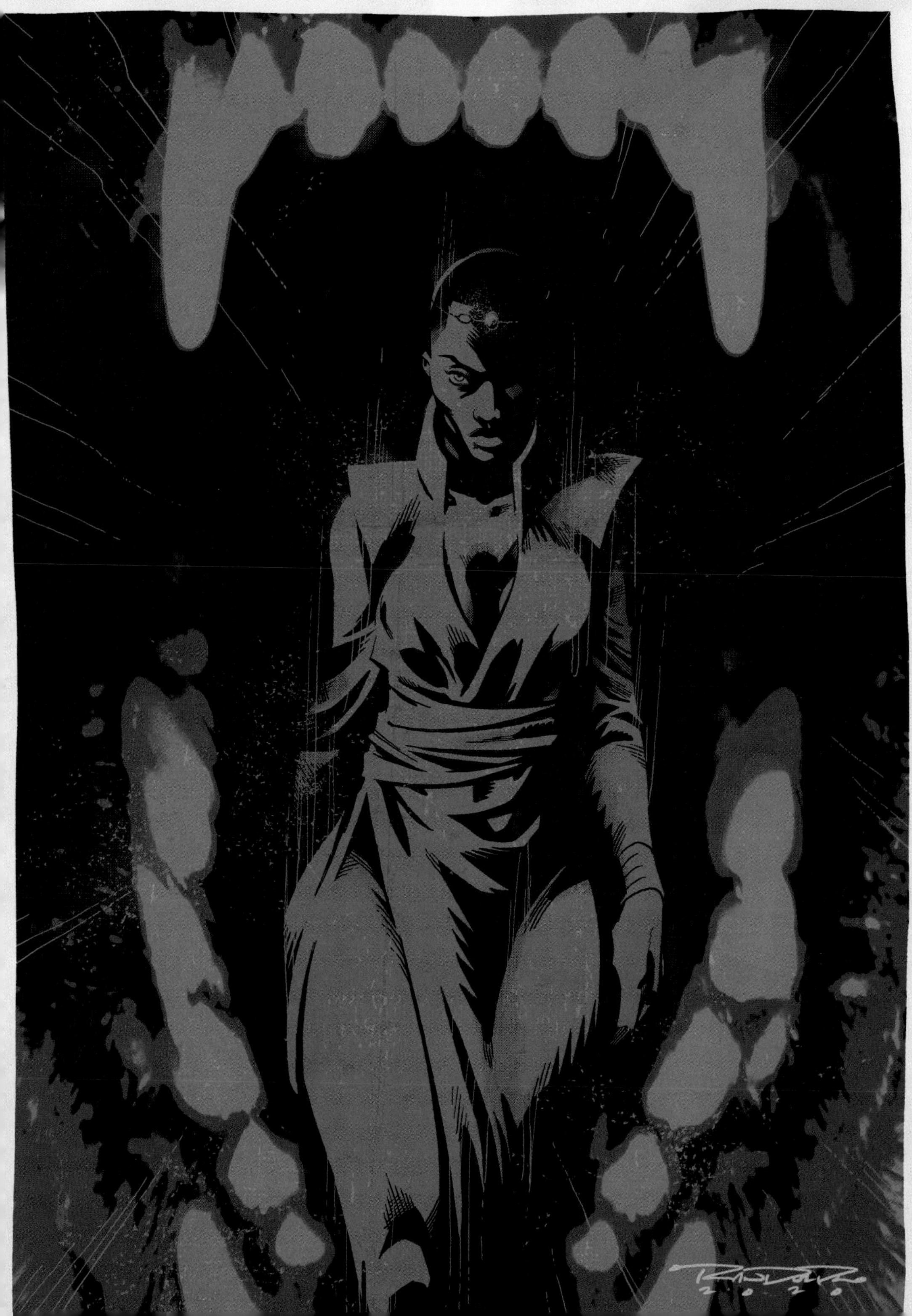

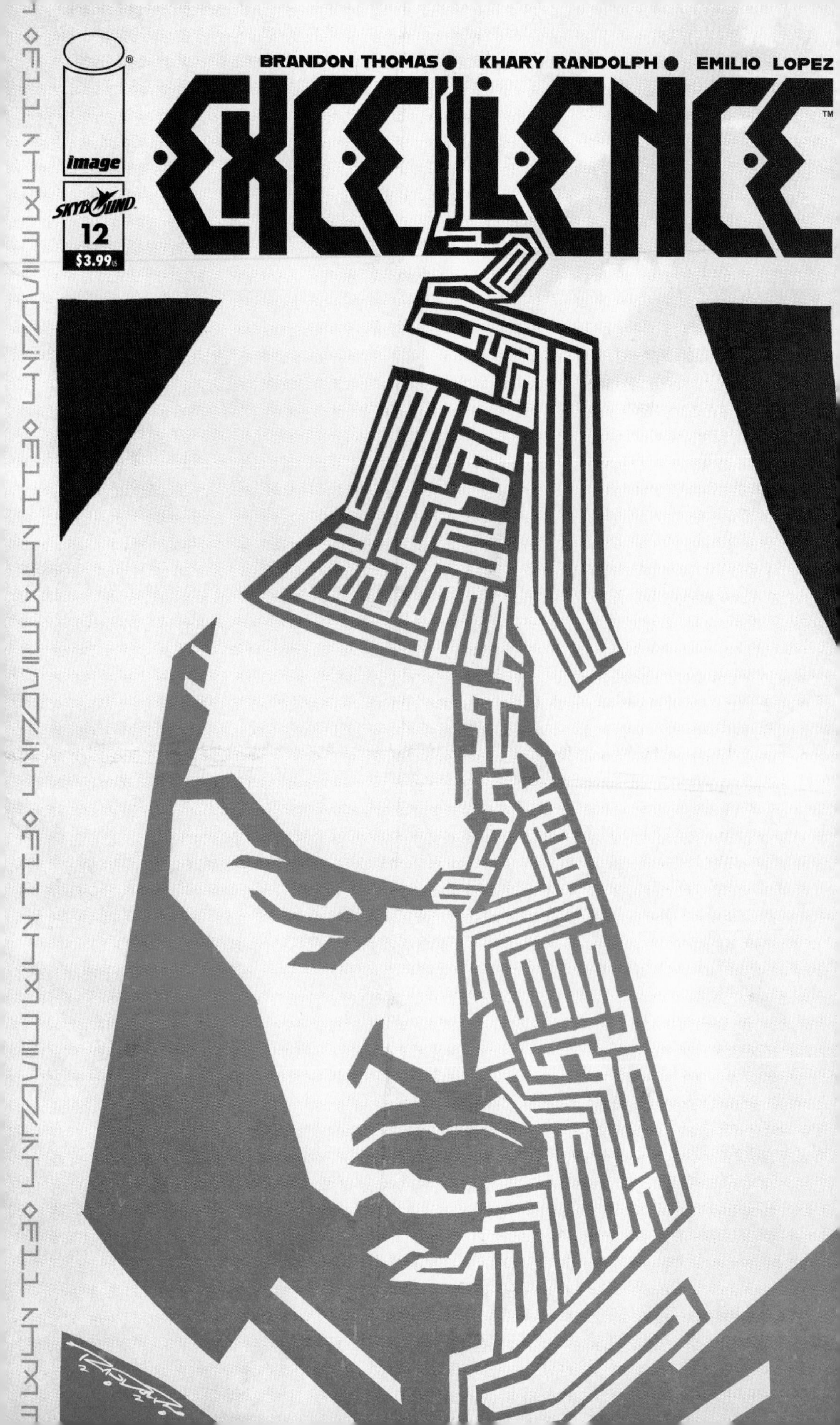
BRANDON THOMAS
KHARY RANDOLPH
EMILIO LOPEZ
EXCELLENCE
image
SKYBOUND
12
$3.99 US

THE CIPHER

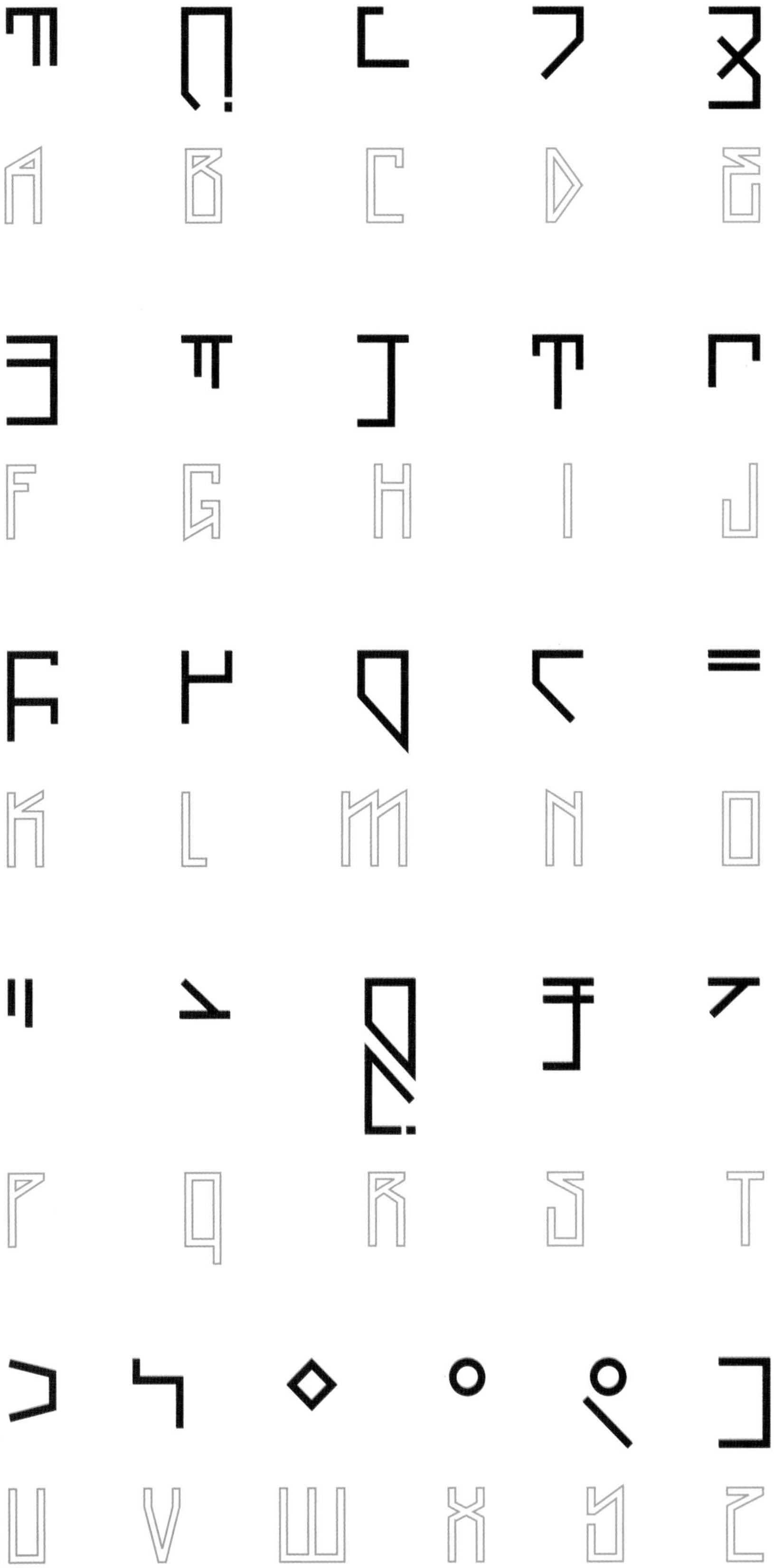
A B C D E
F G H I J
K L M N O
P Q R S T
U V W X Y Z

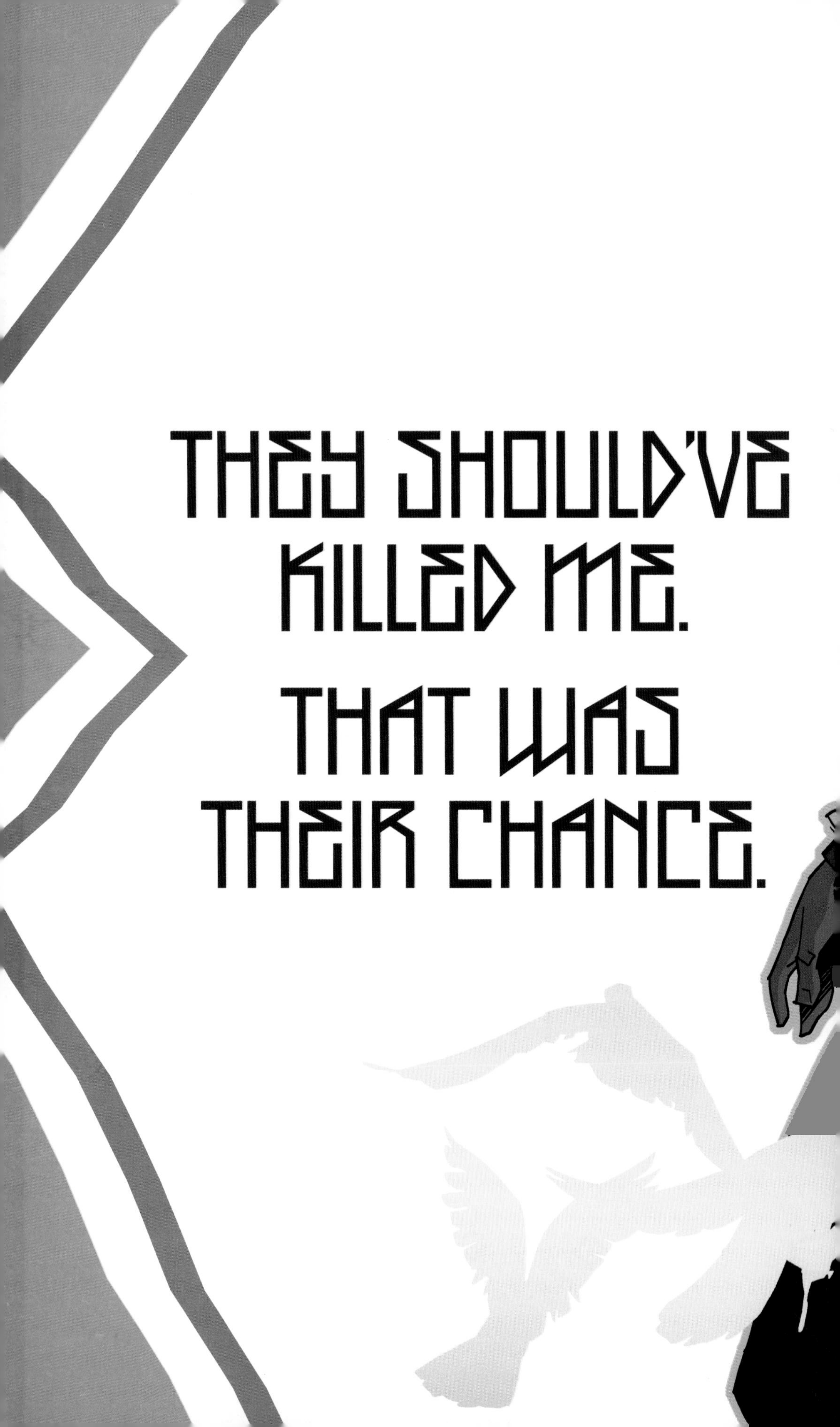
THEY SHOULD'VE KILLED ME.
THAT WAS THEIR CHANCE.

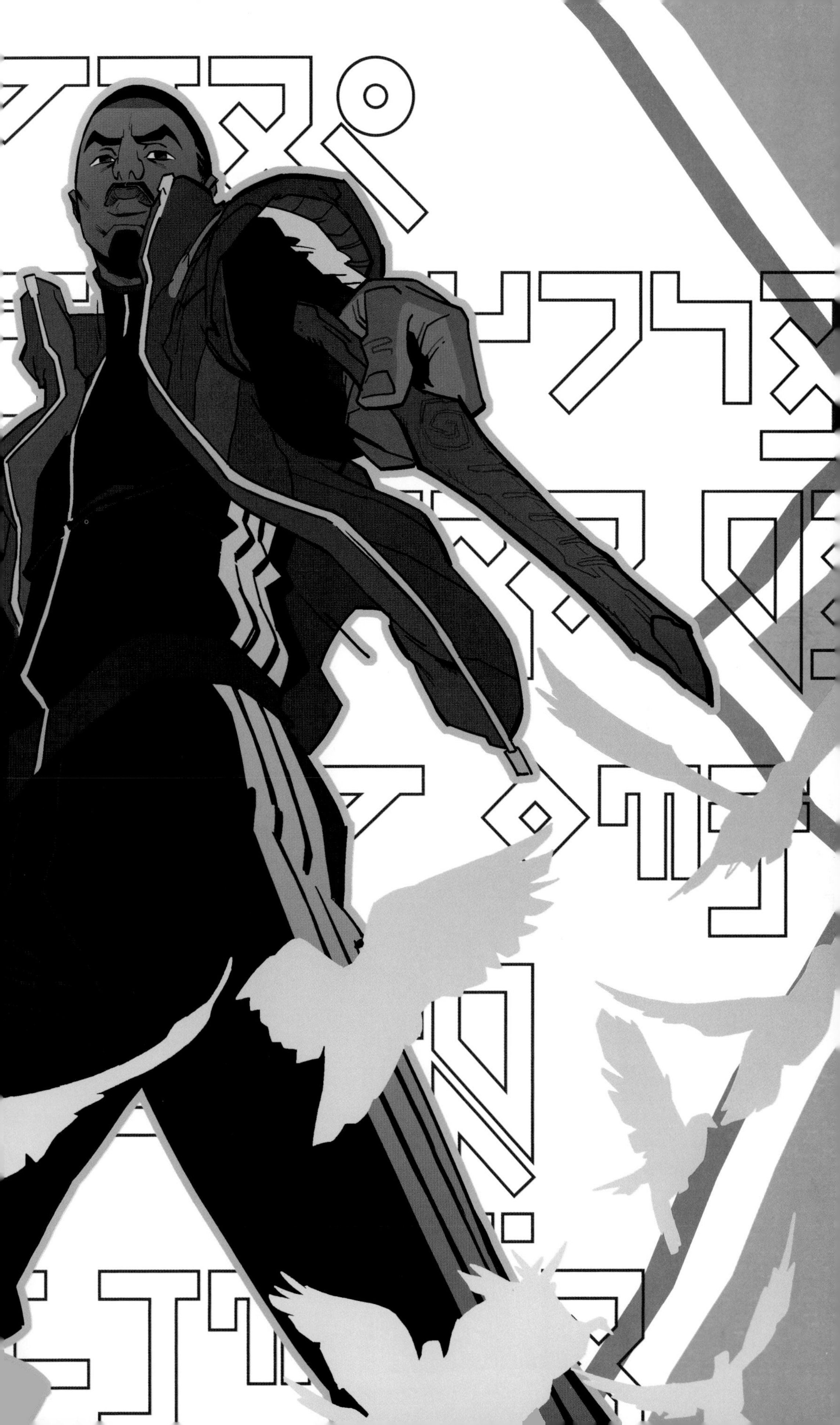

FOR MORE TALES FROM ROBERT KIRKMAN AND SKYBOUND

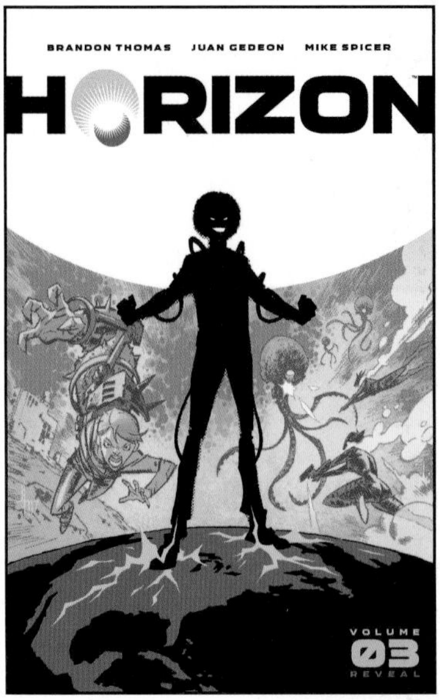
BRANDON THOMAS JUAN GEDEON MIKE SPICER
HORIZON
VOLUME
03
REVEAL

VOL. 1: REPRISAL TP
ISBN: 978-1-5343-0047-7
$9.99

VOL. 2: REMNANT TP
ISBN: 978-1-5343-0227-1
$16.99

VOL. 3: REVEAL TP
ISBN: 978-1-5343-0487-1
$16.99

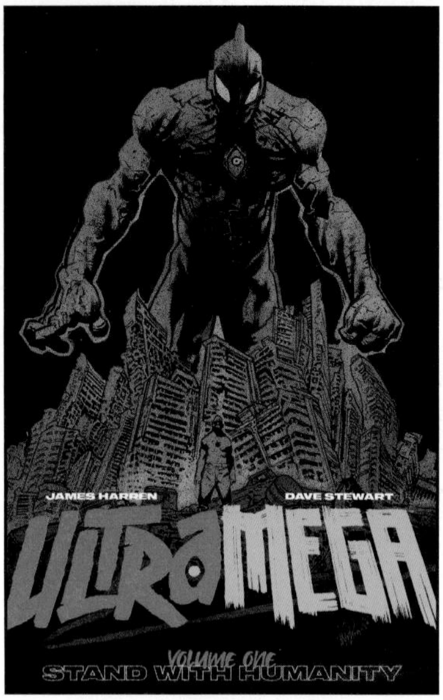
JAMES HARREN DAVE STEWART
ULTRAMEGA
VOLUME ONE
STAND WITH HUMANITY

VOL. 1: STAND WITH HUMANITY
ISBN: 978-1-5343-1984-4
$19.99

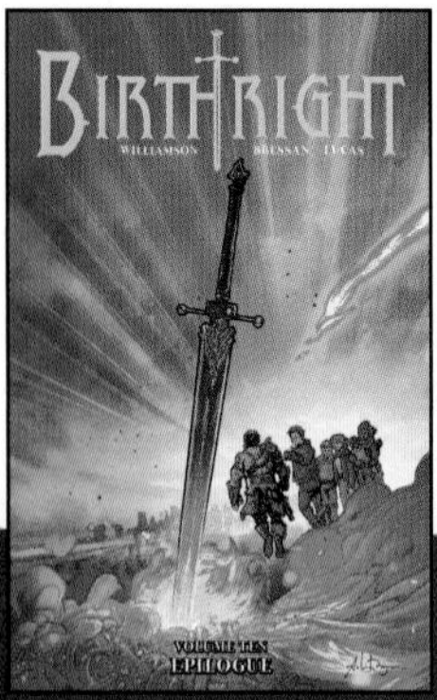
BIRTHRIGHT
WILLIAMSON BRESSAN LUCAS
EPILOGUE

VOL. 1: HOMECOMING
ISBN: 978-1-63215-231-2
$9.99

VOL. 2: CALL TO ADVENTURE
ISBN: 978-1-63215-446-0
$12.99

VOL. 3: ALLIES AND ENEMIES
ISBN: 978-1-63215-683-9
$12.99

VOL. 4: FAMILY HISTORY
ISBN: 978-1-63215-871-0
$12.99

VOL. 5: BELLY OF THE BEAST
ISBN: 978-1-5343-0218-1
$12.99

VOL. 6: FATHERHOOD
ISBN: 978-1-53430-498-7
$14.99

VOL. 7: BLOOD BROTHERS
ISBN: 978-1-5343-1053-7
$14.99

VOL. 8: LIVE BY THE SWORD
ISBN: 978-1-5343-1368-2
$14.99

VOL. 9: WAR OF THE WORLDS
ISBN: 978-1-5343-1601-0
$14.99

VOL. 10: EPILOGUE
ISBN: 978-1-5343-1948-6
$14.99

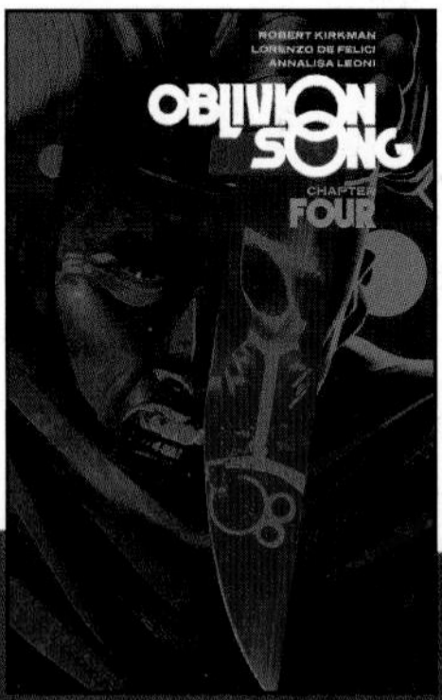
ROBERT KIRKMAN
LORENZO DE FELICI
ANNALISA LEONI
OBLIVION SONG
FOUR

CHAPTER ONE TP
ISBN: 978-1-5343-0642-4
$ 9.99

CHAPTER TWO
ISBN: 978-1-5343-1057-5
$16.99

CHAPTER THREE
ISBN: 978-1-5343-1326-2
$16.99

CHAPTER FOUR
ISBN: 978-1-5343-1517-4
$16.99

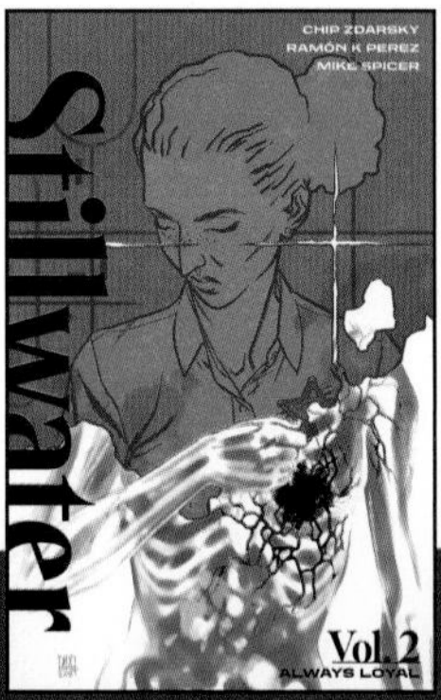
CHIP ZDARSKY
RAMÓN K PEREZ
MIKE SPICER
Stillwater
Vol. 2
ALWAYS LOYAL

VOL. 1: RAGE, RAGE TP
ISBN: 978-1-5343-1837-3
$16.99

VOL. 2: ALWAYS LOYAL P
ISBN: 978-1-5343-2004-8
$16.99

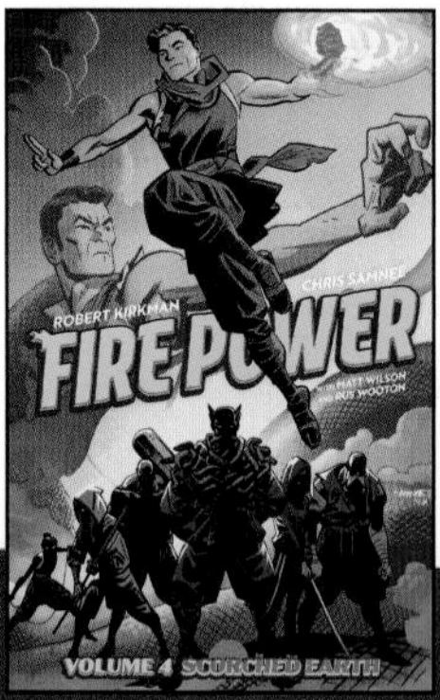
ROBERT KIRKMAN
CHRIS SAMNEE
FIRE POWER
VOLUME 4 SCORCHED EARTH

VOL. 1: PRELUDE
ISBN: 978-1-5343-1655-3
$9.99

VOL. 2: HOME FIRE
ISBN: 978-1-5343-1718-5
$16.99

VOL. 3: FLAME WAR
ISBN: 978-1-5343-1908-0
$16.99

VOL. 4: SCORCHED EARTH
ISBN: 978-1-5343-2103-8
$16.99